Sara's Choice

Book Two In the Romance In the Yukon Series

By

Patty Schramm

First publication 2019
Flashpoint Publications

ISBN 978-1-949096-18-7

eISBN 978-1-949096-19-4

Cover Design by AcornGraphics

Editors Verda Foster and Nann Dunne

Publisher's Note:

Acknowledgments

It really does take a village, especially when writing a book. Thanks to my amazing beta readers, Mary Hettel, Sharon G. Clark and Brenda Adcock. They used their wonder skills on my book and helped me bring the story to live. Verda Foster and Nann Dunne, my amazing editors without whom I would never get my time-line right and I'd certainly never put commas where they belong.

And to Lori L Lake, my friend and mentor. Thanks for everything!

Dedication

To my dear, sweet friend, Sherry Mills. The best hillbilly a girl could ever know. You've enhanced my life in ways that I can never truly describe. I will love you forever!

Chapter One

Sara curled into the warm body next to her. The light from the hallway illuminated Terry's face. Sara trailed her lips along Terry's full cheek to her mouth, where Terry rewarded her with a sultry kiss. The prettiest blue eyes she'd ever seen gazed at her, and her breath hitched.

Her tongue sought Terry's as their kiss deepened. Sara shivered. She brought her hand up to Terry's neck, steadying them both and keeping their mouths in contact.

Terry smiled against her and moved so she hovered over Sara. One arm propped her up while the other hand slid along Sara's abdomen and stopped at the apex of her legs. They paused in their kissing and Terry said, "You're naked."

"So are you."

"Hmm. Thought I might do something about that." Terry's fingers drew tiny hearts along Sara's thigh.

"You've been doing something most of the night." Sara nipped her shoulder. "Not that I'm complaining."

"Good to know." Terry rested her head on Sara's chest, her breath warm on Sara's skin. "I've been thinking, too."

"Oh, not good. You're not supposed to think while having sex." Sara's hand absently combed through Terry's coal-black hair. She enjoyed the feel of the buzz cut at the nape of her neck.

"Call me weird."

"Weird."

Terry tapped Sara's belly playfully and returned to drawing hearts. "I think it's time you met my kid."

Sara stopped her movements as her heart nearly leapt into her throat. Meet her kid? Seriously? The timing was strange, but when she looked at where Terry's head now rested on her chest, Sara's face was nearly swallowed whole by her smile. Terry *would* think now was a good time to chat about something so important. Sara wanted to meet Felicia. She'd been asking to do so for weeks.

Terry propped herself up again and met Sara's gaze. Even in the dim lighting, Sara recognized fear in those eyes. "Have I scared you off?"

"No way. Not the topic I expected you to bring up. I'm shocked is all. And excited and scared and amazed and totally up for this." She cupped the side of Terry's face, and Terry leaned into her touch.

"You sure?"

"I am. As long as you are."

Terry shrugged, the fear no longer evident in her eyes. "There's no point putting it off. I know we haven't been dating very long, but I've never dated a woman I felt this sure about so quickly. Not even Ann, and I was married to her for five years." The look in her eyes turned to sadness at the mention of her deceased wife. "I miss her terribly, but you made me realize I can still live my life. I don't have to hide anymore." She resettled her head on Sara's chest.

"I'm glad, honey. I want to get to know Felicia—be part of her life."

"You'll love her. She's a little diva, but she's a great kid."

Sara brushed a stray lock of hair from Terry's face. "She's *your* kid."

Terry placed several soft kisses on Sara's breast and drew the taut nipple into her mouth.

Sara sucked in a breath. "Done talking?"

"Done." Terry released the nipple and moved to the other breast, tucking one leg between Sara's thighs. "For now."

Her warm mouth clamped down on the nipple and Sara gasped. She dug her fingers into Terry's back as pleasure rolled over her. She bucked her hips a little and rubbed against Terry's thigh.

She held Terry's head in place for a time, encouraging her to continue suckling her breast. Terry pulled away, raked her teeth across Sara's heated skin, and grinned, her eyes dark with passion.

Sara's world tilted when Terry settled between her legs, one hand on Sara's abdomen while the other teased along her left thigh. She let out a gasp and licked her lips in anticipation.

Gentle fingers tangled in her wet curls. Sara's excitement built with every touch, her eyes locked on Terry's. She didn't merely want this moment; she wanted a lifetime of it. Her heart beat triple time, and she thought she might explode before it was over. Terry continued working her magic with her hand and stretched across Sara's torso to capture her lips in a hot kiss.

Sara's heart filled with more love than she ever thought possible. The pressure of Terry's lips against hers was every bit as electric as their first—maybe more.

Fireworks exploded in Sara's brain and spread a feeling of warmth and completion throughout her body. Nothing—no one—could ever compare to this incredible woman.

Tears filled her eyes as she reached the peak of orgasm, her heart full to bursting, her mind fully blown, and her body spent. She trembled. Her muscles clamped down on Terry's fingers and held her in place. Sara wanted nothing more than to keep her there forever, but Terry slipped free and wiped the tears from Sara's cheeks. She kissed her sweetly and said, "Did I hurt you?"

"No." Sara clasped Terry's hand and kissed her palm. "It's...I've never felt this way before."

"What way?"

"It was beautiful. You're beautiful." She leaned forward to kiss Terry passionately, making sure there were no doubts about what she felt.

"I've never made anyone cry before." Terry's voice wavered.
"Well, I've never cried before. A first for both of us."
Terry held her gaze. "First of many new things, I hope."
"I hope so." Sara smiled as they kissed again.
She was keeping this woman.
Forever.

Chapter Two

Three Months Later

Sara heard the damn alarm go off. Both times. Three times. She grabbed her cell phone and tapped the snooze button. She could afford another nine minutes of sleep, right? It wasn't yet seven in the morning, and she didn't need to arrive at Whitehorse International Airport until nine.

Planes never came in on time. Even if they did, the checked baggage needed to be retrieved. She could stretch it to eight-thirty.

She tapped the snooze.

It went off a few seconds later. Or was it minutes? Bleary-eyed, Sara noted the time. Nine-twenty.

"Shit!"

Sara scrambled out of bed and pulled on her jeans and an over-sized sweatshirt, not bothering with a bra or undies. She ran into the living room, grabbed a bright-green wool cap to cover her bed-head, and put on her boots. At the last minute, she realized no socks warmed her feet. Screw it. She didn't have time and grumbled about it while getting into her coat.

Her stomach complained when she ducked into the kitchen to get her purse. The unopened box of Pop-Tarts called to her. She shoved it into the purse, got her keys, and was in her Jeep Wrangler in record time.

At nine thirty-four, she was on the road to the Whitehorse Airport doing her best impression of a sleigh as she slid and slipped along the icy, snowy, Yukon highway. Had she known it was going to snow last night? She couldn't remember. Then again, she didn't remember much about last night.

Except the blue-haired cutie at the bar. She was obviously into Sara and paid for at least four of the beers Sara consumed. Or was it five?

With a sick feeling in her gut, Sara realized the cutie might still be at her house.

"Shit!"

She looked for a place to turn around. Her cell phone rang. She hit the hands-free button on her steering wheel by rote. Her best friend, Liv Templeton's, voice filled the air around Sara.

"You're speeding down the highway as we speak."

"You know me well." Sara glanced at the speedometer. She wasn't exactly speeding at sixty kilometers an hour.

"Be careful. No sense crashing before you get here. We can get breakfast while we wait."

Sara spotted a side road to use as a turn around. "Um, can you make it a longish breakfast?"

"What'd you forget?"

Sara chewed her bottom lip before answering. "I'm not sure what her name is."

Liv paused for rather a long time before saying, "Not Terry?"

Lots of comments entered Sara's brain, none of them worth repeating. Liv knew damn well it wouldn't be Terry. That ship sank three months ago. But Sara caught the sarcasm in Liv's voice and chose to ignore it. "No. Not unless Terry dyed her hair blue in the last week."

"Sara—"

"Don't. I need to make sure she's not at my house. I don't remember most of the night. I left the Pot O' Gold with a cute, blue-haired woman. Lecture me later. I'll text you when I'm in the cell phone lot at the airport." She disconnected the call.

No. The woman who might be in her bed was definitely not Terry Alexander, no matter how much Sara wished she was. Blue-haired, short, muscular... was all she recalled at the moment about the woman. Nothing at all like Terry whose height matched Sara's five feet eleven inches, arms and legs toned without being too muscular, and hair as dark as night, eyes a startling blue with a warmth behind them belied the icy coloring. Even when Terry broke her heart, Sara never saw malice in her eyes.

Sara shook her head against the maudlin thoughts. She pulled into her driveway and parked next to a royal-blue Chevy pickup. How did she miss seeing it when she left? Worse, how did she miss the woman in her bed? Sara exited her Jeep as the woman came bouncing out of her house. She looked quite pleased with herself as she came right up to Sara and kissed her solidly.

"Great time last night. I left my number on your pillow. Call me." She winked, jumped in her truck, and was gone before Sara's tired brain processed what happened.

It was bad enough she didn't know the woman's name. Her cheeks reddened with shame. Her one-night-stand didn't actually look like she was of legal age.

Could the day get any worse?

****

Sara pulled up to the passenger pickup area and jumped out to help Liv and her fiancée, Grace Kato, load their bags into the back of her Jeep. Liv's blue eyes glared at her, and though Sara knew she was in for a lecture, she hugged her bestie, ruffled her wavy, brown mop of hair, and got a hug from Grace. Sara had a few inches on Grace, but you'd never know it the way Grace carried herself.

Her straight, black hair was pulled into a tight ponytail, and her deep-brown eyes held sympathy for Sara, and a hint of laughter.

In the months since Grace and Liv got together, Sara found she and Grace had a lot in common. Sara counted her as a friend. Especially now as Grace shielded her from Liv, slapping her on the arm when Liv started to speak after they got their luggage stowed in the storage area. They climbed into Sara's car and headed to Liv's house.

Sara asked, "How was the trip?"

"Great." Grace met Sara's gaze in the rearview mirror. "I had no idea Olivia was capable of putting away so much food. She was in a turkey coma before dessert."

"I was not," Liv said, her tone playful. "I made it to the second half of the football game, thank you very much. Then I passed out."

"Turkey coma?" Sara asked. "What's a turkey coma?"

"Eat too much turkey and you fall asleep," Grace said. "And Olivia ate too much turkey."

"Turkey doesn't make you fall asleep," Sara said.

"It does." Grace slapped Liv on the arm. "This one ate almost as much as Matthew, and I didn't think anyone could eat more than my twin brother. I'll show you the picture of them snoozing on the couch together when we get to Olivia's house."

"Our house," Liv said. "It's our house."

"Not until we're married," Grace replied. Their mock-argument was an ongoing thing with them. Grace decided she wasn't moving in until after the wedding in April. Liv tried to change the deed on the house to show Grace as half-owner. Sara's intervention stopped the legal process from going through. She knew Grace would call off the wedding otherwise.

"No fighting while I'm driving on ice," Sara said as a way to stop them from bickering. She didn't think they'd seriously argue, but she wasn't taking any chances.

"Tell me about Blue Hair," Liv finally said.

Sara didn't have to see Liv to know her expression was a mixture of worry and anger. "She left as I got home. Nothing to tell."

"You took home a woman you don't know. There's lots to tell."

"She got to my house in her own truck and left in it. I'm sure we had mind-blowing sex all night long, except I can't remember any of it."

Liv said, "What's the point of having mind-blowing sex if you're not going to remember it?"

"I didn't start off not wanting to remember it. I'm sure I intended to remember all of it at some point. Maybe I will later today."

"Doubt it." Liv crossed her arms over her chest and released an exaggerated sigh.

From the back seat Grace said, "Hold on you two. Liv, we talked about this. You don't need to ambush Sara while she's driving. You two can talk this over later. Preferably after Sara has gotten some sleep."

"How do you know I need sleep?" Sara asked.

"Because I'm not blind, and you hardly ever oversleep like you did this morning. Let's not talk about this right now, okay? We'll get to Olivia's, you'll drop us off, and since tomorrow is Sunday, we'll have lunch and talk then."

Liv opened her mouth to speak, but Grace was quick to shut her up. Sara was grateful for that. She said, "Deal. Talk on Sunday."

They rode back in silence, Sara cursing herself for wondering if the day could get worse, because it had.

****

Sara found a note on her pillow, as promised. A cell phone number along with XOX, followed by a signature she couldn't read. So much for learning Blue Hair's name. She started to crumple it up but changed her mind and tucked it into the drawer of her bedside table. Maybe next time she'd be sure not to drink anything stronger than soda.

The state of her bedroom dissipated any doubts about the previous night. She spent ten minutes trying to locate the missing half of her favorite pair of shoes, not sure if she wanted to know why it was in the bathtub. Her bra hung from the headboard, her shirt tucked under the mattress. Had they played hide-and-seek with her clothes?

Mortified, Sara stared at the items in her hands. She never did one-night-stands. She wasn't a prude by any means but at least needed to go out a few times to get to know the woman. She had no idea if the blue-haired girl lived in Whitehorse. Was she a customer at the bank? What if she came in on Monday looking for Sara? What the hell would happen then?

Her job as assistant loan manager was still fairly new. Sara intended to be president of the bank someday. She wouldn't get there if some bouncy, barely legal girl came in looking for her. She sank onto her bed and covered her face with her hands. What the hell was she thinking?

But it was clear what she'd been thinking and how she'd used alcohol to numb those thoughts. The girl was meant to steer her away from them, and for a while, it worked. Inevitably, though, those thoughts returned to Terry.

Five months of happiness squashed in a single sentence. *"I can't see you anymore."*

Sara would never forget Terry's eyes, all puppy dog sad, filled with regret. Yet not one word about why. If you regret something doesn't it mean you don't want to do it? Sara stood like a statue and watched Terry literally walk out of her life.

No more texts.

No more phone calls.

Not even a cordial hello on the street.

On the off-chance Sara noticed her come into the bank, Terry went about her business, giving her a slight nod if she acknowledged Sara at all. Which she often didn't.

Granted, five months wasn't what you'd call a long-term relationship, but Sara lost her heart to Terry early on. Their physical attraction came about easily enough, and Sara found it difficult to keep her mind away from the warmth of Terry's body against hers.

The soft, lavender scent of Terry's skin.

The feel of her fingers brushing through the tufts of Terry's hair.

How Terry's hands knew exactly where to touch Sara to send her over the edge...

Sara spent the last three months mourning their relationship. Her heart belonged to Terry, no matter how hard she tried to reverse course and move on. While neither of them ever said the words, Sara knew Terry loved her. The proof was in her eyes, her kiss, her touch—everything she did.

Why the hell did she break it off? No amount of calling got Terry to speak to her. And Sara was desperate to know. She deserved to know, right? Terry could at least answer her damn phone.

Sara's phone rang, and she nearly jumped out of her skin. She answered it automatically, not bothering to check the caller ID. She instantly wished she had.

"I understand you're single again," a sensuous voice said. It reminded Sara of fingernails on a blackboard.

"It's not any of your damn business, Angel."

"That would be a yes. Look, we didn't exactly get off on the right foot when we went out this summer. Let me make it up to you. Dinner tonight? Your choice."

Sara hardly believed her ears. "Seriously? Are you kidding me? You want to go out? I thought Liv told you to stay away from me?"

"I didn't realize Liv spoke for you. You're a grown woman, Sara."

"And this grown woman is hanging up on you."

"I wouldn't recommend it."

Sara's finger hovered over the disconnect icon. Yet she heard something in Angel's voice and she paused. "Why not?"

"Your new boss."

"What about him?" Sara's stomach twisted in a knot, and she regretted eating the Pop-Tarts.

"Greg Rutherford. He's my cousin."

"And?"

"Can you imagine what he'd do if I pulled my clients from your bank? I can go to Royal Bank of Canada without a problem. They've offered me a good deal. Wouldn't take much to move over there."

"Are you blackmailing me into going on another date with you?" Sara heard herself speak, but the words sounded like they came from someone else.

"No. I'm letting you know where I stand at the moment. I'm sure Greg can work something out for me. I sell a lot of real estate, as you know."

"I'm well aware."

"Think about it. This can work out for you. What have you got to lose?"

"My dignity." Sara winced at her own comment. But Angel deserved it. She'd treated Sara like shit on their disastrous first date. "And maybe an eye."

"I didn't hit you hard," Angel said.

During the long pause Sara knew she was expected to speak, but she kept quiet.

"I apologized. Why can't we get past it? We did have fun, right?"

"Up until the time you decided to be pissed at me for not wanting to have sex with you, yes. We had a nice time."

"That was the wine talking. Let me make it up to you. Please. I promise not to drink too much."

Sara knew this wasn't a good idea. Her brain screamed at her to say no. She heard Liv's voice adding to the cacophony in her head. Could Angel harm her? Was declining one date worth potentially losing a major client for the bank? Angel was the top real estate agent in the city. She could go anywhere she wanted with her clients for mortgages. She was a huge client of The First National Bank of Whitehorse.

"Fine. Pick me up at six." She ended the call and slumped her shoulders in shame. She was so not telling Liv about this. She'd go to dinner with Angel and be done. No harm. Right?

****

"You couldn't wait until tomorrow to talk to Sara?" Grace asked once they were inside.

Liv sighed. "No. I'm pissed she went out alone and got drunk. Anything could have happened. It's lucky the woman wasn't a thief or murderer. What if she was like Angel and got violent with Sara? What would she do then? She can't go around picking up women."

"And yet it was okay when you did it?" Grace narrowed her gaze at Liv, and Liv wilted at the intensity of those dark eyes. Grace added, "Hypocritical much?"

"Hardly the same. And I can handle myself much better than Sara. Plus, I've never been drunk enough I didn't remember anything. She never gets drunk." Liv voiced a horrible thought. "What if the woman put something in her drink?"

"You're being overly dramatic, dear."

"No, I'm being protective."

"No, you're being dramatic." Grace stopped unpacking and moved into Liv's personal space. "None of which happened. Sara's fine. Chastising her or making her feel horrible about it won't solve anything. She can't take it back. She's in a bad place, and you know it." Grace touched her forehead to Liv's. "She needs her best friend, not a lecture on safe dating. Sara's hurting."

"I don't know how to help her. I want to go to Terry and strangle her."

"I know you do." Grace kissed her, and it took away a lot of the anger. "But you also don't know what's going on with Terry. She might have a good reason for breaking up with Sara."

"Sara's amazing. Who the hell would dump her?"

Grace raised her eyebrows. "Seriously? You forgot already you dumped her for me? I'm not complaining, but you did break up with her. And why was that again?"

Liv knew Grace was goading her on purpose. "Because we were too different. We don't have the same ideas on what we want for the future. But we're still friends, and when I met you, we were friends with benefits. There was no dating."

"You are and it didn't happen overnight. Maybe she and Terry need more time to work through this. You don't know they won't be friends later."

"They broke up in October. Three months ago."

Grace laughed softly. "Is there a time limit on these things? I mean, I don't have any ex-girlfriends hanging around to find out."

"Ha-ha. If your ex hung around here, she'd end up in hospital because I'd beat the shit out of her."

Grace's smile faded a little, and Liv's stomach sank. She was an ass for mentioning Carly. She knew better. "I wouldn't let you and you know it."

"I'm sorry, baby." She kissed Grace once more, hoping to soften the blow of her careless words. Though if she did actually see Carly Sanders at any time, she would probably hurt her badly. The scars she left on Grace, both physically and emotionally, were always right there and sometimes hard for Liv to ignore. Like now, when her protective gene went into overdrive. As it did with Sara.

It'd taken Liv a long time to convince Grace to love again. Carly broke her, and Grace had yet to fully heal. Liv would never let anyone hurt Grace again. She'd make sure Grace knew nothing but love for the rest of her life.

Liv kissed her sweetly and said, "I love you."

"I love you, too." The smile returned, and Grace's rich brown eyes reflected her words.

Liv changed the topic. "Want to talk about the wedding now?"

"Sure, but let me get unpacked first. I need to call *Ojiichan* to make sure he's okay."

"Your grandfather is probably asleep in front of the TV. You want to wake him up?"

A week before their trip to Seattle to celebrate the new year with Grace's family, Hariku "Harry" Kato, Senior, Grace's grandfather, turned ninety-four. Harry wasn't up for traveling this year, and Grace called him nearly every day since they left. Liv loved the old man and respected him as a business owner. His mine, Gracie's Glory, always made enough gold profit to keep it a small operation, while paying his employees well and allowing Harry a bit of savings in return. In his words, the mine was his grandchildren's inheritance.

Grace still lived with him in his tiny cabin, when not staying the night with Liv. Most of her stuff, what little she owned, had made its way to Liv's house. Grace planned to move in at the end of the mining season in October. Now it was January and Grace had yet to complete the move. Frustration marred Liv's thoughts. She wanted them to be together now, not wait until after the wedding in the spring.

They'd had this argument already, and Liv had no intention to revisit it. She bit her lower lip as she asked, "Do you need me to drive you home?"

"I was hoping to stay the night," Grace said, her hands now under Liv's T-shirt. Their warmth spread across Liv's flesh, causing her to tremble. "I'm sure *Ojiichan* will be glad to see me, but you and I haven't had much time alone and I thought—I thought I could make it up to you." She placed kisses along the outline of Liv's breasts.

Liv desperately wanted her damn T-shirt off. "Point made." She removed the band from Grace's long, silky hair releasing the ponytail. It fell gently over Grace's shoulders, and Liv ran her fingers through it. She loved the feel of the soft strands on her bare skin. "Call Harry. Tell him, hi, we love him, and we'll be over tomorrow."

"I might have to talk to him for a whole minute," Grace teased, her fingers now pressed against Liv's taut nipples. "Think you can wait?"

"You might need to bring the damn phone to bed." Liv kissed her hungrily, pushing Grace against the wall as she did. She wanted to rip the woman's clothes off right then and there and might have, if Grace hadn't captured her very busy hands.

"Two minutes. You get ready and I'll be right in."

"Two minutes," Liv said, her T-shirt already in her hand. "Two minutes."

****

Apprehension filled Sara the more she thought about the date with Angel. She took an hour to decide what to wear, finally settling on a navy-blue skirt, matching blouse, and flats. Since Angel used her business at the bank as leverage to coerce Sara on this date, she'd make sure she dressed businesslike.

She checked herself in the mirror, happy with her chestnut-brown hair in a French braid.

As she gazed at herself, doubts entered her brain.

What the hell? Last night, she'd been out at the pub, dancing and drinking, and it ended with a great night of sex.

Now she found herself going out with Angel of all people.

Their last date was disastrous. Sara touched her cheek and remembered the sting of Angel's hand hitting her. She hurt more from the action than the act itself. No one, not even her parents, ever hit Sara. Yet Angel had. And all because Sara wasn't interested in sex on the first date.

But last night she'd had sex on the first date with someone whose first name escaped her.

Angel Harrison could be a professional model. Sara knew few people comparable to Angel in beauty and sex appeal.

What, exactly, stopped Sara from having sex with Angel? Some weird gut feeling? Or a complete lack of chemistry?

Did she have chemistry with the blue-haired woman?

Perhaps the beer loosened her up enough to drop the ideal of no sex on the first date.

The moment Terry dumped her, a switch flipped in Sara's brain. Maybe Sara didn't care anymore. The woman she wanted more than anything was no longer available to her. Why bother looking for a new relationship—a new woman to replace her. She was an adult and free to go out with whomever she wished and have sex with her, or not.

Wow. Her life played out like a bad soap opera.

And these thoughts led back to her first date with Terry. She looked handsome in a white golf shirt and black jeans. Her blue eyes twinkled when she opened the door of the nightclub for Sara. Always courteous, Terry even pulled out the chair when Sara went to sit down. At the end of the evening, a taxi waited to take them home. Sensible, in case they chose to drink. Terry dropped her off first, kissed her softly on the lips, and disappeared into the night, but not until she made sure Sara was safely inside.

Sara recalled leaning against her door and remembering the evening. The dancing where their bodies melded together like two halves of a whole. Their movement electric and hot as hell.

But Terry didn't try anything with her, though Sara felt sure she wanted to as badly as Sara did. Like they had an unspoken agreement—sex could wait.

And it did. They slept together on the fourth date, and it was well worth the wait. Like they'd been together for years, they made love well into the morning, watching the sunrise together.

It was the moment Sara knew, in her heart of hearts, she wanted to spend the rest of her life with Terry. Stupid. You can't be in love with someone after a few dates and good sex.

People like Liv and Grace weren't normal. They fell in love in a few weeks and never looked back. Sara recognized her naivete for thinking she and Terry would, or could, do the same. Terry made it very clear after five months. She wasn't in love with Sara.

Except Sara was still in love with Terry and had no idea where the hell to put the damn emotion. She feared it was written all over her face.

The doorbell rang and pulled her out of her reverie. It was a good thing, too, because any more reminiscing and Sara would end up crying over a tub of ice cream and a box of Pop-Tarts.

She straightened her skirt and answered the door, giving Angel her best smile. "Want to come in?"

"Sure." Angel stepped inside, the four-inch heels adding enough to her height she was now taller than Sara, who regretted wearing flats. Angel's black skirt hugged her hips, complemented by a red, satin shirt under her black jacket. Her golden-brown hair hung loosely over her shoulders, and the makeup she wore enhanced the sleek lines of her face beautifully. Sara wondered why the hell Angel wanted to go out with her. She could have any woman she wanted.

"Nice little place you have here." Angel did a quick tour of the living room. The apartment wasn't much: two bedrooms, one bathroom, open-plan living room/kitchen area.

"It suits me. I don't need a ton of space. I'm hardly ever here as it is."

"Ah, wild lifestyle?"

She couldn't tell if Angel was teasing or not. "I like to go out on the weekends sometimes. You know this because you've seen me at the pub or out dancing."

"I have, but I haven't seen you for a few weeks." She spun around and pinned her gaze on Sara. "Rumor has it you're single now."

"I am."

"Good." Angel's grin widened, and alarm bells went off in Sara's brain, but she chose to ignore them. She'd made a date, and she'd damn well stick to it.

"You ready to go?" Sara asked. "I'm pretty hungry."

Angel opened the door for her and waited while she locked up. "I booked us a table at Josephine's. It's a high-end place I take clients to. I thought it might be nice to treat ourselves."

"I've been there on business several times over the years, but it's not usually my thing otherwise," Sara said as she got into Angel's mint-green Jaguar. "I'm a pretty simple person. Burgers and fries are fine with me."

"Yes, but sometimes you have to go outside your comfort zone, right?" Angel got behind the wheel and started the engine. Sara felt a rumble under the seats as the powerful motor came to life.

"Right," Sara said, realizing she was already out of her comfort zone.

"I should also apologize."

"For what?"

"First, for bringing up my business with the bank. I was sure you wouldn't give me the time of day, and it was the first thing I thought of to get you to reconsider. I hope you know I'd never do anything like pull my business. I've got a good deal with First National, and my clients have never had any issues with their mortgages or loans."

"Good to know. I'm sure Greg appreciates it as well."

"He does. He's on the weird side, but he's smart."

"He's a good boss."

Angel's hand rested on Sara's knee after she pulled out of the driveway. "I want you to know I've been waiting a long time to take you out again. I was such an ass the last time we went to dinner, and I can't stop apologizing for it."

"You don't need to. You already did and that's enough." Sara gently moved Angel's hand to her own leg. "But you should know I'm not interested in a new girlfriend. It's too soon."

"I understand. I've been there and not long ago either. I'd broken up with my girlfriend not long before you and I went out. I think it's why I acted the way I did. I took my anger with her out on you."

Sara couldn't see Angel's face very well in the dim, early evening light, but she seemed sincere, which made sense. She'd already dealt with anger over being dumped by Terry, along with the other emotions of shock, hurt, dismay. Why wouldn't Angel have the same feelings over her breakup? "Breaking up sucks."

"It does indeed." Angel stole a glance at her as she entered the highway. "Let's try not to talk about our exes tonight, okay? We deserve a fun evening with overpriced food in a fancy restaurant that will cater to your every whim."

"Every whim?" Sara asked. "Like if I ask them for Pop-Tarts they'll go get me some?"

Angel raised one perfectly trimmed eyebrow. "Pop-Tarts? Blueberry or strawberry?"

"S'mores."

"Wow," Angel chuckled. "It's like a sugar overload."

"No such thing." Sara felt the tension fade and laughed. "Sugar and overload do not belong in the same sentence."

"I wouldn't be able to sleep for a week if I had s'mores of any kind. I love them, but they have too much sugar."

"You're not listening. There is no such thing as too much sugar." Sara kept her tone playful, yet decisive. "And you can never, ever, ever have too many Pop-Tarts."

"Yet I can't see an ounce of fat on you. How do you do it?"

"Good genes."

Angel gazed at her appreciatively as she pulled into the parking lot of Josephine's. "I think I'll have to ask for Pop-Tarts now. I want to see if they'll go get them."

"Excellent." Sara allowed her to open her door and followed her inside.

****

Sunday dawned gloomy and gray, a perfect match to Sara's mood. While the date with Angel went well enough, she remained bothered about the blue-haired girl and the amnesia over what they'd done. She grabbed her coat and purse and trod the few blocks to Liv's house since the sidewalks were clear of snow. The temperature was a lovely two degrees centigrade. Practically summer. A reprieve from the freezing weather they'd experienced the previous week.

She arrived at Liv's door in ten minutes, didn't bother to knock, and regretted it the second she stepped inside.

Liv and Grace were in a serious lip-lock, one Sara envied greatly. Liv's shirt lay on the floor. Grace's mussed hair and flushed cheeks served to add to Sara's embarrassment. Liv smirked while Grace quickly handed her the shirt.

"Sorry. I guess I have to relearn to knock."

"Might save you some embarrassment," Liv said, buttoning her shirt. "You're early."

"I'm hungry."

"When aren't you?" Liv sported the stupidest grin on her face. Sara hated and loved her for it at the same time. "Want to go to the pub?"

"Sure. I don't care where we go as long as food finds its way to my mouth."

"Fair enough," Liv said. She and Grace grabbed their coats, and the trio marched off to the Pot O' Gold. The name was tongue-in-cheek, considering they were located in the heart of gold mining country in the Yukon Territory. The interior resembled an old-fashioned English pub, complete with competition-style dartboards. It happened to be the best lesbian-owned bar in the territory.

None of which mattered to Sara. The pub had great food and was fun to hang out at on the weekends. Maybe not so much lately, as this is where she and Terry went every Saturday. And sometimes on Friday, where they would dance well into the morning.

She'd met the blue-haired girl here, too, and the thought gave her pause as she put her hand on the door handle.

Liv nudged her playfully. "What's wrong? You expended energy. You must be starved by now."

"No. Thinking about Friday night and wondering if I made an ass out of myself in there or not."

Liv grew serious for a moment and put her arm around Sara's shoulders. "It doesn't matter what happened on Friday. New day. New memories. Okay?"

Sara didn't answer but let herself be guided inside. They took up residence at their usual booth not far from the bar. No other customers which was not strange for early Sunday afternoon. Half the regulars were probably still sleeping off their antics from last night.

Izzy, the daughter of the two women who owned the place, arrived at their table before they'd gotten settled. Her spikey hair was green today, though Sara thought it was purple last week. Her short, slightly chubby body practically vibrated with excitement, and she sported a wide grin. The sight of her unnerved Sara. Izzy was the biggest gossip in the territory, and that smile said she was busting a gut to share.

"How'd it go with Bren?" she asked Sara.

Bren. Was that her name? Sara shrugged. "Don't remember much, to be honest. I guess it was okay. She left me her number."

"Stellar! She wouldn't do it unless she was totally into you, Sara. And you two were pretty damn into each other. I threatened to throw cold water on you guys at one point. I think it's when Bren convinced you to leave."

"I guess so." Sara kept her gaze on the table, hoping Izzy would stop talking.

"Hey, Iz." Grace, who was so quiet sometimes Sara forgot she was there, spoke up. She was grateful to her now. "Can we get some colas and maybe nachos to start us off? We're pretty hungry, our usual burgers and fries would be great, too."

"Oh sure." Izzy winked at Sara. "I can't wait to get the scoop from Bren later today. You got yourself a good one there, Sara. Just sayin'."

Izzy went to the bar, and Sara put her head onto the table. She was tempted to slam her forehead against the weathered wood, but Liv's hand on her neck stopped her.

"At least someone remembers Friday night," Liv said.

"Not helping."

"Olivia." Grace's voice held a tinge of humor in it. "Can't you see she's upset about it? Be nice."

"No way. She wouldn't be nice to me if the situation was reversed. Which it was. About two years ago."

"No. No, you don't." Sara pulled her head up and glared at Liv. "You don't get to compare my one night of carelessness to your months of stupidity."

"My months of stupidity started with one night of carelessness." Liv held her gaze. "I don't want you to go there, Sara. You're better than that."

"If I was better than that, Terry wouldn't have broken up with me." Tears threatened and Sara needed to take a few deep breaths before she continued. "And I'm not going down a destructive road. Even if I had a date last night with a woman who wasn't Bren. Or Terry."

"A different woman? Sara…"

Grace reached across the table and laid her hand on Liv's arm. "Don't. Let her tell us."

Sara said, "I went out with someone I know. Someone I've been out with before. For dinner. It wasn't a big deal, and we managed to have a nice enough time. I'm saying I'm not about to jump into bed with the first woman I see. Or the second or the third."

Liv didn't appear at all satisfied with her answer, but she'd have to be. Sara wasn't about to tell her she'd gone to dinner with Angel. When Angel was nice, she enjoyed being around her. Sara forgave her one mistake. Liv wouldn't.

Izzy returned with their drinks and nachos before Liv commented further. Their food arrived soon after. Grace, thankfully, changed the subject, and Sara managed to relax. Right up to the moment Bren entered the pub.

She nearly choked on a nacho.

Bren's face lit up when she saw Sara and changed course to come right to their table. Grace scooted over to allow Bren to join them, after Sara made some quick introductions.

"Pretty cool seeing you here," Bren said. "Did you get my note?" Her eyes lit up with excitement. Damn she was cute. And her hair was very, very blue.

"I did. Thanks." Sara wanted to slip under the table and stay there until everyone left. Maybe even forever.

"Cool. I was hoping you'd text me so I'd get your number. Maybe we should go out dancing next weekend? You're awesome on the dance floor."

Sara thought she heard a chuckle from Liv, whom she none-too-gently kicked under the table. "Uh, okay. I haven't had a chance to text you. It's been a crazy weekend. I'll do it when I get home. I didn't put your number in my phone yet."

"No prob. I can tell you my number right now." Bren's bright blue eyes matched the color of her hair and held an air of mischief in them. She waited for Sara to dig out her phone and carefully called off her number.

Sara obliged by sending her a text. "There you go. Let me know when and where to meet you."

"How about I pick you up? Your house is on the way." Bren stood, said goodbye to them, and gave Sara a wink as she sauntered to the bar. Her conversation with Izzy was immediate, and Sara realized she was screwed.

"Wow. A second date. This is good for you." Liv's goofy grin told Sara she approved of Bren.

"She's a kid. Probably barely legal."

"So? She likes you. Obviously. And she seems nice enough. Why not go dancing? You love to dance."

Sara wanted to glare at Liv. Except Liv was actually right this time. "I guess. It can't hurt anything."

"And maybe this time you'll remember it. Ouch!" Liv rubbed her leg. "Why the hell do you two keep kicking me?"

Grace rolled her eyes. "Because you're being an ass."

"Was not."

"Was, too," Sara said in chorus with Grace. "Thank you." She raised her glass and tapped it with Grace's. "Now, let's talk about something else."

"How about our wedding?" Grace asked. "Is it a safe topic with you two?"

"Don't know. Am I still invited?" Liv asked and got kicked by both women this time. "You two are evil."

"We're not married yet, dear. Careful what you say."

Sara giggled. "I like her for you, Liv. She's going to keep you in line."

Liv grumbled, but Sara knew she was playing. Grace was indeed perfect for Liv. Sara harbored the teeniest bit of jealousy because of it.

Liv said, "Let's take this back to the house. We've got notes to go over."

"Notes? Are you serious?" Sara glanced from Liv to Grace. "You actually have notes about your wedding?"

"Hell, yes. Otherwise, I'd forget half the stuff I'm supposed to do. Especially the stuff I need you to do for me as my best person."

Sara slid out of the booth and put her coat on. "This better be a damn short list."

"It is. And it's your favorite activity." Liv wouldn't look her in the eye, and Sara realized what she was about to say. "You get to plan my bachelorette party."

"Yippee."

Chapter Three

Terry Alexander watched her daughter stubbornly cross her legs and remain in front of the TV. If she didn't get moving, she'd be late for school and Terry late for work. Oh how she hated Mondays.

Her gaze went from Felicia to a picture on the mantle below the TV: she and Ann on their honeymoon at Niagara Falls. They wore those silly, blue-plastic, raincoat things, smiling and laughing while getting soaked by the spray from the falls. Ann's shoulder-length, mousey-brown hair clumped against her head, but the look in her eyes... Ann's hazel eyes captured the happiness of the moment and a lifetime of promises.

Terry's stomach clenched. They never returned to Niagara, much as they often said they would. They'd planned to take Felicia when she was old enough.

Ann died before they could make it happen.

There'd be no trip to Niagara. The memories too painful for Terry to face. Much like the memories running through her brain.

She closed her eyes to force them out.

It didn't work. Terry wanted to push away the image of the Royal Canadian Mounted Police Officer at her door. The kind man gently told Terry her wife was dead. Car accident. On the way to get medicine for Felicia, which the Mountie handed to Terry as she stood in the doorway to their home in shock.

Years later she recovered enough to feel her life was back to normal. Felicia loved her school in Whitehorse, and they both loved living with Terry's mother. She should have been happier.

Terry checked the time on her phone and ended up staring at the wallpaper on it she refused to change. Sara Hyatt smiled at her from her perch on their friend's boat, the lake water crystalline from the sun's rays behind her. She was the only woman Terry dated since Ann.

On some level, she felt unfaithful to Ann. But one look at Sara and Terry was gone. There was something special about her, sweet and loving in those soft, blue-green eyes—Terry found it hard to look away.

Three weeks passed before Terry realized she was in love with Sara. The idea was crazy, but things happened so fast Terry didn't bother to sit and ponder it. She accepted the fact and held that love tightly to her chest, where she kept it still. She'd never told Sara.

Now Sara would never meet Felicia as they'd planned. Never get the chance to know her and be part of her life. Never get the chance to find out if Terry and Sara were meant for each other.

Sara never once shied away from Terry after finding out how special Felicia was. Not even for a second. Most women would have turned away. But not Sara.

Terry closed her eyes and allowed herself to remember the day she showed Sara Felicia's picture.

Terry caught Sara's lips with her own to stop her from talking. They'd been going on and on, back and forth, about what movie to watch, and Sara, being Sara, gave her a rundown of each one and what she did or didn't like about them. Terry didn't care. She wanted to spend time with her, time she didn't have much of. Every minute with Sara was precious, and she felt like they were wasting it on this silly discussion.

"Tell you what," she said once the delicious kissing ended, "you grab a DVD—any DVD—put it in and we'll watch it. I'll sit on the sofa, and with any luck, you'll cuddle up to me and we'll enjoy a restful evening together. Deal?"

Sara grinned at her, and Terry's stomach did a little flip. Happened every time the woman smiled at her. Like a mischievous kid with some very adult thoughts. "I'll put in the romcom," Sara said. "Put us in the mood."

"I'm always in the mood around you," Terry said. Once the movie was going, she held her right arm up and Sara settled next to her. She was delighted with how well they fit together. Sara's head leaned against Terry's shoulder, and Terry rested her head against Sara's. She sighed in contentment and Sara giggled. "What?" Terry asked.

"We're an old married couple already," Sara said.

"How so?"

"Every Friday you come over here after work, and we have dinner and settle in for a movie. How much more domestic can we get?"

Terry thought about it for a moment, and a vision of Felicia came to mind. What would it be like to come home, have dinner with Felicia and Sara, put her daughter to bed, and cuddle with Sara for a few hours? It'd been forever since Terry had enjoyed any kind of domestic happiness. Was it possible for Sara to be the one to bring it back into her life?

"Hey." Sara sat up and leveled her gaze at Terry. The movie paused, and the living room was weirdly quiet. "Did I say something wrong?"

"Huh? No. I mean—I was thinking about the domestic thingy. It's been awhile."

Sara covered her mouth with her hand, and a look of horror crossed her face. "Oh shit. I'm sorry. I wasn't thinking."

"Don't apologize." Terry took hold of her hand and leaned in for a kiss. "I come with baggage, you know? I didn't think I'd ever date again, much less be 'domestic.'"

"Could you? Be domestic again?" Sara's voice was quiet, as if she were afraid of Terry's answer.

Terry was afraid of the answer as well. "I don't know, but there is something I think we need to do."

"What?"

"We never chose a date for you to meet Felicia."

"No, we didn't," Sara said quietly, not looking up at her. "I figured you were waiting for the right time. I know your schedule can be crazy."

"I was thinking of taking her to Burke Park on Sunday. The weather's supposed to be sunny and mild, and I think it'd be the best place to introduce you. She loves it there."

Sara lifted her head and kissed Terry. "It's a date." She leaned into Terry and curled her legs onto the couch. "It'll be awesome."

"I hope so. There's—I haven't told you everything you should know about my kid."

Sara sat up to face Terry. "Honey, stop being such a worrier. Everything will be fine. Even if she's a holy terror."

Terry laughed. "She's not a terror, but she is—different." Terry reached to the side table and picked up her phone. She thumbed through a few pictures and settled on one of Felicia in the backyard, making snow angels in the dry, autumn leaves. She smiled at the expression of glee on her face. Even if with no snow, she'd insisted it was still a snow angel.

With some trepidation, Terry angled the phone toward Sara.

"Oh! How adorable!" Sara took the phone to get a better look. "She's making a snow angel in the leaves."

"How do you know?"

"It's obvious by the way her arms are spread out," Sara said, a very big, goofy grin on her face. "Oh, I like this kid. I like her a lot."

"Sara." Terry's voice lowered to get her attention. "Have you looked closely at the picture?"

"Um, yes?" Sara handed the phone back. "Is there something weird I should see? It's not one of those where something jumps out at you after a few seconds, is it?"

"No. That's, um, creepy. No, I mean did you look closely at Felicia?"

"Should I have?" The question was genuine, and Terry relaxed a little. Had Sara not noticed?

"Felicia has Down Syndrome."

"Uh, duh. It's fairly obvious." Realization must have dawned on her as she said, "Was I supposed to comment on it? Did I do something wrong here?"

"No, no you didn't do a thing wrong. I'm used to people making sure they say something about it."

"Like what?" Sara asked.

"Like how hard it must be, or how sorry they are."

"Why would I be sorry? I mean, I don't know anything about it, but it can't be easy. Then again, is raising a child ever easy? Even if you have both parents?"

"I don't know. It was pretty easy the first few years."

Sara leaned forward and kissed her softly on the lips. "I'm no expert on these things, but all I see is a healthy, happy child smiling up at someone she obviously loves. Honestly, there's nothing else to see. And I can tell by the way you talk about her you're a good mom."

Terry put the phone down and drew Sara in for a kiss she hoped would show her how special she was. There were no words as they pulled apart, eyes locked, smiling at each other. Terry took the remote from Sara and hit the Play button. She turned her attention to the movie and envisioned herself with Sara and Felicia—a second chance for her to have a family again.

Terry shook herself out of her memory-laden thoughts. It did her no good to rehash the past. She focused on Felicia, who was, as with most mornings, being grumpy. It wouldn't last, and it was kind of cute, but not today. She wanted to get to work on time. She tried another tactic, though reasoning with an eight-year-old wasn't always successful.

"I know you want to watch Dora, but Mommy has to go to work and you have to go to school."

Felicia crossed her chubby arms over her chest and stuck out her bottom lip. "School sucks." Her almond-shaped, hazel eyes stared up at Terry. Her round face was set and determined, as usual, showing Terry her ever-present stubborn streak. That streak and the hazel color of her eyes were stark reminders of Ann. As was the mousey-brown color of her fine, straight hair. The slant of her eyes and her short stature set her apart from Ann and everyone else.

Terry considered admonishing her for saying "sucks" but chose to ignore it and grabbed Felicia's backpack. "Maybe, but you're still going." She took her by the hand, gently pulled her to her feet, and led her to her grey, Ford F-350 truck. The one luxury she afforded herself after moving to Whitehorse. The truck was a sturdy four-door with 4-wheel drive. Something she sorely needed in the Yukon Territory.

Felicia grumbled a little in her booster seat but soon was chattering away about the snow when they were on the road. Terry had trouble keeping up with her daughter's moods.

"Music please," Felicia asked in her most polite voice.

Terry smiled and turned up the volume to allow Felicia to sing along. The artist was Lady Gaga and thankfully singing one of her less racy tunes. Terry kept an eye on Felicia as she drove and enjoyed the fun she was having. By the time they got to the school, Felicia was grinning and excited to go see her friends. Terry handed her and the backpack off to Sally Johnson, the assistant principal. Sally was probably the same age as Terry's mother, a bit overweight, with dark-brown skin and a ready smile. Terry wondered how the woman managed to always be in a good mood.

Terry bent to give Felicia a goodbye kiss, but she was already running to the doors of the school.

"She's never still," Sally said with a laugh. "I don't know how you're able to deal with her every day. I'm exhausted after a few minutes."

"If it weren't for my mom, I don't think I'd be able to function. And the school is close to my office. It's a godsend."

Sally gave a mock bow. "We aim to please. Now if you'll excuse me, I have cats to herd."

"And you wonder how I manage."

"At least I get paid for it." Sally intercepted two boys heading for the playground. "Nope. Inside you two. Outside later."

Terry took a moment to watch Sally get the other kids into the building. She'd already lost sight of Felicia, who clearly wasn't bothered to leave her mom behind. It made Terry a little sad to think there might come a time when her child wouldn't need her so much.

She took a deep, settling breath and got into her truck to make the ten-minute trip to her office. She had set no appointments for the morning, but she still hated being late. She unlocked the door at 9:05 and immediately heard her phone beep to let her know of a new voicemail.

She hit the Play button and settled at her desk to listen.

"Mrs. Alexander, this is Warwick Shue from Dresden Diamond Mines. I'd like to set up a conference call with you to discuss your report regarding our new site. Please return my call today to arrange this."

She jotted down the number and did a fist pump. This was the news she'd been waiting on. Her report gave the mine hope of opening a new operation 150 kilometers to the east of Dresden. Currently, they had to use the treacherous Ice Road to get major supplies in and out. Use of the Ice Road was limited to a few months in the heart of winter when the water between Yellowknife and Dresden was frozen.

If they successfully located diamonds at the newly acquired location, they would be able to build a road to use year round, saving the company nearly a million dollars each year. Terry's report highlighted two important things: where the diamonds might be and the cost of looking for them.

She started to call Mr. Shue, but the office door opened and a welcome visitor stepped inside. Frank Trane sported a wide grin as he removed his Indiana Jones fedora and plopped his large frame onto one of the chairs in front of Terry's desk. He practically glowed with excitement.

"Congratulations," he said.

"Thanks. What did I do?"

"Got the Dresden contract. I'd say I'm surprised, but it'd be a lie. I knew you'd get it."

Terry sat back in her chair and stared at Frank. "And you know this how? I haven't called them yet."

"I know people. I keep telling you this." He kept grinning despite the frown she tossed at him. "I knew I sold my business to the right person. You'll be the most sought-after geologist in the territory. Plus, I'm here to make you an offer."

"Frank, did you have anything to do with me getting this contract? Like maybe calling in favors or something?"

"Nope. You done that all on your own. All I did was call Warwick's daddy to see how things were going. Theo and I went to school together."

"I'm not shocked one bit. Is there anyone in the territory you don't know?"

Frank pretended to think about it, and it made Terry laugh. "Pretty sure there are folks I don't know. And I'm sure they don't matter all that much in the scheme of things. At least not to me."

"Gotcha. So, your offer?"

"My wife is glad I sold the business, as you know. Retirement is supposed to be all fun and games and it is—in the summer. But it's winter, and dammit, I'm bored."

"You came here to work, didn't you?"

He nodded. "I did indeed."

"I'd love to, but I can't afford you."

"I don't need to get paid. I want to help out. Maybe with the stuff at Dresden. I'm familiar with those guys and thought you could use a hand. I did some reports for them before you got here, I'm familiar with what they want. Not that I think you're not capable and all, but some of those meatheads can be hard to deal with."

She didn't like how Frank felt the need to protect her, but his heart was in the right place. She was lucky to call him a friend and wouldn't deny the man anything.

"It's a deal. Want to hang around while I call them back? We can make sure to plan the conference call when you're available."

Frank's face lit up, and Terry realized the good thing she'd done. Made him feel useful again. "Perfect. But first, let's get some coffee. And a donut or two. I skipped breakfast."

"Sure, but I'm buying. It's the least I can do."

He got up, placed his hat on his head, and tilted it slightly to the left. "Never turn down free coffee. It's bad luck."

****

Starbucks was crowded, so Terry steered Frank to Liam's Bakery. Frank practically drooled over the amazing assortment of donuts on display. The smell hit them as they entered and nearly gave Terry a sugar rush. Was it possible to gain weight by smelling sugar? Mixed with a hint of fresh coffee, the odor was divine and exactly what Terry needed. Sleep eluded her last night, as it did most nights, and a serious pick-me-up was in order.

She made her selection and waited patiently for Frank to get his. Once finished, he gallantly offered to carry the box of too many confections back to the office, while Terry was in charge of the coffee.

She stole a sip of her drink before leaving. At the same moment, her eyes caught sight of the reason for her sleepless nights. Sara Hyatt opened the door, and their eyes locked. Terry's breath caught, and she was unable to form any words. It wasn't the first time she'd run into Sara, but it was the first time they'd come face-to-face.

Frank deftly avoided crashing into Terry, who had yet to move. He slipped around her and held the door open. "C'mon before the coffee gets cold."

Terry glanced at him, and it was enough to break the spell. Sara moved away from her without a word. Terry didn't blame her. She'd hurt Sara, and there was no way to fix things between them.

Frank muttered something about the coffee. Terry hurried out the door to join him. "There's a microwave in the office. We can heat the coffee up."

"Not the same," he said. "I don't like radiation mixed with my caffeine."

"Have I ever told you how weird you are?"

Frank seemed to enjoy it more than he should. "You haven't. But I like it. I can be weird. It suits me."

"It does." Terry glanced behind them at the bakery. She couldn't see Sara but wondered if she watched them leave. She was probably glad they were gone. And it broke Terry's heart more than she thought possible. Her mind easily slipped back to earlier times…

The sun shone brightly against the lake water and Terry adjusted her sunglasses. They'd borrowed Frank's boat for the day and were enjoying a nice swim with Liv and Grace. Sara was in the water with Liv, and the two of them were splashing and wrestling like little kids.

Grace took a seat on the deck beside Terry. "They'll never grow up."

"Nope. I think it's a good thing, though. Keeps them young."

Grace smirked. "Keeps me feeling like I'm raising two kids sometimes."

"Heh. Try doing it for real. You'd probably find those two much easier to deal with."

"I'm sure you're right. How's Felicia doing?"

Terry sighed. "Her sunburn is fading, but you'd never know it bothered her unless she stops to take a breath. I've never seen a kid with as much energy in my life. Mom practically had to hold her down to put a layer of sunscreen on her this morning. I'm not repeating the whole staying-up-all-night-because-her-skin-hurts thing any time soon."

"I bet not. You know, you ought to bring her over Sunday. We'd love to meet her." Grace studied her for a moment. "You do know she's as welcome as you are, right?"

Terry smiled, glad Sara's friends were accepting of her. "I do and thanks. I want to wait a bit before I introduce her around. She gets attached to people easily, and the move here from Quebec's been hard on her." She watched Liv and Sara still giggling and splashing each other. "I don't want to sound harsh, but I need her to meet Sara first. If things work out, then I'll introduce her around. I know she'd love meeting you two."

"It's not harsh at all. It's smart." Grace leaned forward and grabbed a couple of beers out of the cooler. "You're a good mom, Terry."

"Thanks." Terry clinked her bottle against Grace's. "And thanks for inviting us today. I forgot how beautiful it is in the middle of nowhere."

"It's been an adjustment for me. I've lived in big cities most of my life, and I like the quiet. I used to come every summer to visit *Ojiichan*, but I spent the majority of my time at the mine."

"*Ojiichan?*"

"Grandpa. It's Japanese."

"Oh, cool. Sara mentioned you're something of a linguist."

Grace shrugged. "It's my thing. It's what I did in the army."

"Are you going to do translations here? I don't know how much need there is for Japanese translators."

"Maybe not Japanese, but I'm good with pretty much any language. I'm learning French right now. Thought I'd start there and maybe go back to the Arabic I was studying a few years ago."

"I took six years of French in school and can barely form a sentence. You are officially my new hero."

"Who's your hero?" Sara asked as she climbed onto the boat dripping wet.

"Gracie."

"Ah, well that's acceptable." Sara plopped onto Terry's lap, nearly causing her to spill her beer. She wrapped her arms around Terry, who enjoyed Sara's breasts practically in her face. Her bikini barely covered the important parts.

"You're getting me wet," Terry said as she slipped her arms around Sara.

"Best line ever."

"I got a lot more lines." Terry trailed kisses along Sara's chest, to her breasts, brushing against her taut nipples. "Want to hear them?"

"Hell yes."

"Get a room!" Liv yelled once she joined them. She flicked a towel at Sara and caught her in the arm. "You two are like a couple of randy teenagers."

"Says the woman giggling like a teenager a few minutes ago," Grace said. She got up from her chair and took the towel from Liv before she flicked anyone else with it. "You are a great big toddler."

"Says who?"

"Says me. Now come on. You're going to help me get lunch together." Grace dragged her toward the galley with Liv protesting all the way.

Terry snickered. "I like those two. I'm glad we came out here today."

"They're good people." Sara leaned into her and placed a kiss on Terry's forehead. "It's always fun when we're out. Best of all, Liv made sure to tell me you meet with her approval."

"Was I in need of approval?"

"Sort of." Sara pulled back so they were eye-to-eye. Terry felt a stirring in her stomach at the way Sara's eyes looked right through her. Like she knew her every thought and feeling Terry had. "Livvy's my best friend. Has been since high school. I've never dated anyone she didn't like. I can't explain it, but I always seem to want her approval."

"I don't mind. If it means anything, she meets with my approval as well."

Sara smiled and Terry's heart sped up a little.

"Is it weird I want to kiss you right now?" she asked.

"Nope. I think it'd be weird if you didn't."

Terry met Sara's lips in a long, sultry kiss. She pulled Sara closer as the kiss deepened and wished they were alone. She'd have taken Sara on the deck of the boat. More importantly, she realized her relationship with Sara had moved beyond casual. Right then, in the middle of a lake, with Sara's friends in the galley, Terry realized she was very much in love with Sara.

They pulled apart, and as their eyes met again, Terry wondered what the hell she was going to do about it.

****

Terry sorted through the pile of papers on her desk, glad the day would soon end. Shirley, her mom, had called to let her know Felicia was installed in front of the TV playing with Elmo, her mom's terrier. The little beast loved the little human, and Terry regretted not being there to see them be cute. At least her mom would take pictures.

When she lived in Quebec, Terry struggled to keep a balance between work and home, needing to send Felicia to daycare for at least two hours every day after school. Shirley was the reason Terry moved back to Whitehorse from Quebec. She missed her mom, and in the three years since Ann died, she'd been unable to cope on her own. She was lucky Shirley had flexible hours and stepped in to pick up Felicia when Terry couldn't.

Last year, Terry's father died of a heart attack. She offered to move to Whitehorse then, but her mom wouldn't have it. Terry'd made a home in Quebec, and it would be hard on Felicia to move. At least, that was Shirley's reasoning at the time. But Terry understood the hardship on her mother being there alone. Within six months, she made the decision to live in Whitehorse.

Shirley fought her at first but eventually gave up. Shirley came up with the idea for Terry to speak to Frank about buying his business. He wanted to retire, and she used the money from the sale of her house in Quebec as a down payment.

Frank was well established as a geologist in the Yukon. He'd built a solid reputation over the last thirty years. Because he and

Shirley were friends since high school, he'd happily sold the business to Terry along with his list of clients. He sanctioned Terry's skills to everyone he spoke to. His word alone gave her a decent start. She expected to make a profit in another year or so.

But right now, every extra penny she had went to a lawyer. And it cut her deeper than she expected it to.

She straightened a pile of paperwork and decided it was enough for one day. Her mind wasn't in it, and she'd get little done tonight. It was already dark outside, and she was beyond starved. Two stale donuts did not a good lunch make. She stood to get her coat and, through the window, noticed someone crossing the street in front of her office.

Her heart skipped a beat. The thin figure, wrapped in a long, white coat, was Sara. She had her head down and didn't see Terry watching her. She seemed preoccupied and nearly ran into someone as she trudged along. Terry briefly considered offering her a ride home, but she was certain the kindness would be refused.

And she didn't blame her. Not after what Terry did. Maybe if Sara knew the reason for the breakup, she'd understand. It wasn't like Terry had any real choice. But how could she even begin to explain? Her world was falling apart, and she'd managed to shove away the one person she needed the most.

Terry's gaze fell to a photo of Felicia. She picked up the small, wooden frame with the "World's Best Mom" carved into the bottom. Felicia was nestled in her arms, moments after being born. Terry still wore pale-blue scrubs and looked like hell, but she grinned at the memory. When she and Felicia bonded. They didn't need DNA to be mother and child, just those few seconds of knowing and loving each other.

She put the frame in its place, her eyes never leaving the squirming baby in her arms. Felicia was a handful. She didn't always mind. She was an eight-year-old growing up without both parents. A fact Terry could do little about.

But she would damn well make sure Felicia had one of those parents forever. Even if it meant Terry would have to go around with a broken heart. Or if it meant she had to hurt the woman she loved.

"Damn you, Ann," she said.

Terry didn't think she'd ever be able to move forward with her life, and she sure as hell didn't expect she'd fall in love again. Then Sara came along and made her rethink everything. She decided to let Sara meet Felicia. They'd made plans. Then William showed up. He'd filed for custody of Felicia. When Terry read the documents, she almost couldn't believe what she was seeing.

"Not in the best interest of the child," it read. It stated she'd ripped Felicia from her network of doctors in Quebec. It went on to say William and his wife were better equipped for Felicia's needs—both physically and financially. The fact that she had to sell their home was listed as proof Terry didn't have enough finances to care for her child.

What a load of bullshit.

She cringed when he called her, his voice almost cheerful with his news. Terry finished work on a new site for one of Frank's oldest clients and she was filthy, tired, and not in the mood for any of William's usual crap. "What can I do for you?" she asked.

"I'm filing for custody of Felicia."

"What?" Terry nearly dropped her backpack, laden with tools and equipment. She flung it into the back of her truck and leaned against the quarter panel. "What the hell are you talking about?"

"I'm going to get custody of my grandchild. You're not a fit parent."

"You can't possibly prove any such thing."

"You spend very little time with her, and you refuse to bring her here where we can take care of you both. I always hated that Ann lived far away. You should have let me move you to Vancouver, to live with us instead of moving in with your mother in this backwater town. This is not good for Felicia."

"We live closer to Vancouver now. You can get a flight and be here in an hour if you want. It's not like you can't afford the trip."

"I shouldn't have to."

"And I shouldn't have to raise her on my own, but I am. I already told you this, William. I couldn't afford to keep the house on my salary. Besides, my mom needs me here. I have a new business with established clients, and by next year, Felicia and I will have our own home. It's a good place for us to be."

His eerie silence unnerved her. When he spoke, his voice was as cold as a Yukon winter. "Does it include replacing my daughter?"

"What? I loved Ann."

"No, you loved her money. And now you've found someone else to tap into. I've seen the photos of you out drinking and going to bars. I won't let you bring up Felicia in such an environment."

"Photos? What are you talking about?"

"I hired someone to follow you. These will help me prove you're an unfit parent. I'll also bring up the fact Ann didn't trust you with her money and left it all to her child."

Terry's heart clenched. "Ann knew I wouldn't want your money any more than she did. It's why she put it into a trust for Felicia. I won't touch it, because Felicia will need it when I'm gone. You can't do this."

"I can and I am."

"What would it take to make you stop?" She heard the words come out in a panic. Could he take her child away?

"First step—stop seeing that woman. I won't have Ann replaced by someone like her."

"And?"

"Then we'll talk."

Terry broke up with Sara the next day, but it wasn't enough for

William. He demanded she move to his house in Vancouver. Terry tried to explain she couldn't move Felicia again. Too much change is bad for her—Felicia wouldn't understand.

The next day, he filed for custody.

The little money in her savings account was now tied up in lawyer and court fees. The one thing in her favor was the case had to be heard by a mediator, which was less expensive than going to court. It also meant William was the one to have to fly back and forth from Vancouver. At least it's one expense she didn't have to deal with.

And it hadn't mattered if she was with Sara or not.

Jackie Smith, her lawyer, didn't think William had much of a chance, but his lawyers were tough and Jackie told her up front it would not be an easy fight. She agreed it was in Felicia's best interests to stay with her, not her grandparents.

The energy she put into it all was often overwhelming, and she wanted to go to Sara and hold her and be held and told everything would be okay. Except it wouldn't be. More than once she considered calling Sara and trying to mend the mess she'd created. She never should have turned her back on her. Sara was strong, steady, and reliable—and Terry was still desperately in love with her.

The phone rang and thankfully pulled Terry from her thoughts. "This is Terry."

"This is Terry's mother," Shirley said with a light laugh. "Are you coming home tonight? I'm fixing spaghetti and there's this little monster here who's getting hungry." As if on cue, Terry heard Felicia repeat her grandmother's words.

"Finishing up some paperwork."

Shirley paused. "Are you okay?"

Terry rolled her eyes. How did her mother do that? Was there ever a time Shirley Alexander hadn't been able to read her moods? Terry didn't think so. "Fine. I've been having an up-and-down day."

"We'll talk about the down part when you get home. Don't stay too late, okay?"

"I'll leave in a few minutes."

"Good girl," Shirley said. Felicia repeated her words followed by more laughter.

"Bye, Mom." Terry disconnected and let her gaze rest on the photo again. It was one of the happiest days in her life. Next to the day she married Ann. She touched the empty ring finger of her left hand and sighed. She thought the absence of the ring would help her move on. It had. For a time.

She grabbed her coat and keys, locked up the office, and was halfway to her car when she stopped in mid-stride.

Parked next to her was a shiny, black BMW sedan. The driver stared at her for a moment, and her heart sank. She'd know him anywhere. She wanted to put her head down and pretend she'd never seen the vehicle. Too late. She'd already been spotted.

William Dillson climbed out of the sleek car, dressed as impeccably as ever in black slacks and a gray overcoat that hung to his knees. His leather gloves were pulled tight over his large hands. He trod into Terry's personal space. He loomed a foot taller than her, but she did her best not to allow him to intimidate her.

"You haven't responded to my phone calls."

"Nice to see you, too." She glared at her daughter's grandfather. "What do you want?"

His hazel eyes, much like Ann's, narrowed at her. "I've come for Felicia. I have a right to see her."

Terry's temper neared boiling point. "The lawyers will work it out."

"I'm her grandfather."

"An unfortunate biological fact, but not one which requires me to let you see her. Besides, our lawyers are still fighting this out. Talk to yours, and if I need to know or do anything, mine will get back to me. We're not supposed to discuss this without them present."

She moved past him, but he grabbed her forearm to stop her. His grip tightened. "You won't keep the child from me."

"I never intended to, but I'm glad I moved up here." She pulled away from him. "You touch me again and I'll file charges. Understand?" She didn't wait for a reply. She got in her truck and left.

Her hands shook as she pulled away. Ann used to tell her stories of her father and his anger when he didn't get his way. Sometimes anger had physical manifestations, though he'd never outright hit Ann. His threats were far worse than any physical pain.

He liked to throw around the fact Ann needed him and his money. He paid for university. Bought her a nice car and her first apartment. But he couldn't buy her happiness. Ann being a lesbian was, at one time, a huge bone of contention and the one time Terry knew of Ann's mother stepping in to smooth things over.

William never accepted Terry into their lives. She wasn't rich and worked her ass off to go to university and get her degree. She was still working on her masters, though it was on hold at the moment.

When Ann proposed, William tried to force her to have Terry sign a prenuptial agreement. Terry was more than happy to do it. She didn't give a damn about William or his money, but Ann lost her composure, and for the first time in her life, she stood up to the man. In the end, he cut her off from any money except her trust fund. Ann, being Ann, got a job, and together they found an affordable house, fixed it up, and settled in. Without any of William's help.

Terry knew he was still pissed about it.

Felicia's birth brought him back into their lives, mostly due to his wife, Jennifer, wanting to see her granddaughter. Jennifer was good for Felicia, and Terry knew Felicia missed her. She'd be happy for Jennifer to see Felicia, if she'd do it without William.

Terry pulled into the driveway and took a moment to compose herself before going inside. Felicia could sense Terry's moods. She wanted to be in a good one and see her child's smiling face.

It would make her day.

She wasn't disappointed. The moment she stepped through the door, Felicia wrapped her arms around Terry. "I missed you, Mommy!"

Terry choked back sudden tears and picked Felicia up, twirling her around in the process. "I missed you, too. Did you have a good day?"

"Yep." And that was all the answer she'd get. If Felicia didn't want to talk about it, nothing anyone could do would make her. Terry gave her a kiss on both cheeks and put her down. "You have to eat. Grams says so." She scurried away, plopped on the floor of the living room amongst her crayons and coloring book, and got busy.

Terry set her briefcase down, removed her coat, and entered the kitchen.

"Timing," Shirley said. She held a plate of spaghetti she was about to put into the fridge. "I'll heat this up for you. Grab something to drink. You want some garlic bread?"

"Is it homemade?"

Shirley feigned being hurt, her hand over her heart. "You wound me, child. Have I ever served you frozen bread?"

"If I answer with the truth, do I still get to eat?"

"Maybe."

"Then no. You would never do such a thing."

"Good choice." Shirley handed over the steaming plate of food and got some bread ready for her. "How was your day?"

"Why does it sound like a loaded question when you ask it, but normal from anyone else?"

"Because I know you better than anyone else. And you can't hide the fact you started to cry when Felicia hugged you." Shirley gave her some fresh garlic bread and sat across the table from her. "I got a call from William today."

"Bastard," Terry said under her breath. She glanced to the living room to see if Felicia was listening. She didn't appear to be, but her child had super hearing and she kept her voice low. "He tried to railroad me at the office. I told him to talk to his lawyer."

"That all?"

"He grabbed my arm." Terry watched the color drain from her mother's face. "He didn't hurt me. But I have a feeling he's up to something. I got the impression he's even more impatient, like he wants this all said and done right now. I don't like him being here in Whitehorse, and I'm a little scared he's going to try to take Felicia."

"We won't let it happen." Shirley's eyes hardened as they often did when talking about William. "He doesn't have any rights to her as a grandparent, unless the mediator decides differently." She ran a hand through her short, light-brown hair. "You need to talk to Sally Johnson and make sure the school knows William isn't allowed near Felicia."

"I will." Terry wiped her mouth and pushed away her half-eaten food. Her stomach wanted to reject what she'd already swallowed. "I wish I had as much money as he does. At least that part of his ridiculous claim wouldn't be an issue."

"You don't have to raise her on your finances alone. I told you to have Jackie include my income."

"I can't include your income, Mom. I need to do this on my own. It's not like we're in the poor house. I make enough money to take care of my family. Anyway, I got the impression he's pissed I won't use Ann's money for Felicia unless I have to. But she'll need it later in life. We don't know what her development will be like, and I want to know she's financially secure. Why the hell does he feel he has the right to do this?"

Shirley moved her chair next to Terry's and embraced her. "I don't know. Probably goes back to how he's always gotten his way."

"I guess, but Mom, he doesn't even understand Felicia or what she needs. He thinks she's an eight-year-old infant, and it pisses me off."

"I think it pisses her off as well."

Terry gave a short laugh. "Probably does. She's a damn smart kid."

"She is. Call Jackie tomorrow. Ask her what you can do about him coming to see you today. Mention how he grabbed you."

"It's my word against his."

"Isn't it always? Please talk to her. She'll know what to do."

"Think she can fix my broken heart while she's at it?" Terry asked.

"I wish she could, honey. I wish you'd have talked to me first before breaking up with Sara. I thought she was good for you."

"I wouldn't have set it up for her to meet Felicia if she wasn't." Terry gazed into the living room at her child, certain Felica was listening to them.

"You should talk to Sara."

"I don't think it's a good idea. It's all I can do to make eye contact with her when I see her in town or at the bank. How could I possibly talk to her? What would I say? Sorry, but I was a complete chicken shit and should have told you what was going on? Forgive me and take me back?"

"A little awkward, but it's a start." Shirley kissed Terry on the forehead and got up. "Think about it. Now, try to finish your dinner. I'm sure you either skipped lunch or had something crappy."

"They were good."

"They?"

"The donuts."

"Stale?" Shirley asked.

"Um…"

"Finish your dinner. I'll get Felicia ready for bed. When you're done, you can read to her."

Terry didn't want to eat but felt the need to oblige her mother.

"Thanks, Mom." Shirley nodded before sweeping Felicia off the floor and tickling her all the way to her bedroom.

Terry's stomach complained after a few more forkfuls of spaghetti, and she stopped.

She closed her eyes, and an image of Ann appeared, dressed in her favorite torn jeans and worn-out, k.d. lang T-shirt. Her hair was pulled back in a ponytail, and her eyes twinkled with mischief. Terry wanted to slap the grin off her face. She wanted to throttle her and, at the same time, scoop her into her arms and hold her forever.

She wanted to blame Ann for dying. It would give her someone to be angry at. But the car's brakes locked up on a patch of black ice, sending it into a spin. It slammed against the guard rail, smashing the driver's side against the steel barrier. Ann died instantly of a broken neck from the impact. The RCMP said the crash was over in seconds.

The anger lingered in the back of her mind for years, making itself known when Terry was least equipped to deal with it.

Sara helped Terry realize she needed to move past the anger and allow herself to grieve.

Was it some kind of cosmic joke she had to give up Sara to keep Felicia? What would Ann say if she knew? She'd probably shake some sense into Terry and order her to talk to Sara. But Terry didn't think it was possible now. She'd lost the only two women she'd ever love. She accepted it and would move on. No more dating. No more relationships. The pain was too much to deal with.

She opened her eyes, wiped away the latest batch of tears, and stacked her dirty dishes in the dishwasher. Plastering on the most genuine smile she could muster, she grabbed *Where the Wild Things Are* and went to Felicia's room for her nightly reading.

Chapter Four

"You didn't," Grace said, not exactly hiding her surprise. She sat across the table from Sara at Pot O' Gold for their weekly Wednesday luncheon, and they were the sole customers at the moment. "Tell me you didn't."

Sara tried to hide her disappointment. "My clothes were all over the room, Gracie. I have no damn idea what we did, but I found my shoe in the bathtub and a shirt tucked under the mattress."

"And you still don't remember a thing?" Grace's lovely face pinched a little, like she was trying hard not to bust out laughing.

"Nope." Sara glanced away from her for a moment. "I wish like hell I did. Sounds like we had a great time."

"And you're going out with her next Saturday?"

"I am. Dancing again. It's a new club out on Highway 1, but I've never heard of it. Bren runs in circles I don't."

"Circles for little kids." Grace's brown eyes twinkled. Unlike Liv, Grace found the humor in Sara's weird Friday night. "Is she legal to go places that sell alcohol?"

"Ha-ha. Yes, she is. She's twenty-two, if you must know."

"Wow. You're sure about a second date?"

Sara sighed dramatically. "Sort of. I mean, she obviously wants to see me again. Maybe I'm hoping for a repeat of Friday night—minus the amnesia."

"Then I suggest you stick to soda."

"That's the plan." Sara took a sip of her diet drink and sat back in the booth. "Tell me *your* plans. I assume you've gotten more done on the wedding?"

"Sort of. I don't want it to be very big, but our invite list keeps growing. I swear Olivia knows every person in Canada and wants them to come. At this rate, we'll need to rent the convention center."

"You need to put your foot down. I'm surprised she hasn't invited the whole city."

Grace raised one eyebrow. "I think she has."

"Time for an intervention?"

"Maybe. As her best person, you could talk to her. Gently remind her we wanted a small, intimate gathering of our closest friends and family. Right now the list is over one hundred."

"Shit. It was around fifty last weekend."

"Right. What do you think? Come over Sunday? We'll plan a two-pronged attack."

"You've got this all worked out, haven't you?"

"I have. I need help from the best friend. You in?"

Sara raised her glass in a salute. "You betcha."

"Excellent." Grace returned the salute. She took a sip from her drink and ran a hand through hair so silky black Sara often envied her. "Now, tell me about the woman you had dinner with on Saturday."

Sara nearly choked on her drink. "What?"

"Tell me who she is. You know I'm dying to find out, and I will resort to very low tactics if I need to. It might include asking Izzy."

Sara glanced at the bar, happy no one was there at the moment. Was it possible Izzy knew who she'd been to dinner with? Hell, was it possible Izzy didn't know?

"You don't like her, and I don't really want to tell you."

"I don't know many people," Grace said. "And what does it matter if I like her? You're the one going out with her."

"Once." Sara emphasized the word. "I don't see more dates in the future."

"What's the harm in giving me a name?" Grace leaned forward, real concern etched across her face. Her dark eyes held Sara's for the longest time. "Don't make me worry about you."

"There's no need. Besides, I'd rather be excited about dancing with Bren. At least she's fun, and I know I'll enjoy myself. Might help me forget a certain someone."

"Not likely." Grace reached across the table and took Sara's hand. "You can't simply forget her."

"I can try." Sara smiled at her. "Bren can help me. I don't know much about her, but I get the impression she's good for me."

"I hope so." Grace kept an eye on Sara. She knew Grace wanted to say more and was glad she didn't.

Sara decided to divert the conversation to the wedding. "So, a hundred people?"

Grace sighed, accepting the shift. "One hundred and two to be exact. There's only ten people, other than our families, who I know. I think she might have invited people she went to university with, high school, ex-girlfriends… I have no idea who these people are."

"You can forget the ex-girlfriends. I know all of them. I'm the one she still speaks to. I'll go over the list, okay? We'll get it down to a reasonable number. I think Liv is excited, and let me tell you, I never thought she'd be excited about anything as she is about marrying you."

Grace's dark features lightened with a blush. "You're probably right, and I'm likely overreacting. I'd like to climb onto a cliff overlooking the mountains and have a Justice of the Peace marry us right there. With the three of us present."

"If I knew of a JP who climbed rocks, I'd hook you up."

"That's why I like you." Grace smiled sweetly and glanced at her watch. "Okay. Need to head to the office. Olivia is supposed to help me sort through some of the paperwork for my grandfather's mine. I don't have a handle on Canadian taxes yet."

"You're in good hands. She's awesome with that stuff." Sara got up and handed Grace's coat to her. "I'll see you on Sunday, and I promise to knock this time."

"Good plan."

****

The office for TNT was located in the former Templeton family home. The first floor consisted of an office for Liv, where she ran the business now her dad was retired, a kitchen, and a reception room for business meetings. The three bedrooms and family bathroom were still upstairs, one of the bedrooms occupied by Liv's oldest brother, Dave. It was nice to have him living in the house and always close by.

He was also a great asset as the manager for their largest mining operation.

Her youngest brother, Timothy, was still at university in Toronto and stayed here when he visited. He was due in next weekend, and Liv was excited to see him. She and her brothers were close, and any chance to get the family together was a welcome one.

She sighed, her head not in the work she was supposed to do. Instead she was thinking about her wedding. The reality of it was getting closer. She looked at the silver band on her finger and grinned.

Married. She would be married in a few short months, April, on the cusp of spring. She felt amazed and scared and excited all at once—and like jumping for joy. And maybe adding a few names to her ever-growing list of people to invite. If she could, Liv would have the entire population of the Yukon Territory there to witness her joining with Grace. Ever the romantic, she envisioned herself shouting from the rooftops how much she loved this woman.

Liv closed her eyes and laughed.

What she needed to do was work. Their winter business of renting equipment, ranging from construction equipment to road works, wouldn't run itself. Especially if she didn't get the invoices sorted out. She hated all the paperwork. She'd much rather be at the shop working on whatever vehicle was there for repairs. She loved crawling around the big, heavy, construction equipment the best, getting her hands dirty, the odor of grease and diesel fuel in the air...even her dad thought she was their best mechanic, but she was also CEO of the business. After all, it's what she'd gone to university for.

She sighed and returned to the damn paperwork as the door to the house opened. Seconds later, she smelled French fries and grinned. "If the food is for me, I'll promise to love you forever."

Grace entered the room, her movements slow and deliberate as if she was toying with Liv. She placed two bags on her desk, along with a to-go cup of what she assumed would be cola. "I thought you already promised me? Isn't it why we're getting married?"

"Hmm, I think you might be right." Liv dug into her food, not at all embarrassed when her stomach announced its hunger. "Thanks," she said around a big bite of hamburger. "I needed this."

"I figured." Grace moved some of the paperwork out of the way of the food and settled in a chair across from Liv. She crossed one muscular leg over the other, and the action made Liv momentarily forget her hunger. Her hunger for food, anyway. "You need to stop skipping meals."

"I don't skip them," Liv said. "I forget them. There's a difference."

"Uh-huh." Grace stole a fry and gave her a look Liv was all too familiar with. "I mean it. If you have to pack a sandwich with you in the morning, please do so. You're too tired when you get home, and this will at least give you some energy to get through the day."

Liv knew Grace was seriously worried about her, and it made her heart swell. She was damn lucky to have the woman in her life. "I'll do better. Promise. I'll have to make a note to buy some food though."

"I already did," Grace said with a smirk. "Your fridge and cabinets are stocked up for at least a week. If I'm going to spend any amount of time there, I plan to eat semi-healthy meals."

"How much time are you planning to spend?"

"As much as I can," she said but wouldn't look Liv in the eye. Something was up, and Liv put her food down. "I'm worried about *Ojiichan*."

"Is he feeling bad or something?" Liv asked

"No. I think he's gotten used to having me around all the time. I do a lot for him now because he's too weak. This last heart attack took a lot out of him."

Liv watched the torrent of emotions cross Grace's face. She moved to the chair opposite her. Grace didn't say anything more. Liv took hold of her hands and went to her knees on the floor. She slid her fingers over Grace's dark skin while she considered what to do next. An idea occurred to her, and she wanted to slap herself for not thinking of it sooner.

"You know our house is pretty big, right?"

"I've been there." Grace's brow furrowed. "Define big."

"Big as in it has a guest room with a bathroom right next to it. If we knock a wall down, we can build an en suite." Liv placed kisses on Grace's hands. "What I'm getting at is Harry should move in with us. We'd be a helluva lot closer to the hospital and his doctor in case he needs anything, and you wouldn't have to spend so much time worrying about him. He'd be right there, with us.

"We can look at adding on to the house, too, if you'd like. I'm sure we've got enough space in the side yard we could put in a small living area with a fridge and microwave. I mean, it's not like he can cook so he wouldn't need an oven and—"

Grace cut her off with a soft kiss. "You're serious?"

"Harry's always been like family to me, and it wouldn't be a big deal to have him live with us. It's a win-win. I hate him being far away, and I'm hating it even more you're not with me. I want you there all the time, Grace. Will you please move in with me?"

"Liv, we discussed this already. Once we're married, I'll get settled in. I promise."

"I don't—I hate—dammit. You said you'd move in at the end of the mining season, and that was October. Now it's January." Liv got to her feet, let go of Grace's hands, and sat down again. "If you and Harry move in now, it would save some time and effort. I'll even shut up about putting your name on the deed. Grace, I can't tell you how hard it is on the nights you're not there."

"You think I don't feel the same?" Grace asked, an accusatory tone in her voice.

Liv sat up straighter, knowing the fight was coming but unable to make herself stop. "I don't know. You don't seem interested in moving to our house. You have half your stuff there now. Why is it such a big deal? Why are you stalling?"

"You wouldn't understand."

"I would, if you'd tell me."

"It's not as easy as you think it is. You know it's been hard for me. It took a lot to trust again after Carly." She rubbed the arm Carly nearly crippled. Grace still did the rock climbing she loved, but her arm would never be as strong as it once was.

It's when Liv realized what Grace wasn't saying. *Carly* was the issue. She feared moving in with Liv. She and Carly moved in together early in their relationship and it turned out to be a huge mistake. Carly started abusing Grace a year later and by the time they got married she was beating her. She often wondered if Carly forced Grace into the marriage.

"I'm not Carly," Liv said, and instantly regretted it.

Grace's expression dropped, and her face paled. "I never said you were."

"But you're comparing me to her, whether you realize it or not."

"I'm not. Olivia, I'm honestly scared about all this. Yes, I want to marry you. Yes, I want to be with you the rest of our lives, but it doesn't mean it's easy for me. I feel like I got my freedom back, and in some respects, I'd be giving it up again."

"No, you wouldn't. I'd never ask you to do that."

"You don't have to. Marriage means you have to compromise, and sometimes it means losing out on things. In a sense, I'd be giving up some of my freedom to be with you. And it's damn hard for me."

"I'm having a hard time understanding, Gracie. Tell me what I need to do."

"Back off," she said, her voice soft and low, as if she were afraid to say the words. "Let me have some space. I'll know when I'm ready to move in. It might not be until we're married, or it might be sooner, but the decision has to be mine. Okay?"

"I guess so," Liv said. "What about Harry?"

"I'll talk to him. It'll take some finessing, but I think I can get him to agree to live with us. You're right. It'd be a lot easier on him and me." Grace rose and Liv did as well. Grace stepped closer and put her arms around Liv's waist. "I love you. Don't you ever forget it."

"I won't. I know you do. This other stuff—I didn't expect it to be this hard."

"This is why I have a counselor and go to support meetings. It's damn hard, and when I get scared, I want to run away and hide. To be honest, that's when I go back to Harry's place and stay with him."

"You need to run from me? Gracie, please, tell me what I'm doing wrong here." Liv's heart clenched. She'd been to the support meetings with Grace a few times, talked to her counselor, and thought she had things under control. She thought she was doing right by Grace and being careful with her feelings. Knowing Carly nearly beat Grace to death, all the while saying how much she loved her, still made Liv physically ill. She wanted to kill the bitch.

She rested her chin on Grace's shoulder and pulled her close, holding back the sudden need to cry. "Tell me what to do."

"You're doing it," Grace said softly in her ear. "You're loving me, and it's all I need. The rest will come. I promise." She pulled back to kiss Liv again. The kissing continued for a few moments before Grace released her. "I need to check on *Ojiichan*. Are you going to be all right?"

Liv nodded because she didn't trust her voice.

Grace gently touched her cheek with the tips of her fingers. "We'll talk more later. Promise?"

Liv nodded again.

"I love you."

"I love you, too," Liv whispered as Grace left the office. She dropped back into the chair and cried.

****

Liv came home to an empty house. Harry wasn't feeling good, and Grace opted to stay with him. She promised to call after Harry went to bed.

Liv moved through the living room and right to the bedroom, not bothering to turn any lights on. She stripped down to a T-shirt and undies and slipped under the cool duvet. Her hand touched the empty side of her bed and she sighed.

She picked up her cell phone and called Sara.

"Hey, what's up?" Sara sounded very awake and energized.

"Home alone. Depressed."

"Dramatic," Sara said. "Gracie's at Harry's?"

"Where else?"

"You need to back off on the house stuff, Livvy. You'll end up pushing her away."

"How do you know?" She visualized Sara rolling her eyes.

"Duh. We have lunch once a week. Do you think we sit and stare at each other the whole time? She tells me a lot of stuff. Like how you're still harping on her to move in. How you want her name on the deed."

"It's not a big deal. We're getting married. Her name should be on it."

"And you're a stubborn ass. Why are you depressed tonight? You're usually okay when she's at Harry's."

"We kind of had a fight about the moving-in thing. She said she has to do it on her own terms. I don't know what those are and what I'm supposed to do in the meantime. Plus, I suggested she move Harry in so she can keep an eye on him."

"Wait, what? You offered to move Harry into your house?"

"Sure. I mean, he's family, right? I've got the room, and we can add on if necessary. It's not like he'd be in the way or anything."

"Liv, that's huge." Sara spoke as if admonishing a child. "You popped it on her while you were trying to convince her to move in? You don't think it was a little much?"

"No. I thought it was a solution to a problem."

"You might have compounded the problem, my friend."

"How so?"

"Look, Harry moved here twenty years ago when he bought the mine. He's settled and happy. He might not even want to move in with you two, especially when you're starting out as a couple."

"Sara, Gracie spends most of her free time with him. If she's not at work at Rock World, or the mine, she's taking him to doctor's appointments or to the store or whatever. It's like I hardly see her anymore. It makes sense if they both live here; she's not having to go all the way to his place—especially in winter. His place is over an hour from here, and I guess I don't want her spending all her time traveling to and from. Does it sound crazy?"

"No. I get where you're coming from. You're thinking with your heart. It's a great idea to move Harry in—at some point. Maybe not right after or when Gracie moves in. Damn, woman. She needs to have some adjustment time. You do realize she's never lived on her own, except for a few times she was posted overseas with the US Army? I know you don't see this because I know you, but this is a big step for her. Did it ever occur to you Gracie might feel like she's missing out on the independence of living alone?"

"Um, no. Living alone sucks. Why would she want to do it on purpose?"

"Because it's a chance to spread her wings and be free. No one to answer to, no one to fight over the sink with in the morning…that sort of thing. She was in a horrible marriage for almost a decade and had to live with her brother while she tried to recover her life. Later she moved here and into Harry's house. When has she had time to herself?"

"I—I don't know."

"My point exactly. Livvy, call her. Talk to her. Let her tell you how she's feeling. But don't push her, okay? Be there for her and listen."

"When did you become a shrink?"

Sara laughed softly. "Talking to Gracie has been enlightening. And I can't believe you're not seeing the problem here. Call her, okay? I have an important call in about ten minutes."

"Bren?" Liv asked with a slight grin.

"Yes, actually. We like to chat at night sometimes, before she goes to bed. I don't mind. It's a nice way to end the day."

"Good to know. I'm glad you're enjoying her company."

"I am. You going to be okay?"

"Yes. Later." She hung up and stared at the phone for a moment. She should call Grace and at least make sure she was settled in for the night. She simply wouldn't be able to sleep without hearing Grace's soft voice first.

Liv called and was disappointed when it went to voicemail. She left a message and put the phone onto the night table. Maybe she was busy with Harry. Or maybe she didn't want to talk. With a deep sigh, Liv settled down to sleep, though she realized she'd do anything but.

****

Sara hung up the phone from her chat with Bren. The evening calls were fun, but they did nothing to help her get to sleep. In fact, she usually ended up staying awake longer than normal because they reminded her of Terry. And it sucked.

Not all her memories of Terry sucked. Far from it. They'd had an amazing time together. Sometimes their talks would turn very serious and sometimes not, but they shared a closeness between them Sara had never had before. Not even with Liv, and she was the one person Sara confided in completely. With Terry, however, it was different. Like they knew each other on an entirely different level.

Or so she'd thought. Could it all have been one-sided? It had to be, right? Or else Terry wouldn't have dumped her.

The evening played over and over in Sara's brain like a broken record. Terry stood on the sidewalk outside the park. Little kids played on the swing set, and Sara recalled saying something about Felicia. What was it? That she looked forward to meeting her?

"I don't think it's a good idea," Terry said. She wouldn't face her, and something in her voice caused the hair on the back of Sara's neck to stand up.

"I thought we were headed to the park this weekend. Are you afraid I won't like her or she won't like me? I'm good with kids, Terry. I promise I won't bite." She tried to joke, but it didn't lighten Terry's mood at all. In fact, Terry seemed pissed at her.

"No. I think she'd like you," Terry said. She finally faced Sara, and the pain in her eyes gave Sara a shock. "I planned to wait until after dinner, but I can't."

"Wait for what? What's wrong? Are you hurt? Sick?"

Terry raised her hand to ward off any more questions. She kept her eyes on Sara, and when she spoke, Sara swore her heart broke into pieces with each word. "We can't see each other anymore."

Nothing came out of Sara's mouth, though she tried hard to speak. She must have looked like a fish sucking air.

Terry didn't say anything more, and after a beat, she walked away. They were no longer a couple.

The weight of the breakup was too much, and Sara sank to her knees. She could still see Terry's retreating form, pretty sure she literally ran away. She stared after her until her vision blurred. Tears streamed down her face, and she sat on the sidewalk and sobbed.

She called Liv when she could manage to keep her hand steady enough to use her cell phone.

Liv picked her up, and they went to Liv's house, where Sara cried herself to sleep.

Sara told her boss she was sick with the flu and took a week off work. It was a lie, , but anyone who might have seen her would have believed it. The same day Terry walked out of her life was also the day she'd planned to tell Terry she loved her.

Sara'd had her share of relationships, her longest being with Liv, but she never truly fell in love with any of those women. She always loved Liv, but on a friendship level. Never anything as deep as what she felt for Terry.

She ended up spending the week in one of Liv's spare rooms. Going home would remind her of the romantic evening she'd planned. Liv brought her a few changes of clothes, and Sara's mom and dad checked in on her every day. Grace was in and out as well. Liv made sure someone was there all the time to watch over her. She was damn lucky to have such great friends.

Barely five weeks later, she still felt the hit of those words as if Terry said them yesterday.

She stared at the ceiling of her bedroom and wondered if she'd ever feel whole again.

Chapter Five

Liv paced around her office, unable to rid herself of her nervous energy. She'd still not heard from Grace. Their fight was two days ago, and she didn't think they'd ever gone that long without talking or texting each other. Maybe Liv was moving too fast. Grace clearly wasn't ready to live together.

She tried like hell to understand Grace's reluctance. Though they'd talked about it many times, Liv would never fully understand what Grace went through at the hands of Carly. The physical abuse was evident, but the mental abuse…

Right now she felt like an ass, with no way of redeeming herself.

She returned to her desk, grabbed the phone, and called Sara, who answered on the first ring.

"Morning," Sara said. She didn't sound any happier than Liv.

"Hey. You busy?"

"Nope. You?"

"Nope." Liv hesitated. She got the impression calling Sara wasn't such a good idea.

"What's wrong?" Like always, Sara read her like a book—without being there to see her.

"I haven't heard from Gracie."

"Have you called her?"

"Three times last night and a text this morning. I know she worked late at Rock World yesterday, and she's off today."

"She needs time, Livvy. We talked about this. Besides, it's not like you don't know where she lives. If you want to talk to her, go to the cabin. Face-to-face works best every time."

"I don't think—" Liv stopped when her cell phone showed a text coming in. She stared at it for a few moments, not sure what to do since the text was from Grace.

"What?" Sara asked.

"Uh, she sent me a message."

"Cool. Job done."

Liv didn't reply right away. Instead, she stared at the phone, the message very simple. A telephone emoji. Their shorthand to say "call me."

"What did she say?" Sara's voice was quieter as though she didn't want anyone to hear her. "Tell me."

"She asked for you to call her."

"Don't scare me. I thought she was breaking up with you."

"She might still be," Liv said, even though her brain told her it was a completely irrational thought. Grace loved her. Right?

Sara said, "Don't be stupid. She's not breaking up with you. I'm hanging up so you can call her."

"No, don't!"

"Why? Liv, do I need to come over there? Why are you all freaked out?"

Liv didn't have an answer. Probably because there was no logic to it. Only a deep-seated fear of being without Grace. Her hands shook a little as she stared at her cell phone. She finally had to put the damn thing on top of her desk.

"I can't, Sara. I'm afraid of what she'll say."

"She'll say she loves you and together you'll work out the issue of her living in your house. It really is that simple. Trust me, okay?"

"I want to. I seriously want to."

"Text her back to let her know you got the message. She's reaching out. Don't ignore her." Sara spoke to someone in her office, her voice muffled for a few seconds. "I have to go. Will you be all right?"

"Sure."

"Don't you ignore her, Olivia. You hear me? You pick up the phone and text or call her right after you hang up with me. Got it?"

"Yeah." Liv placed the receiver on her desk phone and hung up. She didn't actually promise she'd call Grace, and it was a good thing, because she couldn't do it. Not even a simple message to say she'd gotten the damn text.

Liv desperately wanted to hear Grace's voice, but if she was leaving her—Liv would put it off as long as possible. She turned her cell phone off and dove into the pile of paperwork on her desk, hoping to bury herself in it and forget the ache in her heart.

****

Grace was already at the pub when Sara breezed in on Saturday afternoon. They'd missed their usual Wednesday lunch and agreed to make it up on the weekend when they were both off. But Sara decided to stop at the bank to get something she'd forgotten and got caught up in a minor issue. She made a mental note to never show up on a Saturday again. She slid into the bench across from Grace and released a dramatic sigh. "I didn't think I was going to make it. Sorry I'm late."

"No worries," Grace said.

Sara put in her order with Izzy, who was quieter than usual, then turned to her friend. Grace wouldn't look at her and kept picking at a groove in the wooden table. "Let me guess. Liv's still on you about moving in?"

"Not really." Grace sighed heavily. "We kind of had a spat about it last week, but it wasn't all bad. At least I didn't think so. But I've been trying to call her since then, and she won't pick up the phone. I guess it's my own fault for not answering when she tried to call me."

"I am officially going to kill her," Sara muttered.

"Why?"

"Because we talked about this. I told her to back off, not ignore your calls. Gracie, I don't think she understands what's going on in your head. You need to spell it out for her. You know she can be pretty damn thick sometimes."

"I do." Grace smiled a bit. "But it's difficult to talk to someone who's ignoring you."

"Well, there is that." Sara waited for Grace to keep going, but she didn't. "Hey, go over to her office. I know for a fact she's there because I saw her going in on my way here."

"I don't know how to make her understand."

"Open your mouth and tell her."

"I've tried. It's hard because this is super important to her, but for me—when I was with Carly, I felt trapped being in the same house with her. I wasn't able to leave without her permission. I know Olivia isn't Carly, but it doesn't stop the feelings I'm having." She met Sara's concerned gaze, and Sara realized Grace hadn't been sleeping. Grace said, "I'm afraid. It's all overwhelming me in ways I never expected. I should be excited to marry her. I love her. But instead I'm terrified."

"You have to tell her, honey." Sara reached across the table and patted Grace's hand. "She won't understand why you're scared, because she can't. But she'll try like hell. Plus, I think it might be good if you two have a talk with your counselor, Abby."

"I know. I've got an appointment with her later today." Grace sniffled. "It's like I have claustrophobia, and she wants me to move into a shoe box. It's irrational because I know it would never be like it was with Carly. It's a house. Our house. It means a lotz to her. I know I'm hurting her feelings with all this. I want to talk to her, but I don't think she wants to talk to me right now."

"Bullshit. Doesn't matter what she wants. It's about what you need, and you need to talk to her. Let's go." Sara got up and tugged on Grace's arm.

"What? Where? We haven't eaten yet."

"We can eat later." She glanced over at Izzy. "Hey, Iz, would you please box our lunches? I'll get them in a little bit."

"Sure," Izzy said. She never looked up from wiping down the bar, and Sara got a very weird feeling something was off.

She couldn't worry about it. She needed to fix Grace and Liv first.

"We're off to Liv's office," Sara said once Grace had her coat on. "I'll get her to stop whatever the hell she's doing, and you two will talk about this."

"I don't know if that's such a good idea. There's got to be a reason she's dodging my calls. I'm not sure barging in on her at the office will fix anything."

"We won't know until we try." Sara took her hand and led her out the door and toward Liv's office. "She's shutting down because she's hurting, Grace. It's what she does, and if you don't confront her now with the issue, it'll fester."

Grace stopped when they were across the street from Liv's office. "Sara, I appreciate what you're trying to do, but I can't. I'm sorry. It's not—the timing is off. I think I should go home, and by home I mean *Ojiichan's*. I need to Skype Abby and maybe get my head around things. Sometimes it sucks my counselor is in another country, but Abby gets me."

"Okay, but are you sure?" Sara hated the sadness in Grace's eyes. She wanted badly to fix things.

"I'm not sure of anything except I need to talk to Abby." She hugged Sara tightly. "Thanks. Sorry about lunch."

"I don't care about lunch. Call me if you need anything."

"I will," Grace said and walked away.

Sara stared at the office and contemplated going in. She wanted to get the food from the pub and hand lunch over to Liv and get her talking about the situation. But something told her to back off. As much as she loved Liv, she knew it wasn't her place to get between her and Grace, especially not on an issue this big.

She returned to the pub, where she found Izzy still wiping down the bar. By now it should be shining like glass. "Hey there," Sara said, startling Izzy.

"Hey. You want your food?"

"I guess so." Sara waited and once the boxed lunches were handed to her, she paid Izzy. "You okay?"

"Yeah, why?" Izzy said without looking at her. Something was very wrong with the way she hunched her shoulders forward. Like she was defeated.

"Because you're not okay. I've known you most of your life, Izzy, and I know when something is off. Spill."

Izzy shrugged. "Girl troubles. No biggie."

"I'm sorry to hear that. Want to talk about it?"

"Michelle broke up with me. Said she's not into me anymore."

"Michelle sucks." Sara waited for Izzy to look at her. There was a tiny smile on her face. "I know you guys were together for about a year, and it's gotta hurt, but let me tell you it gets better."

"She says she thinks I'm, like, into someone else."

Sara raised her eyebrow. "Are you?"

Another shrug.

"Maybe it's good Michelle broke up with you. Makes you available for this other woman, right?"

"Nope. She's now dating someone else."

Sara almost laughed at the irony but kept her expression sympathetic. She patted Izzy's hand. "She's not married. Tell her how you feel. Let her know you're interested and see where it leads you. You never know. She might be dating the wrong woman."

"I wish." Izzy sighed. "Thanks, Sara. I appreciate the talk."

"Any time." Sara wasn't sure she'd done much for Izzy, but at least she smiled a little. "Catch you later."

"Later," Izzy said and moved her polishing down the bar.

Sara took both lunches and walked home.

****

Grace sat at the tiny kitchen table at Harry's cabin later that evening and thumbed through her text messages to Liv. All of them unanswered. It wasn't like Liv to shut her out this way. They'd had a few disagreements before, but nothing like this. Had she hurt her feelings? Why was her moving in now such a blasted big deal to Liv?

Grace wanted to ask her, but Liv wouldn't take her calls. Grace was tempted to go to Liv's house and make her talk to her. She was hurting, too. Every minute apart from Liv was like a minute she couldn't breathe.

Harry settled into the chair beside her and put his hand on her arm. His once dark skin was lighter now because he no longer spent most of his time outside. His wrinkled hand reminded Grace of how fragile her beloved *ojiichan* was. Grace looked up at his kind face and smiled for him.

"Gracie Lee, you must go to her. This does you no good to sit here and be miserable. Talk. Tell her how you feel."

"I want to, but she doesn't. I can show up, sure, but it won't make her talk to me. I don't know what to do. She's never done this before."

"You have not had this issue before. How were you to know how she would react? Likewise, I am sure she does not understand your reaction."

"Did you ever have this kind of problem with *Obaachan*?" Her gaze drifted to a photo of her grandparents on the mantle. Their wedding day. *Obaachan* wore a satin-white dress that ended at her ankles. The photo was black and white, but Grace could easily see how happy they both were.

"There were times we did not agree. We married later in life, as you and Olivia are doing, which meant we were both independent— set in our ways. You two have a lot to learn about each other."

"I thought I already knew her."

"You do, but this is different. Bringing your lives together will change your relationship, Gracie Lee. It will make you stronger. You will get past this."

"It hurts."

"I know."

A knock at the door surprised them both. Harry had no immediate neighbors. Grace noted the time was close to ten at night. She exchanged a glance with him before answering the door.

Liv stood there in jeans and a sweatshirt, despite the near freezing temperature.

"Hey," Grace said, too stunned for words.

"Hey. Can I come in?"

"Sure." Grace stepped aside. Liv looked terrible. Her eyes were puffy, her face drawn and pale.

Harry greeted Liv from the kitchen. "I'm going to bed," he said. "G'night, Olivia."

"G'night, Harry." She waited for him to close the door to his room.

They stood there, a few feet between them, letting the awkwardness fill the room.

Grace motioned to the twin recliners, the only real furniture in the living area of the cabin. "Want to sit down?"

"No. Thanks." Liv shoved her hands in her jeans pockets but not before Grace noticed she was trembling.

"This is crazy, Olivia. We have to talk about this. Please don't shut me out."

"I—I'm sorry. I don't know why—it's crazy and stupid, and I should know better." Liv paced the small room. "I should be more sensitive to your feelings, Gracie, but I don't know how to tell you mine."

Grace stopped her and waited for Liv to look at her. The desperation she saw in her eyes pressed on her heart. "First, I love you."

"I do. I love you, too."

"Second, I want to spend the rest of my life with you."

"Me, too." Tears filled Liv's eyes.

"Third, I'm terrified and it has nothing to do with you or how I feel about you. I want to be with you—all the time. It hurts to be apart, and I don't sleep worth a damn when I'm not with you. But it's hard. Carly had so much control over me—I still get scared."

"Of her?"

"No. That's not what I mean. I get scared because to live with someone else you have to give up some control. I feel like I'm finally back in control of my life, and giving up any of it is terrifying. I know in my heart you're not Carly, but sometimes my brain doesn't want to accept it. It's like I'm fighting with myself over it, and it's damn hard."

"I'd never hurt you, not on purpose." Liv's hand touched the side of her face. "I don't want you to give up anything, Gracie."

"But that's not how it works." Grace covered Liv's hand with her own. "I have to give up some control because it would be our house, our lives. Not mine or yours. I want to—it's—I have to find a way to remind myself it's okay if I do."

"What can I do?"

"Talk to me. Tell me how you're feeling. Don't shut down, Olivia. Please."

"I'm sorry I hurt you." Liv leaned forward and placed a sweet kiss on Grace's lips. "I got scared, and I was afraid if I talked to you, I'd make it worse. I'd already botched the job of explaining it to you in my office."

"But that's when we need to keep talking. We can't work things out otherwise."

"I know. It's tearing me up inside. I guess I wanted you to move in badly enough I forgot how you might feel about it. I mean, I know you want to or half your stuff wouldn't be at my place now. I want to share my life with you, Gracie. I guess waiting until April seems like a long time."

"It's a couple of months."

"Yeah. And if I lived in the States, I'd be the kind of lesbian with a U-Haul who moves in on the second date." She gave a self-deprecating laugh.

Grace opened her arms, pulled Liv into them, and embraced her as tightly as she could. "I promise we'll work this out. I'm not letting Carly win."

"You sure I can't go kick her ass?"

Grace laughed. "I'm sure. You'd have to break into prison and end up in the cell next to her. Then we'd never be able to move in together. It would suck."

"True. I don't like it when you're right."

Grace wiped the tears from Liv's cheeks and smiled. "Get used to it. I'm going to be the wife who's always right."

"Oh joy. I guess I'll be saying 'yes, dear,' a lot, huh?"

"If you're smart."

"I'm very smart."

Grace kissed her gently. "And sexy."

"I'll trust you on that one."

"You should." Grace deepened the kiss, making sure Liv understood how she felt. "How about I come by the house tomorrow afternoon? I've got to get some stuff done for *Ojiichan*, then I'm all yours."

"Sounds good. We can have lunch and talk more."

"We can. There's a lot of planning to do." Grace kissed her again. "I think the idea of expanding the house so *Ojiichan* has his own living area is great. And he's offered to pay for it."

"Seriously? Harry's going to live with us?"

"He is."

The smile nearly split Liv's face and warmed Grace's heart. Liv initiated the next kiss, and Grace's knees buckled.

"This is great," Liv said. "I've got a contractor in mind. I'll call him on Monday." Her eyes held Grace's and her stomach did a little flip. "Stay tomorrow night with me?"

"Plan on it."

"I better go. I'll call you when I get home to say goodnight." Liv stopped at the doorway. "G'night, Harry," she called out.

Grace shook her head when he replied, "G'night, Olivia." She should have known he'd be listening in. He always did, and it brought one thought to mind. She leaned close and whispered to Liv, "Ask the contractor about soundproofing the walls."

****

The wind picked up, and Terry nearly lost her grip on the office door as she walked out. She hated Mondays and couldn't be happier this one was over. There was an icy patch on the sidewalk, and her left foot slid and knocked her off balance. She tried to use the door to right herself, but her grip wasn't strong enough and she fell on her ass.

And missed taking someone else with her. Terry muttered an apology as she glanced up into Sara's concerned gaze.

Terry, mortified, scrambled to her feet and carefully closed the office door. She turned to go to her car, surprised Sara was still there.

"You okay?" Sara asked quietly.

"Hurt my pride, I think. Thanks."

"Sure," Sara said, but she didn't make a move to leave.

Terry desperately wanted to get out of there. Her legs, however, refused to obey the commands from her brain. "You doing okay?"

"I'm great," Sara said, but the words fell flat. Terry read the hurt in her eyes, and it pulled at her heart.

"I'm sorry," Terry said.

"For what?"

"Hurting you."

"Pfft." Sara waved her arm as if to shove the idea away, but her eyes told Terry a different story. "You didn't. I'm fine."

"Good, good." Terry edged toward her truck. "I should go. I need to get Felicia from school."

"Okay."

"Okay," Terry said and went to her truck. She took one last look at Sara before getting in the vehicle and driving away.

No matter how hard she tried, the expression on Sara's face stayed with her. Lost. Hurt. Angry. All mixed together. All caused by Terry.

She wanted to turn the vehicle around and find Sara. Talk to her. Let her know why she'd been forced to break up with her. Let her know she still cared.

But would Sara accept Terry's reasoning for the breakup? Or would she be angrier?

Terry took a shaky breath as she pulled into the parking lot of the school. She had to get her emotions under control before Felicia saw her.

As if on cue, Felicia ran to the truck, followed by Sally Johnson, who held Felicia's backpack in her hand.

Felicia wrapped her small arms around Terry's waist and held on for dear life. "I miss you, Mommy."

"I missed you, too." She cupped Felicia's face in her hands and smiled down at her. "Did you have a good day?"

"Nope." Felicia pulled back and opened the rear passenger door of the truck. She climbed onto her booster seat and waited to be buckled in.

Terry caught the exasperated expression on Sally's face and walked a few steps away, hoping Felicia wouldn't be able to hear her. "What happened?" she asked as Sally handed her the backpack.

"She tried to kiss a boy today."

"Oh? Which boy?"

"Bryce Preston. They play together a lot, and I guess Felicia decided she needed to kiss him."

"Please tell me she kissed his cheek."

"Um, no. She went for a full-on lip lock." Sally's face gave away how much humor she saw in the situation. "I've seen it happen before. They see older kids, or their parents, doing it and decide that's how you show affection."

"How did Bryce react?"

"As you'd expect. He shoved her away, wiped his mouth like it was full of mud, and stomped off. He hasn't talked to her since."

"Oh, no. First kiss and first rejection all at the same time." Terry sighed. "It's going to be a long night. How has she been?"

"Quiet. She's upset. I think her little heart is broken."

Terry glanced at the truck, where Felicia sat patiently waiting for her. Felicia's little heart would mend. Probably by tomorrow when she chose a different boyfriend. Terry wished it were as easy for a grownup. "Thanks. I doubt I'd have gotten much information out of her. When she shuts down, she means it. No more talking."

"So I've learned. Good luck," Sally said and walked away.

Terry got Felicia buckled in and pointed the truck toward home. "Want some music?"

"Nope." Felicia stared out the window, her arms crossed over her chest. She often used her arms as a shield to protect herself. It worried Terry how she was able to close herself off.

"Not even Lady Gaga?"

"Nope."

"You want to talk about it?"

"Nope."

Damn. Terry wasn't getting anywhere. She let the silence hang heavily in the car for the short drive home. Once inside, Felicia hugged Shirley, went to her room, and closed the door behind her.

Shirley gave Terry a puzzled look. "What happened?"

"She kissed a boy." Terry relayed the whole sordid tale. "I'm sure she'll be fine. There'll be another boy tomorrow, or next week, but that's not what's bothering me."

"Let me guess. It's how she's closed herself off and won't talk about stuff bothering her."

"Exactly. I don't know what to do, Mom. Is she like this because Ann died? Did I do something to make her think she can't talk to me about her problems? I can't let her do this. What if she's like this as a teenager and gets into trouble because she won't come to me for help? Or what if—"

"Stop." Shirley pointed to the couch. She took a seat and patted the cushion beside her. Terry obligingly sat down. "It could be a phase she's going through. Or related to Ann's death. There's no way you'll figure it out. What you need to do is go into her room and make sure she understands you're there for her. Even if it means sitting in the room without saying a word."

"Are you sure?"

The look on Shirley's face might have been comical in another situation. "You do know what I do for a living, right? I've told you this before?"

"Counseling juvenile delinquents is different. Felicia's a good kid, and she's eight."

"Psychology is the same, and you know my job is more than dealing with delinquents. You also know Felicia's age has little to do with anything. She's not likely to ever be mentally equal to her physical age. Now take my advice or not, but let me know what you're going to do. I'm starved and want to get dinner going." She got up and entered the kitchen, signaling the conversation was over.

Sometimes Terry hated that her mother was a psychologist. Why couldn't she be a regular mom with a regular job? Like at the local grocery or something.

She stood and headed toward Felicia's room but paused at the kitchen doorway. "You do know I hate it when you're right."

"I do. I'll come get you when dinner's ready."

"Thanks, Mom." Terry walked to Felicia's room and knocked on the door softly. "Can I come in?"

"Yep," Felicia said. She was sitting on her bed, her legs crossed and a book in her hands.

"Mind if I sit in here with you?"

Felicia shrugged and Terry made herself comfortable, sitting in a similar position as Felicia. They faced each other, but Felicia didn't look up from her book.

Terry knew she could read it, because they'd practiced doing it a few days ago. But Felicia hadn't turned a page in a while, and she suspected Felicia was simply staring at it. "Want to read it to me? Or maybe the new book Grams got you? The one about the monkey who gets into all kinds of trouble?"

Felicia didn't answer right away, her eyes never leaving the book. But something in her posture changed. She loosened up a bit. Before Terry said another word, Felicia started reading aloud.

Chapter Six

Josephine's was packed, and Sara was thankful she managed to get reservations at the last minute. Weekdays were busy enough, but this was Saturday. Reservations usually had to be made weeks in advance. The owner happened to be a client of hers, and for the first time ever, she used it to her advantage. She felt the need to pamper Bren a bit, and by the look on her face, Bren was well and truly impressed, if not a little intimidated. She doubted Bren ever had the opportunity to go to such an elegant place.

Sara couldn't help the stupid grin on her face as she oogled Bren. She was absolutely adorable in black slacks, white Oxford shirt with long sleeves, and a black jacket. A bright-blue bowtie complemented the outfit. And not the kind that clips on. An honest-to-God bowtie.

Sara touched the tie, pretending to straighten it. "You're too cute for words."

Bren laughed. "And you're stunning." Her eyes roamed appreciatively over Sara's body, lingering on the low neckline of her red cocktail dress. "You turn heads everywhere you go."

Now Sara was blushing, and she hated it. Her makeup wouldn't be able to hide it either. She knew her cheeks were blood red, but her insides were even hotter as she locked eyes with Bren. There weren't any big fireworks or butterflies, but Sara definitely felt the attraction between them. She had a sense they were good in bed and maybe, just maybe, good for each other, too. She looked forward to finding out about how good the sex was. No way would she be getting drunk tonight.

"Does flattery get you places with other women?" Sara asked.

"Usually."

"Huh."

"Is it working right now?"

"It might be."

Bren opened her mouth to comment, but the maître d' interrupted her. Sara chuckled and followed him to their table.

"I was about to tell you I have a lot of other lines I enjoy using," Bren said as they were seated. "Some damn sexy moves, too, which you'll find out about later on the dance floor."

"Promises, promises." Sara ordered a bottle of wine, knowing the best selection without looking at the menu. How very different this date was to the one she'd been on with Angel last weekend.

"Wine?" Bren asked as she perused the food choices. "I thought we weren't going to drink much."

"A glass or two would do. Then coffee before we hit the dance floor. Trust me, the wine here is incredible, and you'll thank me for ordering it."

"I might thank you, but I'll need a loan from the bank to pay for it."

Sara hadn't given any thought to what Bren might do for a living. Sara herself wasn't rich, but she saved her money and did okay. Coming to a place like this wasn't something she did often, but the costs never entered her mind. "Don't worry about it. It was my idea to come here for dinner. I'll pay for everything. You can buy me a soda at the club."

Bren didn't look up from the menu, and Sara got the sense she was more than embarrassed. Mortified maybe? "I'm sorry," Bren said. "I didn't think about who was paying tonight. I figured the place wouldn't be cheap, but I was like, they got to have salads, right? Those are cheap. But damn. The salads cost more than it takes to fill up the gas tank in my truck."

"Bren, it's okay. I meant for this to be a nice treat for you. I feel like you deserve it."

"I probably should have told you I don't have a job yet. I recently graduated from university, and I'm living at home with my parents. I have some money left over from my college fund, but I'm trying not to spend too much of it."

Wow. Sara knew she was young, but she was still living at home? It made Sara not only feel old, but like a cradle robber. Since they met up at the pub before coming to Josephine's, Sara had no idea where Bren lived. "I have a job, so tonight is on me." She watched Bren reading the menu for a few moments before asking, "What'd you study?"

"I have a double major in education and journalism. I'm certified to teach, or I could work for a newspaper. I'm not sure which way I want to go. I thought I might try both and see what happens."

"At the same time?"

Bren shrugged. "Why not? I pulled off a double major, and it was like having two full-time jobs. Plus, I minored in history and English. I'm pretty sure I can at least get a job as a substitute teacher to start with."

"But something's stopping you?"

"Yeah. My heart's not in it or journalism. I did my internships, and they were okay I guess. I don't know. How'd we get on this crappy topic anyway?"

Sara gave her a smile. "There are no crappy topics. I'd like to get to know you better. It's what going on a date is for, right?"

"I suppose so."

"I'm totally impressed with a double-major. I barely pulled off one."

Bren shrugged. "It wasn't hard. School's always been easy for me. What was your major?"

"Business administration. I'm a geek when it comes to crunching numbers and dealing with paperwork. I got a BA with the intention of working at a bank. Seems like a weird dream job, but it works for me."

"I don't think I ever met anyone who liked working in a bank. What do you do?"

"Assistant loan manager right now. Eventually I'll be bank manager—maybe higher. I don't know yet."

"Wow. Tell me more about yourself."

"Like what?" Sara took a sip of her wine after the waiter filled her glass. The sweet rosé made her taste buds do a happy dance.

"Like how you know what wine to order." Bren raised her glass to Sara. "This is amazing."

"I know about the wine because I've been coming here for a couple of years now. My boss and I bring big clients here to keep their business or to convince them to bring in more business to the bank. I saw a client ordering wine one day, and she was sure and confident about the flavor I have to say I was a little jealous. I decided to study up on the subject in order to impress the client instead of it being the other way around."

"And did you? Impress, I mean?"

"I did, and it happened to be the same woman. Afterwards she agreed to give us all her business. She owns a car dealership. My old boss was impressed, but she was always nice like that."

"You have a new boss now?"

"I do. He's okay, but I'm expecting him to move on soon. I don't think he's the kind of person to stay in one place too long."

Bren raised her glass in a toast, clinking it with Sara's. "Here's to you either getting a new boss or a promotion in the very near future."

"Hear, hear." Sara took a sip of wine and grinned. "You're good for my ego."

"I have a hard time believing you need help."

"Oh, I do. My ego is very tiny. So tiny in fact you can't see it. I hardly let it out and make sure to hide it from anyone I run into."

"Too bad. I think you could use a good ego. You're smart, beautiful, fun—why aren't you married?" Bren said with a teasing note to her voice, but the comment saddened Sara a little.

If Terry hadn't broken up with her, would she be well on her way to being married? They'd have an instant family with Felicia, and even if Sara had never met the kid, she had a feeling they'd get along well. Maybe if she'd told Terry how she felt they'd still be together.

"Earth to Sara." Bren's voice broke into her thoughts. "Did I say something wrong? You sort of zoned out."

"No, you're fine. I went through a bad breakup recently, and I guess I'm still thinking about her—it."

"Breakups are never good, are they?"

"I had one that was sort of good. We were together two years, and we're still best friends. But I think it's a one-off. I don't think it happens all that much."

"Me either. But for the record, let me state the woman who dumped you was a blind asshole. If she couldn't see how awesome you are, then you're better off without her."

Bren took Sara's hand into her own. She placed soft kisses on Sara's fingers. "I mean it, Sara. I don't know where the two of us might be heading, but I know your ex had no idea what she was letting go of."

Sara fought to hold back her tears. "You're very sweet. Thanks."

"You're welcome." She kissed Sara's fingers again and let her hand go.

Funny, but Sara didn't miss the contact the way she would have with Terry. Dammit. Was everything Bren did going to remind her of Terry?

"What's good to eat here? I don't even know what half this stuff is."

Sara, glad to have a distraction, pointed out a few dishes and made their order. Their easy banter returned, and Sara knew, without a doubt, no matter what happened between them, she'd found a new friend.

****

"You need to get out and meet people. You need new friends," Shirley said as she put the clean dishes away. "It's Saturday night. Go to the pub you like, or go dancing. Anything to get you out of this house."

Terry leaned against the breakfast bar, hands stuffed in the pockets of her worn, comfy jeans. Her mother started the lecture not long after Terry got home from work, and apparently, she wasn't finished.

"Mom, I don't have time to go out and make friends. I tried it once and look how it turned out."

"You were wrong to break up with Sara."

"Didn't we go over this the other day? You've been telling me this for the last two months. I had to break up with her."

"No, you didn't." Shirley spun around and the look in those blue eyes, eyes identical to Terry's, gave her a chill. She was in for it. "You didn't give her a chance to make up her own mind about how involved she may or may not want to be. How do you know she wouldn't have had a better solution to offer? How do you know she didn't love you enough to maybe cool her heels for a while and wait for you? Did it ever occur to you to ask her?"

"You know—"

"You didn't think before you acted. God, you're like your father. Leap and hope the net is there. I'm here to tell you it's not always going to be there. Sara was good for you, Terry. You know this as well as I do. You wanted to introduce her to Felicia. That alone tells me you loved Sara on some level and saw a possible future with her."

"Yes, but—"

"I'm not finished." Shirley put the last of the silverware in the drawer and took a seat at the table. Terry thought she looked more tired than usual and pale as well. "I don't give a damn what asshole William does or how long he takes to do it. I won't let him take Felicia from you. I promise you. Whatever he thinks he has against you is bullshit. You're a normal woman, going to work, coming home to spend time with your family, and on occasion enjoying a night out with friends—or girlfriend, as it once was. You've got to stop living your life in fear. William cannot hurt you or Felicia. You've got an amazing lawyer in Jackie, and I have confidence she'll get it settled for you."

Shirley stopped and took a sip of her cooled coffee. She made a face at what must have been a bitter taste.

Terry said, "I'm terrified of William. And I have good reason for it. He pushed Ann around her entire life, and there was damn little she could do to stop him. I don't want him influencing Felicia in any way, but I know I can't get out of him having contact with her. I'm terrified he'll get her for a weekend, and I'll never see her again."

Tears welled in her eyes as pain spread across her chest. "I can't lose her, Mom. She's my daughter. She's all I have left of Ann. If being a hermit and never making new friends—or a new girlfriend— helps me keep custody of her, then I'll do it. You know how close I am to moving to Vancouver? If I do, he says he'll drop everything."

"He said he'd do it if you broke up with Sara and filed for custody anyway."

Terry wouldn't look at her, her throat tight with emotion. "He told me to come to Vancouver after I broke up with her. It was his second demand, but I couldn't. I can't uproot Felicia and I can't leave you, Mom. I need you."

Shirley quieted as she played with her coffee mug for a few moments. She didn't look up as she spoke. "Which is why I'm here, trying to help you, sweetie. You don't have to move to Vancouver." She took a sip of her coffee. "I didn't see how I'd ever go on after your father died, and if for one minute I'd have thought someone could take you away from me, I'd have turned into a momma bear. I'd have ripped out the throat of anyone who came near you. Still would."

"I believe you," Terry said as she sniffled and wiped the tears away. "I can't go after him or I would. I have to let the lawyers work it out for me, but every day makes it that much harder. I miss Sara. I miss her friendship, and I miss having her to lean on. If I thought it was possible to get our friendship back, I'd be at her doorstep in a flash."

"Why wouldn't she? If you were such good friends, wouldn't she be willing to talk to you? Let you lean on her now and again?"

"I hurt her, Mom. She barely makes eye contact when she sees me. The other day we literally almost bumped into each other, and neither of us could form a full sentence because it was too damn awkward."

"Then make it unawkward."

"Is that even a word?"

Shirley met Terry's gaze and gave her one of those all-knowing-mother looks. "Try again. And again, until it's not awkward and you can actually talk to her. It might take a lot of work, but wouldn't it be worth it in the end?"

Terry knew she was right, even if it was maddening. Probably why she was damn good at her job. "I'll try to speak to her. Maybe I'll see her on Monday when I go to the bank to deposit a couple of checks. I got an advance from Dresden, and I think Frank had something to do with it."

"He's a sweet man." Shirley smiled shyly, and suddenly Terry needed to know more about Frank Trane.

"You guys went to school together, right?"

"Yep." Shirley got up and put her cup in the dishwasher. "And it's all you're getting, nosey girl."

"Wait a minute." Terry did her best to sound indignant. "I laid my heart out to you, and now you're shutting me down?"

"There are things a child should never know about her parent." Shirley winked at her and left the kitchen.

Terry had a sudden vision of Frank and Shirley, a very vivid one. She now regretted bringing the subject up.

****

Sara had a slight buzz from her wine and enjoyed the sensation of dancing with Bren. She moved against Sara like they'd been lovers for years. Her body, solid and warm, pressed along all the right places. The blue in her hair sparkled in the strobe lights. Sara molded her body to Bren's and ran her fingers through her short hair, which was damp from sweat. The look in her eyes shot tingles through Sara.

The music stopped, but they didn't move. Bren wrapped her arms around Sara's waist and pulled her a fraction closer. When their lips met, Sara knew exactly how much Bren enjoyed their dance. Bren left no doubt she wanted much, much more.

Sara took her hand and led her off the dance floor. She was tempted to get a fresh drink but worried she'd end up drunk again. The dancing wore her buzz down, and she looked at Bren with fresh eyes. Eyes that took in the view with a hunger she hadn't felt in a long time.

Okay, two months, give or take, but it felt like forever. It probably accounted for why she ended up with Bren in the first place. Not that it mattered now. The adorable woman staring back at her should be the one on her mind.

But she wasn't. As always, Terry was right there. Ready to kiss her and make love to her in ways no other woman ever could.

"You're doing it again," Bren said. She leaned closer in order for Sara heard her over the new song playing.

"Doing what?"

"Thinking about your ex."

"How the hell do you know?"

Bren shrugged, but Sara knew it bothered her. "I've seen it before. You're not the first woman who's come to me after a breakup. I guess I'm the rebound girl."

"No you're not." Sara tried very hard to convince herself she was telling the truth. "Why don't we get out of here? Go back to my place for a while. I'll drive. We can get your truck later."

"Sure. Let me settle up our tab." Bren kissed her on the cheek and paid for their drinks. She was quiet as they trekked to Sara's car. "You good to drive?" she asked when they got there.

Sara nodded. "The wine wore off a bit ago. I'm good."

"Good."

Bren kept some distance between them as they drove, and Sara felt the chasm opening up. Was she using Bren as a rebound girlfriend? This was their first real date, and she was messing it all up thinking about Terry. She simply had to fix this.

Sara put her hand on Bren's knee and gave it a gentle squeeze. "I was with Terry for about five months. I thought we were perfect together. We talked about everything, went everywhere together. I thought she was the one."

Bren covered Sara's hand with her own. "But she dumped you."

"She did. Without any explanation. She simply said we can't see each other anymore and walked out of my life. It's damn hard to deal with, you know? I mean, where do I put all those feelings? How do I forget her and move on?"

"I don't think you forget her. But you do have to move on— unless you think there's still some chance she'll come back."

Sara shook her head. "No chance. We've seen each other enough times since and she's had ample opportunity to talk to me. She can't even look me in the eye."

"Coward." Bren lifted Sara's hand and placed soft kisses on the back of it. "I'm sorry she hurt you. You don't deserve that."

"No one does." Sara cast a brief glance at Bren. "I don't want to hurt you."

"You won't."

"I'm not even sure I should be seeing you. Hell, we're about ten years apart in age and—"

"It doesn't matter. I like being with you."

"It bothers me. I'm worried I'll hurt you." Sara pulled into her driveway, turned off the ignition, and twisted in her seat to face Bren. "You're probably right. About being a rebound girl. But I don't want it to be like that. I want to be with *you*, Bren. It's damn hard."

"And complicated." Bren gave her a shy smile. "Like I said, I understand. I've been here before." She leaned in and kissed Sara so sweetly it brought tears to Sara's eyes. "Shall we go inside?"

"Sure."

Sara unlocked the front door, and after taking off their coats and hanging them up, the two walked hand-in-hand to the living room. Bren went right to the fireplace and got a nice fire going before she joined Sara on the two-seater settee. Sara leaned her head on Bren's shoulder and enjoyed the warmth of her and the fire.

"Did we have wild sex the last time we were together?" Sara asked. She felt Bren chuckle.

"We had sex, yes. I'm not sure I'd call it wild."

"My clothes were in places they shouldn't have been."

"I think the word 'playful' would work better." Bren ran her fingers through Sara's hair and kissed her temple. "You were pretty drunk and frisky. I wasn't sure if I should stay or not. I knew I had to get you home. My friend Izzy drove your car here."

"I wondered," Sara mumbled. The rhythm of Bren's fingers was making her sleepy.

"You did this funky striptease and shoved your clothes here and there like you were playing hide-and-seek."

"Seriously?" Sara closed her eyes. Did she want to hear all this?

"Oh, yeah. Once you were naked, you decided I had to be naked, too. You're very horny when you're drunk?"

"I'm not sure I've ever had drunk sex before," Sara said, now mortified.

"I'm happy to be your first. Do I win a toaster?"

Sara slapped her playfully in the stomach. "I don't remember it, so no. I think both parties are required to remember."

"I'm sad you don't remember." Bren's hand brought Sara's face closer to her. "Very memorable." Her lips met Sara's in a fiery, passionate kiss.

Bren was very sexy in her blue bowtie and suit. Her body was lean and young and taut with muscles Sara wanted to see. The problem was Sara didn't ache to see them. She didn't ache to touch Bren in a way that made it more important than breathing.

Terry elicited those feelings with one look. When she touched her, Sara felt like her body was on fire.

Shit.

She pulled back from the sexy kissing and smiled sadly at Bren. "I can't."

"It's okay," Bren said, but the look in her eyes said otherwise. "Want to sit here for a while?"

"Can we? I like you, Bren, but I need more time."

"It's fine. I promise." Bren put her arms around Sara and held her snuggly as they sank into the softness of the couch.

"You'll make someone a great wife someday."

Bren placed a kiss on the top of Sara's head. "I've heard of this phenomenon, yes."

"It's true. You're a beautiful soul, Bren."

"Thanks. Let's stop talking and enjoy the fire. Okay?"

Sara heard the hurt in Bren's voice. She forced herself not to cry. She never wanted to hurt Bren, but if she couldn't stop thinking of

Terry it's exactly what would happen. Maybe she needed closure. If she confronted her, would Terry at least tell her why she'd left her? Would it help Sara move on?

If nothing else, maybe it would help Sara stop thinking about her. It wasn't fair to Bren, and it sure wasn't fair to her. One way or the other, she had to speak to Terry.

Chapter Seven

Terry glanced at her phone while in line at Starbucks. She had a full day ahead of her, starting with a video conference with the guys from Dresden. Frank said he'd meet her at the office, but only if she brought him coffee. He was very specific about the coffee he wanted; thus Terry was wasting time in line. Why the hell he had to have the cappuccino whatever was beyond her. It never tasted much like coffee.

She remembered the last time she'd been in Starbucks. Sara, who also liked the cappuccino stuff, was with her. She got a kick out of the barista who made cute little swirls in the foam. The smallest, weirdest things made Sara smile. The barista was adorable. Sara was a shameless flirt, and it was one of many things Terry enjoyed about her.

Try as she might, Sara was always on her mind. At every turn, every building in Whitehorse reminded her of Sara. Had they been to every damn place in the city? Maybe her mother was right, even if it was a bitter pill to swallow. Maybe she should talk to Sara and try to repair their friendship.

Terry stepped up to the counter, finally, and placed Frank's order, along with a mundane coffee for herself. She moved to the pick-up area at the same time someone else stepped in to grab a napkin. "Sorry," Terry said, and her heart sank when she realized it was Sara. Words failed her as they stared at each other, the awkwardness filling the space between them like water in a sinking ship.

"I—hey." Sara's voice trembled slightly. "I didn't expect to see you. You hate the coffee here."

"I don't hate." Terry swallowed against the lump in her throat. "Frank loves it, and because he's helping me out, I'm treating him. He's a nice guy and deserves a treat now and again. For helping me, especially." God, she was rambling.

"Good. It's good to see you."

"You, too."

"Okay." Sara clearly had more to say, but she didn't appear comfortable in their current surroundings. Her eyes nervously searched around them.

"Are you busy tonight?" Terry heard herself ask. "I think we should talk."

"About what?"

"About us."

"There is no us." Sara's voice softened as she looked around them. "And there's nothing to talk about. You left me."

"I did. But I had my reasons, and I think you should know them."

"Hello there." The new voice belonged to someone Terry didn't know. She had to look up to see the woman's dazzling green eyes. Her hair was pulled neatly into a French braid, and her makeup was as gorgeous as a professional model's. Which she could easily be. She was stunning.

"Hey," Sara said. She looked as surprised to see the woman as Terry. "I'm leaving."

"Let me walk with you." The woman slipped her arm around Sara's waist. "I have a meeting at the bank this morning and was hoping I'd see you. How about lunch today?"

Sara, for an instant, looked like she'd refuse, but when she met Terry's gaze, something changed. "Sure. Lunch sounds great. Shall we?"

The woman ushered Sara out of the building, leaving a shocked Terry behind.

The barista called her, and when Terry turned around, she had the feeling the girl had been trying to get her attention for a while. She thanked her, took the coffees, and headed for her office, now sure talking to Sara was a mistake. There was nothing left to mend, and it broke her heart all over again.

****

Sara slipped away from Angel's arm once they were out of the building. Why the hell had she accepted Angel's offer to go to lunch? She was busy as hell today and planned to eat at her desk. This wasn't going to work.

"Before you retract our lunch date, you should know I did it to help you out back there."

"You did?" Sara nearly stopped in her tracks, but she was running late and forced herself to keep going. "Why?"

"I saw you were having trouble with that woman and could use saving. Was I right?"

"Sort of. She's my ex."

"I figured. Her loss."

"Thanks." Sara wished she'd seen Terry someplace less public. Maybe she wouldn't have been on the defensive. Maybe she'd have gone ahead and talked to her. She'd practically written her speech should the opportunity present itself. And yet she walked away with Angel's arm wrapped around her. What was that about? Was she trying to make Terry jealous?

They reached the bank, and Angel gently touched Sara's shoulder before she walked in. "Let me take you to dinner. I'm busy today, or I'd keep the lunch offer open. But I like you and you should know there are women who can appreciate someone like you."

Sara felt defensive toward the barb clearly meant for Terry. She didn't think Terry was a bad person, but it didn't stop her from being hurt or angry. She felt slighted at Angel's judgmental comment. The look in Angel's eyes, however, told Sara she'd meant it as a compliment. It felt nice to know she was appreciated, though she'd rather be spending her time with Bren.

She paused a moment to recall Bren's schedule. She'd said something about hanging out with Izzy. They were going out tomorrow night for sure, and Sara figured tonight would be okay. No reason she couldn't go out with more than one woman. "Thanks. That's nice of you to say."

"Tonight? I can pick you up around six?"

"Sure." Sara gave her a winning smile and headed to her office. Inside, she felt like she'd made a deal with the devil.

****

Frank left with his coffee and took off to meet with a client regarding surveys he'd done during the summer. It was fine with Terry. She needed a moment to herself. But didn't get it because the phone rang. She recognized Jackie's number and picked it up immediately.

"This is Terry."

"Hi, Terry. Jackie. Do you have a minute?"

"Sure," Terry said, her stomach clenching. "What'd he do now?"

"It's what you're going to do that I need to talk to you about."

"Okay."

"I got a call from Shirley. She told me Mr. Dillson grabbed you the other day."

Terry closed her eyes and leaned back in the chair. "Dammit. He didn't hurt me. I shook it off and went home."

"It doesn't matter if he hurt you or not. It's still assault. I need you to file a police report. Today if possible."

"What good will it do? It won't make him stay away from me."

"Yes, it will. I plan on using it to force his attorney to keep him in line. We'll file a restraining order if necessary. And this will work in our favor. The mediator won't look kindly on Mr. Dillson's actions."

"Fine. I'll call when we're done." Terry paused, her eyes drawn to her picture of Felicia. "Any idea how much longer before we get this settled? It's getting harder for me to keep the stress away from home."

"I understand. His attorney and I are going through the list of mediators right now. It usually takes a couple of weeks to get it scheduled, once we decide on the mediator."

"And his word is final? No court?"

"Correct. The court referred us to mediation, and since Mr. Dillson agreed, then the mediator's decision is final. That's not to say he can't refile or try to contest the decision, but these are rarely overturned. I doubt his attorney will recommend it."

"You sound like we're going to win."

"I know," Jackie said. "You keep a positive attitude, Terry. We'll get through this. Now call the police and get a report filed."

"Will do. Thanks, Jackie."

****

Dinner with Angel went well and afterward they decided to go to the bar attached to the restaurant for drinks. Sara limited herself to a glass of wine, but it was still enjoyable. Angel was an interesting companion, talking about her work in realty and a gold mine near Yellowknife she had part ownership of. She'd never set foot there and certainly never had the urge to work any of the equipment, unlike Liv who would spend every day at one of her mines if she could.

Maybe Angel was showing off for Sara, but it didn't bother her. Angel paid for everything and Sara enjoyed being spoiled. She could get used to it, but she wasn't about to allow it to happen. As much as she liked this side of Angel, Sara knew the relationship couldn't go anywhere. There was no spark, no desire on her part.

In all honesty, she'd much rather be out with Bren dancing. They definitely had sparks between them, and Sara was eager to explore them. With Angel she felt nothing, and Sara hoped like hell she could avoid hurting Angel's feelings.

Hours later they settled into Angel's Jag, and Sara noticed the time on the radio was well past midnight. No wonder she was tired. The late hour and two glasses of wine had done her in. She put her seatbelt on, relaxed, and enjoyed the rumble as the sporty engine came to life.

Angel set the radio to some soft jazz and headed in the direction of Sara's house. "Did I mention how lovely you look tonight?" Angel asked.

"You did. Five times at least." Sara laughed, even though she felt a blush creep up her neck to her cheeks. "You don't have to keep saying it."

"It's true. You shouldn't devalue yourself. You're a beautiful woman."

"Thanks," Sara said.

"I'd like to see you again," Angel said. Her hand rested on Sara's thigh, not demanding, but it didn't do anything for Sara. Not a single twinge or wave of heat. Only the gentle pressure of her touch.

"You're very sweet, Angel, but like I said last time, I'm not up for dating you. It's great to meet you for dinner sometimes, but I'm sort of seeing someone."

Angel's touch turned to a painful grip. "Who?"

"No one you know," Sara said and removed Angel's hand from her thigh. "We're taking it slow, and I'm not sure where it's going, or if it'll even work out."

"Why can't you go out with me, too? You've not made any commitments to this woman, right?"

"Right, but it doesn't mean I want to date two people at the same time. I did consider it, but I don't think I want to. It wouldn't work."

"Make it work," Angel said, as if it were so simple.

"No. Absolutely not. Bren's too kind for me to do that to her. I'm sorry, but—"

"But nothing. Make. It. Work." Angel shocked Sara by pulling off the highway. She parked the car and faced her. She couldn't see Angel's face very well, but in the dim lights of the dashboard, she saw her anger. "I want to see you, Sara. I want you to give me a chance. I think you owe me."

"I owe you? What the hell are you talking about? I don't owe you anything."

"You do. I brought in five more businesses to your bank. Each one coming to you for their client loans because I sent them there. Plus, I graciously saved you from having to deal with your ex today."

"I don't care about the business, but you didn't *save* me from anyone. In fact, I think if you hadn't butted in Terry and I might have had a chance to talk. I need closure from her, and I might not get it if she thinks I'm not willing to sit down and listen to her."

"You want to go back to her? Is that it?"

"No. Yes. I don't know!" Sara stared out the window into the dark night. "I need to end things properly with her. Then I can move on."

"Then get it done. Tomorrow." Angel put the car in gear and sped off down the highway again, as if the conversation were now over. It wasn't over for Sara.

"You don't get to order me around, Angel. I'll do what I want on my own time. I think going to dinner tonight was lovely, but it's the last time. I'm not interested in seeing you anymore."

"Seriously?"

She heard something very scary in Angel's tone, and Sara wished she were anywhere but in Angel's car. "Yes. You're not my girlfriend or my wife, and even if you were, I wouldn't let you talk to me like this. No one orders me around. I don't want to see you and that's final."

"You don't want to see me?"

"No. I don't."

"Fine." Angel pulled off the highway again, reached across Sara's lap, and opened her door. "Get out."

"What?"

"You heard me. You don't want to see me, so get the fuck out of my car."

Sara hesitated, not sure if Angel was being serious or not. When she pressed the button to release Sara's seatbelt, she knew. An air of violence hung in the car, Sara got the hell out of it. She slammed the door closed, and Angel pulled out and spun her tires on the icy patches and slid onto the road in a reckless manner.

Sara grabbed her cell phone and pulled up the first person she thought of. Her heart hammered in her ears when she realized who she'd called.

****

Terry stretched and lowered the leg rest of her recliner, the book on her lap still unread. Her brain refused to stop thinking about the run-in with Sara earlier in the day. She looked beautiful as always, but something was missing. Her smile didn't reach her eyes, and she seemed—off. Maybe their chance encounter startled her.

It'd certainly thrown Terry for a loop. She'd thought over and over what she would say if she saw Sara. Yet none of those rehearsed words fell from her mouth. Instead, she sounded like a babbling idiot.

At least she'd tried to get Sara to make a time to talk to her. It sucked her girlfriend walked up on them. It sucked more how Sara had moved on so quickly. Terry certainly hadn't expected it. Then again, what had she expected? For Sara to become a nun?

Her cell phone rang. She grabbed it and thumbed the Answer button by habit. She didn't bother to check the caller ID. "Hello?"

"Uh, hi, Terry. It's Sara."

As if she wouldn't recognize her voice. Terry's throat constricted as she tried to form words. "Hey."

"I'm sorry to call late, but I need help. I sort of got dumped along the roadside."

"What?" Terry was on her feet and almost outside before she realized she didn't have her shoes on, or her coat, nor did she know where she was going.

"Yeah. Look, can you come get me? I'm on Highway 1, about twenty minutes south of Whitehorse."

"I'll be right there." She shoved her feet into a pair of boots and grabbed her jacket. She moved the phone away from her mouth to shout at her mom. "I need to go help someone out. I'll text you to let you know how long I'll be."

She heard Shirley's voice but not her words as she was already in the driveway.

"I'm putting the phone on Bluetooth. Don't hang up."

"Don't worry," Sara said. Terry heard a tremor in her voice. "You're the closest person I know to where I am. I'm sorry I had to call you."

"Stop apologizing." She hesitated, not sure this was exactly the right time for the talk she wanted to have. "We broke up, but it doesn't mean I'm not willing to help you."

"Thanks. I guess I wasn't sure."

"You were sure enough to call me." Terry didn't bother to check her speed as she raced along the highway. "Are you on the west or east side of the road?"

"Um, northbound. Coming into town, the east side of the road."

"Got it." Terry kept her high beams on and told Sara as much.

"I'm on my way."

"Good. It's kind of creepy out here."

"You'll be okay if you stay close to the edge of the road."

"I'm practically standing on it right now."

"Good." Terry's heart was racing. She wanted to beat the crap out of the person who'd done this to Sara. Had they no idea how dangerous this could be? A person, alone, in the dark, along a highway without streetlights late at night. Who does that?

"Terry, are you still there?"

"Yes, sorry. I'm wondering what kind of asshole dumps someone on the side of a dark road."

"Trust me, I'm as surprised as anyone. We had a nice dinner and—oh! I think I see your truck."

Terry looked toward the opposite side of the road and indeed saw Sara waving at her. Relief flooded her when she pulled alongside her and Sara climbed into her truck.

"Thank you," she said again.

Terry disconnected the call and took a moment to give Sara a quick once-over. She didn't have any visible injuries. "You okay?"

"I am now. Take me home, please?"

"Sure." Terry eased her truck onto the road and drove a normal speed to Sara's house. They were quiet on the ride there, despite the fact Terry ached to talk to her. It didn't feel like the right time, but perhaps this was a step in the right direction. Sara had needed someone and chose to call Terry.

She pulled into Sara's driveway and parked. Terry turned to her as Sara opened the door. The interior light made her face look unnaturally pale, and Terry was sure she spotted tearstains on her cheeks.

"You sure you're okay? Do you need me to come in with you? Does she know where you live?"

"How do you know it's a she?"

Terry smiled and pointed to the black, form-fitting dress Sara wore. "You wouldn't wear it unless you were on a date."

"It wasn't an actual date. It was dinner with someone I thought was a friend."

"She was an asshole for doing this to you, but I'm glad you called me. I'm glad I could be there to help you out."

"Me, too." Sara's voice was quiet, and she got out of the truck. "Thanks."

"Wait." Terry had her attention, and it was now or never. "Can we please set up a time to talk? I need a few minutes. Your office or mine, or somewhere else. I don't care. I need to explain myself."

Sara hesitated and Terry practically held her breath as she waited for an answer. "Sure. I'll text you tomorrow."

"Great."

Sara closed the door, and Terry watched her until she was safely inside the house. It was definitely a start.

****

Sara couldn't sleep. She tossed and turned most of the night. Her cell phone informed her it was four thirty-five in the morning. She'd gotten home around one and should be well on her way to sleep after an exhausting night. Plus, today was Saturday. She wanted to sleep in on her day to be lazy and not get up until at least nine. This was ridiculous.

The reason for her restlessness was easy enough to figure out. First, Angel being all possessive and dumping her on the highway late at night. Then Terry coming to her rescue like some hero from a romance novel.

She should have taken advantage of the time together and talked to Terry. But now she feared facing her. Could they talk? Or would it end up being another fight? With all the hurt hanging between them—was it even a good idea to see her? She'd have to text her later today regardless.

Sara couldn't stand it any longer and got up. She made some Pop-Tarts, grabbed a Diet Coke, and settled on the settee. It reminded her of the night last week when she cuddled with Bren.

Shit!

She retrieved her cell phone from her room and called Liv. She simply had to talk to someone.

Grace answered the phone. "Hey, Sara." She had obviously been sleeping.

"Hey. Can I talk to Liv? It's important."

"Sure." Grace sounded very awake now, and Sara heard her rousing Liv. A few seconds went by, and Liv was there.

"What's wrong?"

"I need my bestie. It's been a rough night."

"Want me to come over?"

Sara hesitated. Grace was with Liv, and she didn't like the idea of interfering with their time together. "I—"

"Give me fifteen minutes," Liv said and disconnected the call.

Sara put the phone down and leaned her head back against the settee. She was damn lucky to have such good friends.

Ten minutes later, Liv was in the living room with her. They were seated on the floor in front of the couch, as they'd done many times over the years. Liv looked exhausted, and Sara felt extra guilty.

"You didn't have to come over," Sara said.

"Yes, I did. I heard it in your voice. Now, tell me what's going on."

And Sara did. Every dirty little detail. To Liv's credit, she was quiet during Sara's story, though Sara saw the storm brewing behind her expressive eyes. She finished with the trouble she'd had sleeping and tossed the conversation firmly into Liv's lap.

"I can't believe you went out with Angel and didn't tell me. Twice."

"This is what you're taking away from what I said?"

"Partly, yes. I mean, Angel? Seriously? What the hell were you thinking?"

"I was thinking about my job at first. She has a lot of pull. And her cousin is my new boss, at least for now. But it doesn't matter. I went with her willingly. I never thought it'd get this bad. I mean, I didn't see either time as a date, but I guess she did."

"And she got pissed about you sort of going out with Bren?"

"Yeah. It's not any of her business, but for whatever reason, she decided she can control me. I mean, she wants to go out with me. Liv, I can't handle her. I thought if I went to dinner a couple of times she'd back off, but it's the opposite. I'm worried she'll cause trouble for me at work, or trouble with Bren."

"Want me to talk to her?"

"God no. I think you'd make things worse." Sara took a bite of her Pop-Tart while she watched the emotions pass over Liv's face. She loved her dearly, but she had a bad feeling Liv was going to do something they both might regret. "Promise me you won't talk to her. I mean it, Liv."

Liv hesitated. "Fine. But if she comes near you again, I won't be responsible for my actions. She has no right to do this to you. You might have been hurt or killed. It's so damn dark a car could have plowed into you or you could have been kidnapped or—"

"Trust me. I've been through all the 'ors' in this scenario."

"But you called Terry first?"

She hated it when Liv changed gears like this. "Yes. I called Terry first."

"What do you think it means?"

"Am I a shrink now? I have no idea. It means I called Terry first."

"It means, when you needed someone most, you called your ex-girlfriend before you called your best friend, who happens to live about as far away as Terry does from where you were. Don't you think it's significant?"

"Maybe. I mean, I was sort of thinking about her."

"Oh?" Liv perked up. "Tell me."

Sara sighed dramatically. "I saw her at Starbucks, and she asked to see me. Says she wants to tell me why she dumped me. I told her it didn't matter, which is nuts because I need to know. I want closure."

"Call her and tell her otherwise."

"I did call her, remember? She came to my rescue. When we got to my house, I promised to text her a time when we could meet up."

"Did you?"

Sara shook her head. "Not yet. This thing with Angel has me rattled. Why didn't I call Bren? She'd been texting me. I knew she was still awake."

"Bren lives an hour away. Terry was twenty minutes, max. It wouldn't have made sense to call Bren."

"I chose to call Terry instead of you or Bren. How will it feel to

Bren? I'm already worried I'm hurting her. It's a big fucking mess."

"No, it's not." Liv put her arm around Sara and hugged her close. "Talk to Bren. She'll understand. Let her decide if it's hurting her too much to keep seeing you. She's a big girl, and I'm betting she knows what she can and can't handle. As for Terry..." She paused until Sara looked up at her. "Meet up with her. Get it over with."

"Okay. Why did you and I break up?"

Liv laughed softly and kissed Sara's forehead. "We work better as friends. And it's good, too, because I think we both need a solid friend in our lives."

"Sadly, I agree with you. Do you think I'll ever find someone like you have? Someone who makes me smile the way Gracie makes you smile?"

"I hope so," Liv whispered. "I really hope so."

"Want a Pop-Tart? I've got another box."

Liv helped Sara to her feet and gave her another hug. "I love you, weirdo."

"I love you, too. Let's eat."

Chapter Eight

Liv got home with enough time to shower and change for work. She hated working on the weekend, but the mine owner she was meeting was only available today. If it weren't for the promised sale of three new pieces of equipment, running in the six-figure price range, Liv would have told him no. Weekends were usually off limits for work. But she was a businesswoman, and sometimes it sucked. Like now when she'd much rather be going to bed.

She found Grace in the kitchen, holding a cup of coffee and staring out the window over the sink. Liv stood behind her, unable to see whatever Grace found interesting.

"How's Sara?" Grace asked, not moving or looking at Liv.

"Better." Liv slid her arms around Grace and rested her chin on Grace's shoulder. "Want to tell me why you're staring out the window with a cold cup of coffee in your hand?"

"I've been thinking…" Grace poured the contents into the sink and set the cup on the counter.

"About?"

"It's not important." She finally moved so she and Liv were facing each other. Grace rested her hands on Liv's hips. "Tell me what happened to Sara."

"Angel happened."

"Angel? Angel Harrison?"

"Yep."

"I thought you got her to leave Sara alone?"

Liv shrugged. "I did, but then Sara agreed to go out with her again. Twice."

Grace grew very quiet and moved away from Liv to pace the length of the kitchen. "Oh God. What did she do? Did she threaten Sara? Did you call the police? Is Sara okay?"

"Whoa, calm down." Liv tried to stop her movements, but Grace pushed past her. Her face was pale, and her hands shook. "Gracie, please. Sara's fine. I promise."

"She can't be fine, Olivia. The woman hit her, or don't you remember?"

"How could I forget? The date went fine, she went home, and everything was good."

"It's clearly not good if she called you in the middle of the night to come to her house." Grace's voice rose with each word. "What the hell happened, Olivia?"

"Angel got her to agree to a second date. Sara thought it'd be okay—they got along fine the last time. Except Angel wanted more.

Acted like Sara should break up with Bren and go out with her. Apparently, Angel didn't get the memo they weren't on a romantic date." Liv shook her head, still not able to wrap her brain around most of this weird situation. "When Sara told her, in no uncertain terms, she has no romantic interest in her, Angel dumped her out on Highway 1 sometime last night—well this morning. I guess she was too far out to walk home. She called Terry to come get her."

"Angel dumped her out of her car, in the dark, on the highway? How far out was she?"

"About thirty kilometers or so, I guess. I'm not entirely sure, but Terry was there in about twenty minutes to get her. Sara was shaken over it, but not hurt. Angel never touched her."

"She doesn't have to," Grace said, now stopping in front of Liv. Her eyes relayed a mix of anger and fear, and Liv's stomach clenched. "You don't have to touch someone to be abusive. Sometimes the suggestion is enough. Her body language, her words. She left her in an isolated area where anything could have happened to her."

"I know." Liv tried desperately to keep her voice calm. "And I want to go right now and kick her fucking ass over it, but I promised Sara I wouldn't. I promised her I wouldn't even speak to Angel."

"Did she call the police?"

Liv realized neither Grace's anger nor the fear had dissipated. "No. And she won't. She says it's not a big deal. I don't like it, but it's her choice to make."

"Bullshit. Call her right now and tell her to make a report. Even if nothing happens and there are no charges, a report should be made and kept on file. Believe me, she will do something like this again. People like her don't stop, Olivia. Sara's my friend, and I'm not going to let her get hurt." Grace stomped out of the kitchen, Liv hot on her heels. She was in time to shut the door after Grace opened it.

"Where are you going?" Liv asked, even though she knew the answer.

"To speak to Angel. You might have promised Sara, but I didn't."

"And what'll that prove? Are you talking her out of seeing Sara again?" Liv stopped fighting the urge to be gentle and let her own anger flare. "I did, and it clearly didn't work. And I threatened violence, Gracie. You won't—can't do that. What makes you think you'll get to her?"

"Because I know her. Better than any of you ever will." Grace had tears in her eyes and angrily swiped them away as they fell along her cheeks.

Liv flinched at her words, knowing full well she was speaking about her ex-wife, Carly. Images which sometimes haunted Liv's thoughts came to the surface. Grace's twin brother, Matthew, once described the injuries Grace suffered under Carly's abuse. How she was in a coma for days after being hit in the head with a baseball bat. Liv's gaze went to the scar on Grace's forehead, now faded a little, but prominent enough to remind Liv of what she'd gone through.

She got between Grace and the door and gently pulled her into a loving embrace. Liv didn't speak as she waited for Grace to relax against her. Then the sobs started, and Liv held her through them, whispering words of comfort to the woman she loved most in the world. If anyone deserved receiving retribution, it was Carly. Prison simply wasn't enough punishment. Not to Liv.

Once the sobs faded, Grace met Liv's gaze. Her eyes were bloodshot from crying but no longer held the fear or anger in them. Liv kissed her lips softly and swiped away the remaining tears with her thumb. "I love you," she said, holding Grace's eyes with her own, searching them to see the love she knew was there. Hoping her eyes relayed the message in her heart.

Grace gave her a tremulous smile. "I love you, too."

"We're calling in sick today," Liv said, kissing her again. "I think we both deserve a day off...play a bit of hooky."

"I job at Rock World is new, dear. It might be part time for now, but I'm sure calling in sick isn't a great idea. Much as I'd love to do it. Plus you have a client to meet."

"I'll call for you. Tell them you woke up sick and need a day to rest." Liv got the cell phone out of her pocket and punched in the numbers. "You're in no shape to be climbing walls and stuff. Not today. And I can call David to meet the client. I'm sure he can handle it. Trust me."

"I do trust you, Olivia." Grace cradled Liv's face in her hands. "I'll always trust you."

"It's the most wonderful thing I've ever heard," Liv said and called them both in sick for the day, arranging for David to handle their client. Once finished, she tenderly escorted Grace to their room where they settled onto the bed. Grace was asleep in minutes, curled on her side with Liv's arm firmly holding her close. Liv glanced up at the ceiling and sighed. She wondered if there would ever come a time when Carly wouldn't haunt Grace anymore.

****

Bren, as always, was ten minutes early for their date. She wore faded jeans with rips along the thighs and a bright-blue T-shirt hugged her girly figure. The famous blue hair was shorter, with little spikes in the front. Such a refreshing sight after the disaster with Angel the night before.

Sara sighed. Could this woman be any more adorable?

"Heya," Bren called out as she walked up to Sara's door. "You look amazing."

"Do I?" Sara wanted to comment how she wasn't wearing anything special, but neither was Bren. She glanced down at her black jeans, matching boots, and white polo shirt. "Thanks."

"You're welcome. Are you ready to dance the night away?"

"I am, but can we talk for a bit first?"

"Yeah." Bren's expression changed slightly, the fun no longer there.

"It's nothing bad, I promise." Sara led her to the settee and sat beside her, holding her hand. "Something happened last night and I want to tell you about. I don't want you hearing about it from the lesbian rumor mill."

"Did you get back together with Terry?"

Sara gave her a smile, but it didn't do much to change the sadness in Bren's eyes. "No. I went to dinner with a woman who I work with, and she got pissed off when I told her I wasn't interested in dating her. She dumped me out of her car on Highway 1 last night."

"What the hell? Are you okay?"

"I'm fine," Sara said. "I was pretty upset when it happened and luckily had my cell phone with me. I called someone to come get me, which she did, and got me safely home."

"Terry."

"Yes." Sara looked away from Bren, afraid to see if she was hurt by this or not. "She lives on Highway 1, outside the city. I knew she'd be close."

"It makes sense. I couldn't have gotten there for at least an hour or more. Are you sure you're okay?"

Sara met her worried gaze and nodded. "I—I'm sorry I didn't call you. I consider you a friend."

"But you still have feelings for Terry." She kissed the back of Sara's hand. "And here you are, still willing to give me a chance. Are you sure about this? About going out with me?"

"Honestly? No. I'm not sure about anything, except I don't want to go out with Angel—the one who dumped me on the roadside. Yeah, I still have feelings for Terry. I don't think it'll change anytime soon. Though we are supposed to get together next week. She wants to tell me why she broke up with me."

"Do you want to hear it?"

"I do. I want closure. I need it to move on."

Bren was quiet for a moment. "When you decide to move on, do you think I'll have a chance?"

"I think you have the best chance of anyone I know." Sara kissed her on the cheek. "But right now, I need for us to be friends more than anything. I want someone I can go out with, have a good time with, and not feel any pressure from. Can you be that person?"

"I want it more than anything." Bren held Sara's face in her hands and drew her closer. "I have strong feelings for you, Sara. I'll do whatever it takes to be with you. Even if it's as friends." She placed a soft kiss on Sara's lips, and the gentleness nearly made Sara cry.

"You're a special woman. Don't let anyone ever tell you different."

Bren shrugged. "I'll take it. So, dancing?"

"Hell, yes. I have stress to get rid of."

Bren stood and pulled Sara with her. "Friend dating then?"

Sara laughed. "Friend dating."
"Cool."

****

Terry stood at the back door and watched Felicia and Elmo run around in the snow. They'd gone from snow angels to a very lopsided snowman, and now Felicia was tossing snowballs and Elmo was trying desperately to bring them back. He'd bite the snow and come up with a face full of fluff, his expression hilarious. Felicia giggled, and the sound warmed Terry's heart.

She wished Ann were there to see it. Or Sara. She glanced at her phone and checked the text message she'd gotten from Sara. They'd be meeting Monday after work, around five, at Terry's office. At least a dozen times since she got the text, Terry thought over what she'd say to Sara. How she'd explain things so they made sense. Except they didn't, because, as always, her mother was right. She should have been upfront with Sara and worked it out together.

But her impetuous side won out, and she made the biggest mistake of her life. Was it even possible for her and Sara to be friends again? Did she dare hope for anything more? Terry pressed her forehead against the cold glass of the window and sighed, creating a mist on the smooth surface.

She heard Shirley come in the front door and waited for her to join her in the kitchen. Her mom left early on an emergency call, and it was now past dinnertime. When Terry saw her, she looked exhausted and her skin was unusually pale.

"Mom, did you eat today?"

"I had a candy bar at around noon. I didn't have time. I had to get intake done on this kid the police picked up. He needed to get into the hospital today, and you know that stuff is never quick. Make it a Saturday, and the system slows down to a crawl. It was awful."

She slid onto a chair at the kitchen table and put her head in her hands.

"Let me heat up something. You need to eat." Terry pulled out the leftover chicken casserole and popped it into the microwave. "Have you checked your blood sugar?"

"Are you the mom now?"

"If it's what I need to be, then yes." Terry knew her mother well enough to know her blood sugar was too low. It couldn't be in a danger zone, or Shirley wouldn't be able to walk, much less sit at the table. "You have to keep better tabs on it, Mom. You're working too much, and you're going to make yourself sick."

The microwave dinged, and Terry placed the dish in front of Shirley. She was unusually quiet as she set about eating and accepted a glass of orange juice without a word.

"I'm worried about you," Terry said. She was standing by the door again, keeping an eye on Felicia and Elmo, while making sure her mother ate. "I think you need to tell them you can't be on call anymore. These all-day deals and late-night and early-morning calls are too much for you."

"It's my job," Shirley said. Her tone made it clear the discussion was over.

But Terry wasn't ready to stop. "I know, and I know you love it, but you have to consider your health. You won't do anyone any good if you're in the hospital again."

"It wasn't bad. I had something from McDonald's for breakfast on my way to the office. It always tides me over for a while. The candy bar wasn't ideal, but I was fading and needed a fast boost of sugar. I do know my own body. I can handle it."

"You do realize if I said those same words to you, you'd take my head off? As soon as you tell me you can handle it, I know to worry even more. I can see by the look of you right now you're not handling it, Mom. Far from it."

"Grams!" Felicia screamed and ran to Shirley. She threw her arms around her as best she could in her snow-coat onesie. "We played all day today. How come you weren't here?"

"I had to work, baby. But I promise to play in the snow tomorrow, okay?"

"Yep." Felicia was off and outside again, Elmo trailing on her heels.

Shirley said, "That dog loves her more than any other human, and I'm the one who rescued him."

"And you're changing the subject." Terry took a seat across from her. "Will you please consider what I'm asking you? Back off on the extra work. Let me."

"You need to spend time with Felicia. That's more important than work or money."

"I agree, but right now I need the money. And I won't work a lot extra. Maybe the occasional weekend. I have some new clients who come for the gold season and could use my help during the off time. Three of them can only meet on Saturdays because they all work during the week. I'll set up those times this week, but I need you here with Felicia. Please, Mom."

"Fine. I'll take myself off the call-out list for now. There's a chance I might get called in as a backup person, but I guess we'll deal with it if it happens."

Terry got up and hugged her tightly. "Perfect. Now, finish your dinner and check your sugar before you go to bed."

"Who said I was going to bed?"

"Your daughter did. You've taken care of me my entire life. Time I turned the tables on you."

Shirley squinted both eyes at her in mock anger. "Are you saying I'm an old lady who needs taking care of?"

"You're not old, but yeah, you need looking after," Terry said. "I'm going to try to pull my child and your dog in from the snow. I'll keep them quiet while you rest."

"You're a good kid."

"And you're a good mom."

Shirley smirked and went back to her dinner.

****

Terry paced her office. Sara was late. Which wasn't like Sara at all. She was never late, and Terry wondered if she might not be planning to show up. Terry watched the snow fall on the street and wished she'd picked a different day to do this. It would be a long drive home if the snow didn't let up soon. She couldn't have been more surprised to see the damn Beemer pull up and park next to her truck. Again. What the hell did William want? Hadn't his lawyer told him to leave her alone?

She stalked outside without her coat and was there as he got out of his car. "Get the hell away from me, William. You know you're not allowed to be here."

"I came with an offer." He had a look on his face that told Terry he expected her to accept whatever he was going to say. "You give me full custody of Felicia, and I'll allow you visitations during the summer holidays. You'll have to come to Vancouver, but—"

"No. Offer rejected. Talk to my lawyer, not me."

"I wanted to do this in a civilized manner."

"Little late, isn't it? You've been hounding me for months. I've tried to make deals with you, but you rejected everything we've brought to the table. If you keep harassing me, I'm calling the police. Go home. We'll deal with this at mediation."

Terry spun around and stomped back toward her office, shocked to find Sara standing in the doorway. Had she heard the entire exchange?

"I'm going to prove you're an unfit parent."

Terry ignored him as she passed Sara and went inside. Sara followed and closed the door.

Terry shut her eyes against the tears she desperately needed to shed. "I'm sorry you had to see that."

"Who was he?"

"My father-in-law. Ann's father."

"Oh." Sara remained standing, her hands clasped in front of her in a move Terry recognized as nerves.

"You want to have a seat?" Terry steadied herself against her desk in an attempt to gain her equilibrium. Sara's face was a mixture of sadness and confusion, and she didn't know what to say to her.

"I can't stay long. I promised Liv I'd stop by for dinner tonight."

"Sure. I understand."

"Did I hear him right?" Sara asked. "Is he trying to take Felicia away from you?"

"Yes."

"Why didn't you tell me? All the times we talked—talked about Ann and Felicia. You never said a word."

"He filed for custody after we broke up." From the concerned look on Sara's face, Terry saw her words fell short. "At first, he told me if I broke up with you he'd call off the lawyers." Terry choked back a sob. "So I did. But he also wanted me to move to Vancouver. I considered it, but I don't want to uproot Felicia again. Plus I need my mom as much as she needs me. I said no. He decided to file for custody. He's trying to say I can't take care of Felicia on my own.

"I don't have as much money as he does—he's richer than God. There's more specialized care in Vancouver than here, and he claims it's harmful for Felicia to be away from those doctors. He says I'm keeping her away from him to hurt him, and the last bit he's come up with is pictures of you and me going out dancing and he's trying to use them to say I have some wild, partying lifestyle."

"He's using the fact you were dating me against you? He forced you to break up with me?"

"He is and yes, I guess." Terry gave in and sat behind her desk. She put her elbows on the top of it and held her head in her hands. "He's been an ass since Ann died. Like it was my fault she went out late at night to get medicine for Felicia. Like I was the one who caused her to go off the road." Terry ran her fingers through her hair and tried to get her thoughts in order. "He wanted me to give him Felicia. He said he could provide for her better than me. I stayed in Quebec for almost three years trying to prove him wrong.

"When he told me he'd stop this custody battle if I broke up with you—I didn't see myself as having any choice. I love my daughter, and there's nothing in this world I won't do for her."

"You should have told me." Sara's voice was unusually quiet, cold even. "But I guess you didn't trust me."

"That's not true."

"Isn't it? If you trust someone, you tell them these things. I mean, you asked me not to meet Felicia for a while until you were sure about us. Then right before we were set to go to the park together, you broke up with me. What kind of message do you think it sends to me? What did I do wrong?"

"Nothing." Terry was on her feet now and tried to go to Sara, but she backed away. "Sara, please. I didn't have a choice. You have to believe me."

"I do believe you, Terry. I believe you did what you thought was right, but I don't understand why you didn't tell me. I was stupid to think you might actually love me."

Sara quietly left the office.

Terry froze, unable to stop her.

She stared after Sara for what felt like forever, shaken out of her shock by the ringing of her cell phone.

"Honey," her mother said, "take your time getting home. I'm already here and picked up Felicia for you. The roads are getting bad."

Shirley paused, but Terry's voice caught in her throat. "Hey, you there? Hello?"

"Uh, yeah. Thanks, Mom."

"What's wrong? Wait, weren't you supposed to talk to Sara? Am I interrupting?"

"No, you're not interrupting anything. There's nothing, Mom."

"Oh no."

"William was here. She heard me arguing with him. It was bad."

"Come home and we'll can talk about this."

"I need some time first. I don't want Felicia to see me like this. Tell her I'm working late, and I'll be home in a couple of hours."

"Will you be all right?"

"I don't know." Terry let the tears fall. She wished her mom was there to hold her, but she couldn't chance Felicia seeing her this upset. "I love you, Mom."

"I love you too, honey. Let me know when you're on your way home."

"I will." She disconnected the call, slid to the floor, and cried.

Chapter Nine

For once, Sara remembered to knock on Liv's door. She didn't need a repeat of the last time she barged in on her and Grace. Liv was there in a few seconds, her slightly flushed face letting Sara know it'd been wise to knock first. She scooted past Liv, hung up her coat, and sat at the kitchen bar. The tears came before she could speak.

Liv's arms were around her as Sara sobbed uncontrollably. She heard Grace move around, felt her gentle touch on her back, and cried harder. Her friends had a ton of love and trust between them. Why the hell couldn't she have it for herself?

"What's wrong with me?" she finally asked after she soaked Liv's shirt and emptied half a box of tissues.

"Nothing. Why would you think that?" Liv still held Sara and kissed the top of her head. She always felt safe in Liv's arms.

"There must be something. I thought—I thought Terry and I had something special, but apparently she can't trust me. I'm trustworthy, right? I don't gossip about people, except to you. I don't tell lies, and I don't share secrets."

"All of it is true or you wouldn't be my best friend." Liv hugged her a little tighter. "I don't know why Terry can't trust you, but if that's the case, you're better off without her."

"Exactly." Sara heard her own voice, and she sounded pathetic. Which was fine since it's how she felt. "I don't think I am better off without her. I love her, Liv. What am I supposed to do?"

"I don't know."

Grace spoke up. "Did you tell her?" Sara pulled away from Liv and glanced at Grace, who sat across from her at the bar. "Does she know you love her?"

"I don't know. I never said the words, but I thought my actions would speak for me, you know? I thought we had this connection…we were made for each other. How is it I'm always wrong? I mean, I went out with Angel twice knowing she could turn on me in a heartbeat, which she did. I'm dating this young kid who dotes on me, but I can't give her anything in return. I feel like I'm stringing her along. It's all fucked up."

"It's not," Grace said. She handed Sara another tissue. "First, Angel doesn't count in any of this. You went out with her because you were trying to make nice and keep a client. It backfired, but it's not the same as with Terry or Bren."

"How so? I still made a colossal mistake."

"But that was about work more than anything else. Bren knows how you feel because you told her outright. She's a grown woman capable of making decisions for herself. If she says she wants to keep going out with you on a casual basis, then good. Go with it. I personally think she's what you need right now."

"And Terry?" Sara asked between sniffles. "She told me she couldn't trust me with something so major. Something that will affect her life forever—literally."

"The reason she broke up with you?"

Sara nodded and spilled the entire story in one go, nearly in a single breath so she wouldn't be able to stop herself. "I kind of get why she stopped seeing me, but if she'd told me, we might have worked something out. I would have waited for her."

"Maybe she was afraid," Grace said. "I'm not trying to stick up for her, but if she's scared of losing her daughter, maybe she's also scared of losing you."

"She did lose me."

"And maybe that's the problem. She had to choose one of you, and she chose her child. Given her circumstances, I can't fault her for choosing Felicia over you. Clearly she felt like she'd been backed into a wall."

"I suppose." Sara wanted to stay angry at Terry, but Grace wasn't making it easy. "I still think I deserved to know."

"And I agree." Grace gently held Sara's hand. "Which is why I'm suggesting you go back and talk to her some more."

"What?" Sara and Liv chorused the question.

"Are you nuts?" Liv said. "She doesn't need to put herself through any more of this. Terry had a chance to explain herself, and she did."

"But Terry also didn't have all the information at hand, either," Grace said. "She has no idea how Sara feels about her. Maybe if she did, the outcome would have been different. Maybe she'd never have broken things off."

"How could she not know Sara loved her? I mean, this is Sara we're talking about. She's the most affectionate, loving person in the world. Terry would know exactly how she felt."

Sara said, "Um, you two do know I'm right here?" They stopped talking around her and gave her their full attention. "I don't know if I can talk to Terry right now. I need time to think about all this. Do you guys mind if I skip dinner? I think I need to be alone for a while."

"Skip dinner? Seriously?" Liv looked suitably horrified. "Now I know you're more upset than you're letting on. Do you want me to come home with you?"

Sara looked briefly at Grace, whose expression was neutral. She knew Grace would never stop Liv from coming with her, but she had the feeling Grace might not always like it. "No. I'm good. I need to lie down, maybe go to sleep. It all sucks right now."

"It's okay if she goes with you, Sara," Grace said in the kindest of ways. "Seriously. You don't have to be alone. I do understand how close you two are. If she's what you need, take her up on the offer."

"Grace, you are one in a million, and I'm glad Liv has you. But no. It's something I need to work out for myself."

"At least let me fix you something to take home. You'll want to eat eventually."

"Sure." Sara got up while Grace moved about the kitchen, on a mission to make sure she ate a good meal. She pulled Liv into the living room and kept her voice to a whisper. "She's really special."

"I know. It's why I'm marrying her." Liv held Sara's gaze for a few moments, her expression one of concern. "I love you. Tell me what I can do to help you."

"I love you, too, and you've already done it. I don't know if I'll ever get over Terry, but I have to figure out how to move on. One day at a time, one step at a time, I guess."

"What about Bren?"

Sara shrugged. "She's sweet and fun and a pleasant distraction from all the drama. If she's willing to hang out with me, I'll take it. Maybe you two can come to the club with us on Saturday. I'd love for you to meet her and get to know her. I know you'll like her."

"We'll make it a tentative yes. I'll check with the wife-to-be."

Sara chuckled. "You're already whipped, aren't you?

"I was whipped after our first kiss." Liv laughed and Sara joined her.

"Now that's a sound I like to hear," Grace said. She handed Sara a plastic container big enough to hold two full meals. "Left over lasagna and salad. Eat it all, or I'll come over and kick your ass."

"Do I have to eat it all tonight?"

"No, but you have to eat a lot of it tonight and the rest can be lunch tomorrow. I'm not working, by the way. If you'd rather have lunch out of the office, call me."

Sara hugged them both. "I will."

"Text me when you get home," Liv added as they walked her to the door.

"You do know I live like two minutes from here, right? You can practically see my house."

"If I had X-ray vision, I could see your house." Liv gently pushed Sara onto the porch. "But since I don't, text me when you get home."

"Weirdo."

"Text me."

"Fine." Sara smiled as she left their house. Her love life was in turmoil, but at least she had friends.

****

Sara didn't get much sleep that night. Her thoughts remained on Terry and whether or not she should talk to her again. Their chat didn't give her any closure. In fact, it made things worse. Terry couldn't trust her. Clearly, Sara didn't know Terry as well as she thought she did.

She settled at her desk the next day and opened the container of lasagna from Grace. It smelled heavenly, but Sara's stomach was at odds with her about eating. Yesterday, she skipped breakfast and had a few small bites of the lasagna for dinner. She poked and prodded the food with her fork. She stopped when her cell phone buzzed with a new text message from Bren. A string of smiley faces followed by a dozen red roses and two pink hearts.

She couldn't stop the grin that covered her face.

She sent back two giant smiley faces.

Want to hang out tonight?

Sara didn't have to think about it at all. Not after the shitty few days she'd had. *Yep. Should be home around sixish. Come over?*

Be there. Chinese takeout?

Hell yes.

Later!!!

Her last text was followed by more goofy emojis.

Sara dug into her lunch, happy to have someone like Bren to brighten her day, as always, right when she needed her to. Funny how a few little emojis brought her appetite back.

Maybe the sad faerie would leave her alone after all.

****

The takeout was delicious, and Sara patted her very full belly with a sigh. "I know I'll want more in a couple of hours. Thanks for getting extra."

Bren smiled, clearly proud of herself. "No problem. I'll want some, too. You know, I never believed the whole thing about being hungry after eating Chinese food until you talked me into getting some. There's a lot of it. I don't get how you can be hungry two hours later."

"Don't know, but it's a sin. Or a good thing because it's so damn tasty I don't mind eating more later."

"Hey, I got hired today as a substitute teacher for Whitehorse Elementary."

"Cool, congrats. But I thought you weren't going to do the teaching thing?"

Bren shrugged. "I don't know yet. I need something so I can have money and eventually move out on my own. I accepted the job. I've had applications all over the place, and this is the first one that panned out."

"It's a start. Have you thought much about what you want to do with your life?"

"Not really." Bren got up, cleared the table, and placed the leftovers in Sara's fridge. "Tell me more about how you decided to work at a bank. Did you choose the job before going to school?"

"I figured it out at university. I took all those required courses the first year. Turns out I was very good at two things—math and management. I've always liked math and never once thought about working in any kind of management. However, like you, I needed to do something and I wasn't like Liv, who was driven to get her degree in business administration.

"But, since that's what she was doing, I followed her. I had the biggest crush on her. Anyway, I didn't have any idea of where I might want to work, but an admin job was open at the bank, and I applied. Been there going on ten years now, and I love it. Most people think it's a boring job, but for me it's a challenge. Every day is different, and on some level, I'm actually helping people out."

"Unless you have to decline a loan."

"Yes, but it doesn't happen as much as you'd think. I like the clients I work with, and I've got my own office. I won't be doing loans forever, and there are lots of other jobs I want to try out before I get to bank manager."

"Is it weird to say I want more? Like, I can do any job and get enough money to live on, but I don't want any job. I want my job to mean something. I don't want to sound full of myself or anything, but I want my job to be one that changes the world."

"You're not full of yourself." Sara joined her at the sink and stopped Bren from doing the dishes with a gentle hand on hers. "You're a sweet woman who's trying to find her spot in the world." Sara put her arms around Bren and pulled her close for a soft, slow kiss.

"Thanks," Bren said. "I'm a little lost on what job it is I ought to be doing."

"Don't stress about it. Concentrate on the teaching job for right now. You'll figure it out. You might find out you love teaching."

"Could happen I guess, though my internship sucked."

Sara kissed her again, pulling Bren's lower lip into her mouth. When she let it go, she said, "Don't say 'sucked' when I'm standing this close to you. It gives me ideas." And Sara was suddenly full of a lot of ideas concerning Bren. It might be the proximity or how incredibly sexy Bren was in her cargo pants and blue T-shirt, but it got very hot in the kitchen.

She'd been thinking about Bren since lunch when she got all those emojis. One emoji was a couple locked in a passionate kiss and got Sara thinking about more than kissing Bren. She wanted to explore their new relationship now she was sober enough to remember every little detail.

Bren smiled as if she could read Sara's thoughts. "Have you been drinking?" she asked with a tease in her voice.

"Nope. My mind is clear as a bell, and my body is getting more worked up by the minute." She ran her fingers through Bren's short hair and clasped her hands behind Bren's neck. "I like you, Bren. And I'm attracted to you. But I'm not in a place for a relationship. As long as you're okay, but I need to be sure. Friend dating, remember?"

Bren was difficult to read, and Sara wondered if she was going to walk away.

When she spoke, there was a slight tremor in her voice. Her eyes never left Sara's. "I like you, too, and if that's the deal I need to make to be with you, I'll do it. No relationship. Strictly casual. Got it." Bren wrapped her arms around Sara and kissed her for all she was worth.

Sara moaned into the kiss as their hips rubbed against each other.

No fireworks. No explosions of overwhelming need. But enough spark existed between them that Sara felt the kiss all the way to her toes. Her body was ready, willing, and able. And for now, she told herself to stop thinking. Feel.

The trip to the bedroom was made in record time. Bren's hands were gentle and precise as she removed Sara's clothes, piece by agonizing piece. Each new bit of bared skin was kissed lovingly and slowly. Bren's movements were deliberate, and she knew exactly where to touch Sara to bring the most excruciating pleasure. Bren gently pressed her onto the bed, where her kissing continued down Sara's body.

Sara's hands tore at Bren's shirt. She wanted skin-on-skin contact, but Bren had other ideas. She stopped Sara with one hand, then leaned on her forearm to lever herself over Sara's body. Bren returned to kissing Sara's very sensitive thigh, her lips moving closer to the apex of her legs while her free hand went from one breast to the other, massaging them in equal measure.

Sara's hips rose as Bren's tongue found her in the most amazing way. The first touch was electric, and she wanted nothing more than for Bren to take her. She couldn't believe how much she wanted— needed— this. How was it Bren knew exactly what to? The intensity was more than Sara expected, and the pleasure she brought her was divine.

As she reached her breaking point, Bren put her hand to work and Sara bucked the moment she entered her. Bren kept one arm around Sara's hips as she pumped her other hand. Sara gripped the duvet with her fists and called Bren's name as the orgasm ripped through her.

Bren stilled her fingers while Sara rode the last of the orgasm, her senses heightened and her legs twitching. Bren kept her hand still as she slid up Sara's body, a very satisfied grin on her face. She kissed Sara deeply, curling her fingers a bit as she did.

"Amazing," Sara said, her breathing not yet normal. She wiggled her hips when Bren began to tease her. "I wish you were naked right now."

"I will be." Bren nibbled along the edge of Sara's collarbone. "Later. Right now, it's all about you."

"Why?" There was something in her eyes Sara couldn't quite figure out.

"I want to do this, Sara." Bren kissed her slowly. "I want to please you."

"You have, baby. You have."

"But I'm not done," Bren said and wiggled her fingers again.

Sara leaned her head back and moaned. "You're not?" she asked, her voice husky.

"No way." Bren kissed her throat, moving to the valley between her breasts. "I want to explore every inch of you." She continued her kissing, taking a moment to lavish attention on each breast, her teeth grazing each nipple.

Sara was in agony and ecstasy all at once. She wanted more, and she didn't care if Bren was fully dressed or not. "Bren," she ground out between gasps of pleasure. "I need—"

Bren cut her off with a kiss, then worked her magic once again. She took Sara over the edge and into a blissful moment of joy she hadn't thought she'd ever have again.

Moments later, or it could have been an hour, Sara wasn't sure of the time, Bren was naked and wrapped around her from behind. Her head rested on Sara's shoulder, and Sara felt her warm breath by her ear.

"Thanks," Sara said, still enjoying the tingling feel of Bren's touch.

Bren placed a kiss behind Sara's ear. "I've been wanting to do it since the first night we were together."

"Really?"

"Oh yeah. Did I forget to mention you didn't let me touch you? Not even once?"

"Huh?" Sara turned to look into Bren's eyes. By the dim light from the street, she could barely make out her expression. She was smiling. "I think it's time you told me, in detail, what the hell I did."

"Details, huh?" Bren chuckled. "Might take a while. I mean, you undressed yourself like a stripper and hid all your clothes."

"I know. You told me that part."

"Then you undressed me, but I made sure my clothes were in a pile by the bed." Bren laughed softly. "Once we were both naked, you practically threw me onto the bed and had your way with me. And trust me, I had no intention of making you stop. It was amazing."

"I had my way with you?" Sara turned around so she didn't have to see the smirk on Bren's face. "Oh my God. I've never—I'm never aggressive..."

"You were that night. I actually had to make you stop because you wore me out. I mean, I'm young and healthy, but seven times—"

"Seven times?" Sara sat up and glared down at Bren. "You're making this up."

"Nope. Seven hot, wonderful orgasms. You even joined me for one of them, though it was your own doing. It was kinda weird how I had to be hands-off, but you were doing pretty into it and, honestly, I didn't care. I've never had sex like that before."

"Fuck."

"Yep. And it was great." Bren sat up beside her and pulled Sara in for a gentle kiss. "Besides, I don't think I'd have done much to you anyway. You were drunk. I didn't want to take advantage of you."

"You let me take advantage of you instead?"

"More or less. Look, you did what you wanted, and I didn't exactly think it sucked. Just sayin'."

"And you still wanted to see me after? I mean, you must have thought I was acting like some crazy nymphomaniac."

"Nah." Bren cuddled her and Sara sank into her embrace. "We didn't talk a lot, but I could tell you'd had a bad breakup. I figured you needed to let off some steam, and I was happy to help you out. Trust me, Sara, it wasn't a bad experience. Not for me. I'm sorry you don't remember it."

"Me, too."

"Why don't we get some sleep? If you're a good girl, I might let you ravish me in the morning."

Sara laughed as they snuggled down, spooning again. "I might take you up on that."

"Awesome."

Chapter Ten

"I think it's time we invite Bren to dinner," Grace announced at their weekly luncheon at Pot O' Gold. She was staring at Sara, but her voice held a playful tone. "Sunday sound good to you?"

Sara kept quiet for a moment to consider her response. "Are you trying to get me to subject Bren to you and Liv? For an entire night?"

"I wouldn't put it that way, but she's pretty damn important to you, and I thought we should get to know her better. A quiet dinner would be perfect, and I promise I'll cook."

"The promise of your cooking does get me a step closer to the table." Sara took a sip of her diet drink and pushed her empty plate aside. "I like Bren a lot, but I'm not in love with her."

"I didn't say you were," Grace said, her expression suddenly very serious. "But you talk about her a lot, and you see her a few times a week. Is there something I'm missing here?"

"I don't know. We're keeping it casual. I can't commit to anything, and I don't think I should. Bren's a sweet woman, but she's also much younger than me." Sara leaned back in the booth and sighed. "We're having fun, but I'm still a little worried I'll hurt her in the end."

"Why would you hurt her? You've told her it's a casual thing. You're not girlfriends or partners. Is she seeing anyone else?"

"I don't think so, though I kind of get the impression sometimes she's not completely present when we're together. I guess we have that in common."

"What do you mean?"

"Truth?" she asked and Grace made a face at her which said "duh." "The sex is amazing with Bren, but there's no real connection there. When we're done and cuddling, it's wonderful and I feel comfortable enough. But if I'm not careful I end up thinking about Terry."

"Terry?"

"Yes. I think about how warm and safe I always felt with her around. The things she could do to me—the ways we'd make love… It's not fair to Bren, and she can tell I'm thinking about her. Maybe not while we're having sex, but sometimes I sort of stare off into space because something reminds of Terry. When I look at Bren, she'll have this look like she knows what I'm thinking about, and I can see the hurt in her eyes.

"I still love her, Gracie. How can I move on when I'm feeling like this?"

"You can't."

"Gee thanks."

"Sara, you can't move on until you resolve your feelings for Terry. Maybe it means being depressed and sad for a few more months. Maybe it means going back to her office and having it out with her. Obviously, you've got some pent-up emotions about the situation. Regardless, you have to confront how you're feeling or you'll never move on. Assuming it's what you want to do."

"Huh? Why wouldn't I move on? There's nothing left where Terry is concerned."

"I don't know. Why was Terry the first person you called when Angel dumped you out on Highway 1?"

Sara couldn't honestly answer. She'd hit Terry's number more from instinct than anything, even if it'd been months since she actually called her for anything. Why did she think of Terry first?

"She doesn't live far from where I was."

"Neither does Liv." Grace took a sip of her drink. "Try again."

"I guess—maybe she was on my mind. Again."

"Which brings me to my point. You have to resolve your feelings for her one way or the other. I know you still have them. I can see it in your eyes when you talk about her."

"Seriously?"

"Yes. You're the easiest person in the world to read. I mean, you already said Bren can tell when you're off thinking about Terry."

"I know and I hate it. It's like Terry's haunting me, but she's not dead. I can't stop thinking about her, and it's gotten worse since I've been going out with Bren. What the hell am I supposed to do?"

"Talk to her again. And don't hold back how you feel. Get it out of your system. You might not be friends when you're done, but you'll have told her what's nagging at you and you'll feel better."

"I don't know. I'll have to think about it."

"Don't take too long. I think you're right about Bren. It is unfair to keep her hanging on like this. Eventually she'll need to know where she stands with you."

Grace was right. And no matter how many times she and Bren talked about it, she felt Bren was becoming way too attached to her. "Now I know why Liv always says she hates it when you're right. I'll figure out a way to talk to Terry. Okay?"

"Sounds good." Grace patted her on the hand. "I wanted to ask you the other day when you were over, but you were too upset—have you heard anything more from Angel? Is she leaving you alone?"

"Not really. I get text messages sometimes—not a lot of them. She's called the office three times this week, but I ignored her. I think if I keep ignoring her, she'll go away eventually. I mean, she's the one who dumped me out of her car. What could she possibly want now?"

"To apologize," Grace said. The words were simple enough, but Sara heard something else behind them. "Women like her apologize every time they hurt you. It's like if they apologize, it erases the past and they get a fresh start. If she convinces you she's sorry, she might get you to see her again. The next time, it might not be her telling you to get out of her car."

Sara didn't understand the fierce look in Grace's eyes. It was scary. "What do you mean?"

"Next time she might get physical. Not a slap like last summer, but physical. Yelling, pushing, shoving—she might hurt you. You need to file a police report, Sara. Let them know she's harassing you."

"It's my word against hers, Gracie. And I haven't answered any calls, so how is she harassing me? I ignore her and move on. I blocked her number from texting me, but she calls from an unknown number to my office. I can't block those types of calls. The one time I did pick it up, I realized it was her and slammed the phone down."

"It's still harassment. Please, take it to the police. You have to make sure they know what she's doing."

Sara felt at a crossroads right then. Her friend was right, but she also had to protect her job at the bank. "If she keeps it up, I will."

"Promise?"

"Promise."

The commitment seemed to satisfy Grace. She finished her drink and got up. "I'll stop pushing, for now. I need to get to work to finish some paperwork regarding my work visa." She tossed some money on the table and gave Sara a heartfelt hug. "Call me if you need to talk, okay?"

"I will," Sara said, never happier Grace had become such a good friend. "See you on Sunday."

****

February brought more snow and a new tradition for Sara. Sunday dinner with Liv and Grace was fast becoming a regular thing, and she normally looked forward to it. Until today. With Bren. She was all kinds of nervous and gripped Bren's hand a little too tightly as they meandered from her place to Liv's.

"Um, Sara, are you worried I'm going to run away?" Bren asked.

"No. Why?"

"Because you're holding my hand like you think I'm leaving you."

"Sorry." She released Bren's hand, but Bren took hers back right away. "I'm nervous is all."

"About what? It's dinner."

"You don't know Liv. I mean, you've met her once, but you don't know her like I do."

Bren stopped their progress and placed a gentle kiss on Sara's lips. "I'm sure I can handle whatever she's got planned. From the look on your face, I'm guessing I'm in for a question and answer session?"

"More like the Spanish Inquisition."

Bren shrugged as they started walking again. "No worries. I got this."

"I hope so," Sara muttered.

They reached Liv's house and stepped in after Sara knocked once. She figured if they walked in on Liv and Grace it would serve them right. But this time they were in opposite parts of the house, getting things ready.

Her friends welcomed Bren, and it wasn't long before they were seated at the table enjoying Grace's lovely home cooking.

Bren took a bite of the melt-in-your-mouth roast beef and sighed. "This is amazing. I wish my mom cooked like this."

"It's nothing," Grace said. "One good Instant Pot and you're all set. Does everything for you."

"I disagree," Bren said around another bite. "A good cook puts a lot of effort into the meal. Heart and soul kind of stuff. The Instant Pot is the tool, but you're the one making the art."

Grace laughed softly. "I don't think I've ever heard anyone say it quite that way before."

"Thanks. I have a way with words and a passion for food." Bren was already going for seconds.

Liv nudged Sara while Bren refilled her plate. "I think you two are good for each other. She eats almost as much as you do."

Sara kicked Liv under the table. "Asshat. She's a growing woman with a decent appetite. Besides, she'll need the energy for later." Sara nearly spit her drink out at the shocked look on Liv's face. "What? You know damn well I'm sleeping with her."

"I did—or do," Liv stammered. "I didn't expect you to say so with her sitting next to you at the table is all."

Sara leaned over to Bren and said, "Liv is a bit prudish sometimes. Pay no attention to her."

Bren saluted her with her glass of tea. "Noted."

"Hey," Liv said in her best put-out voice. "I'm not a prude."

"Yes you are," Sara and Grace chorused the comment and did a fist bump across the table. Bren looked back and forth between them, a bemused smile on her face.

Liv slumped slightly in her chair. "You people suck."

"I wasn't going to—" Sara grinned when Bren covered her mouth to stop her smart comment coming out. She kissed Bren's palm before pulling it away. "You asked for it."

"Did not."

"Did, too."

Grace sighed dramatically. "Bren, as you can see, when these two are together they revert to adolescence. Sometimes infancy."

"I think they're cute."

"Sometimes," Grace said. "Until you've seen it for the hundredth time. Then, not so much."

"I'm not cute?" Liv asked her, batting her eyelashes at Grace.

"You know you are, honey." Grace kissed her on the cheek. "Now behave. We do have a guest, you know."

"Yes, right." Liv sat up straighter. "I hear you're working at the elementary school. How's it going?"

Bren shrugged. "It's okay. I think I'd rather be around the slightly older kids, maybe pre-teens. But it's good experience if nothing else."

"You're young enough you have time to choose your career," Grace said. "I went through a couple myself. It's hard to settle on one thing, and I'm not sure you even have to."

"I do if I want to retire young enough to enjoy it," Bren said. "My parents retired last year, and they've been traveling and loving every minute of it."

"Retired?" Sara asked. "They can't be much into their fifties. How'd they manage it?"

"You're not the only one who's good at math. They put every penny away possible since they were nineteen, when they got married. Despite having me and paying for my education, they saved enough they won't have to worry about anything. And they're gearing up for a big trip to Jamaica. My mom says it's their second honeymoon."

"Make sure they talk to Dana Smith," Sara said. "She's amazing and the best travel agent in the city. Tell her I sent them. and she'll give them a good deal."

"Cool. Is there anyone in the city you don't know?"

"No," Liv replied for Sara. "She's probably dated half of the women. Including Dana. Hell, I think Dana lasted a couple of months, right, Sara?"

Sara felt the heat of the blush creep up her neck to her cheeks and tried to kick Liv, but her idiot friend dodged her. "Gracie, you sure you want to marry this one? She's a pain in the ass, you know?"

"I know, but she's my pain in the ass." Grace gave Liv a kiss and said to Bren, "She's a big brat and horrible at making a good first impression. You'll have to ignore her."

"It's cool. I suck at first impressions, too." Bren ran her hand through her blue hair. "People see the hair and think I'm some punk who doesn't have two brain cells to rub together. I'm still shocked I got the job at the school. I was sure they'd turn me down since I made it clear I'm not changing my appearance for anyone."

Liv raised her glass in salute to Bren. "Good for you. I'd hire you. I like your attitude."

"Oh? Hire me for what?"

"Nope. Not happening," Sara said. "Trust me, you don't want to work for her. She's mean."

"I'm not mean," Liv said. "I'm a good boss, and I run a huge company. Have you heard of TNT?"

"Sure. I've lived here my whole life. How could I not? Wait, you're a Templeton?"

"Yep. And I run the company. Okay, we're not huge, but we're pretty damn big. You need a job, come to me. I'll hook you up."

"Seriously?"

"Why not?"

"I—okay. I will if the teaching thing goes bust. Thanks."

"Sure." Liv got up and began the process of clearing the table.

"Anyone want a beer?"

Sara also got up and nudged Bren. "No, thanks. I think I'd like to take off and give Bren a break from Livvy."

"I'm not that bad," Liv protested even as she escorted them to the closet for their coats. "But I'm serious, Bren. Come to me if you need work."

"Thanks, Liv. I will. I had fun tonight. Thanks for inviting me."

Liv and Grace said their goodbyes, and Sara happily tugged Bren out of the house and toward home. "Congrats. You survived," she said when they were outside.

"It was fun. I like those two. Especially Grace. She's super sweet."

"She is."

"Hey." Bren stopped her and took Sara's hands in hers. "Thanks for tonight."

"I didn't do anything."

"You brought me to meet your closest friends in the world."

"If you and I are going to be friends, it makes sense for you to get to know Liv and Grace. They're family to me."

Bren kissed her soundly. "Like I said. Thanks."

"Bren, I—"

"Don't." She placed a finger over Sara's lips. "I know we're casual. Friend dating and all. I get it. But I can't help if I feel something, Sara. Please let me, okay?"

"I don't want to hurt you."

"You won't." She kissed Sara, and this time, Sara felt the emotion in Bren's words. "You can't."

"I probably will."

"Then I'll deal with it."

"Bren, it's not fair to you. If you feel something for me, and I'm over here saying it's a casual thing…what's that make me?"

"Honest."

"Bullshit."

"I'd rather you be honest with me than tell me you feel something you don't." Bren smiled her sweet smile, and Sara's heart constricted. "Promise you'll always be honest with me. It's all I need."

"Got it," Sara said around the lump in her throat.

"Good. Now let's get to your house before we freeze to death."

The sound of tires squealing caused them both to stop and look toward the street. A green Jaguar sped by, sliding on an icy patch as it passed. The driver righted the vehicle and increased speed until disappearing a few blocks away.

Sara knew the car, and her stomach clenched at the thought of who was driving it.

"Someone you know?" Bren asked.

"Angel."

"The bitch who dumped you out on Highway 1? Angel?"

"Yeah."

Bren stared in the direction Angel went, and Sara wondered what was going through her mind. She squeezed Bren's hand. "Hey, I thought we were heading to my house to get warm?"

"Sorry." Bren strolled ahead and maneuvered herself between Sara and the street. "It's a damn fancy sports car. Can't miss it."

"No. She owns a realty agency, Harrison's."

"I've heard of it. I think my folks bought their house from them."

"Most of Whitehorse has at one time or another. Anyway, she thinks her money gives her special privileges. Like getting whatever woman she wants."

"Not this time."

"Nope." Sara bumped shoulders with Bren. "How about you steer clear of her if you see her, okay? I wouldn't put it past her to cause trouble."

"I think Izzy's told me a bit about her. She's not known for being the nicest person ever."

"That's an understatement."

"Why'd you go out with her?" Bren asked. "She hardly seems like your type from what you've told me."

"It's a long story."

Bren stole a kiss as they turned onto Sara's street. "I got time."

"I'd rather spend it doing something else."

"Depends on what you have in mind."

"It's a surprise." Sara enjoyed teasing her, and when they reached her doorstep, Bren pressed her body against Sara's, making it difficult to unlock the door.

"Bet I can guess what it is." Bren nibbled on her lobe and sent pleasant tingles along Sara's body. "Do I get a prize if I do?"

"Yes. Oh yes."

****

"I like Bren, but she's not right for Sara," Liv said as she cleared the dishes from the table. "I mean, she's sweet and all."

"But she's not Terry?" Grace said. "Honey, Terry broke Sara's heart. You can't expect her to get back together with her, and don't tell me it's not what you're thinking in that adorable head of yours."

"It is and I think she's still in love with Terry. And, I think the feeling is mutual. I wish I could get them to see it."

"And getting them to talk to each other has worked so well you think you can make it happen?" Grace took the plates from Liv, set them on the counter, and took hold of her hands. "You're a good friend, but this is one time you need to butt out. Let Sara deal with this on her own."

"Right. She's not dealing with it at all. She's going around with Bren and pretending like she's not hurting. All the while I see her looking at Bren, I can tell she's wishing it was Terry."

"You can't know that, Olivia. You're not psychic."

Liv let go of Grace's hands and returned to her cleaning. "I am when it comes to Sara. You don't know her like I do, Gracie. Trust me, she's heading down the wrong path right now. The longer she stays with Bren, the harder it'll be when she has to break it off."

"What if she doesn't break it off? Maybe she's planning to stick with Bren for a while. I can't blame her if she did. Bren's a lot of fun, and I think she's good for Sara."

"It'll hurt Sara more than it will Bren when she stops seeing her." Liv was insistent. She wanted Grace to understand. "Sara looks at Bren like a friend. Nothing more. Bren, however, looks at Sara like she's found her soulmate."

"You're exaggerating, as usual." Grace flicked a tea towel at her. "Honey, Bren's young and maybe she is falling for Sara, but there's nothing you can do to stop it."

"And you're wrong."

"No, I'm right." Grace stepped in front of Liv and stopped her going into the kitchen. Her eyes cut right through Liv. Instantly she knew trouble was coming. "You are not trying to get Terry and Sara back together. This can't be one of your little matchmaker schemes."

"Matchmaker schemes? Seriously? I don't do that."

"Bullshit. I think Emma and Gail would disagree."

Liv rolled her eyes. "Those two were making me crazy sitting around pining for each other. I had to do something."

"No, you didn't. Sometimes you need to let people come together naturally."

"Those two weren't going to do it naturally. They needed a push."

"You literally shoved them together!" Grace took over the dishes while Liv packed up the leftovers. "I thought poor Emma would break her ankle when you bumped her into Gail. You have a serious problem, my dear. You're worse than Izzy with her gossip."

"Oh no. No one is worse than Izzy and her gossip." Liv laughed, recalling the moment Emma literally fell into Gail's arms like something out of a romance novel. The scene still made her smile.

"That's the look I'm afraid of," Grace said, pointing at her. "The smile says you're good at your matchmaking and you're moving forward with it."

"I did convince you to give me a chance, right?" Liv kissed her as she walked past. "It's gotta count for something."

"It does. I don't think you should be messing with Sara. It's been hard on her."

"Exactly why I'm doing this. I have a meeting set up with Terry next week. I'm heading to her office early to talk to her."

"Please do one thing for me," Grace asked, pausing until Liv looked at her. "Promise me you'll not go to Sara. If you insist on talking to Terry, fine. But don't bring it up to Sara. Let her be happy for now, okay? If it's with Bren, then so be it. I think she needs more time to think things through. Besides, I'm already trying to get her to talk to Terry and get some closure, one way or the other. Sara will talk to her in her own time. Don't push her."

Liv carefully considered Grace's request. She'd been wanting to talk to Sara, but Grace was right. It would probably end up in Sara either crying or yelling at her. Neither of those options were pleasant. But it didn't stop her from wanting to do something.

"I promise. I'll talk to Terry."

"Good. Now, let's get this finished up then you can help me knock off a few names from our guest list."

"How many is a few?" Liv asked.

"At least half."

"Seriously?"

"Yes. We can't have the whole city at our wedding. It's too many people. Don't you remember how we talked about having a nice, small gathering of family and friends?"

"My list *is* family and friends."

Grace bit her lower lip, a sure sign she was carefully thinking about her reply. Liv waited uncomfortably for her to continue. "I know you have a big family and a lot of friends, but can't we find a compromise here? I don't think I can handle a big crowd."

Liv saw the genuine look of concern on Grace's features and dropped what she was doing to pull her into a warm hug. "I'm sorry. I didn't think."

"Why would you? You're excited, same as me, and when you get excited, you go overboard a little bit." Grace rested her head on Liv's shoulder. "We've got way too many people, honey. Still. I'm serious about cutting the list in half. If it means family only, then okay. Let's do it. I want to marry you in the worst way but not in front of a ton of people."

Grace was trying hard to compromise, and Liv loved her for it. She wanted to smack herself for not thinking of Grace's fears when putting things together for the wedding. She should have remembered big crowds were a huge problem for her.

Liv tightened her grip before pulling away from Grace. She kissed her lips and said, "I'll break up the list. Maybe we can have an extra party the day before we leave for our honeymoon. Sound like a plan?"

"Perfect."

"I love you," Liv said.

"I love you, too."

Chapter Eleven

Once a month, Pot O' Gold held a ladies-only dance night. The pub was pretty much known as a lesbian bar, but most weekends there was a mixed crowd. However, the first Friday of the month belonged to the ladies, and Sara loved it. She ordered their drinks and joined Bren, Liv, and Grace at their usual booth, far enough from the dance floor to be able to speak above the music but close enough she could see the dancers.

She tapped her feet to the latest Adele song and smiled when Bren leaned over and kissed her on the cheek. "Want to dance?"

"You have to ask?" Sara jumped up, held Bren's hand, and pulled her to the dance floor.

Bren molded herself to Sara, and their bodies gyrated as one. Their hips rubbed together in the most pleasant way, and Sara wondered how long her libido would last. She wanted to dance all night, yet the look in Bren's eyes told her she had more on her mind than dancing.

Was it her youth that brought out the sex maniac in Sara? She'd done casual many, many times in her life, but this was something different. Something about Bren kept her wanting more. At the same time, she couldn't. Because, ultimately, they weren't right for each other. She and Bren were good right now but not in the long term. But the sex—whoa. Sara tingled all over thinking about how their night would end.

The music stopped while the DJ took a quick break. Sara held Bren's hand as they left the dance floor. They slipped back into the booth, and Sara took a long, slow drink of her beer.

"I love ladies night," Bren said with a huge grin. "We should have these every night."

"Amen." Liv clinked beer mugs with her. She turned to Grace when a slow song started up. "C'mon, babe. We need to dance to this one."

"We *need* to?" Grace asked.

"Yep. I need to dance with my future wife. Get some practice in for the wedding."

"In that case…" Grace laughed and allowed Liv to pull her to the dance floor.

Sara watched them hold each other, eyes locked in a way that said no one else existed. She wanted to have someone look at her like that again.

She pulled her gaze away from Liv and Grace and took note of the women at the bar. The place was steadily filling up, and for a split second, she thought she saw a very familiar woman wearing blue glasses and a distinctive leather jacket. But it couldn't be, right? Terry never came to the pub anymore. Not since their breakup. At least, Sara didn't think she did. Not after those pictures her father-in-law had.

But she knew Terry as well as she knew herself, and she was damn sure it was her at the bar. Several women now swarmed the area she'd seen Terry in, yelling out orders.

"Hey, you okay?" Bren rested her hand lightly on Sara's thigh. "You've been staring at the bar a long time. Do you need me to get you something?"

"No. I thought I saw Terry. Sorry."

"It's okay." Bren removed her hand, and her eyes reflected sadness. "You want to go see if it was her?"

"Yes, but I'm not going to." Sara put her hand over Bren's. "I'm not here with her. I'm here with you. It's important to me."

"You're sweet."

Sara shrugged. "It'd be super rude to leave you sitting here so I can chase down my ex, don't you think?"

"Maybe. But I'd understand."

"No. I got my closure with her, Bren. It's over now."

Bren squeezed her hand. "No, it's not. Sara, we haven't known each other very long, but you have to know you're very easy to read. I mean you practically telegraph your thoughts with your facial expressions." She brought Sara's hand to her lips and kissed her fingers. "Yes, you talked with Terry. But it was more a fight than anything else. I don't think you got any closure. I think it confused you more."

"How old are you?" Sara teased her. "You sound like Gracie. Have you two been talking?"

"Nope. I'm very observant. And practical."

"Don't forget adorable." Sara touched the side of Bren's face with her fingertips, wishing she could fall into those sweet eyes of hers. But she couldn't because Bren was right. No matter what happened between them, she was still very much in love with Terry.

"I might be adorable, but you're beautiful and you've got the attention of a lot of women in here. Especially the knockout at the bar."

"You're full of shit. No one notices me unless I'm up there dancing and making a fool of myself in the process. Not that I care, mind you."

"I'm serious," Bren said and pointed to the woman in question. "She's been staring at us for the last couple minutes."

At the bar, sipping a glass of wine, sat Angel. She was indeed watching them. More like glaring at them, Sara thought. She didn't acknowledge her and turned away. "Fuck."

"Who is she?"

Sara considered her response. Bren reminded her a bit of Liv when it came to her protective streak. She wasn't as bad as Liv—few people were. Though she wondered what Bren might do. "Promise me you won't go near her."

"Is she Angel?"

"Dammit. Yes. Promise me you won't go over there. Do not engage her, Bren. I'm serious."

Bren's eyes were on Angel. Sara saw the indecision and was glad she was blocking Bren from sliding out of the booth. Bren said, "I'll promise to be good tonight. But I can't say I won't respond if I see her somewhere else. Like on the street or something."

"Thanks, but don't waste your time on her. Okay? She's not worth it." She pulled Bren's attention back to her with a kiss. "Let's do some more dancing. We came here to have fun. Let's not allow the bitch to ruin it, okay?"

"Sure." Bren motioned for Sara to get up, and they returned to the dance floor. Bren pulled Sara close enough there wasn't air between them. "Better?"

"Much," Sara said and leaned into her. She closed her eyes and allowed Bren to lead her to the beat of another slow song as she shut out all thoughts of Angel and Terry and tried very hard to be present for the sweet, kind woman who held her in a loving embrace.

****

Terry went to the restroom at the pub, closed herself into a stall, and leaned against the door. What did she honestly expect? Sara sitting at home pining away for her? She was a vivacious, fun-loving woman who deserved to move on with her life. She deserved happiness.

The blue-haired girl with Sara was damn cute, and the way they danced together very much reminded Terry of the way she and Sara danced. Sara loved to be all sexy and fun with her movements, and she was. Damn. She certainly hadn't lost her talent.

Terry was torn between being happy for Sara and being angry she'd moved on. Obviously she and the girl were together, sharing little touches and kisses as they sat at the booth with Liv and Grace. Terry felt like a damn stalker watching them, but it was hard to pull her gaze away. The timing was perfect when a crowd of women came into the bar. She was pretty sure Sara had seen her.

Terry cursed her mother for being insistent she go out tonight. The pub was the last place she wanted to be, but it was also the one place she felt even a little comfortable going to. She'd taken a cab here, as always, and hoped William no longer had someone following her. Still, even if she had one drink she wouldn't chance driving home.

But the beer caused her stomach to roil and threatened to make her puke. Hot tears streamed down her cheeks as she realized she wasn't ready for any of this. It was hard enough to date after Ann. Even harder to think of doing it after Sara. And really, how could she?

No one would ever replace Ann, though Sara certainly filled a hole in Terry's life quite well. Now it was empty again, and she didn't think she'd ever want to fill it.

She was probably being overly dramatic, but Terry's feelings spilled out as she sobbed. She covered her mouth to stifle the sound when she heard someone come into the restroom.

She closed her eyes, held her breath for a moment, and forced herself to get a grip. This was not the place to fall apart. If she were going to do it, she should do it at home when Felicia was asleep. Or maybe in her car in the driveway.

The woman who entered the restroom finished her business and left. Terry opened the door of the stall and went to the sink to splash cold water on her face. Her reflection mirrored how she felt inside. Miserable. And without friends to talk it over with.

She took a deep breath and released it slowly. Time to leave. No sense staying there and wallowing in self pity. She could do it at home.

Terry reached for the bathroom door and nearly ran into Liv Templeton. "Sorry," she mumbled and kept going.

Liv stopped her. "Hey, you okay?" She looked at Terry for a very long moment, her brow furrowed.

"No. I'm not."

"I know it might not be comfortable, but you can join us if you'd like. You don't have to be here alone."

Terry gave her a tight smile. "I can't. Sorry, Liv. Being around me—it's not what Sara wants or needs right now."

"But what do you need?" Liv asked. Her concern was clear, and for a moment, Terry considered whether Liv was someone she could talk to. But as Sara's best friend…she didn't think it'd be a good idea to cry on Liv's shoulder.

"I don't know. Probably time to figure out what the hell I'm going to do with my life."

She made another move to leave, but Liv stepped in front of her, gently pushing her aside to let someone else through the door. "Terry, you don't have to do this alone. We're friends, right?"

"You're Sara's best friend."

"But I'm your friend, too. I mean, I'd like to be."

Terry patted Liv on the shoulder, this time maneuvering to open the door. "You're a good person, Liv. I'd like to think of you as a friend, yes."

"Then use me as one, too. You've got my number. If you need to talk, call me."

"I will. Have a fun night," Terry said and got the hell out of the restroom. She pulled her phone out of her pocket and tapped the app to call a cab. She couldn't help watching Sara and her girlfriend as she passed them. Grace was there as well, and the three of them were having a good time.

Terry heard the sound of Sara's laughter in her memory and held onto it as she left the pub to wait for her cab.

****

Monday came around and offered Terry a fresh start to her week. She'd put the weekend behind her and looked forward to the work she'd be doing at one of TNT's claims, a rare piece of land yet to be mined. She couldn't wait to get out there and survey the area. Even in the frozen ground they could drill through it to get a good sample of dirt. Her job was to find the dirt they needed to drill through.

Her mind was pulled back to reality when the office phone rang.

"This is Terry," she answered.

"Terry," Warrick Shue said, "can you come up here next Monday? We'd like to go over your reports to take back to the board of directors. If Frank can come as well, that'd be great. I want to talk about the work he did last year and compare it to what you found."

Terry paused to consider this. The timing was awful. Dresden was a thirty-hour drive from Whitehorse. She'd have to fly even if she didn't want the expense of it. Jackie wasn't yet sure when the mediation with William would take place. Could she afford to be gone a couple of days? Could she afford not to be?

"Let me get with Frank, though I doubt he's got anything going on," she finally said. "I'll be happy to come up there and go over the reports. I'd need to return on Wednesday."

"Perfect. We'll meet with you on Monday and do a site visit on Tuesday." She heard him typing on his computer. "I'll book hotel rooms for both of you."

"Thanks. I appreciate it, Mr. Shue. I'll get with Frank and send you an email."

"Excellent. Have a good day."

"You, too." Terry hung up and sighed. No way would she let anything slip with this contract. They paid very well, and it would increase if her findings were correct. And she was sure they were. She sort of wished she was a miner and could get busy digging up diamonds for herself. A handful ought to be enough to get her through this damn mediation and keep William off her back.

She dialed Jackie's number, left a message, and did the same with Frank. For a retired guy, he was busier than she was. She considered calling her mom, but the thought was derailed by a call coming in from Felicia's school.

"This is Terry."

"Hi, Terry, Sally Johnson here. I'm sorry to call you, but there's been an incident with Felicia."

"An incident?"

"Yes. You remember when she kissed Bryce Preston?"

"I do."

Sally hesitated. "Something happened and Bryce shoved her. He said some hurtful things, and Felicia shut down. She won't speak to anyone."

"Do you know what he said?" Terry asked, already tossing paperwork into her briefcase.

"One of the teachers overheard Bryce calling her ugly names. Referring to her as a retard. I've already called his parents, and they're on the way."

"I'll see you in a few minutes." Terry locked her office door and raced to her truck. On the way, she noticed someone across the street, watching her. The woman was bundled up in a thick winter coat, her face obscured by the fur-lined hood, but Terry thought she knew her somehow. She brushed the thought aside and left.

She arrived at the school in record time and went directly to Sally's office. Sally gestured her to come in and closed the door behind her. Felicia was seated on a chair in front of Sally's desk.

Terry went to her child. She knelt in front of her and put a hand on her knee. Hazel eyes tracked to her face, and she saw the pain in them. "Hi, sweetie. Bad day?"

Felicia nodded.

"Mrs. Johnson told me what happened with Bryce."

Felicia didn't blink; she kept her eyes on Terry. Terry waited, knowing the wheels were turning in Felicia's brain as she tried to figure out what to say. Or not say.

"You don't have to talk right now. I'll take you home, but I need to talk to Bryce's parents first."

"Okay," Felicia said, her voice softer than usual.

Terry pulled her into a hug and kissed the top of her head. "I love you, baby. You wait here for me. I won't be long."

Felicia hugged her back for all she was worth, put her hands in her lap, and went back to staring straight ahead. Terry stood and motioned for Sally to step outside the office. Once the door was closed behind them, Terry said, "Are his parents here?"

"They got in after you. They're in with Principal Gillam right now."

"Can I speak to them?" Terry asked, nearly biting her tongue to stay calm. She wanted to hit something.

"I think it's best we all sit down to discuss this." Sally put her hand gently on Terry's arm. "Are you sure you're up for it? We can take a few minutes if you need to."

"No. I want to get it over with and I can take Felicia home. Please?"

"Sure. C'mon." Sally led her to the office across the hall and knocked. Mr. Gillam called them in, and Terry entered first.

Mr. Gillam was seated behind his desk, a man and woman across from him in faux-leather chairs. Sally moved two more chairs to the desk, and they sat down after brief introductions were made.

Mr. Gillam was in his late sixties; a hint of grey stubble lined the bottom of his bald scalp. His dark brown eyes were sharp as they took in the group seated before him. He folded his hands on his desk, his face a mask as he spoke.

"I want to say, first off, Whitehorse Elementary has a zero-tolerance policy. This applies to the use of epithets such as the one used by Bryce. What I find most disturbing is his lack of empathy at the use of such a word. I'm suspending him immediately."

Mrs. Preston, a short, round woman, looked as though she was going to cry. She said, "Mr. Gillam, is this necessary? He's eight."

"Zero tolerance, Mrs. Preston, doesn't have an age limit."

Mr. Preston spoke up. "This is bullshit." His hands were balled into fists in his lap, his angry expression directed at Terry. She returned the anger. The man was a behemoth, but Terry didn't blink. "My kid called her kid a retard. So what? Doesn't mean anything. Besides, she *is* a retard. What's the big-ass deal?"

Terry opened her mouth to speak, but Mr. Gillam stopped her. "The big deal is your son deliberately used that word to hurt Felicia. And he doesn't seem to understand or care she's hurt. I'm sorry, Mr. Preston, but it's an issue we need to address. He has to understand one cannot use such words."

"Why? Not politically correct? Is that it?" His glare never left Terry, even though he was addressing Mr. Gillam. "Why the hell is she here anyway? She needs to go to one of those special schools."

"She's here because she lives here, and this is her school district," Terry said, her voice sounding calmer than she felt. Her insides were churning, and her legs twitched with angry energy. "She's got every right to come here for her education. Same as your son."

"She's mentally retarded. It's probably why she kissed my boy. She's the one who ought to be suspended."

"She kissed him because she likes him," Terry said, "She's different than the other kids, yes, slower to learn, but more self-assured than any of them. She knows what she wants, and she's not afraid to go for it. She kissed him and he shoved her away. Point made. Why did he decide to call her names? What did she do to him?"

"She doesn't have to do anything. She's in his class. She's disruptive and he got mad." Mr. Preston seemed satisfied. Terry wasn't.

She turned her attention to Mr. Gillam. "Can you tell me exactly what happened?"

"Felicia was playing football with some of the other kids. The ball got away from them and ended up in front of Bryce and some of his friends. He picked it up, threw it a bit harder than necessary to Felicia, and used the 'R' word. His friends laughed when he did it. Mrs. Grey, who was standing a few meters away, saw the entire exchange."

"What did Felicia do?"

Mr. Gillam gave her a small smile. "She took the ball and went back to playing. After recess, Mrs. Grey made Bryce apologize to her, but she refused to speak to them. She hasn't said a word since."

Terry nodded. "She does it when she's upset. Shuts down."

"Because she's retarded," Mr. Preston said.

Terry found it hard to remain in her seat. She wanted to slam her fist into his idiotic face. "My child has Down Syndrome. I would ask you to stop saying she's mentally retarded. It's derogatory, and I won't sit here and let you get away with it."

"Then leave," he said. "I think it's the best thing you can do. Take your kid and put her into another school."

"What other school? One where she isn't with children her own age? Where she doesn't get the social experience of being around other people? Where she might not learn she's part of society and not someone who needs to be shunted away? I want what's best for my child, something I assume you want for yours as well. The very best thing for Felicia is for her to be here. To make friends, grow up with these kids, and enjoy her childhood.

"Kids with Down Syndrome don't always need special treatment. Felicia's lucky she's high functioning enough to go to public school. Trust me when I say if I thought this wasn't best for her I wouldn't have her enrolled here. But here she is. And your kid has to get used to it, and he has to learn he can't go around using those kinds of words. To anyone. If you don't stop him now, he'll grow up and keep using those words, hurting people as he goes through life. What kind of man do you think he'll grow up to be?"

Mr. Preston wouldn't look at Terry. His wife, tears streaming down her face, said, "I'm sorry, Mrs. Alexander. I promise I'll speak to him. We'll sort this out. I promise." To Mr. Gillam she said, "Is it okay if we take him home now? I think we should go."

"I think it's best," Mr. Gillam said. "His suspension is for three days. We'll speak again after he returns. Please let me know if you have any questions."

Mr. Preston kept his mouth shut, shook Mr. Gillam's hand, and followed his wife out of the office.

"I'm also sorry, Mrs. Alexander," Mr. Gillam said. "If there's anything we can do for Felicia, please let me know."

His expression was sincere, and Terry accepted he meant what he said. She appreciated it. "Thanks. I think I need to go as well."

Mr. Gillam stood to take her hand. "If she needs to take a day or two before coming back to school, please let Mrs. Johnson know."

"I will." Terry left and stopped at the door to Sally's office. "Do you think this was a one-off?" she asked Sally, who'd followed her. "Maybe Bryce getting back at her for kissing him? I'm having a hard time accepting an eight-year-old kid using that word."

"So am I. I've never known Bryce to use bad words before. He must have heard it from someone older. I'm guessing it was his father. I'm hopeful it won't happen again."

"Me, too."

The ride home was quiet, as Terry expected. Felicia went right to her room and closed the door. Terry took a few minutes to put their coats away and send a text message to her mom, giving her a heads up about the trouble they'd had. She also needed a moment alone to process Everything. It was the first time Felicia was confronted with such behavior and Terry knew it wouldn't be the last. How the hell could a kid be so cruel?

Then it hit her. To her knowledge, no one had ever used the word in front of Felicia. How did she know what it meant? And she had to know, or she wouldn't be upset.

Terry went to her room, knocked softly, and entered. As expected, Felicia was seated cross-legged on her bed, staring at a book without changing the page. Terry sat across from her, in the same position, and waited.

It didn't take as long as she expected for Felicia to speak. "I'm retarded."

"No, you're not. You're smart. It takes you longer to learn stuff sometimes, but it doesn't mean anything. You're smart, silly, beautiful, sweet, and so many more things I can't list them all."

"I'm retarded," she said again, still staring at her book. "Bryce said so."

"He did, but he was wrong."

"Gramps is never wrong."

"What?" Terry thought she misheard her. William wouldn't use that word. Would he?

"Gramps said so. And it's bad. He was yelling when he said it."

Terry gently pulled Felicia onto her lap and cradled her against her chest. "He's wrong. I promise you, he's wrong. I love you, Felicia. No one has the right to call you any bad words, and I'll make sure Gramps never says it again, okay?"

Felicia didn't speak. Terry looked down and saw her tears. She gently wiped them away and held her close. She tamped down her anger—for now.

****

As soon as Shirley got home, Terry unloaded all the details of the incident at school, including the revelation William used the 'R' word around Felicia. Her anger simmered most of the afternoon, and once Felicia was asleep, it reached boiling point.

"I tried to call him, but it went right to voicemail. If the bastard were to show up now, I'm pretty sure I'd slam my fist into his mouth. How could he do that to her?"

"Take a deep breath and calm down," Shirley said. They were sitting in the kitchen, and it was all Terry could do to keep her voice from carrying to Felicia's room.

"I've been trying, Mom, but it's damn hard. It was bad enough I had to deal with asshole Preston, but to find out William has called Felicia retarded? I don't know where to even start."

"How about something positive? It sounds like Mrs. Preston was genuinely sorry it happened. Maybe she'll be able to get something done."

"I doubt it." Terry stood up from the kitchen table and prepared a fresh pot of coffee. "I mean, she was nice and all, but I have to wonder how successful she'd be at standing up to the caveman she's married to. I'd bet money it's where little Bryce heard the word. I hope she at least explains to him what it means."

"I'm sure she'll try." Shirley was using her psychology voice, and it grated on Terry's nerves a little. She was mad, and she wanted to stay mad. Especially at William.

"I'm going to make sure Jackie knows Felicia heard William use the 'R' word. It's got to count against him, right? Aside from the fact it's unconscionable he did it, I can certainly use it to sway the mediator."

"You can." Shirley accepted her coffee but didn't make a move to drink any. Terry steeled herself for what was next. "But you have to be careful what you're saying right now. Don't call William. Period. If he needs to know something, I'll call him or we'll get Jackie to tell his lawyer. That's number one. Got it?"

"What's number two?"

"You be careful what you say. I know you're pissed at him, and you have a right to be, but he's still Felicia's grandfather and she loves him. Don't let your anger paint him ugly for her. He may end up doing it on his own, but don't you do it for him. She deserves to have her gramps, no matter how you feel about him. Be extra careful until the mediation is over and you've gotten their decision. You certainly don't want William to find out you went off the rails about him within earshot of Felicia. Or how you did the same with the parent of another child at her school." Shirley paused to sip her coffee, never taking her eyes off Terry. "Are you following me?"

Terry nodded. Her mother always managed to make sense and get her to toss her anger away no matter how much she wanted to keep it. "You're right." She sank into a chair across from Shirley. "I'm over-the-top pissed off, and I'm sick about it. I know I can't keep her from being hurt by other people's careless words or actions, but I should be able to rely on her grandfather to do the same. Right?"

"Yes. You should. I'm sure Jennifer probably had words with him right after he said it. And if she'd had any inkling Felicia heard them, she'd have talked to you about it. She's sensible and kind. Did Felicia say if she heard it from him any other time?"

"No, but I'm not sure if she would have told me. She was pretty upset after she figured out it was the same word she'd heard William use. She didn't fully understand what it means, only it wasn't a nice word. I explained it to her as best I could."

"What'd she say?"

"She's retarded, and by definition, she is. I tried to make sure she understands no one has the right to use that word around her—ever. She cried herself to sleep. I was going to wake her for dinner, but she's had a hard day and I'd rather see her resting. I kind of doubt she'll want to eat anyway."

"What about you? How are you doing?" Shirley was firmly in psychologist mode, and Terry sighed.

"I'm hurting for her. Mostly because there's little I can do. I can rant and rail all I want, but in the end, people will be cruel to her. I'm scared she'll lose that beautiful trust she has in people, the piece of her that loves everyone."

"She won't, honey. Not as long as she has you to rely on." Shirley got to her feet and urged Terry to stand and accept a big hug. "She'll be fine. As long as she keeps talking to you, it'll be all right. You can be her advocate and rant and rail whenever you feel the need to do it. It won't always work. There will always be assholes."

Terry guffawed at her mother's language. "You sound funny when you cuss. It's rare to hear it."

Shirley ran her fingers through Terry's hair and held her face gently. "The words have more impact then. You good?"

"I am. Thanks, Mom."

"You're welcome. Now sit down and let me fix dinner."

"No way. You've had a hard day. I can tell by the slump in your shoulders." Terry moved her to one side. "Take a seat. I'll refresh your coffee, and you can tell me about your day while I fix food."

"Who's the psychologist now?"

"I am. I think I learned it by osmosis or something." Terry laughed. "Or maybe it's in my DNA, and if it is, consider yourself at fault."

"Is that so?"

"Yep." Terry turned to prepare dinner and hid the smile the finally crept across her face.

****

Sara shut her computer down, leaned back in her chair, and closed her eyes. It'd been a helluva day, and she was glad it was over. Actually, most of the week sucked. A headache worked its way up and threatened to be fully blown if she didn't get out of there and find something to eat.

She put on her coat, grabbed her purse, and waved at Greg, who still sat in his office. She nearly ran out of the building, not wanting her workaholic boss to think of something for her to do at the last minute. The temperature was typical for March at minus nine centigrade. She briefly wondered if it were possible to freeze before she reached her house. It sure felt like it by the time she walked up her driveway.

A smile spread across her face when she saw Bren standing on the porch, hiding something behind her back. Her grin was huge, and when Sara got to her, Bren pulled her close and kissed her soundly. "Welcome home," Bren whispered and produced a bouquet of yellow roses. "Yellow is for friendship."

Sara inhaled the sweet scent. "Thank you. It's sweet of you. Is there a lesbian anniversary I'm missing?"

"Not that I know of. Do lesbians have special anniversaries?" Bren followed Sara inside.

Sara placed the flowers on the table and removed her coat. "You're such a kid. You've got lots to learn about how lesbians do things. I mean, there's a ton of rules."

"I had no idea." Bren hung their coats up and leaned against the counter while Sara put the flowers in a white, tapered vase. "No one ever said there were rules."

"Tch. I guess I'll have to mentor you." Sara stole a quick kiss. "One rule is you shouldn't bring out the U-Haul until at least the third date."

"Got it. Third date."

"Then you have to make sure you remember the calendar dates of all your firsts."

"All of them?"

"Yep," Sara said in her best business-like voice. "First time you meet, first kiss, first dance, first date, first time you have sex—everything."

"Damn." Bren took her phone out. "I've got this Calendar app I've never used. I think I better take notes."

Sara laughed and put her hand over the phone. "This is for very serious relationships, dear. You'll make note of these things when you find Ms. Right."

Bren's gaze locked with hers, and Sara felt a tightness in her chest. Bren's eyes telegraphed her thoughts. Sara's smile faded. "Oh, Bren, don't."

"Too late."

"No." Sara covered Bren's hand with her own. "You're going to get hurt. I don't think—"

"Don't think. Please. Sara, I can't help what I'm feeling for you."

"But we're supposed to be friend dating. Remember?"

Bren shrugged and found something interesting on the floor to stare at. "I know you don't feel the same about me, and it's okay. Honestly. I'll take what I can get."

"Don't ever do that, Bren. You deserve better than what I can give you. I'm serious." She touched Bren's chin, but she refused to look up. "Please. This isn't right. I can't do this to you."

"You're not doing anything to me. I want to be with you for as long as I can." Bren pushed away from the counter and took a few steps toward the door. "I'll leave if it's what you want, but you have to know I'm okay with our arrangement. It's the most important thing in my life right now."

Sara hugged her from behind and rested her chin on Bren's shoulder. "Don't go. Not until we've talked this through. Please. Come sit with me on the settee." She took Bren's hand and led her to the living room. They sat together, but Sara felt the awkwardness grow between them.

"You're a catch, Bren. Any other woman would fall for you in a second."

"But not you."

"No, not me. I'm still struggling with my feelings for Terry. I thought going out with you would help me figure things out, and I guess it did. I know I'm not over Terry, and until I am, I can't try going out with anyone else. I'd be substituting for Terry, and it isn't fair to her—you—or me. I'm sorry I can't be who you need me to be."

"It's okay. I told you I understand about being the rebound girl." She finally looked at Sara with unshed tears in her eyes. "You've been sweet and kind and a lot of fun to be around. Sometimes think it's all a dream." She glanced at her hands, knotted together in her lap. "Maybe it is."

"It's not. It's all very real. I promise you. And what you feel is every bit as real. I'm sorry I can't return those feelings. I'm serious when I say you deserve someone better."

"I don't want anyone better." Bren brushed her fingertips along Sara's cheek. "I want you."

Sara captured her hand and kissed it. "I'm sorry."

"Is this us breaking up?" Bren's voice wavered as she spoke. "It feels like it is."

Sara thought carefully about it. Was she breaking up with Bren? They'd had such a great time together, but was it fair to drag this young woman along indefinitely? It sounded crass and mean and not at all like Sara and she knew right then what she had to do. "Yeah, I think we are."

"But we're still friends?"

"You couldn't get rid of me if you tried. And I hope you don't try, because I genuinely like you, Bren."

Bren nodded and was very quiet for the longest time. Sara continued to hold her hand, gently rubbing it with her thumb. She watched a myriad of emotions play across Bren's face before she eventually gave her a sad smile. "I love you, Sara."

"I know, honey. I know."

"What do I do now? What do we do now?"

"We are going to have pizza delivered, pop in a stupidly funny movie, and enjoy the evening together. You order the pizza, and I'll get a couple of beers from the fridge. Deal?"

Bren leaned closer and kissed Sara tenderly. Sara felt the goodbye in her touch. "Sure. Pizza, beer, and a movie. Sounds fun."

Sara playfully mussed her hair and got up. "It will be. You and me are good for each other. You've been nursing my broken heart for a while now. Time I returned the favor."

"Ironic, right? Since you're the one breaking it?" Bren's smile took the sting from her words, and Sara returned the gesture.

"Probably. But I'm doing it anyway. Once we get through the pizza, we'll dig into a tub of chocolate ice cream and have a proper cry over it all. Okay?"

"Deal."

Chapter Twelve

Terry arrived at her office an hour early. She needed to get her equipment ready for a site survey later in the afternoon. She'd be going to one of TNT's mines with Liv and a surveyor to talk about potential areas to mine. After a two-hour meeting with Frank yesterday, and based on the information he'd gathered last year, Terry was confident she could help Liv find the right spot to excavate. Once layers of earth were pulled away, Terry could examine them and best tell Liv and her team what to do.

Winter wasn't normally busy, but she had a feeling Frank was sending people to her. Not that she minded, but with the stress from William, Sara, and now the ordeal at Felicia's school, Terry got precious little sleep. She rubbed her tired eyes and felt the thin plastic of her right contact lens touch her fingers. Before she realized it, the damn thing was on the floor, or her desk. It was hard to tell with one good eye.

She gently moved her hands around her paperwork, searching for the tiny blue circle. Nothing. Probably on the damn floor. She carefully pushed her desk chair out of the way and ended up on her hands and knees.

Terry heard the front door of her office open and waved from her position on the floor, next to her desk. "Be with you in a minute."

Seconds ticked by, and whoever came in made themselves comfy in the chair across from her desk. She got her penlight from the side pocket of her cargo pants, turned it on, and caught a reflection against the concrete floor. She retrieved the wayward lens and settled into her chair again.

"Sorry. Dropped my contact. Hang on a sec." She cleaned it and put the stupid thing back in. She hated them, but it was much easier than wearing glasses when in the field.

Her eyes focused, and she was surprised to find Liv sitting in front of her. "Did I miss an appointment? I thought our site inspection was at two today?"

"It is. That's not why I'm here."

Uh-oh. Terry saw the determined look on Liv's face, and her heart sank. "You want to talk about Sara."

"I do." Liv shifted in her seat. She'd yet to meet Terry's gaze. "I didn't get a chance to talk to you the other night at the pub."

"I was sort of in a rush to get out of there."

"I got that impression. I meant what I said. I'd like to be your friend."

"Thanks. I may end up taking you up on it."

"Good. You should also know I appreciate what you did for Sara last week. You drove out there to pick her up when Angel dumped her, and you didn't question why she was with her or lecture her about seeing Angel. You simply showed up and took her home."

"What else could I do? It's not my business who she sees, but I'm not about to say no if she needs my help. It might not seem like it, but I still care about her."

"And this is why I'm here. I didn't want to talk to you at the job site later today, because I need to ask you something very personal. I know it's none of my business, but can you please tell me how you feel about Sara?"

"It's complicated."

"It usually is."

"I care a lot about her. I'm guessing she told you about my situation with Ann's father?"

"She did and I'm sorry to hear about it."

"Thanks. It's been a very rough road, and on some level, maybe I didn't want to trust Sara with all of it. I wasn't sure if she'd go running for the hills. Most women would take off the second they found out I have a kid. But Sara didn't, and that should've been a clue. She wanted to meet Felicia as soon as I showed her a picture. Did she tell you Felicia has Down Syndrome?"

"No, but I haven't gotten Sara to talk about you. I had to pick her up at the park when you dumped her."

"You had to pick her up? She drove there…"

Liv's smile was grim. "She was a mess and collapsed on the sidewalk. Took me ten minutes to figure out what she was sobbing about."

"Oh, God. I never meant—I kept going—practically ran away. I had no idea."

"I figured. But trust me when I say I was a hair's breadth from coming after your ass. I wanted to kick it into next week."

"I deserved it," Terry said.

"No, you didn't. You were acting in the interest of your child. But you have to admit you could have gone about it differently."

"I'm hearing it a lot lately." Terry heard her mother's voice echoing Liv's words. "I panicked. The day before, I'd been wondering what it might be like to live with Felicia and Sara. If Sara would love Felicia as much as I do."

"She loves kids, and she'd make a great mom."

"You're not making this easy."

Liv shrugged. "Not my plan. I guess I came here to be Sara's advocate. Though if she knew I was here, she'd kick my ass."

"I'm sure she would."

"But I am here, and I want you to know you should talk to her again." Liv leaned forward, and something in her eyes confused Terry. A mix of sadness and regret maybe? "She cares about you, too. More than she should, and she doesn't know what to do with it. You've got to talk to her. Really talk to her."

"I tried. We fought and she left. I couldn't do anything more."

"You could have followed her. I know Sara. She'd have turned around and given you another chance. She was in shock, and who the hell can blame her?"

"It certainly wasn't how I wanted to tell her. William being here threw me off completely."

"Who's William?"

"Ann's father. Didn't Sara tell you about him?"

"Yes, but she didn't say he was here."

Terry sighed. "He was here all right. She showed up while I was in the middle of an argument with him. I was angry—he came all the way from Vancouver to harass me. I think he's staying somewhere local. I've seen him twice, and I doubt he's going back and forth. His lawyer told him to stop coming around me, but he won't. He seems to think if he shows up, one of these times I'll give in and do what he wants. William isn't used to losing. He's had anything he wants delivered to him on a silver platter his whole life. What's worse is I'm afraid he'll accost me when I have Felicia in the car."

"Sara saw you fighting with him?"

"Oh, yeah. She heard him say how he was going to use my girlfriend against me and prove I was an unfit mother because of how we were out partying all the time. It was another tactic of his. He knows we're not together anymore."

"Partying? Sara? Does he not know anything about her?"

"He hired a private detective to follow us," Terry said. "He sent photos of Sara and me going to a couple of clubs. You know how she loves to dance...and it's all we were doing. Dancing. We might have had a few beers, but every time we went out, we took a cab to and from. He didn't bother to put it into his report to William, though. The guy made it sound like I was neglecting my child.

"I couldn't have that. I *can't* have that. I know William well enough to know he'd bring Sara into the whole mess. Use her as an example of my lifestyle. He told me if I broke up with Sara, he'd drop everything. I broke up with her, and he said I had to move to Vancouver. I started thinking about moving, but I can't up and go unexpectedly. Felicia isn't equipped for more disruption in her life. Things need to be consistent for her. It was too much and I put my foot down and said no. Then he filed for custody. He's come here twice now and made threats about taking her from me."

"Sara didn't tell me. Seriously, what does he have against you?"

"Nothing substantial according to my attorney, but it doesn't change the fact I didn't want Sara to have to deal with all this. I thought I was doing the right thing. I mean, I guess I could have gone to her when he filed and ask for her forgiveness."

"What an asshole."

"A rich asshole who lorded his wealth over me and Ann our entire marriage. When she died, he tried to say he should get Felicia because

I'm not her bio mom. Then he said how he's got the money to give her a proper, safe life. I moved from Quebec, but it took me three years to do it. I was drowning on my own, and I needed my mom's help. William's idea of help is hiring someone to care for Felicia. When I got the chance to come back here, I took it. Honestly, I think I didn't go back to Sara because a part of me thought I was protecting her."

"Take it from me," Liv said, "she doesn't need protecting. It pisses her off. You need to talk to her. Make her understand how scared you were—are. I can tell she means a lot to you. Right now, she's hurting and there's nothing I can do to help her. But you can."

"What can I do? I'll end up messing things up and making it worse. Besides, she's with someone. I saw that very clearly at the pub."

"They're not in a serious relationship. Casual dating is what Sara called it."

Terry scoffed. "I know Sara, and I'm sure she wouldn't dance like that with someone she's casual with. They're lovers, and for Sara that's a big deal."

Liv sighed. "Talk to her. Please. Tell her how you're feeling. Tell her how you feel about her. She needs to hear it. Trust me on this. You might even manage to be friends when you're done."

"Friends?" The idea hurt more than Terry expected it to. She didn't want to be friends with Sara. She wanted to spend the rest of her life with her. Could she settle for friends?

"Yeah. Don't say it like it's a dirty word. She and I managed to make it work. I'm sure you can do the same. Sara's the most forgiving person I've ever known. Hell, she went out with Angel twice after the woman fucking hit her. I can't believe she wouldn't at least consider being friends with someone she loves."

"She still loves me? After everything I did?"

Liv had the decency to look sheepish. "Oh, did I say that out loud? Huh. Well, look at the time." She got to her feet and headed for the door. "I have a meeting in ten minutes. See you later today." And she was gone. But not before she had dropped her bombshell.

Sara still loved her? Did Terry still have a chance with her? If she begged, pleaded, groveled, whatever? For the first time in a long while, Terry allowed herself a smile. She'd find time to see Sara and plead her case. If nothing else, she needed a friend right now.

****

Later that night, Terry scrolled through her months worth of text messages to Sara. Most of what they said to one another held no real importance. Times and places to meet up, maybe a note about how the workday was going, whether they could have lunch at the pub. She'd read them a hundred times and wondered why she kept them.

Four months ago, she'd have said she kept them for posterity. Or to remind her to poke fun at Sara over something silly. Maybe to remember a specific moment they'd shared. But now? Now it was torture, plain and simple.

She switched from the text messages to her photos. Mixed in with pictures of Felicia and the occasional work-related shot were images of Sara. Dancing, laughing, smiling at Terry with so much love in her eyes it hurt Terry to look at it. But she figured it was her penance, right? She deserved to see how happy Sara once was in order to know what she'd ripped away. What kind of person was she? Why didn't she trust Sara with the truth?

And why couldn't she let her go?

Liv was convinced she needed to talk to Sara more, but she'd moved on. Terry saw her twice walking through town, holding hands with the blue-haired woman. The subtle touches and little smile told her they were lovers. She could still read Sara's body language, even from a block away. She should be glad Sara's moved on, not wallowing in pain over it.

She tucked the phone into her hip pocket and got up from the table. The snow came down hard now, and she leaned against the doorjamb to watch it. The white faded as the sun set, but she continued to stare at it until it blended into the darkness. Her vision blurred, and she realized there were tears on her cheeks. More crying. She didn't think she cried this much when Ann died. Lately she cried when the door shut too hard, or Felicia looked at her funny, or she thought of Sara.

Familiar arms wrapped her in a warm hug from behind, and Terry leaned into her mother's embrace. Once again, Shirley's intuition was spot on and she showed up when Terry needed her most.

"If I tell you to go talk to her, will you think I'm crazy?"

"No. I'd think you were right. I love her, Mom. It's not going to change. And I made a colossal mistake by pushing her away. You didn't see the look on her face when I tried to explain myself to her. I never expected Sara to think I didn't trust her, but I guess she's right. I mean, if I had trusted her, where would we be right now?"

Terry turned to face her mother. "Would she be at my side helping me to get through this crap with William? Or would she have run screaming for the hills because she didn't want to get involved?"

"I think you can disregard the latter statement, dear. From what you've told me about her, I can tell Sara is a loyal person. She'd have stayed by your side. She still might, if you give her a chance to."

"I'm pretty sure that ship has sailed. She's done with me." Terry peered at her hands, surprised at how hard they shook. "I convinced myself I was protecting Felicia, and it's cost me more than I thought possible. I want to go to her, Mom. Tell her how I feel, but I'm scared. I don't know if I could handle a rejection from her."

"You can. You're a strong woman who's dealing with more stuff than anyone should ever have to. You were thinking of Felicia. Did you make a mistake? I think you did, but it doesn't mean you can't fix it. You're only human. Give it a go. I'll watch Felicia. She's almost ready for bed anyway."

"Right now? You think I should call Sara right now?"

"No. I think you should go to her house right now." Shirley hugged her again and pointed Terry toward the door. "Go and don't come back telling me she wasn't home. You have to actually knock on her door and wait for her to open it. If she kicks you out, that's one thing. If not, you open your mouth and spill your guts."

Terry stared at her mother for a few seconds, not sure whether to be angry or thankful. For once, she chose thankful, grabbed her coat and keys, and left.

****

Sara finished putting the clean dishes away and decided to settle in for the evening to watch a bit of television. She'd not had much time for her usual binge watching, but tonight she would make an exception. Now to figure out what to watch.

Her phone dinged to let Sara know she'd gotten a text message. Bren sent her smiley faces—several different ones. She was comforted by Bren's friendship. They were going dancing this weekend. She couldn't wait.

The woman was such a breath of fresh air and a balm for Sara. It saddened her she wasn't what Bren needed. Such a sweet, loving woman deserved more than someone partially present. On some level, Sara was glad she wasn't the one for Bren. No matter how she examined it, she was still very much in love with Terry. Even after their fight and how much hurt and anger poured out over it, Terry Alexander owned her heart.

But to find out Terry dumped her without ever coming to her with the truth—Sara didn't think Terry could break her heart all over again, but she had. Even with all the "I'm sorry's" she said, Sara was amazed by Terry's lack of trust in her.

They'd shared countless nights talking about everything, especially Ann. How could they share those moments without a word about Felicia and Terry's fears she'd be taken away from her? The child meant everything to Terry. And so, Sara thought, had she.

The doorbell interrupted her. Sara peeked out the window before opening the door. Instantly the air was sucked out of her. Terry stood there in her worn jeans, her leather jacket opened enough Sara noted she wore her favorite kd lang T-shirt. Her hair was longer than usual, almost covering her ears. She looked sexy as hell, and Sara hated the way her body suddenly responded to Terry's presence.

She did her best to ignore it and got right to the point. "What do you want?"

"We need to talk," Terry said, as if it was reason enough. "Please."

"We've done enough talking, don't you think?" Sara started to close the door, but Terry stopped her and stepped partially inside.

"You're not taking the hint, so let me be clear. Go the fuck away. Now."

"No. This is too important. I should have told you this a long time ago, but I didn't have the courage to do it. Please, Sara. I need to talk to you about Felicia and the custody stuff. You can kick me out when I'm done, but I'd rather do this inside."

Sara's heart melted at the hurt in Terry's eyes. It mirrored the hurt she felt every time she saw Terry, thought of Terry, walked by Terry's office. Did she even care to hear Terry's explanation?

Deep down, she knew she did. She motioned Terry in and closed the door. "Why do I need to hear this? You don't trust me. There's nothing more to say."

"That's not true." Terry stepped forward and stopped herself. "It wasn't a matter of trust. I was scared."

"You should have told me. I'd have understood."

"I—I did what he wanted me to do, expecting it to be enough. I can't ever risk losing Felicia, Sara. She's all I have left of Ann, and she owns my heart."

"You're planning to lie down and let Ann's father run over you? Was it as easy to toss me away?"

"No." Terry's voice shook with emotion. "It wasn't easy. It was one of the hardest things I've ever done."

"He can't take your child from you. You're a good mom. Anyone with eyes can see it."

"You don't know him. He won't stop until he gets his way. He's got a lot of money and determination. It took years for Ann to get out from under his thumb. She had to fight to take the money she inherited from her grandma and put it into a trust for Felicia. It nearly bankrupted us. When she died, it bankrupted me because William refused to help pay for the funeral. He was still angry she refused his money."

"Sounds like a right bastard."

"He is. And he's used to getting what he wants. I never thought he'd do this. He was angry that, although I sold the house in Quebec, I wasn't moving to Vancouver. And why would I? I'm from Whitehorse, and my mom needed help. It made sense to come here. He said if I came to Vancouver, he'd take care of us, and we'd want for nothing."

"Why didn't you do it?" Sara fought the urge to wipe the tears from Terry's face. It killed her to see the sadness in her eyes.

"Ann wouldn't have wanted me to. She hated his money and how he throws it around to get what he wants. She didn't want Felicia exposed to that."

"So he threatened you?"

"He flew to Quebec and tried to take Felicia home with him. I nearly called the police to stop him. Since then, he's been on the phone harassing me at every opportunity. I offered to let him come to see her in Whitehorse, but he made excuses for not coming here. Twice my mom flew to Vancouver to let Felicia see her other grandparents. Both times he tried to buy Felicia's affections, which says right there how little he knows about her. She's not into material things at all."

"Terry, you should have told me all this from the beginning. You should have told me. All those times we stayed up all night talking—did you think I wouldn't want to stay with you or something?"

"No. Never that." Terry's voice softened, but Sara heard a slight tremble in her words. "I can only say I'm sorry. I made a huge mistake, and I've missed being with you every minute of every day since. I don't know what else to say."

Say you love me, Sara thought. If Terry would say that, she'd be in her arms in a nanosecond. But those words weren't forthcoming, and Sara knew it. The chasm between them was bigger than the Grand Canyon.

"I don't know either."

Terry sniffled as fresh tears slid down her cheeks. "I need you as my friend. I've missed you, and I know I screwed up, but I need you. I have no one to go to. No one understands or knows me the way you do."

"Friends?"

"Yeah. Do you think we could try? Please?"

The hurt in Terry's eyes was heart wrenching. Could Sara be satisfied with a friendship with Terry? Did she even want one?

Yes. She did. She wanted nothing more than to have Terry back in her life. She loved her with all her heart, and if there was a tiny chance Terry would one day see that, Sara was willing to take it. But the road to trusting her again would be a long one.

"You'll have to earn my trust," she said. "We can't have a friendship without it."

"I'll try. I promise I've told you everything. There are no more secrets."

"Good." Sara swept her arm toward the kitchen. "Why don't you come in? Want some tea? I've got jasmine."

"I don't think I can say no to jasmine tea."

"Then don't. Hang up your jacket. I'll get the tea ready, and we can talk about this mess. And you can tell me why you were at the pub last night."

"I was hoping to run into you," Terry said. She stared at her hands like they held all the answers in the world. "I saw you with that girl and left. I didn't want to intrude on your date. You looked like you were having a good time."

"We were. She's been good for me."

"I'm glad. Um…may I use your bathroom?"

"Sure."

Terry retreated down the hall.

Sara didn't know what to say. She busied herself and placed the cups and saucers on the table, along with the tea. She reached for the kettle at the same moment a knock sounded at her door.

She answered it and was nearly bowled over as Angel shoved her way inside. "Hey! What the hell are you doing?"

"Who is she?"

"What? Angel, get the fuck out of my house."

"I want to know who she is." Angel shoved her way into the living room, pushing Sara back as if she were a nuisance. "You said you didn't want to date two women, but that was clearly a lie. I saw you with the blue-haired chick, and then I saw a different one come in here a while ago."

"Get out of my house." Sara tried hard to keep her voice steady. "I don't want you here."

"I don't give a shit." Angel spun around and came at fast and Sara found herself backed against a wall. Angel loomed over her, one hand grasping Sara's shirt. "Who the fuck is she? What's she got I don't? I saw the shitty truck she's driving. You into trailer trash now?"

With a frightening glint in her eyes, Angel's hand raised as if to strike Sara.

Before Sara could answer, Terry was there. She pulled Angel away from her and shoved her toward the door. Sara realized how dangerous Angel could be. As it was in the car, Sara felt a wave of violence come from her and instinctively tried to keep Terry away.

"Stop. Angel, you need to leave. Right now."

Angel lunged toward Sara, but Terry shoved her, causing Angel to stumble backward. She caught herself on the door frame. Terry spoke through clenched teeth. "She said leave."

"Who the fuck are you?" Angel glowered, but Terry didn't budge.

Terry's calm voice belied the shaking Sara felt under her hand, which rested on Terry's arm. "None of your business." She opened the door, keeping Sara behind her. "Out. Now."

The expression on Angel's face scared Sara. She seemed indecisive—fight or leave. "Go, Angel," Sara said, "Now."

"Call the police, Sara," Terry said without taking her eyes off Angel. "She's trespassing and I'm pretty sure what she did would be considered assault and battery. It's time you pressed charges against her."

Angel locked gazes with Sara, who made no move for her phone. Angel edged toward the door. "This isn't over," she said to Terry. "You have no idea who you're fucking with."

"I don't care who you are. You need to leave. Right now." Terry gently pushed Sara back a few steps as Angel headed for the door.

"You're going to regret this, Sara," Angel said as she left the house. "I'll be meeting with Greg first thing in the morning."

Sara's gut tightened at the thought. She wanted to stop her. "Angel—"

"Don't worry. I'll take care of this one, too." She pointed to Terry and left.

Terry gently closed the door. She stood at the small window beside it for a few moments before letting her gaze rest on Sara, the angry lines on her face now softened with concern. "You okay?"

"Yes. No. Both?"

Sara let Terry lead her to the kitchen table. Terry reheated the water while Sara sat down. "I'm sorry," Sara said. "I went out with her a couple of times, and she decided we were a couple. She's the one who dumped me along the roadside."

"That was her? I should have kicked her ass when I had the chance."

"No don't. You'll make things worse. Her cousin is my boss at the bank, and Angel's realty company brings a lot of business in. She's used that fact a couple of times to get me to have dinner with her. I haven't talked to her since she kicked me out of her car. I thought we were done."

"We should call the police."

"Why? She didn't hurt me. There's nothing to tell them."

"She's harassing you, and if I hadn't been here, she might have hurt you."

"I think it would make things worse if I reported her. She has pull at the bank. What if she tells my boss I'm harassing *her*? What if she pulls her accounts? Then what?"

"You beat her to the punch." Terry removed her cell phone from her back pocket and dialed. "I'm going to help you do this." She spoke into the phone. "Yes, I'd like a police officer to come see me. I need to report someone for harassment and assault."

Sara waited nervously while Terry gave information to the police. When she was done, Sara didn't know if she should hug her or hit her for taking matters into her own hands.

"Done." Terry finished her tea. "You want another cup?"

"I haven't touched the first one."

"Then I'll reheat it."

"I don't know if this is a good idea."

"Sure it is. Cold tea is gross." Terry got up and put the cup in the microwave, a hint of a grin on her face. "As for the police, it's totally a good idea. Angel needs to be put in her place, Sara. I don't give a shit who she knows. If she talks to your boss, then I'll talk to his boss."

"You don't have to try so hard to win my trust back, you know?"

"Yes I do." Terry put the steaming tea in front of her, leaned down, and kissed Sara on the cheek. "I wouldn't be a good friend if I didn't do this."

"Will you stay until the police get here?"

"I'm not going anywhere."

Sara wanted to read much more into her statement. Terry not got rid of Angel and was ready to protect Sara from her at the same time. When had Terry become her knight in shining armor? It's not like she needed it. Sara was sure she could handle Angel on her own, but the idea Terry felt strongly enough about her to get right in Angel's face, be ready to rush to Sara's defense against anyone she needed to—it tipped the balance for Sara. She'd work on the friendship and see where it led.

Sara sipped her tea and asked, "You really don't have any other friends?"

"I'll accept the change in topic for now." Terry gave Sara a small smile. "And no. I don't. I mean, Frank sort of counts, but he's more my mom's friend and a super sweet guy who likes to help me out. He wasn't ready to retire when he sold me his business, but I guess his wife sort of pushed him into it.

"Anyway, I don't go out, ever. The people I meet are clients, and I'm not interested in any of them. The friends I had were your friends. And most of them are too pissed off to have anything to do with me."

"You need to go out once in a while. Meet new people. Have some fun."

Terry laughed. "I have lots of fun with Felicia. Maybe not the kind of fun I had with you, but it'll have to do for now. Though I would love to be able to call you now and again to talk. We used to be good at talking to each other."

"We were, until I found out the huge secret you were keeping from me." The smile faded from Terry's face, and Sara regretted her choice of words. But she was angry and hurt all over again and wasn't about to let Terry off the hook for it.

Terry's eyes dropped to her teacup, and she looked utterly defeated. "I'm sorry."

"Can't you at least help me understand why you did it?"

"I don't fully understand myself. I know I have to protect Felicia at all costs. Even if the cost is my own happiness. Everything I do affects her. Even she can see I've been miserable since I broke up with you. She wanted to meet you, and she was upset she didn't get to. I still hear about it because Felicia never forgets anything."

"Then let me meet her." Sara hardly believed what she was saying.

"You want to meet her?" Terry's expression was somewhere between fear and shock.

"I do. I think it's best we pick up where we left off—in a manner of speaking. I should meet your family. I think it's a good start. You've met my family, such as it is."

"I met your mother the one time."

"That wasn't enough for you? She wore you out dragging you around the mall while she shopped for shoes."

"She does love her shoes." Terry gave her a lopsided grin.

"She does, but she's not the topic of discussion here. What do you say? Let me meet Felicia?"

Terry didn't seem like she needed to give the idea much thought as her answer was immediate. "Yes. What are you doing Sunday afternoon? I can make lunch, and you can join our Sunday picnic/teatime in the living room."

"A picnic in the living room?" Sara asked, her smile mirroring

Terry's. "Sounds cute."

"Trust me, it is. Felicia gets all dressed up for it and usually puts a bow in Elmo's fur. We get out her best plastic China and make a very big deal out of it."

"It's a date."

"Sunday at one?"

"I'll be there."

Terry smiled sweetly and the expression made Sara weak in the knees. Her heart raced and she wanted badly to take Terry into her arms and kiss her forever. But she held those emotions in check.

"Too bad I have to work tomorrow."

"How so?" Terry asked.

"I'd ask to come over. I don't want to wait until Sunday."

"It's been a couple of days," Terry inched closer and Sara was tempted by the proximity of her lips…

Hearing a knock at the door, her thoughts switched back to Angel, cooling her hormones like a cold shower. She watched quietly as Terry opened the door and led an officer into the living room. Sara trudged after them, hoping like hell this wouldn't come back and bite her in the ass.

****

Greg called Sara into his office first thing the next morning. Greg Rutherford might not be as tall as his cousin, but he was no less imposing. His dark eyes observed everything, and Sara doubted anyone, or anything, ever got past him. He was brilliant at his job, even if he lacked personality.

His blond hair, cut close to his scalp, revealed the hint of a receding hairline. Greg didn't appear to care about such things. He always came to work in crisp, white, button-down shirts and a black tie that matched his black slacks and black shoes. As a boss, he was fair and always had Sara's back.

He didn't say a word when she walked in and pointed to one of the plush chairs in front of his over-sized oak desk. He waited for her to be seated then sat up straight and gave her his full attention.

"Thanks for coming in. I know you're busy. I'll get to the point. I had an interesting conversation with Angel Harrison on my way to work this morning."

Sara braced herself. In her hand, she held a copy of the police report she'd filed. Charley Townsend, the Royal Canadian Mounted Police sergeant who responded to the call, was kind enough to fax it to her first thing this morning. It helped she and Charley went to school together. Sometimes living in a small community was useful. She looked up at Greg, who, as usual, sported no particular expression on his face. She waited for him to continue.

"What may or may not go on between you two outside this building is none of my business. However, Angel is threatening to take her clients to the Royal Bank of Canada. It wouldn't be ideal for us, but it's not the crushing blow she thinks it is. Nor is it of much concern to me. What is of concern is she claims you've sexually harassed her here, in your office."

Sara started to speak, but he held up a hand to stop her. "I haven't worked with you very long, Sara, but I know you well enough to believe you would never be anything less than professional in the workplace. Angel filed a formal complaint, and I have to investigate it, and I am. She claims this happened several months ago, after you went on a date together. She says you pressured her to go out again and made calls to her during work hours so often she's had to block your office number and your cell number.

"Now, this is all her side of things. I'd like to hear yours."

"She's lying. Several months ago we went out, but when I made it clear I wasn't going to sleep with her, Angel hit me."

For the first time since they'd started working together, Greg reacted to her words. His eyes narrowed and Sara could sense his anger building.

"I refused to see her again, even after she apologized to me. I had another relationship, and I didn't hear anything from Angel until it ended. She came to me and said I should go to dinner with her. She kept saying she could easily pull her clients from our bank and how bad it would be for me if she did, and I agreed to go out with her. Twice. The second time, when I made it clear I wasn't interested in a relationship, she dumped me out of her car along Highway 1, in the middle of the night, about twenty kilometers south of here.

"Last night, she showed up at my house." She placed the police report on his desk. "You'll find everything you need in there. The officer did suggest I take out a restraining order against her, but I don't want to. I think this ought to be enough. The officer told me they'd investigate things, and I suspect, given she called you this morning, the police have already spoken to her."

Greg read over the report, and Sara tried to be patient while he did. She kept her hands in her lap, clasped tightly to hide the trembling.

After a few tense minutes, Greg put the report down. When he looked at her, she was certain she saw genuine concern in his dark eyes. "May I keep this report?"

"Certainly."

"Sara, let me say I'm sorry this has happened. I will make sure this accusation of Angel's goes no further than my desk. You're good at your job, and I won't allow her, or anyone else, to make false accusations. If you need anything from me regarding this matter, please let me know."

"Maybe a copy of her complaint? I should probably tell the police."

"I'll have it to you before lunch. Thank you, Sara."

"Thanks, Greg."

Sara barely made it to her desk when the phone rang. She sank into her chair and glanced at the caller ID to see Liv's office number.

"Morning, Livvy."

"Tell me what happened."

"What makes you think something happened?"

"You do realize I know everyone in this city, right?"

"I thought that was my line."

Liv sighed loudly and dramatically. "Let me try this again. Charley Townsend is a police sergeant. You know?"

"I do. Handsome butch—"

"Who was at your house last night taking a report about Angel harassing you."

"She shouldn't have told you that."

"Not the point. Sara, why didn't you call me? I'd have come over there right away. Well, maybe not right away. I might have stopped and beat the shit out of Angel first. Still might."

"No. You are expressly forbidden from speaking to her. Period."

"What happened?"

"She pushed the situation too far," Sara said. "Terry was there, and for once we were talking through things. Angel literally stormed into the house. If Terry hadn't been there..." Sara let the line drop. She tried not to think of what Angel was capable of doing. It hadn't happened and it was over. "Terry called the police, and I told them everything. About the night she hit me, threatening my job, getting in my face at my own house. And this morning, I found out from Greg she filed a complaint against me saying I sexually harassed her in my office."

Liv kept quiet for a moment. "What'd Greg say?" Liv asked.

"He plans to drop it and took the copy of the police report Charley faxed me this morning. Now, how the hell did you find out?"

More silence and Sara had the impression she wouldn't like Liv's answer. "I asked Charley to watch out for you. She didn't call last night because it was late when she left your house, so she waited until this morning."

"You had the cops watching me?" Sara loved Liv's protective streak, but sometimes she felt it went too far.

"I did, and I'm not apologizing. Besides, it wasn't like I asked the whole entire Whitehorse division of the RCMP to watch out for you. Charley lives two streets over from your house. It's not a big deal for her to drive past now and again."

"I should be pissed at you," Sara said. "If I didn't love you, I'd kick your ass right now."

Liv huffed and promptly changed the subject. "How'd it go with Terry? Aside from the fact she tossed Angel out on her ass."

"It went well. I'm going to her house on Sunday to meet her mom and Felicia."

"Oh?"

"Stop right there. We're trying to be friends, and if I'm going to be her friend, I should at least meet her family. She's got a long way to go to fix the trust issues."

"But?"

"But I want this, Liv. I want her in my life, and I'll take whatever I can get." As soon as she said the words, Sara was struck with a very sad thought. "Which reminds me I need to phone Bren. We're supposed to go out Friday night."

"You're canceling?"

"No. I want to firm up the time she's coming to get me."

"So, you're still going out with Bren?"

"No. We're friend dating, remember? Besides, I told her we had to stop any kind of dating."

"When?"

Sara sighed. "Couple of days ago. Bren said she's in love with me."

"Uh-oh."

"You have such a way with words."

"Sorry," Liv said. "How'd she take it?"

"Like the dear, sweet woman she is. With a smile. We're still friends, and we're going dancing on Friday. I think we both need each other. She's been good for me, Livvy. I feel like such an asshole."

"Don't you call my best friend an asshole. I'll have to beat you up."

"It's true. You didn't see the look on her face."

"I know it sounds trite, but she's young. She'll be fine. You don't know she won't fall in love with someone else next week."

"Actually, I do. She's not like that. Bren's very serious about her feelings."

Liv was quiet for a lot longer than Sara thought possible. "You're a good woman, Sara Hyatt. You will find someone perfect for you. I know it."

"I already did. I love Terry, and I want nothing more than to be with her again, but I don't see how. And I'm not even sure she wants to get back together. I mean, there's still this whole thing with her father-in-law. I think the choice is hers."

"No. It's your choice. It's always your choice."

"There's no choice for me. I love her. I want a life with her."

"Then go for it, my friend." Liv spoke to someone in her office. "Look, I've got a very important geologist in my office, and she needs my undivided attention."

"Tell Terry I said hello."

"Will do. We'll talk more later."

"Bye."

****

The day couldn't end fast enough for Terry. She had a ton of things to do before flying to Yellowknife on Monday. She knew her mother could handle things at home for a few days, but Terry felt uneasy leaving her and Felicia alone. Most of all, she worried about how Felicia would react to her absence. At least she had the weekend to figure it all out.

Then her mind shifted to thoughts of Sara and how the timing for this trip sucked. They were talking again, and there was definitely a chance they'd mend their relationship. All she wanted was to spend every minute with Sara. She had a feeling Sara would like it, too. She looked forward to having her over on Sunday.

And it made her smile as she locked the door to her office. The smile, however, was wiped off her face by the fist that slammed into her cheek. She stumbled a few steps backward, stopped by the solid frame of the door at her back. The hit stunned her, and she didn't see the second one coming. Her head bounced off the door frame.

Someone spoke, but it took a few seconds for Terry's scrambled brain to understand what the hell was going on. She squinted through blurry vision. A woman stood in front of her, gesturing with her arms as she spoke. The woman was a bit taller than Terry, with long, golden-brown hair pulled into a thick braid. She ought to know her but couldn't bring any names to the surface.

Terry's briefcase became too heavy, and she let it drop to the ground. She managed to stand straighter and slid a few steps away from the woman. "What—"

"You fucking bitch!" She shoved Terry against the wall. "I told you I'd come after you for what you did."

With the next punch, Terry doubled over and grabbed her stomach. The air left her lungs, and she stumbled to her knees. She struggled to breathe while the woman continued her tirade.

She pulled Terry to her feet, and Terry saw her arm cock to deliver another strike. Terry'd never hit a person in her life, but a rush of adrenaline ran through her. She brought her right fist up and jabbed the woman in the face. Blood spurted from her nose.

The woman screamed and grabbed her face .

"I'm calling 9-1-1!" a new voice yelled.

Terry recognized Mark, the manager of the electronics store next door.

Blood soaked the front of her white blouse, and for a moment, Terry thought the woman would come at her again. But her attacker glared at the store manager, who spoke into his cell phone, then she spun around, and left.

The adrenaline rush faded as fast as it came on, and Terry leaned against a parked car, unable to hold herself up any longer. Gentle hands helped lower her to the ground, and she gazed up into Mark's concerned face.

"You okay?"

"My head hurts. Who the hell was that? Did you see her?"

"No. I heard someone screaming and ran out here. I called for help."

"Thanks." Terry patted the hand resting on her shoulder.

It felt like forever before an RCMP car pulled up. Terry watched as a tall, well-built, female officer climbed out of the vehicle. She put a hat over her short, midnight-black hair and strode quickly to Terry's side. Her dark eyes assessed Terry instantly.

Terry gave her a weak smile when she realized it was Charley Townsend kneeling next to her. "Didn't I see you last night? Don't you have an angel you can send to do all the dirty work?" Terry tried to joke.

Charley smiled. "I wish. I happened to be in the area. Got another car on the way. You okay?"

"I don't know. I feel like I got hit by a truck. My face is throbbing, and my hand hurts like hell." She tried to flex her swollen right hand.

"Did you get a good look at the assailant?" Charley asked.

"No. She blindsided me. After she hit me, my vision sort of blurred and I couldn't make out much about her. I think I know her. She seemed familiar. She's taller than me by a few inches and had long hair in a tight braid. Kind of blonde. I got in at least one good punch. Think I broke her nose." She looked at her shirt. "The blood's hers."

"You might have a concussion," Charley said. "I'll have the paramedics come and check you over. Which way did she go? Did you see a vehicle? Was she alone?"

"She went south, toward the park," Mark said.

Charley spoke into her radio, and her authoritative voice had a calming effect on Terry. She glanced at Mark. "Do you know who she was? Did you get a good look at her?"

Mark shook his head. "I heard shouting and saw her beating up on Terry. I called 9-1-1 and stepped outside, but by then she had a hand over her face. I'll get you the CCTV security camera footage."

"Thanks." Charley placed something cold against Terry's cheek. "Keep this on there. It'll help with the swelling. Paramedics will be here in a few minutes. Is there anyone I can call for you?"

"Not yet. I don't want to scare my mom."

"Sure."

"Do you think you can find her? The woman who attacked me?"

"We're going to try," Charley said.

Mark came up to them, though Terry didn't remember him leaving. He handed a USB drive to Charley. "Here's the footage you need. Doesn't give a great view of her or her face, but maybe it'll help." Mark turned to Terry. "I'm sorry I didn't get out here sooner."

"No worries. It's not your fault."

"Want me to lock the office for you?

"I think I did already, but I'm not sure." Terry patted the pocket of her coat. "I don't know where my keys are."

"You probably dropped them. I'll go have a look," Mark said and walked away.

"I think I know her, Charley," Terry said quietly. "I kind of recognized her voice, but I can't be sure. She was making threats like I'd done something to piss her off."

"Hmm." Charley appeared pensive for a moment before carefully saying, "Tall and light brown, almost blonde hair, right?"

"Yeah."

"And she was pissed off at you specifically? She didn't try to take your wallet or get into your office?"

"No."

"I can make an educated guess." Charley hesitated as the ambulance arrived. "Angel Harrison. Description fits, though it also fits a few thousand other people. But we know she's angry with you and was incredibly pissed off when officers showed up at her house this morning."

"I need to call Sara." Terry reached for her phone.

"Let me." Charley took the phone from her. "You let the medics take a look at you. I'll have Sara meet you at the hospital. Deal?"

"Deal. Don't scare her to death, okay?"

****

Sara ran into the emergency room, heart hammering in her chest. Even though Charley said Terry wasn't badly injured, the idea she was in the hospital at all shook Sara. She started for the information desk when Charley intercepted her.

"Hey, I told you she's okay."

"I know, I know." She gripped Charley's arm. "Was it Angel?"

Charley's dark eyes narrowed, but her expression gave nothing away. "I'll take you to see Terry." Charley gently disengaged Sara's grip and led her through the doors to the emergency room.

Sara kept her eyes on Charley instead of the rooms and beds filled with sick and injured people. She'd been in the emergency room once, when she was a little kid. She had to get stitches in her foot when she stepped on broken glass. The place gave her the creeps then, and it still did now.

They stopped at a wooden door which stood out in contrast to the white walls. There was an elongated window panel above the handle, but Sara couldn't see over Charley's shoulder. The Mountie was a good ten inches taller than her. Charley peeked in and said, "She's going to look worse than she is. But I promise she's okay."

Charley watched Sara for a moment as if she were picking up on Sara's fears. Sara nodded. Charley opened the door for her and followed her inside.

Terry sat on the bed and held something against the side of her face. Her right hand was wrapped in a tan bandage. A huge red mark stained her shirt, like someone tossed paint at her chest, the spatters going to her left shoulder. Their eyes met, and Sara calmed down.

"Hey, thanks for coming," Terry said.

Sara went to her side and rested her hand on Terry's thigh. "I had to repay the favor. How are you feeling?"

"Like I got hit by a bus." Terry removed the cold pack and set it on a table beside the bed.

Sara's trembling hand reached up to almost touch the reddish patch on the side of Terry's face. The skin wasn't cut, but it was already purple and swelling around her eye. Sara dropped her hand. "What happened? It was Angel, wasn't it?"

"I'm not sure, but I think so. If you see her with a broken nose, you'll know for sure." Terry held up her bandaged hand. "I got at least one good hit in before she took off. She came at me as I was leaving the office and started hitting me. I didn't have a chance to do much— not even call the police. I'm lucky Mark was still at work. He heard her screaming at me and called 9-1-1."

"Oh, Terry, I'm sorry." Sara covered her mouth to stifle a sob. "It's my fault. I shouldn't have let you confront her—I should never have gone out with her in the first place. I didn't know how unstable she was."

"We don't know it's her for sure, Sara. Let Charley figure it out." Terry gently took Sara's hand. "The doctor says I have a mild concussion, but I'm getting a CAT scan anyway to make sure nothing else is wrong. My head hurts, and I think my eye's trying to swell shut, but otherwise I'm good. I promise. The worst is I can't see well because they had to take my contacts out."

"How can you be calm about this when I'm freaking out?" Sara brought Terry's hand to her lips to kiss her fingers. She held the hand in both of hers and rubbed circles on Terry's palm with her thumb.

"I don't know. I've never been attacked before, and I've never hit anyone in my life." She looked down at her injured hand. "I guess the fight or flight thing kicked in, and I chose fight. Besides, she had me up against the wall—literally. I couldn't run. I don't think she was trying to kill me, maybe she wanted to send a message."

"And that was…"

"I messed with the wrong woman, I guess. She kept calling me bitch and saying I fucked up her life or something. I don't remember all of it."

"Miss Alexander?" A young woman wearing dark slacks and a maroon golf shirt came in. "I'm here to take you to radiology."

"Okay." Terry smiled at Sara and pulled her hand away. "Can you wait for me? I didn't want to tell Mom everything about what happened. She's got Felicia, and I don't want to scare them. I told her I fell. I hope you don't mind sticking around."

"Terry, we're friends." Sara kissed her lightly on the cheek, mindful of the bruising. "I'll be right here when you get back. Promise."

"Thanks." Terry gave her a little wave as she was wheeled out of the room.

Sara sank into a chair and released a deep breath. Terry might be calm on the outside, but she had a feeling she wasn't calm on the inside. How could she be? Someone attacked her. No, not someone. Angel. Sara was sure of it. She took her phone out of her purse and stared at it for a moment. She could call Angel and talk to her. Though she had no idea what she'd say when she did. Hello, did you beat up my ex? Is your nose broken?

"Do you need anything?" Charley squatted next to Sara's chair, and they were nearly eye-to-eye. "You want me to call anyone?"

"I was thinking of calling Angel."

Charley's face revealed her compassion. "Don't. If it was her, it'll stir up more trouble. Let us handle it, okay?"

"I guess." Sara put her phone away. "Has anyone gone to her house yet? Talked to her?"

"No. I will once I know Terry's status and if she intends to file charges. I have to get a report written up, but I promise we'll speak to Angel."

Sara accepted that. At least something would finally be done about her. "How did you end up here? I mean, handling all this. Are you our personal police officer?"

Charley grinned and Sara found it absolutely charming.

"Maybe," Charley said. "Guess I was in the right place when the call came in." She stood up. "I'm getting some coffee. These scans can take a while. Want to come with me?"

"I told Terry I'd be here when she got back."

Charley helped Sara to her feet. "We've got time. I promise."

****

"If I'm fine, why do I need a wheelchair?" Terry groused as she was rolled out of the emergency room several hours later. She was as grumpy as Felicia on a school morning. Bad enough she wore scrubs a size too big since the police needed her bloody clothes as evidence. She had to be rolled around like an invalid and was embarrassed. "I can walk." She didn't bother to keep the irritation from her voice.

"Sorry, hospital policy," the nurse said. He was very nice about it, and Terry felt a little guilty for her attitude. She wanted to go home. Her mood lightened a lot when she spotted Sara waiting for her on the curb in front of the main doors. "Is this your ride?" the nurse asked.

"Yep." Terry wanted to jump out of the chair and hug Sara, but her nurse put a firm hand on her shoulder to keep her still.

"Take it easy. The concussion is mild doesn't mean you get to act like you're not hurt."

"How do you know what I was going to do?"

He leaned over her and smirked. "Years of practice. Now let me help you into the Jeep. Once you're out of here, you can run around all you want. But don't be mad at me when you end up back here because you don't feel good."

Terry was grumpy again as the strong young man helped her out of the wheelchair and into the Jeep as promised. He even buckled her seat belt, though she thought it was more as a joke than anything else. He was still smirking when they pulled away.

Sara patted her on the knee once they were underway. "You sure you're okay? I think he's right. You do need to take it easy."

"I'm fine. Honestly. I feel like I got my brains jumbled, but otherwise I'm good. I hope I broke her damn nose."

"I can't believe Angel did this." She glanced quickly at Terry then kept her eyes on the road. "She's pissed at me and taking it out on you—I'm sorry, Terry."

Terry's head pounded like a kid in her skull was practicing the drums. It made sense Angel attached her. At the time, Terry felt like she knew the woman, and even though she met Angel only the one time, she thought she recognized her voice.

Terry sighed and leaned back. "It's not your fault. You don't have to keep apologizing. Hell, I didn't expect she'd follow up on what she said. It felt like an empty threat, you know?"

"I do and I'm still sorry this happened." Sara fell silent until she pulled into Terry's driveway.

Terry reached across the seat and laid her hand on Sara's arm. "It's not your fault. The bitch has issues, and we'll get it all sorted out."

"She went after you because of me." Sara faced her, and Terry saw the tears in her eyes. "I never should have gone out with her. If I hadn't, none of this would have happened. She's still mad because I filed a police report, and she's going after you because she can't come near me."

"Charley said they're looking for her. It won't be hard to find her with her nose messed up. If I'm right and it is Angel, it'll be pretty damn obvious."

"I hope they find her soon." Sara's fingers trailed the uninjured side of Terry's face, and Terry leaned into her touch. "I don't want anything to happen to you. You don't deserve this."

"No one does," Terry said. "But I'm okay. I promise. Doctor said to get rest, and I've got all weekend. Mom's already promised to help me get my stuff together for the trip to Yellowknife this week."

"You're still going there? Are you sure you'll be up for it?"

Terry shrugged. "I have to be. I can't afford to lose this contract." She smiled at Sara and kissed the fingers as they fell from her face.

Sara exited the Jeep, hurried to the other side, and helped Terry. Terry had a bruised abdomen, and when she stood, it hurt like hell. If she hadn't had a concussion, she'd have at least been allowed to take some damn pain meds.

"You okay?" Sara asked as she helped her to the door of the house.

"Nope. I want to start the evening over again. Go back to when I was leaving the office and not get beat up. You know?"

"I wish I could make that happen." Sara opened the door and kept one hand on Terry's arm as she entered the house.

"Where do you want to go? Living room? Kitchen? Bedroom?"

Terry opened her mouth to answer, but her mother was already speaking.

"Bedroom. She's going to lie down and rest." Shirley helped Terry out of her coat. "I'm Shirley, Terry's mom."

"I'm Sara." She helped Terry remain upright. "Tell me where it is, and I'll get her there."

"Down the hall, first door on the right," Shirley said.

"Sorry you have to meet like this," Terry mumbled. "Not the grand introduction I was hoping for."

"It's not a problem," Sara said. They entered Terry's room, and Sara took a moment to pull the duvet back. She helped Terry get seated on the bed. "Can you take your shirt off?"

"Um, don't know." Terry shrugged and tried to lift the scrubs over her head, but the pain in her abdomen stopped her. "I don't think I can."

"Okay." Sara tugged the bottom of the scrub top and carefully lifted it over Terry's head. She tossed it on the floor and knelt to remove Terry's shoes, then pulled the scrub pants off without asking.

Shirley arrived and handed her a nightshirt, which she helped Terry put on. Once Terry was settled on the bed, Sara lightly tucked the duvet around her.

"Better?" Sara asked.

Terry's mouth went dry. Sara's touches were soft and light as she undressed her, and if not for her foggy brain, Terry knew she'd be incredibly turned on right now. "I'm good. Thanks."

"Good." Sara turned to Shirley and handed her a folded-up piece of paper. "This is from the nurse at the emergency room. Terry has to rest, but if she falls asleep, wake her up every two to four hours through tonight. If she doesn't wake up, call 9-1-1. No medicine of any kind for pain, but she said a cold washcloth might help if her head hurts." Sara met Terry's gaze, and Terry was touched by the concern she saw.

"I can stay here if you need me to," Sara said.

"We'll be okay, dear. Thanks." Shirley placed the paper on Terry's dresser. "You look like you could use some sleep yourself. Why don't you go on home? You can call me later if you want to check up on her. I'll keep her phone so she isn't tempted to use it."

"Hey, I'm right here you know? I'm perfectly capable of not playing with my phone."

"No, you're not," Shirley and Sara chorused. Shirley said, "I'll call you if there are any problems, Sara. Feel free to stop by if you'd like to check up on her."

"Thanks." Sara lovingly touched the uninjured side of Terry's face, holding her gaze. "Be good and rest. I'll call you tomorrow, okay?"

"You better. Why don't we reschedule our Sunday tea for next week? I'd rather you not have to meet Felicia like this. It's easier for her when there's not much going on. I have a feeling my mother's will hover over me all weekend. Felicia is going to freak out when she sees my face."

"Are you going to tell her the truth?" Sara whispered.

"I don't know. Probably. I can't lie to her. Even if she won't understand."

"Good plan."

"I know my kid." Terry tried to smile, but the movement made her face hurt.

"Rest. Talk later." Sara kissed her forehead and walked out of the room.

Shirley had a huge, knowing grin on her face. "Tomorrow morning you're telling me everything, young lady. I want to know who you got into a fight with." She also kissed Terry's forehead before leaving the room.

The whole incident sucked, but Terry felt she and Sara had taken a huge step forward. Maybe it was worth it. Terry closed her eyes and fell to sleep, hoping to dream about Sara undressing her.

Chapter Thirteen

Terry double-checked her plane ticket and stuck it into the liner pocket of her coat. Her packed overnight bag and briefcase sat by the door.

She turned her attention to Felicia, who sat in front of the TV watching a cartoon. Except Terry knew she wasn't actually paying attention. Felicia refused to speak to her upon finding out Terry would be leaving for a few days. Only twice since Ann's death were they separated and both times Shirley took Felicia to see her grandparents in Vancouver.

Shirley waited with the keys to her car in hand ready to take Terry to the airport. Terry gave her a wry smile and settled on the floor beside Felicia, who stared at the TV. Terry tried to wait her out, but the clock was ticking on her flight and she needed to leave.

Terry gave in. "I won't be gone long, honey. I promise. I'll do a video call with you when I get to my hotel room. I can read to you over the phone every night before you go to bed. I packed two of your books in my suitcase."

Felicia didn't even blink.

Terry reached out to her, but Felicia pulled away. It hurt more than Terry expected. "Honey, tell me what's wrong."

"Mommy never came back."

"No, she didn't."

"You won't come back."

"Yes I will. I promise."

"Mommy promised."

Terry heard her mother moving around behind them. The door opened and closed, and she assumed Shirley took her luggage to the car. She considered cancelling the trip. Was it right to do this to her child? Felicia was somewhere between hurt and terrified, and Terry didn't know what to do about it. If she didn't go, she'd lose a lot of money.

Could she give in to Felicia? Her posture and actions suggested it's exactly what the girl wanted her to do. No. If she did, Felicia would give a repeat performance before her next trip up north. Terry addressed what she hoped was the real issue. "I know Mommy promised, but she didn't know there'd be an accident. She didn't want to leave us."

"Don't go." Felicia touched the bruise on Terry's face. "You got hurt. What if you get hurt again?"

The words cut through Terry like a knife. "I won't get hurt. The person who did this won't be where I'm going. Besides, this is my job.

I have to go." She pulled Felicia onto her lap and held her close. Despite her attempts at staying mad, Felicia relaxed into her embrace. "I love you, baby. I know it's scary, but Grams is here and she'll take good care of you. I'll call you, and we'll see each other on the phone every night. Okay?"

"Promise?"

"I promise."

Felicia's gaze locked with Terry's, and for a moment, Terry saw Ann in their child. She nodded once and said, "'K."

Terry helped Felicia to her feet and took her hand as they walked to the closet for Felicia's coat. They were both quiet on the short trip to the car. Once Terry had her secured in her booster seat, she found her mom standing behind her. As if the woman read her mind, Shirley pulled Terry into a warm hug.

The ride to the airport was short, and after a few more hugs, Terry got her luggage and went inside. She checked in and got through security in short order and settled onto a very uncomfortable chair to wait for her flight.

The image of Felicia watching her as Shirley drove away stayed in her head. Felicia's sad expression imprinted on the backs of her lids when she closed her eyes. She felt like the world's worst parent.

A text message pulled her from her maudlin thoughts. Sara wished her a safe flight. Terry smiled and decided to call her. Sara answered on the first ring.

"Hey. How're you feeling?"

"Still kind of tired but okay enough. My face looks like I was in a boxing match, though."

"I bet. Hope it won't put off the people you'll meet in Yellow-knife."

"Frank says it won't," Terry said. "He's knows them pretty well."

"Have you heard anything from the police? Did they talk to Angel?"

"No." Terry sighed. "Charley called me last night. No one's seen Angel in a couple of days. The detectives want a DNA sample to check against the blood on my shirt, and they're hoping she'll give them one willingly. Otherwise, they'll have to get a subpoena and it takes time. Until they find Angel, nothing more can be done. The CCTV didn't show her face clearly enough to ID the woman who attacked me. If it's not Angel, we're back to square one."

"I'm willing to bet it was Angel," Sara said. "I'm so—"

"Don't you dare say you're sorry. It's not your fault, Sara. I mean it. Let the police do their thing. I'm not worried about it. Honestly."

"You're not?"

"No. It's over. I'm fine. I promise."

She heard a faint sigh on the other end of the call and almost laughed. Sara was most certainly annoyed. "You're being difficult on purpose, aren't you?"

Now Terry laughed. "I am. If it diverts you from the topic of Angel."

"It almost did."

"What if I tell you I'm bored and need something else to do but talk about Angel?"

"You bored?"

"I'm at the airport. What do you think?"

"You're bored." Sara released a nervous laugh, and Terry was glad she allowed the change in topic. "And Whitehorse Airport is damn little, if you got up to walk around, you'd make a circuit of the whole place in ten minutes."

"A tiny exaggeration but close enough. Are you busy?"

"Nah. I just finished up some paperwork and was thinking of getting a snack before lunch."

"I wish I could eat like you do. I look at food between meals and gain weight."

"It's a gift," Sara said. "You don't sound like you're happy. Is something wrong? Plane delayed? Hard time getting through security?"

"None of that, but you're right. I'm not happy. Felicia was upset this morning because I'm leaving. She said Ann left and never came back. She's freaked out. She thinks I'm not coming home."

"Poor thing. It's hard for both of you."

"It is. And she's got good reason to worry, you know? But how do you tell a kid the odds of me not coming home are pretty damn slim? It took a while for her to adjust to me going to work every day. She's not been like this in a very long time, but I get it."

"Doesn't make it any easier to deal with, though. But she's got your mom with her. She'll be okay, won't she?"

"If she'll talk. I'm worried about her. I promised we'd do a video call when I get to Yellowknife. I packed a couple of books so she can pick one for me to read to her."

"It's adorable. You're a good mom, Terry."

"Thanks," Terry said, feeling a little better for talking to Sara. "I think I needed to get it all out."

"This's what friends are for, right?"

"Right. Speaking of friends, how are things with Bren?" Terry hoped she didn't sound like she was prying. If they were going to be friends, Terry needed to let Sara know she was interested in her life.

"We're going out dancing again on Saturday, though I gotta say she wears me out."

"No way. You're like the Energizer Bunny."

"But I'm not twenty-two and fit like an athlete. And she's healthy, too. It's awful."

Terry rolled her eyes at Sara's overly dramatic tone. "You poor dear. I hope she doesn't rub off on you."

"Me, too! I'd miss my junk food."

"There's that."

"When you get home from your trip, maybe we could go see a movie or something? Hang out for a while."

Wow. Terry's heart did a little flip. The prospect of spending any amount of time with Sara was awesome and scary at the same time. But she'd take it. No matter how much or what they were doing, as long as they were in the same space at the same time. "I'd love to. I'll even let you pick the movie."

"You know I'll go for the sappy romance," Sara teased.

"I do indeed." Terry welcomed the idea. The last time they saw a sappy romance together, it led to a lot of other, very pleasant activities and she allowed herself a moment to remember them.

Maybe Sara was, too, because she got very quiet for a time. "Done. I have to get a hotdog and popcorn for dinner. Bren always makes a frowny face when I do it, but I know you'll smile and pay for it."

"Oh, I'm paying, am I?" Terry laughed softly. "If I'm paying, does that mean I get to eat crappy food, too?"

"It's a movie, and a movie demands crappy junk food while you sit in a comfy seat and watch. It's a rule."

"We wouldn't want to break the rules. They called my flight. I need to go. Thanks for talking to me."

"I'm here for you, right?"

Terry mulled the comment over for a moment. "Right. Talk to you later."

"Bye."

She tucked the phone into her pocket and gathered her stuff. For the first time in weeks, a weight was lifted off her shoulders and she perked up as she got in line to board her flight.

****

A dozen text messages flooded into Terry's phone the moment she powered it up at Yellowknife Airport. Most of them were from Jackie, though a few came from her mom. The ones from her mom said to call Jackie right away.

She gathered her luggage, and once in a cab and on her way to the hotel, she pulled up Jackie's number. "Hey, Jackie. I'm in Yellowknife. What's up?"

"How soon can you get back here?"

"Two days." Terry's heart sped up. "Why?"

"William is causing more trouble. He's demanded to have the mediation brought forward by two weeks even though we don't have a firm date. He's demanding we meet on Wednesday if the mediator agrees."

"Can he do that?"

"If the mediator says it's okay. I already put in my two cents about it. I think he's doing this on purpose because he knows you're not going to be home. And he mentioned something about you hitting a woman in front of your office on Friday."

"How the hell does he know?"

"It's true?" Jackie's voice got quiet. "Terry, did you get into a fist fight?"

"Not exactly a fist fight. I mean, I fought back, because she jumped me when I walked outside. She slugged me a couple of times, and my business neighbor called 9-1-1. I ended up with a mild concussion and a sprained wrist from when I hit her. All of it was recorded on CCTV."

"There's a police report, right?"

"Yes. We think it's a woman named Angel Harrison, but the video isn't clear enough and they haven't found her to talk to her."

"Seriously?" Jackie asked. "I know her."

"Yeah, so does half of Whitehorse."

Jackie didn't speak, and Terry heard her typing on a computer. "Okay. I'll get the report. We'll prove him wrong. It might be what prompted him to ask for this to be moved up. Might also be enough for the mediator to consider doing it, too."

"Asshole," Terry muttered. "I'll be back in time for it, no matter when it gets scheduled for. Even if it means I cut my trip up here short." She cussed under her breath. "Before I forget, Felicia told me something the other day that's got me concerned. A kid at school used the 'R' word toward her. I didn't think she knew what it meant, but apparently she does."

"How awful."

"That's not the worst part. She told me she knows the word is bad because she heard Gramps yelling it a few times and she knew he was referring to her."

"Do you think she can remember when or where he said it? Or anything about the context?"

"No. She told me he said it when he was angry. He was probably yelling at his wife, who always takes the brunt of his abuse."

"Abuse? Is William abusing her?"

"Not physically—at least not that I know of. And before you ask, Felicia has never come home with bruises or anything. The one time I saw him get physical was after Ann and I got married. He grabbed her upper arms and literally shook her. We didn't see or hear from him for a year."

"This is stuff you should have told me a long time ago, Terry. We can use it for sure."

"I don't want to make him out to be some kind of monster. Especially if there's a chance Felicia might hear what gets said. If she's in there—I can't have her seeing my hatred for him."

"She won't. I'm not allowing her to be present. They can do a video interview if the mediator thinks it's necessary. But I want as much detail as you can give me about his use of the 'R' word. Did you file a police report about him grabbing your arm when he came to your office?"

"I did. I also have the one from the assault. I'll fax them both to you. I got busy with this trip and completely forgot about them."

"Don't worry about it. Get them to me as soon as you can," Jackie said. "I'll call or text you when I know the mediation date. Be ready to get your butt back here. Okay?"

"Yes, ma'am." Terry hung up and wanted to slam her fist into something. Typical of William to pull a stunt like this.

The taxi arrived at the hotel, and Terry paid him and got out. A few minutes later, she was in her room and stretched out across the bed. She had an hour before she needed to meet with Warrick at the Dresden offices. She sent off a quick text to her mom to let her know she was there, safe, and had called Jackie.

Then she left a message for Frank to let him know she'd arrived and would be at the meeting.

Her mom replied to her text, and Terry gave her a quick call.

"Hey, Mom. Let me talk to Felicia?"

"Sure." Shirley called for Felicia and within seconds she was on the phone.

"Hi, Mom," she said, sounding much happier than she had when Terry left. Then again, it was an in-service day for the teachers. She didn't have to go to school. Terry would have felt the same at her age. "We got to see a pink limousine on the way home!"

"Cool. Was the driver wearing pink, too?"

"Nope. Black."

"Luckily, black matches everything. Listen, I need to talk to you for a minute. Don't hang up." She paused to make sure Felicia was still there. She heard her breathing and continued. "Remember when you told me you heard Gramps yelling that bad word?"

"Yep."

"Do you remember when it happened? Or why he was yelling it?"

"It was my birthday when Grams took me to his house. Granny D made me a cake with Dora on it. Gramps wasn't happy I was there and said I had to go home. Granny D wouldn't let him send me home. But he said I was retarded, and he didn't want me in his house. I don't know what retarded means, but it's a really bad word."

"How do you know it's bad?"

"The way he said it. All angry and stuff. Granny D said I could stay, and that was that. I still don't know what retard means, but Bryce knows it's bad. He had to tell me he was sorry for using it."

Terry hesitated. She should have been more specific with Felicia when she explained it before. Now Felicia would probably keep coming back to it if she didn't. "It means slow to progress or to hold something back. Some people will use it to describe you because you're different from them, and they don't understand different. But the word has no power over you, sweetheart. It never will."

"I am slow. But I do my best and I get good grades. Can I stay in school? Bryce said they will make me leave because I'm a retard."

Damn the little bastard, Terry thought. Less than a week after using that horrible word, the little shit was at it again. What the hell did he have against Felicia? Or was it the prejudice of his father he was echoing?

"You're not going anywhere. It's your school from now on. Even after we get our own house, you'll still go to school there. Bryce doesn't know what he's talking about."

"He got suspended because he used the bad word," Felicia said.

"I know. And I hope he never uses words like that one again. You make sure to tell me if he does. And I don't want you saying it either. We'll call it the 'R' word from now on. Okay?"

"Yep. I'm gonna go play now."

Shirley came on the phone, and after a few minutes, Terry hung up, feeling very proud of her kid. A lot had happened to her, and she handled it better than her mother.

Who now realized if she didn't don a business suit, trot down to the lobby, and catch a cab, she'd be late for her first meeting.

****

Sara stared at her cell phone. A bit past ten at night, she was lying in bed thinking about Terry. Vivid memories of the nights they would lie awake and talk on the phone flooded her brain, and she longed to repeat them. Better still, she'd love to have the woman in bed with her. Right now. She'd contemplated making the call for the better part of half an hour.

She slid her finger across the screen and pulled up Terry's number. Again. Why did she hesitate? They were friends, right? It wouldn't be weird to call her at night to chat before they went to sleep. Would it?

Her finger hovered over the Call button. Before she could press it, a call came in. She answered it without looking at the caller ID. "Hello?"

"Did I wake you?" Terry asked.

"No. Weirdly, I was lying here trying to decide whether or not I should call you."

"Great minds. Why were you trying to decide? Should I maybe hang up?"

"No, please don't," Sara said. "I wasn't sure if you'd be awake. I know you're up there for work, and I didn't want to bother you."

"You never bother me. I could use a friendly voice."

"Things go badly up there?"

"The guys here are great. Frank gave them a ringing endorsement about me, and they're already treating me like one of them." Terry hesitated. "No, it's to do with home. William wants to move our mediation hearing to Wednesday, and I'm not supposed to return until Wednesday morning. He found out I was up here, and we know he's doing it on purpose. Plus, an issue came up at Felicia's school. This boy she likes apparently got mad when she kissed him. She decided to do it again, and he shoved her away and called her the 'R' word."

"The 'R' word?" Sara asked. She felt a bit dense not knowing what Terry meant.

"Retard."

Sara gasped. "What?"

"It came from a boy her age at school."

"What did the school do?"

"Suspended him for three days, but I'm not sure his parents treated it like punishment. At least not his father. They were in the office with me, talking to the principal, and his dad used some not-so-nice language regarding my kid. I wanted to punch his face in."

"Is Felicia okay?"

"She is, but I had to tell her what the word meant. After I explained it, she said, 'Well, I am slow.' Like that made it okay some-how. I'm not sure she understands the harshness of it, and for now, it's probably a good thing."

"Is he in her class?"

"He is, and he's harassing her. She told me today he said she has to leave school and go somewhere else."

"What?"

"I'm sure he got it from his father, who thinks she needs a special school."

"And you still managed to keep from punching him? I'm proud of you. I'm not sure I would have."

Terry laughed softly. "I'd pay to see that, but it's okay. I'm call-ing them tomorrow. The assistant principal's been helping me with it, and she's set up a phone conference at noon. I guess it's when Mr. Preston has time."

"I'm sure you'll give them something to consider, but do you think you can get Felicia moved out of his class?"

"I could, but I'm not sure that's the answer. He might see it as a win, you know? Like she got moved, and he's getting away with it. His kid might do it again to another kid he doesn't like."

"I get your point. Are you sure Felicia doesn't fully understand what's going on? From what you've said, she sounds smart."

"She is, and I'm not a hundred percent sure. She knows it's a bad word because she heard her grandfather using it. He was talking about her, though not to her at the time. He doesn't know how good her hearing is."

"What a bastard. Can you use it against him?"

"I can even if I hate doing it."

"Terry, he's playing dirty, and he clearly doesn't care about Felicia the way a grandparent should. It ought to be brought up to the mediator. Might be enough to make her see he's not good enough to take custody of Felicia. How did you put it? It wouldn't be in her best interest?"

"Exactly what my lawyer said. You two talking to each other?"

Sara laughed. "I don't know her name, so probably not."

"Jackie Smith."

"Oh! I know Jackie."

"Of course you do."

"Hey now, I don't know everyone."

"So you say." Terry was clearly teasing her, and Sara loved it. It warmed her heart.

"You can blame Liv. She set me up with Jackie years ago. We went out a couple of times, but there wasn't anything there. She's good people, though. Does a lot of work with the community and some of it pro bono. I'd be very surprised if she loses your case."

"Good to know. On both counts."

A blush crept up Sara's neck to her cheeks. Was Terry flirting? "Did you tell her what Felicia said about William?"

"I did. She might have Felicia do a video statement. She's not going to allow her in the mediation, thank God. I don't want her to ever know this is happening. She loves her grandparents, and I'd like to keep it that way."

"You really are a great mom. I mean, William is trying to tear your family apart, and you're worried Felicia won't love him anymore. That's—that's amazing."

"It's something I promised Ann." Terry grew quiet for a moment. "At her funeral, when I was alone with her, I promised her I'd always keep her parents in Felicia's life. Especially her mom. I can't go back on it."

"No, of course not." Sara thought she heard a tiny sob, and her grip on her cell phone increased. "Hey, I wish I could hug you right now."

"I need one."

"I can guarantee you'll have one soon as you get back. But, and listen very carefully, if you need me I'll be on the next flight to Yellowknife. I mean it."

Terry didn't speak, and now Sara was sure she was crying. "I—I wasn't... Sara. I can't expect those things from you. Not after what I did."

"What you did is in the past. And it was a kneejerk reaction to something that scared the shit out of you. If it helps any, let me say you're forgiven. We're moving past it. Okay?"

"I don't deserve your friendship. I'm afraid I'll mess it up again."

"You won't." Sara sat up, as if doing it would put more emotion into her words. "You have my friendship. I'm not going anywhere, unless you need me on a plane. I'm serious. If you say yes right now, I'll book it and be there in the morning."

She heard Terry's uneven breathing, sniffles, then Terry blew her nose. Sara was ready to switch to the Internet and make the flight arrangements right now. Terry needed her.

"It's okay. I'll be okay. Sometimes it gets overwhelming. I don't know what to do first. I've got a job that needs my attention, but Felicia needs me more, and I have to keep William from taking her away. When I did a video chat with Felicia tonight, she looked sad. Mom was there to give her a goodnight hug, but it's not the same, you know?"

"I can't imagine what you're going through, but I can tell how hard it is for you. But you're a damn strong woman. You'll be fine. I'm sure of it."

"This is why I called you. I needed to hear someone tell me that. Mom says it a lot, but she's my mom. I think she has to." Terry made a self-deprecating laugh. "Most of the time, I feel good—I know I can do what needs to be done. I guess it all sort of crashed in on me today."

Sara stared at the Internet icon, wavering over booking the flight. She could skip a day or two of work or work remotely. She was confident Greg would be okay with it.

"Sara? You there?"

Always. Forever. "I am."

"Tell me what you're thinking."

"I should fly out first thing in the morning and be at your hotel room for breakfast."

"You'd have to be here around five. I'm meeting the guys at Dresden around six for a site inspection, after which we go to the main office to review my findings from the summer samples I took."

"I would be there right now if I could. I want to hold you, Terry. I want you to know you've got someone to lean on."

"I already do, or we wouldn't still be on the phone."

"True enough." Sara settled back in bed and pulled the duvet up to her chin. "Are you sure you're going to be okay?"

"As long as I have you, yes."

"Then you'll be fine. Call me tomorrow night before you go to sleep."

There was no hesitation this time. "I will."

Chapter Fourteen

"How many names do I have to cut from the list?" Liv asked again. She'd already removed ten people, but she wanted to be sure.

"Small wedding, dear. Small. As in less than fifty people." Grace poked her head around the bathroom door. "You've heard of small, right? The community center doesn't hold more than sixty. Genta told us three times."

"I know, I know." Liv stared at the list. Down to ninety. How the hell could she strike another forty people from the most important day of her life? Instead of cutting names, she needed to add at least two more. Terry and Bren. She liked Bren well enough, but she intended to make sure Terry and Sara were a couple by the time the wedding happened.

Grace came out of the bathroom, fresh from her shower, and settled behind her on the bed. Her long, damp hair fell over Liv's shoulder as she peered at the notebook in Liv's hands. "Ninety-two. You added two names. You don't understand how subtraction works, do you?"

Liv kissed Grace on the cheek. "No. I always sucked at math."

"Liar. It's your strongest subject. Okay, I know you want to invite all your employees, but can we knock most of them off the list? It would get us closer to the number we need."

"I don't know who. I've been around most of those guys for years. I don't want any hurt feelings."

"Hmm." Grace slipped her arms around Liv's waist.

"You think we could get the community center for two days?"

"I'm sure we can even though it's next month." Grace kissed Liv's bare shoulder. "I'm sorry I'm making this difficult."

"You're not being difficult, I am." Liv put the notebook away and resettled in order to fully embrace her fiancée. "Besides, I know you're not keen on big crowds, especially when you don't know most of the people in them."

"And I'm assuming everyone we invite will show up, which almost never happens."

"It probably will. They'll love an excuse for a good party."

"Especially if someone else is paying the tab?"

"Especially." Liv kissed her longingly, no longer interested in the wedding planning. "I love you."

"I love you, too." Grace returned her attentions for a moment but stopped when Liv nudged her to lie down.

"What?"

"I talked to *Ojiichan* about moving in here. He's already packing."

"He's awesome." Liv wanted to go back to kissing, but something in Grace's eyes stopped her. "But?"

"But he's a lot more enthusiastic than I expected. And, being a pushy old man, wants to move in next week."

"Seriously? Next week? That's great, right?"

"For him, yes. I didn't get much choice in this one, though. He pretty much told me to pack and get it over with."

Liv brushed a strand of hair from Grace's eyes and tucked it behind her ear. She held her face with that hand, and Grace leaned into her touch. "Are you good with this? You can stay at the cabin if you need to—until we get Harry settled. Unless he plans to sell it right away."

"He's not selling it. He wants to keep it for Matt or my parents when they come to visit so they don't have to go to a hotel."

"You can still stay there."

Grace shook her head. "No. He's not having it. He used his army voice and ordered me to pack. He said it's tough love time. I have to get past my insecurities and move in with you." She smiled. "He reminded me most of my stuff is here anyway. What's the difference?"

"The difference is your independence, right?"

"I won't be losing anything." Grace kissed her lightly on the lips. "I'll be gaining a life with you, instead. I should have seen it all along, Olivia. I'm sorry I didn't. I never know when the damage from Carly will crop up and make me afraid to walk down the street by myself. But I promise you I'm working on it."

"I know you are. It's never been a question for me. I don't want you to do something because Harry or I pushed you into it. Got it? Promise me you're good with this." Liv searched those deep brown eyes before her and found no trace of doubt. But she needed to hear it.

Grace didn't let her down. "I promise. It's about time we started our life together, don't you think?"

"I do." Liv kissed her again, this time with a much lighter heart. To think they'd be together all the time, in the same space—incredible. She almost wished she could go to the cabin and get Grace's stuff right now. Almost. The woman kissing her clearly had other ideas, and Liv was not about to disappoint her.

****

Warrick was kind enough to give Terry an empty office to make her noon phone call. Her nerves were rattled at the prospect of a confrontation with Preston. Sally's calm voice greeted her after two rings.

"Hello, Mrs. Alexander. I've got Mr. Preston here in my office. Mrs. Preston couldn't come. Are you all set?"

"I am. Thanks, Mrs. Johnson."

"Now, it's my understanding Bryce told Felicia she has to attend a different school and she can't stay at Whitehorse Elementary. Is that correct?"

"It's what she told me. And apparently he used the 'R' word again." Terry thought she heard someone in the background and assumed it was Mr. Preston. "I'm sorry, I didn't quite catch that."

"I said, how the hell can you know anything she says is true." Mr. Preston was unnecessarily loud, and Terry had a sudden urge to hit him.

"Because she isn't a liar. I know my daughter."

"And I know my son. Your kid keeps trying to kiss him. I should file sexual harassment charges on her."

"Are you kidding me? They're eight years old. They don't know anything about sex. Like any kid, she sees people kissing and thinks it's how you tell someone you like them," Terry said.

Sally said, "I think we need to take a step back. Let's discuss the issue of Felicia kissing—or trying to kiss—Bryce. Mr. Preston, I have to agree two eight-year-olds kissing is hardly sexual in meaning. Mrs. Alexander, I trust you'll speak to Felicia and explain she should not do this again."

"I already have."

"Mr. Preston, I must impress upon you we will not tolerate any kind of bullying. Which would include your son's use of inappropriate language."

"So what? Her kid gets off scot-free?"

"It's hardly—"

"It's not the same," Sally interrupted her. "She didn't hurt Bryce with words and taunts. There's a difference, Mr. Preston. We can't allow children to think for one moment it's okay to use derogatory words of any kind against other children. Nor can we allow them to think taunting another child is okay. It may seem like nothing to you, but to a child it can be everything. Were you ever bullied as a child, Mr. Preston?"

"No. What's that got to do with anything?"

"Maybe everything," Sally said. "Did you know there are documented cases of children under the age of ten who have committed suicide due to bullying?"

"That's crazy. Little kids don't know how to kill themselves." Mr. Preston didn't sound like he believed his own words. Terry heard his doubt plain as day.

"The Internet gives them a lot of information. As do other kids. My point is we don't know how any child will react to a bully, whether it's a hurtful word or physical harm. We have to stop it the minute we know it's happening."

An uncomfortable silence hung in the air. Terry hoped it meant Sally's words had sunk into Preston's thick brain.

"I'll tell him to stop."

"It's a start, but please do more," Sally said. "Tell Bryce why he needs to stop. Explain the consequences of his actions. It will go a long way coming from his father."

"I'll try," Mr. Preston said. Terry heard the distinct sound of a chair scraping across the floor. "I have to get to work."

Terry released the breath she'd been holding and spoke when the door to Sally's office opened and closed. "Thanks, Sally. I don't know how you do it."

"Unfortunately, I've had a lot of practice. It will probably happen again, too. Might not be Bryce, but I'm sure some other kid will pick up on the word and its use."

"At least I've got you in my corner."

"She's a sweet child, but I think you already know that."

"I do." Terry smiled. "I should get back to work, too. Thanks for doing this."

"My pleasure."

Terry disconnected and stuck the phone in her pocket. It sounded like Mr. Preston got the message. Now if things with William could be as easily resolved.

****

The following Wednesday afternoon, Liv and Grace went to the community center. After getting their lists figured out, they needed to secure the building for a second day. Grace arrived at Liv's office before lunch, and they walked, hand-in-hand, to the center.

Liv had a giddy feeling in her stomach as they approached the building. The planning for the wedding had gone on for a few months now but looking at the center made her realize it would soon be a reality. Amazing.

Grace squeezed her hand, and Liv returned the gesture. She had a smile on her face as big as Liv's. Maybe she was thinking the same thing. It was going to happen. Liv gave her a quick kiss before they entered the center.

Genta Dubois, the center manager, greeted them. "Hello, you two. To what do I owe the pleasure?"

Grace said, "We hit a tiny snag with our wedding plans, and we need your help."

Genta's expression was dubious. "I can try."

"We need to book the center for an extra night." Grace gave Liv a significant look. "Someone plans to have half the city attend, so we need to split up the festivities."

"Two parties?" Genta laughed. "Sounds exhausting."

"But fun," Liv said. "Seriously. I can't get married and not invite the guys I work with."

"Is that who the second party is for?"

"Mostly, yes. I mean, they're important to me. Besides, the first time I got married—mistake it turned out to be—we eloped. The guys at work were upset about it. Let me say I never knew men could be so sensitive. I heard about it for weeks."

"So, you want the night right after your wedding reception?"

"Yes, please." Grace held a little tighter to Liv's hand as they followed Genta into her tiny corner office. They waited patiently while she checked her planner.

"Done. Under one condition." She grinned up at them. "You let me provide the drinks. I could use an excuse to enjoy a good party."

"Deal." Liv shook her hand once Grace released it. "Thanks, Genta. Seriously. You have no idea how much this helps us."

"If it keeps the newlyweds-to-be from having a fight, I'm all for it."

"Oh, there was no fight," Grace said. "I told her no more than fifty guests. Period. And like a good fiancée, she said, 'Yes, dear,' and came up with this crazy idea of a second party. I have a feeling I'll be asleep on the flight to Avignon."

"Avignon? In France? Seriously?" Liv was surprised by Genta's sudden fit of laughter. "Gracie, I hope you speak French, because if you rely on this one to do it for you, you'll end up on a boat ride to the middle of the Mediterranean with no way home."

"Ha-ha." Liv stuck her tongue out at Genta. "My French is passable."

"Your French is horrible," Grace said. "I've heard it. Don't think for a moment I'm going to live here and not learn French. In fact, I've been taking classes."

"And I'm just finding this out why?" Liv wondered if some weird conspiracy existed to make her look like an idiot.

"I was going to surprise you, but now I'm thinking you should come with me. It wouldn't hurt to at least try to speak French while we're there."

"They all speak English," Liv said. "And when did this discussion become about my language skills?"

Grace shrugged and gave her a conciliatory kiss. "Because it's fun to tease you. You're easy. No worries, babe. I got this. Languages are my thing, remember? *Je t'aime*, Olivia."

"I love you, too. Thanks, Genta—for the room booking. Not for busting my ass over my French."

"I was taking Gracie's side. I like her better than you."

Liv resisted the urge to flip off her friend as they left the center. She didn't mind the teasing and was honestly glad to know Grace was making friends of her own. Liv thought it was important for Grace to be comfortable in Whitehorse. She wasn't even a little surprised to learn Grace was taking French lessons.

"Want to get something to eat?" Grace asked, taking her hand as they meandered toward Liv's office.

"Got a spot in mind?"

"There's this new restaurant I'd like to try out. It's the one near Burke Park."

"Anything you want, honey." Liv kissed Grace on the cheek. "Thanks for letting me have a second party. It means a lot to me."

"I know it does." Grace pulled Liv into a quick embrace. "And as for the French stuff, it's something fun I decided to do. I planned to speak French once we got to Avignon. Thought it'd be cute to see the look on your face, but I got the reaction I wanted."

"And? Was it cute?"

"It was." Grace sounded very satisfied with herself. "But I'm biased because I think you're cute all the time."

Liv chuckled. "Nice save. I'm glad we're having a real, honest-to-God wedding with all our friends. I missed it when Jane and I eloped."

"You never told me you two eloped," Grace said.

Liv faced Grace. She didn't appear mad, but Liv sensed her disappointment. Liv hated talking about Jane, especially after the woman nearly ruined her relationship with Grace. "I try not to think about it. It was the most impulsive thing I've ever done, and my parents—my mom especially—were furious. Not to mention the shit I got from my brothers."

"Because you ran off or because of Jane?"

"Both. We were together all of a month before we eloped. Spent the weekend in Toronto and flew back to what I thought would be well-wishers, but no. A lot of hurt feelings. Sara didn't talk to me for two weeks. I don't know what the hell I was thinking."

Grace brought their linked hands closer and placed soft kisses on Liv's knuckles. "You weren't thinking, you were feeling. It's what you do."

"I guess. I wish I hadn't. I know I told you about her sleeping around on me and how she up and left one day without a single word, but I never told you the hardest part."

"What?"

"I had to take care of the annulment and clean up all her messes. Unpaid bills, money missing from our joint account, and the savings all gone. Not to mention I was a complete basket case the entire time. If it wasn't for Sara and my family, I don't know what I'd have done."

Grace kissed her tenderly. "I love you."

"I love you, too."

"And if I ever see Jane again, I'll slap her."

Liv smiled. "No you won't. But thanks for the sentiment. I hope she's gone for good this time. I did hear she was headed to British Columbia. They can have her."

"Still, if she comes back…"

"Gotcha." Liv laughed, but the sound died in her throat. Parked a few blocks from them was a very distinctive green Jaguar, close enough to First National Bank the driver could see the front door. Liv recognized Angel seated behind the wheel, though she was too far away to tell what she was doing.

Something in her gut told Liv this was bad. The police still needed to talk to her about the assault on Terry, and Liv didn't trust Angel to leave Sara alone. Before she realized it, Liv was halfway to the street corner.

Grace jogged to catch up to her, clearly surprised by her sudden dash.

"Olivia, what are you doing?" she asked when she reached her. "What's wrong?"

"Angel," Liv said as if it were all the explanation needed. In her mind, it was enough.

Grace grabbed her arm and stopped her. "Oh, no, you don't."

"Oh, yes I do." Liv was determined. Her protective button was pushed, and with one thing was on her mind: Angel Harrison. "I want to talk to her, Gracie."

"You told Sara you wouldn't. You can't go back on your promise."

"You don't know Angel like I do. I can get her to leave Sara alone."

"I'm sure you think you can, but I won't let you." Grace's grip was strong, and Liv found it hard to free herself. "You're a good friend, and Sara knows it, but she's also a big girl. She's told the police and her boss what's happening. As long as Angel stays away from her, everything is fine. If you go over there, you'll end up in a fight with her or make threats that might come back to bite you in the ass. And you'll make more trouble for Sara. Is this what you want?"

It wasn't. She wanted desperately to protect her best friend, but she also really, really wanted to smash her fist into Angel's face. She almost wished she'd hit her the last time she confronted her over Sara. But Grace was right. Confronting Angel was a bad idea.

Liv took a couple of deep breaths to calm her temper. After a few moments, she pried Grace's fingers off her arm. "I'm sorry."

"Don't be. You're a good friend, Olivia. And Sara knows it." She pulled Liv so close they were sharing the same air. "Don't be sorry. I'm not."

"I would have probably slammed her head into the steering wheel."

"I doubt it, even though you might want to, but there's no point arguing with her. She'll do what she wants."

"I know. But I might have enjoyed it."

"For a few seconds, sure. But you know being violent never fixes anything."

The emotions in her words were reflected in Grace's eyes, showing her sadness now. Liv pressed her lips to Grace's in an attempt to remove the sadness. "It doesn't," she said, her lips hovering over Grace's. "Thanks for stopping me."

"You're welcome." Grace kissed Liv back. "Want to go to lunch now?"

"I do. After I call Charley. She needs to know Angel's in town." Liv kept an eye on Angel's car while she waited for Charley to pick up.

"Hey Liv. What's up?"

"Angel Harrison is sitting in her pretty little sports car in front of National right now. Thought you'd like to know."

"Do not engage, Templeton. You hear me?"

"Damn. Does everyone think I have a hair-trigger temper?"

Charley and Grace chorused, "Yes."

Charley said, "I'll get someone over there to make contact with her. You wander off in the opposite direction."

"Yes, ma'am," Liv said and disconnected the call.

"Ma'am? She's two years younger than you."

Liv shrugged. "Can't help it. She's got the authority thing down to a science. Ordered me to wander off in the opposite direction of Angel."

"Good plan."

Liv stole one last look at Angel before giving Grace her full attention. "Can we wait until the police show up? I know the bank has security people, but I'd feel better—"

"We can wait." Grace directed her to a bench near the bus stop. "I worry about your impulsive streak sometimes."

"I've heard that more times than I can count. From Sara, my parents, even David, and he usually encourages my impulsiveness."

"Your brother is worse than you are. He's a bad influence."

"But he's a fun influence sometimes. You didn't mind when he impulsively started dancing with you at the pub a few weeks ago."

"He's a good dancer." Grace bumped shoulders with Liv. "Must run in the family. Plus, he's kinda cute."

"God, don't tell him. I'll never hear the end of it. Did I ever tell you he used to try to steal my girlfriends when we were in school?"

"Seriously? Wasn't it a little awkward? Did it make you mad?"

"Both," Liv said. "He was successful twice. The second time I gave him a black eye and was grounded for a month."

"Matt and I never fought when we were kids," Grace said. "Maybe a disagreement here and there, but never an outright fight, and certainly not over a girl." Grace twined her fingers with Liv's. "We never could agree on women. Our tastes are very different."

"But you're twins. Aren't you supposed to be the same? You guys finish each other's sentences."

Grace gave her an indulgent smile. "We finish each other's sentences because we've always been close. When you grow up as a military brat, you don't get a lot of long-lasting friends. Maybe a year or two here and there, but Matt and I always had each other. I think we'd still be close even if we weren't twins. Being the same age made things easier is all. We liked being in the same class and having the same homework and stuff."

"If David and I had been in the same class, we'd have killed each other. Even though I hated him sometimes, and wanted to punch him a lot, I will say the dumbass has had my back whenever I needed it. Even when we weren't speaking."

"What about Timothy?"

"He was too much younger than us. We were in middle school when he was in kindergarten. And once we were done with uni he was finishing high school. Our social circles never met, except for the time

Timothy came out to me." Liv grinned at the memory of her younger brother taking her by the hand and leading her into his room, his expression serious as he closed the door and blurted out he was gay.

Liv giggled. "I wish you could have seen the look on his face. I mean, he had posters of the latest boy bands all over his bedroom walls. And it's not like he was ever subtle about things, like checking out cute guys. He tells me he's gay and I said, 'Duh. Was that all you wanted to tell me?'"

"Poor guy. He obviously thought it was important to tell you, and you burst his bubble."

"He did, but then we both started laughing and spent a few hours talking about it. He already knew Mom and Dad wouldn't care, but I guess he looks up to me so he told me first. He made David figure it out on his own."

"How long did it take?"

Liv grinned. "Two years, when Timothy took his boyfriend to prom."

Grace laughed hard enough tears came to her eyes. "That's mean."

"No, that's David. He's a dumbass. Remember?"

"I believe you've told me once or twice."

An RCMP patrol car passed them and parked at an angle in front of Angel's Jag to block her from leaving. Two officers got out and approached her. When Angel rolled her window down to speak to one of them, her gaze met Liv's.

Liv gave her an instant smile and stood up, pulling Grace with her. "Well, our work here is done."

"Ready for lunch?"

"I have a better idea." Liv pressed her lips to Grace's, not caring about the people walking around them or the idea Angel might be watching. Kissing her was deliciously sexy, and when her hands found their way under Grace's coat she stopped. Grace wasn't complaining.

Their gazes met and they shared a laugh. Grace took her hand and tugged her in the direction of the restaurant.

Chapter Fifteen

The moving van arrived at Liv's house at one o'clock on Tuesday afternoon. She found it a little weird Harry refused to wait until the weekend, but she didn't mind. She watched while Grace directed the movers with each box and piece of furniture, first placing everything of Harry's in his room. The room would be a little crowded until the extension was built.

Harry, thanks to Sara, was having lunch at Marge's in Blue River and wouldn't be back for another couple of hours. Liv waited to approach Grace until the movers were finished, which didn't take as long as she thought. Maybe all of half an hour. She wrapped her arms around Grace from behind and pulled her close, enjoying the feel of her lean body. "Did Harry leave half his stuff at the cabin? Didn't seem like a lot came out of that van."

"He didn't need the stuff in his kitchen, since he never used anything besides the microwave. He and *Obaachan* never did have a lot of stuff. She made sure of it because they were always moving around while he was in the Army. She taught my dad to make do with minimal stuff and did the same for us as kids. Kinda handy when you're moving around your whole life."

"Your grandma always gave good advice. I liked her a lot."

"Me, too. So, other than a healthy collection of musicals on DVD, it's mostly clothes and pictures."

"Then it won't take long to get him settled." Liv nibbled on Grace's ear, eliciting a groan from her.

Grace gently pulled away and twisted around to face Liv. "The sooner we get moving, the sooner we'll be done. I do have stuff of my own to put away."

"But can it wait?" Liv waggled her eyebrows and got the expected laugh out of Grace. "Fine. All work and no play..."

"Makes Olivia a frustrated girl. I know." Grace patted her cheek. "You'll live."

"I don't think so. I can feel myself dying right now."

"Uh-huh." Grace slipped away when Liv tried to pull her into another embrace. "You're not helping."

"I am helping. I'm helping celebrate you're finally here. In *our* home."

Grace opened a box of clothes and started putting them into the chest of drawers they'd purchased for Harry. "It is. And once we're married, I'll let you make it official."

"Seriously?" Liv sat on the twin bed and watched Grace, who kept her back to her most of the time. "Can I ask you something? I've been thinking about it, but I'm not sure how you'll react to it."

"Sure," Grace said, continuing to work. "You can ask me anything, you silly woman. I don't mind."

"Uh, you might." Liv waited until Grace finished and stopped her from opening another box. "I mean it. It's not all that easy to ask, because I'm not sure you'll say yes."

"Olivia, ask me." Grace touched the side of her face, her fingers gentle against Liv's skin.

Liv leaned into the feel of them and sighed. "I'd like you to take my last name. We have to finish the application for our marriage license, and I'd be honored if you would share my name." She stared into those deep, brown eyes in front of her and searched for the answer. She was surprised to find them wet.

"Yes. I'll take your last name." Grace closed the space between them, wrapped her arms around Liv, and kissed her tenderly. "What took you so long to ask me?"

Liv stole another kiss. "I was afraid it would sort of turn out like when I asked you to move in. I don't want you to feel like I'm smothering you. But—I don't know. It's kind of important to me we share a last name. And I'm proud of my name so...are you sure?"

"I am. I've been thinking about it. I chose not to take Carly's name because it didn't feel right. Maybe it was a premonition. But this time it feels right. Like it's something I need to do." She held Liv's face in her hands and kept their gazes locked. Liv fell in love all over again.

"Thanks. I don't know what I did to deserve you, but I'm damn glad I did it."

"You showed up at my grandfather's mine at a time in my life when I was open to something new. The crappy part is your dad and *Ojiichan* played matchmaker and now they're both insufferable on the subject."

Liv chuckled. "Maybe after we're married they'll shut up."

"They won't shut up until we give them grandchildren."

"How many?"

"How many what?" Grace asked.

"How many grandchildren? I like the idea of even numbers. I had two brothers, but Timothy was much younger and more like a baby sister than a brother. But I think two of each would be nice."

"Do you? And who will give birth to these children?" Grace raised one eyebrow, her mouth lifted in a smile.

"Both of us." Liv surprised herself with the proclamation. She'd never actually thought about the subject, yet it felt completely right and natural. "We can flip a coin to see who goes first."

Now the tears flowed from Grace's eyes, and if not for the beautiful smile on her face, Liv would have been worried. It took a moment for Grace to speak, and when she did, her voice held a slight tremor. "You—you're amazing. I love you. And yes, we can totally flip to see who gets pregnant first." She kissed Liv again, slowly, tenderly, as tears streamed down Liv's face.

"We'll be cool moms," Liv said. "I'll be the cool mom for sure. You'll probably be the mean one."

"Thanks a lot." Grace playfully hit Liv in the arm. "Maybe I'll be the one to spoil them."

"I think it's Harry's job. But probably we'll both spoil them a little."

"A lot."

They shared a laugh. Liv said, "Now that we've got our future planned out, should we maybe get Harry's stuff in order? It'd be a nice surprise when he gets home."

"It would be," Grace said, not making a move. "But I kind of think I have other ideas on how to spend the next hour or so." Her eyes tracked to Liv's lips, and she pressed her mouth against them, leaving no doubt as to how she wanted to spend her time.

Liv guided her to their bedroom without a single complaint.

****

Terry stood outside the designated meeting room at the community center. She was dressed in navy slacks, black shoes, white blouse, and dark-blue jacket. It was the tenth outfit she tried on, hoping to appear as professional as possible. Jackie seemed confident about the mediation, but Terry's heart hammered in her chest.

William hadn't managed to get the date moved to Wednesday, but it was moved up to the following Friday. Still too soon for Terry, but also not soon enough. Her brain couldn't settle on which was better. Jackie assured her they were ready. Hell, Jackie would probably need a box to bring all the paperwork she and Terry put together yesterday.

She paced to get rid of her nervous energy. It was her own fault for being damn early. Jackie said she'd meet her at quarter to nine. The clock read eight fifteen.

A door opened down the hall, and Terry was shocked to see Sara stroll toward her. Their eyes met and held as Sara came to her without a word and embraced her. She leaned into Sara's body and allowed the tension to melt away.

"I promised you a hug when you got home."

"I needed to meet with Jackie…"

"I know." Sara placed a kiss on Terry's cheek but didn't let her go.

"Thanks." Terry closed her eyes and rested her head against Sara's shoulder. "How'd you know?"

"That you needed me? I had help."

"My mom sent you a text message."

"Bingo." Sara stepped out of their embrace, and Terry shivered at the loss of warmth. "I told my boss I had a meeting and I'd be late."

"I kind of hate it when my mom does this stuff, because she's always right. I'm glad you showed up. I needed a hug."

"There's more where that one came from."

Jackie joined them, though Terry never heard her come in. "I didn't expect you this early. Sara? What're you doing here?"

"Hey, Jackie." Sara gave her a quick hug. "Terry needed a friend. She's over the top nervous about this whole thing."

"I know." Jackie grinned at Terry. "We've got this. I'm sure of it."

"How can you be sure?" Terry asked.

"I have a statement from Jennifer Dillson regarding Felicia." Jackie glanced behind her as if to see if anyone else were around. "Is it okay to talk about this in front of Sara?"

Terry didn't hesitate. "Yes."

"Jennifer is disputing his claims. She says it's not in Felicia's best interest to be with them. She belongs with her mother."

The blood drained from Terry's face. Was it possible? She'd not talked to Jennifer since this whole mess started. Was she on Terry's side? Sara put her arm around Terry's waist and helped her stay on her feet when she swayed. "You're serious?"

"I am. She offered to come here today. I told her the statement would be enough for now. We can always do a video conference if the mediator wants to hear from her."

"Wow. How did William take it? He's got to be pissed."

Jackie's grin nearly split her face. "He doesn't know. We're surprising him with it in"—she glanced at her watch—"twenty minutes. I need to step in and speak to the mediator for a moment. You'll be all right out here for a bit?"

Terry nodded, unable to form any sensible words. Once Jackie was in the office, Terry sought a chair along the wall and sat down heavily. Sara stayed with her and held her hand. "Talk to me," Sara said. "I can see a lot is going on in that brain of yours."

"I don't know. I didn't expect this. I mean, I've always had a good relationship with Jennifer. She and Ann were close, and she adores Felicia. I guess I thought she'd be all for getting custody of her. It's been hard seeing Jennifer since Ann died. They're so much alike. They always cowed to whatever William said—until Ann and I got together. Then Ann was done with him."

"Maybe Jennifer is as well." Sara bumped shoulders with her. "This is a good thing, right?"

They both looked up in time to see William confidently stroll down the hallway, his lawyer at his side. He barely acknowledged Terry before going into the meeting room. Terry saw the smug expression, and her confidence renewed. This was happening, and she was about to see that smug look wiped off his face.

"Yes. This is a very good thing."

****

Two hours later, Terry stood in her office. She immediately

changed into more comfortable work attire and settled behind the desk. She had a lot to do regarding the Dresden project, but her mind and heart weren't in it. Her concentration simply wasn't there. After almost an hour of nothing getting done, she chose to leave. A glance at the clock told her it was nearly lunchtime. She wondered if Sara had plans.

She made the short walk to the bank in no time and lightly rapped on the doorframe to Sara's office. The door was open, and Sara looked up from a pile of paperwork and smiled. Terry found herself captivated by blue-green eyes. When she looked at them, she saw love.

"Hey there. You hungry?"

Sara laughed. "Does a bear shit in the woods?"

"Sometimes he shits in a field. Or in front of a mine office. Or next to the miners' trailers. You never know. They're sort of unpredictable."

"Well, I'm not." Sara stood up and grabbed her coat. "I'm always hungry. Head to the first restaurant you see and buy me food."

"Why do I have to buy?" Terry asked, following her out of the bank.

"Because you're the one asking me out."

"I'm asking you out? I said are you hungry. How is that asking you out?"

Sara tossed her a fake mean look and Terry laughed. Sara said, "Because the question was rhetorical. Therefore, you were asking me out." She kept walking, taking a right turn out of the bank and toward a popular restaurant two buildings down. They were quiet as they entered and were seated almost immediately.

Terry didn't bother looking at the menu. They'd been there dozens of times while they were dating, and she remembered what to order. "So, it's a date is it? That why we're here?"

"We're here because it's closest to the bank and I'm starved. Feed me."

"Wow, grumpy much?"

"When I'm starving." Sara didn't read the menu either, and they made their orders as soon as the server arrived. Once he left, Sara reached across the table and took Terry's hand in hers. "How'd it go? I wish I could have gone in there with you. I'd have held your hand the whole time."

"Talk about me, not you. Got it. The mediator was nice enough, and she didn't bat an eye when William tried to do his usual I'm-better-than-you shit. She asked a lot of questions and took a ton of notes, even though she recorded the meeting. William didn't like the stuff she asked and got pissy when she brought up his use of the 'R' word. I think he showed his true colors, to be honest."

"What'd Jackie say?"

"She's confident our case was strong enough to prove I'm a good parent and Felicia ought to stay with me. She gave her statements from Felicia's teachers as well as Sally Johnson, the assistant principal at her school. She talked to a lot of people."

"It's her job and she's damn good at it. I'm glad she was there to help you out. If she's confident, I'd say it's pretty much a done deal. When will you know for sure?"

"Could be a week, could be a month. Depends on how busy the mediator is. In the meantime, I have to play nice with William and let him see Felicia, though I did get them to agree he can't see her alone. Mom or me have to be there. Mom's letting him come over tomorrow afternoon. I'm going to make myself scarce. I'm afraid I'll end up in a fight with him, and I don't want Felicia to see it."

Sara squeezed her hand and let go when the server brought their food. They ate in silence for a few moments before Terry spoke again. "Tell me about your morning. I get the impression it wasn't a nice one."

"Nope, though the day started out nice because I got to give you my promised hug." She winked at Terry, who found the gesture adorable. "But then I got a phone call, and sometimes it takes one call to turn the day into shit."

"Who was it?"

Sara hesitated and the fries in her hand landed back on the plate. "Angel called me."

"Angel? What the hell did she want?"

"To apologize. I told her to go to hell and hung up on her."

Terry's fist clenched so tightly her knuckles turned white. "I'm going to kick her ass."

"No, you're not." Sara gently put her hand over Terry's fist. "It won't solve anything, and you'll end up hurting your hand. Maybe worse."

"She's supposed to leave you alone. You have a protection order. She's not allowed to call you."

"I know, but she did and it's over. I promise."

"You sure I can't go after her?" Terry asked, almost pleading for Sara to let her beat the crap out of Angel. Not that she was prone to violence, but Angel seemed to bring those thoughts out in her.

"No way," Sara said. She touched Terry's cheek, her fingers soft as they brushed Terry's skin. "I'm serious. It's bad enough she hurt you once. I don't want it to happen again. Please, promise me you'll stay clear of her."

"I promise." Terry met Sara's concerned gaze and knew she'd promise Sara anything.

"Good. Between you and Livvy I think I've got the best protection service around."

"She wants to beat up Angel, too? I knew I liked Liv."

Sara rolled her eyes. "She does and I made her make the same promise. I told Greg about her calling me, and I think he might say something to her. Anyway, I'm trying to not let her ruin my day."

"But you should tell the police. I heard from Charley she refused to give them a DNA sample. They're waiting for a judge to issue a subpoena for it. Might take a while, and they need to know she's called you."

"I'll file a report when I get back to the office, okay?"

Terry kissed her on the cheek and leaned back in her chair. "Yes. Now, no more talk of Angel or William. Deal?"

"Deal."

"Since this isn't a sort of a date, how about you let me take you on a real sort of date."

"A real sort of date?" Sara laughed. "What, exactly, is a real sort of date?"

"One where I take you to dinner, maybe a movie, and spend quality time with you, just the two of us. It's about time we got to know each other properly."

"Wow. So friends going out for a nice night. Right?"

"Something like that. It's a start at least."

Sara's smile reached her eyes, and it warmed Terry's heart. "When?" Sara asked.

"Tonight?"

"Oh, I can't. Bren's coming over. It's beer, pizza, and a sappy movie night. It's the least I can do after breaking her heart."

"How'd you break her heart?"

"I told her I can't go out with her anymore. I mean, we weren't seriously dating—at least I wasn't—but I was always honest with her. I'm sad I hurt her feelings, but we're still good friends. I like having her around. I'd like you two to meet up eventually."

"I'd like that, too."

She took Terry's hand in hers, her touch gentle, intimate. "But I'm free tomorrow. You said you need to make yourself scarce when William shows up. How about being scarce with me?"

"It's a date."

"It certainly is."

****

It was well past seven, and Terry had yet to arrive. She was never late without a text or phone call. The roads and weather, for once, were clear. Sara checked her phone. Nothing.

Something didn't feel right. She started to call Terry as her phone rang. She answered right away. "Hey there. I thought we were heading to the pub tonight?"

"I was." The voice didn't belong to Terry. The unmistakable sound sent shivers down Sara's spine—and not in a good way. "I'd hoped you'd be there, since it's where you like to go with your women."

"You need to stop calling me, Angel. I'll tell the cops—"

"Don't give a shit what you tell them. It doesn't matter anymore." Angel sounded drunk. Sara wanted to hang up on her, but she hesitated when Angel said, "I had to take the one shot I had. Kind of messy, but you best believe I'll get you eventually."

"No, you won't. I'm calling the cops now, Angel. Goodbye."

"Hope the blue-haired chick makes it."

"What?" Sara's knees suddenly gave out, and she sat on the floor. "What are you talking about?"

"I'm coming for you next." Angel disconnected the call, and Sara's entire body shook. What did she mean? Was she talking about Bren?

Without another thought, Sara called Bren. But it wasn't her voice that answered the phone.

"Sara? This is Izzy."

"Izzy? Why are you on Bren's phone?" A million thoughts went through Sara's mind, but she did her best to quash them all as she waited for Izzy to respond.

"You need to get to Whitehorse Hospital right now. Bren's in the emergency room."

"What? What happened?"

"Some maniac ran her down in the parking lot of the pub. She stopped by for a minute to talk to me, and when she walked out to her car, bam! This car comes out of nowhere and runs her down."

"How bad is she?" Sara knew who the maniac was.

Izzy didn't respond. Sara heard voices in the background but couldn't make out what they were saying.

"Izzy, talk to me. Is she okay?"

"I don't know. They won't let me back there. I'm not family."

"I'll be there in ten minutes. Have you called her parents?"

"Yeah, but they're on vacation in Hawaii. They're trying to get a flight home, but it might not be until tomorrow or later. I don't know what else to do."

"It's okay. Do your moms know where you are?"

"Mom does, but she had to stay and deal with the cops. *Maman's* on her way, but she was at a friend's house, and it's going to take her two hours to get here. Sara, I'm scared. I don't know what to do."

"Take it easy. I'll be there in a few minutes."

Sara hung up and got into her car. She took a couple deep breaths to try to calm down. It didn't work. She shook hard enough she couldn't get her keys into the ignition. "Dammit!"

She rested her head on the steering wheel and took a few more deep breaths. She would not hyperventilate. She needed to get to the hospital and be there for Bren and Izzy. How the hell could this happen?

Her brain went into autopilot, and she dialed Terry's number. Before she answered, Sara said, "Terry are you on the way? I need you. I have to get to the hospital. Bren's been hurt, and I—I can't stop shaking."

"I'm on your street. Don't move."

Terry arrived at the house in minutes and tapped on the window of Sara's car. She opened the door and had her arms around Sara immediately. "It's okay. I'm here. Want me to drive?"

"Please," Sara said against Terry's shoulder. "I don't know why I can't stop shaking. I need to be strong for her. Terry, someone ran her down on purpose. In the parking lot of the pub. I'm pretty sure it was Angel."

"Fuck." Terry helped her into her truck, and they were off to the hospital. Sara filled her in on as much information as she had. "And her parents are stuck in Hawaii?"

"Yeah. Shit!" Sara sent a quick text to her friend, Dana Smith, and explained to Terry she was the travel agent booked the McAfferty's vacation. Dana was quick to reply. "Dana says she's working on a flight for them, but no matter what, she's can't get them out of Hawaii before tonight. Best she can do is get them here in two days. Fuck. Two days."

"I can't imagine being that far from Felicia and needing to get to her. Those poor people."

"Yeah." Sara fell silent. They pulled into the parking area of the emergency room, got out of the truck, and Terry took her hand as they rushed inside. Sara immediately sought out Izzy and was greeted with a strangling hug. Izzy sobbed, and it took everything for Sara to calm her down. "Where is she?"

"I don't know. They won't tell me anything. I saw it happen, Sara. I saw her get hit—she flew over the hood of the car like a ragdoll. I thought she was dead!"

"Shh. Let me find out what's going on."

"They won't tell you anything," Izzy said. "You're not family."

"Watch me," Sara said with renewed strength. "You stay with Terry."

Izzy didn't argue as Sara marched up to the Information desk. "Hello. My name is Sara Hyatt. I understand my girlfriend was brought in. Brenda McAfferty?"

The man wore a name badge that said Miles, Volunteer. He smiled kindly at Sara and consulted his computer. "Yes. She came in by ambulance about half an hour ago."

"Can I see her?"

"Let me check for you." Miles picked up his phone and spoke quietly while Sara watched. When he got his answer, he said, "A nurse will come for you, but it might be a few minutes. You can have a seat while you wait."

"Did she tell you how Bren's doing?"

"She didn't. I'm sorry."

"Thanks."

Sara returned to Izzy and Terry, both of whom were now seated in the plastic chairs closest to the Information desk. "A nurse will come out in a few minutes to get me." She took Izzy's hand in hers. "It's going to take at least two days to get Bren's parents here. Dana's working on it, but I thought you should know right now you and I are her family. Okay?"

"The guy at the counter didn't think so. He wouldn't tell me anything."

"I told them I'm her girlfriend. It got me in the door. Once I find out what's happening, I'll make sure you see her, too. Promise."

"She's my best friend," Izzy said through her tears. "I don't want to lose her."

"Me either." Sara pulled her into another hug and spoke to Terry. "Thanks for getting me here. I'm not sure I'd have made it otherwise."

"You would have. I'm sure of it." Terry's grin reassured her.

"Miss Hyatt?" A woman dressed in light-green scrubs entered the waiting area.

Sara glanced at Terry. "Can you stay?"

"Yes."

"Thanks." She joined the woman at the Information desk. "Hi. I'm Sara. Bren's girlfriend."

"I'm Dr. Lynn. Let's go somewhere more private so I can update you on her condition." She led Sara into an unmarked room and sat down with her on a grey, vinyl couch. Sara's stomach clenched at the expression on the doctor's face.

"Please tell me how she's doing."

"She's stable right now but headed for surgery. There's internal bleeding, and she'll probably need her spleen removed. But the head injury is the worst of it. She's not been conscious since she got here."

Sara's breath caught in her throat. It sounded like a death sentence. "Can I see her?"

"For a few minutes before we take her up, but I need you to be prepared."

"Will she die? Please, tell me the truth."

Dr. Lynn hesitated. It wasn't much, but enough Sara knew her next words would be hard to hear. "She should be fine after the surgery, if she wakes up. There's a lot of pressure on her brain right now, and while surgery isn't optimal, there's not much choice. We have to stop the bleeding." She took Sara's hand and tried to smile, but it didn't reflect in her eyes; Sara saw sadness. "We found her ID and know she's a donor. But what we don't know is if she'd want to be on life support. Is it something you ever discussed?"

"What? No! She's twenty-two years old!" Sara jumped to her feet as did the doctor. "Why—you have to put her on life support. You can't let her die."

"That's not what I'm saying at all. It's something we need to know, in case a decision has to be made."

"Her parents are in Hawaii. It'll take a couple of days to get them home. Will she make it until then?"

"I can't say. Head injuries are difficult to predict." Dr. Lynn put a hand on Sara's shoulder. "I'm sorry I had to ask. Would you like to see her now?"

"Yes, please."

"Okay, but understand she looks bad and you can only be there for a few minutes. If you're ready, we'll go back."

"I'm ready," Sara said, even if she was anything but. She badly wanted to ask Terry to go with her. She needed her comforting presence.

Dr. Lynn opened the door and guided Sara through the chaos of the emergency room and into a large, single room with a dozen people moving around doing God knows what to Bren. She saw a hint of blue peeking out from white bandages as she got closer. She wanted to hold Bren's hand, but something was attached to her finger. She settled for touching her wrist instead. The bandage on her forehead was bloodstained, and Bren's right eye swollen and discolored. Her left hand was wrapped in bandages, and a weird, solid, red thing hugged her left leg from the knee to the foot.

"Hey there, cutie," she whispered in Bren's ear. She choked on a sob. She didn't want to cry in case Bren heard her. "Don't you dare leave me, Bren. You promised to stick with me through all this crap, and I'm not letting you go. I'll be right here, by your side, until they make me leave. You'll be fine. You hear me? You're going to be fine."

Dr. Lynn gently put her hands on Sara's shoulders. "I'm sorry, we need to take her now." She pulled Sara back a few steps, and before Sara knew it, the bed carrying Bren was whisked away. She stared at the empty space and took note of the medical debris scattered around the room.

"She'll be in surgery for a while. One of the volunteers will show you to the waiting area. It's where the surgeon will come looking for you when he's done. Will you be okay?"

"No. Not until she's okay. But thanks."

"I'll take you back to the main lobby for now and get someone there to take you upstairs as soon as I can. Your friends can go with you. I imagine you won't want to be alone."

Dr. Lynn guided her through the maze of hallways until she was with Izzy and Terry. She thanked Dr. Lynn and filled them in on the situation.

By now Harriet, one of Izzy's moms, was there. She said, "I hope they find the bitch who did this. If Marion finds her first, she's a dead woman."

"You know who did this?" Sara took a seat next to Terry.

"Blue VW with no license plates. Some bitch behind the wheel. It's all the CCTV could get. But I'll never forget the car or her, what I could make out anyway. She looked familiar, and I'm sure I'd recognize her again if I saw her." Harriet kissed the top of Izzy's head, never letting go as she continued to cry. "Marion had me close down the pub. She's still an hour away. I wanted to get Izzy home, but she won't leave."

Sara said, "I need to talk to the police. I might know who it is." She told them of her phone call with Angel. Her stomach roiled and she wanted to throw up. "It's my fault. I mean, if I'd—"

Terry grasped her hand. "No way. If it was Angel, then it's all her doing. You couldn't have known this would happen. You went out with her a couple of times. No way you'd know she'd go all crazy on you like this. Harriet, can you give me the contact info for the officer you talked to?"

"Sure. I've got the number in my cell phone. I'll text it to you."

"Thanks," Terry said. "Once we get to the surgery waiting room, we'll give the officer a call." She gently squeezed Sara's hand. "Okay?"

"Yeah." Sara glanced down at her phone and checked the messages she'd gotten from Dana. "It looks like Dana has Bren's parents leaving on a flight in about an hour. I think I'll call them to update them."

"You okay to do this?" Terry asked.

"No."

"Want me to?"

"You're sweet, but I think I should be the one. I've never met them, but I did talk to her mom, Judy, on the phone once." Sara wiped fresh tears from her face. "But I wouldn't mind if you stay next to me while I do it."

"Not going anywhere." Terry slipped her arm around Sara's waist and held her while she made the hardest phone call of her life.

****

Four hours later, Terry, Sara, Liv, and Grace, along with a few people Terry recognized from the pub, were crowded into a tiny waiting area. Marion Nelson showed up about an hour into their vigil with enough food to feed half the hospital. Terry was grateful for it, as she doubted Sara would be leaving anytime soon and neither of them had eaten.

Terry observed Liv settle beside Sara, her arm firmly around Sara's shoulders. Whatever Liv said caused a tiny smile on Sara's haggard features. Terry wanted to move Liv out of the way, take Sara into her arms, and promise everything would be okay.

But she couldn't.

She considered leaving. It didn't seem like she was doing any good for Sara being there. They'd not talked since Liv and Grace arrived. Actually, the only ones to speak were Marion and Harriet.

Charley, their personal Mountie, made it a point to come to the hospital and speak to Sara and left a few minutes ago, after getting a written statement about her call from Angel. As Terry watched the people gathered in the tiny room, she wondered if Angel might come for her next.

Or worse—if she'd come after Sara.

"You okay?"

The soft voice in her ear startled Terry. She found Grace standing beside her, her gaze on Liv and Sara.

"I don't know. I mean, it probably should have been me. I'm the one that got her all pissed off the other day. And I broke her nose, too."

"Maybe. We don't know what was going through her head. Sara told me she thinks Angel's been watching her for a while now."

"Since when?"

"Since soon after you guys called the cops on her at Sara's house. I don't think it would have mattered if it was you or Bren or me or Olivia. Angel purposely went after someone Sara cares about." She faced Terry with a determined expression. "And it's why we're not leaving her alone for a single second until Angel is in jail. I'm heading home as soon as Bren's out of surgery. I'll get some sleep and trade places with Olivia and she can do the same. One of us can bring fresh clothes and toiletries for Sara. There's no sense in trying to get her to leave."

"Good. She needs you guys right now."

"She needs you, too," Grace said. "I think it'd be a great idea if you sat with her for a while. I'd like a few moments alone with Olivia."

Terry hesitated. Would Sara want her to? Their situation was up and down right now. But it's what a friend would do, right? Go sit with her. Be there for her. Right?

"I will."

"Good." Grace gave her a one-armed hug. "Olivia, can I see you for a minute please?"

Liv and Grace shared some unspoken communication as Liv rose to join them. She nodded at Terry and said, "Go. She needs you," then left the room with Grace.

Terry settled next to Sara. "How you holding up?"

"I'm not." Sara's shoulders slumped. She leaned forward and rested her arms on her knees. "It's all my fault. I should have kept my mouth shut and never told Angel I was seeing someone. Maybe she wouldn't have gone looking for her."

"She was stalking you, Sara. None of this is your fault. How could it be? You can't control that crazy bitch. No more than you can control the weather." Terry covered Sara's hand with hers. "Please don't waste your energy on her. Think about Bren and keep good thoughts she'll be okay. She's young and healthy and pretty soon a doctor will come in here and tell us she's fine."

"It's hard not to beat myself up."

"I get it." Terry put her arm around Sara and pulled her close. Sara's head rested on her shoulder. "You're a beautiful person, Sara."

"Why do you think she did it? Was she getting back at me?"

"Angel's the only one who knows that, honey. And I doubt you'll ever hear the truth of it." She gently lifted Sara's face. The hurt in Sara's eyes cut Terry like a knife. "Ultimately, it doesn't matter. She did a horrible thing, and right now we have to be here for Bren and her family. Angel we can deal with later. With any luck, she'll be in jail soon."

"I hope so. You think I should tell my mom it's okay to come here? She's called twice, but I told her dozens of people have been in and out already."

"Sure," Terry said. "She wants to be here for you. Everyone needs their mother sometimes. Want me to call her for you?" She placed a soft kiss on Sara's temple.

"You don't have to, and you don't have to stay here." Sara's eyes pleaded with her to stay, and Terry happily got the message.

"I'm exactly where I want to be." Terry kissed her head again. "Tell you what, you call your mom and I'll get you a plate of food. I haven't seen you touch any of it, and you have to eat."

"I'm not hungry," Sara said, her voice so small it reminded Terry of Felicia when she was cranky.

"It wasn't a request." Terry got up. "Call your mom. I'll be back with food in a minute."

"Thanks." Sara's eyes filled with tears as she met Terry's gaze. "I'm glad you're here."

"Me, too."

****

Liv handed Sara her third cup of coffee and pointed to the couch, such as it was. "Last one and then you sleep. You can't keep using caffeine to stay awake."

"I can." Sara stubbornly stepped away from the couch. Bren now rested in an ICU room, and her exhausted friends moved to the family area located a floor above the surgery wing. The doctor spoke to Sara briefly. They'd removed Bren's spleen and stopped the internal bleeding. At the moment, she was in a medically induced coma. Her left wrist was broken, and both bones of her lower left leg were shattered. She'd need surgery on the leg, but the doctors wanted to wait for the brain swelling to go down. Sara barely comprehended it all and didn't want to consider Bren might not wake up.

Liv's eyes drooped from lack of sleep, but her voice was strong as she said, "I'm putting my foot down. If you won't go home, the least you can do is lie down in here. Look, I got you a pillow and blanket. Sometimes they have cots you can use, but the nurse told me they didn't have any available right now. I'll try to get one of those recliner things they sometimes put in the patient rooms. It'll be more comfy, I think, but for right now, you're going to lie here and like it."

"Pushy much?"

"You know I am." Liv took the coffee from her and tossed it into the trash. Sara's eyes were bloodshot, and her skin so pale it scared Liv. Bren's accident was two days ago, and among Liv, Grace, and Terry, they'd seen Sara nod off a couple of times. Getting her to eat was even more difficult, and unlike Sara it was scary. Liv said, "I do this out of love. Lie down. I promise to wake you if anyone comes out here with news."

"What if Bren's parents call?"

"Then I'll answer your phone." Liv put the phone in her pocket, keeping it away from Sara. "Problem solved."

"I don't think I can sleep."

"Then lie there with your eyes closed and rest."

Sara finally capitulated and was getting comfortable when Charley and Grace walked in. Charley held her RCMP hat in one hand, and her arm rested on the grip of her pistol. She looked worn out and nervous, and Liv's gut clenched at the thought of her giving them more bad news. Grace stood next to her and took her hand. Obviously she already knew what it was.

Sara leapt to her feet, and Liv clutched her other hand. "Hey, Charley."

"Hey." Charley ran her fingers through her short, straight hair and turned her dark eyes to them. "We arrested Angel Harrison an hour ago. I thought I should come tell you in person."

"Good." Sara's grip tightened on Liv's hand.

"She's already got a lawyer."

Liv's protective streak raged. She wanted to kill the bitch. "Do you think there's enough to convict her?"

"Yeah. The CCTV footage Marion gave us was enough to confirm Angel was driving the car. The techs did some magic with it and were able to zoom in on her face. She used a rental car we found abandoned a few kilometers north of the city. It took us this long to find her because she bought a new car and was halfway to Alaska. They're bringing her back here tomorrow. We'll get a DNA sample and confirm she assaulted Terry. She's not going anywhere for a long time."

"Why?" Sara spoke through her tears. "Why would she do this? What did Bren ever do to her?"

"I wasn't there when she was arrested." Charley shifted from one foot to the other. Liv dreaded what she was having trouble getting out. "Let's say she's got some serious mental health issues."

"It's because of me," Sara said.

Liv watched the little bit of color drain from Sara's cheeks. She quickly got her arms around Sara and helped her sit down. "Hey, it's okay. No way is this because of you."

"Yes it is. I told her I didn't want to see her. She knew I was going out with Bren. We saw her the night we had dinner with you and Gracie. She'd been following me, I guess. Anyway, it's not hard to find Bren, you know? Angel saw us at the pub on ladies night. I never thought—I mean why would she do that? I get she's mad at me, but Bren never did anything to her."

Charley shrugged. "It's not about you, Sara. Angel's messed up. If it hadn't been Bren, it might have been someone else at the pub. We can't know for sure. She was looking for someone to hurt."

"It should have been me. I'm the one she's pissed at." Sara lifted sorrowful eyes to Charley, and Liv saw Charley flinch. "Can I see her?"

"Who? Angel?" Charley asked.

"Yes. I want to talk to her."

"Not happening. Sorry. Not unless you're her lawyer. Besides, Bren's the one you should concentrate on. She needs you more than you need to talk to Angel. If something changes, and I can, I'll tell you guys. Deal?"

Liv stood and gave Charley a quick hug. "Thanks. I owe you big time."

"No, you don't," Charley said. "Let me know if you need anything."

Once Charley was gone, Liv re-joined Sara on the couch and put her arms around her. "She's right. It's not your fault."

"Do you think I pushed Angel too far by filing a police report? Should I have backed off?"

Grace sat on Sara's other side, her face drawn. "No. You did everything right. This isn't your fault, Sara. You have to listen to us. Angel was going to do whatever she wanted to do regardless of what you may or may not have said or done. Remember when we talked about her a few weeks ago? I told you she's an abuser?" Grace didn't continue until Sara nodded. "I told you this isn't your fault. You could have said no, and Angel would have probably done all this stuff anyway. You don't have any control over her. None. The important thing here is she's been arrested and she can't hurt anyone else."

"It's so—overwhelming. It's hard not to feel guilty."

"I know." Grace pulled Sara into a tight embrace, and Liv saw she was very close to tears herself. "I understand. It won't go away easily, but we'll work on it. Okay? Promise me—promise us—you get it."

"I do, sort of. I mean, I hear what you're saying."

"Good enough for now." Grace released her and stood on shaking legs. Liv moved closer to make sure Grace didn't fall over. She had no idea Grace would react strongly to the situation and wanted to get her home.

But she couldn't leave Sara.

"I hate her." Sara spoke softly and Liv barely heard her. "She hurt that sweet girl for no other reason than to get at me."

"It that why you want to go see her?" Liv asked, putting her arm around Grace. "Think they'd let you beat her up or something?" Liv tried to keep her tone light, though she was seriously wishing that's exactly what the police would let Sara do.

"No. I don't know. Maybe I want to hear her say it. She hurt Bren because she wanted to hurt me. Or maybe she ran Bren down because she couldn't find me. I guess I want to know for sure."

"Doesn't matter," Liv said. "She can't hurt anyone. If she needs help, she'll get it. If not, she'll end up in jail where she belongs."

"Will it get better?" Sara asked Grace.

"It will. I still blame myself sometimes, but it's a process. It'll take a while."

"Well, you've got Livvy. I'm sure you'll be fine."

Liv moved closer, hugged Sara, and gave her a kiss on the top of her head. "And who do you have, Sara?"

"She's got me," Terry said as she joined them. Sara burst into tears and practically leapt into Terry's embrace.

Liv watched them and knew, deep down, those two were right for each other. That it took such an awful event to bring them back together sucked, but at least they were together. And Sara wasn't alone.

Chapter Sixteen

Judy and Andy McAfferty arrived thirty-seven hours after Bren came out of surgery. Sara managed to convince Izzy to go home with Harriet around the twenty-hour mark. For the last seventeen hours, Terry was in and out, going between Sara and home to check on Felicia and her mom, then to her office. Liv and Grace were "on shift" when the McAfferty's got there.

Sara greeted them first and introduced everyone. She'd kept them up-to-date on Bren's condition throughout their grueling journey home. Now they were here, Sara felt a weird sense of loss.

Judy grabbed her up in a bear hug. "Thank you. You have no idea how much it's meant for us to have you here."

"It's the least I could do for her. Bren's very special to me."

"I know." Judy released her and took Andy's hand. "Can we see her?"

"The nurse has been strict about one at a time and only for a few minutes. She's in Room Five."

Judy and Andy exchanged a quick glance, and he went in first. Judy took a seat next to Grace. "Have you all been here this whole time?"

"No, we've been taking shifts. Mostly to make sure Sara eats and sleeps."

"Shifts?" Judy asked.

"Unlike my dear friend," Liv said and gave Sara a significant look, "we all decided to come in shifts to make sure someone was here at all times. Sara, as you can see, thought it did not apply to her."

Judy looked ready to cry, and Sara wanted to slap Liv. Good thing Grace sat next to her.

Grace rose and pulled Liv with her. "And our shift is up. Terry should be here in a few minutes. I'll take this one home. Judy, is there anything we can get for you and Andy? Have you had a chance to go home? Do you need anything to eat? I can come back once I get Liv out of here."

"Marion took care of our luggage when she got us from the airport. And I don't think I can eat right now."

"If you need anything, let us know. Sara's got our number. I'm sure she won't be leaving anytime soon." Grace kissed Sara on the cheek and pulled Liv out of the waiting room.

"Sorry about those two," Sara said. "Sometimes, well, most times, Liv opens her mouth without engaging her brain."

"I think it's amazing you've been here all along. You didn't have to do. None of you did."

"That's not true," Sara said. "Bren's my friend, and by extension, she's friends with Grace and Liv and Terry. We're a team. And they're right. There's no way I was leaving before you got here."

"We're here now. Why don't you go home? Get some rest. I can call you if anything changes."

Sara considered her options. It would be nice to sleep in her bed instead of the lumpy, vinyl couch she now sat upon. But it didn't feel right. Something told her she needed to stay. "How about if I get you two something to drink? There's coffee and tea in here and a vending machine in the next room with water and sodas. I don't want to leave yet. I hope it's okay."

"Of course it is." Judy hugged her again. "I'd love some water, thank you."

"Sure." Sara headed to the adjoining room and met Terry in the hallway.

"I heard they got here. I ran into Liv and Gracie at the elevator. They doing okay?"

"Her dad's with her right now." Sara continued on to the vending machine. She stared at it for a long time, trying to remember what she was supposed to be doing.

"Hey." Terry gently took her hand. "Tell me what you want."

"I want her to be better," Sara cried. "I want my friend to wake up."

"Me, too." Terry held Sara as a fresh bout of tears started up. "Do you want to leave or stick around?"

"Stick around. But you can go." She sniffled and cuddled closer to Terry. She didn't want her to go but understood if she needed to. Not everyone was capable of shutting down their lives to wait for news on Bren. It had to be Sunday by now, though Sara wasn't completely sure. "Don't you have a date with Felicia today?"

"I do, but she knows what's going on." Terry kissed Sara's cheek and held her tighter. "She's disappointed, but she understands. My kid's pretty damn amazing. Besides, Grams is a good enough substitute for me. She lets her have more cookies."

Sara allowed herself a soft laugh. "I was hoping you'd stay."

"No place I'd rather be. Now, let's get something to drink and head back in. I'd like to meet Bren's folks and see if there's anything new to report."

****

Sara held Bren's right hand in hers and rubbed small circles over the back of it. Her turn to sit with her was almost over now. They were well into day five of their vigil, and the exhaustion took its toll on Sara. She desperately needed real sleep. But the one night Liv managed to get her to go home, Sara paced for several hours, got in her car, and came back. It was no use. She had to be at the hospital.

"I miss dancing with you," she said. "I miss that I can't text you because I'm feeling down and need your cute emoji responses. I miss my friend."

She felt a slight tug on her fingers, and Sara looked down at their linked hands. It couldn't be. The doctors warned them Bren's muscles might contract and it would appear as though she moved. But this couldn't be a contraction. She was no longer in a medically induced coma, and they were simply waiting for her to wake up. Sara tensed. Please let her be coming around.

Bren's fingers gripped Sara's.

Shocked, Sara turned her tired eyes to Bren's battered face and let a smile slip through her tears. Baby blue eyes looked back at her questioningly. Bren opened her mouth, but no sounds came out. "Shh," Sara told her. "Don't try to talk. Let me hit the Call button."

She pressed the button for a nurse. The door opened seconds later, and a flurry of activity followed. Sara was pushed out, happy to tell Bren's parents what happened.

Time slowed. It felt more like hours than minutes before a doctor came to speak to them. He had a cautious smile on his face. "She's awake. It's hard for her to speak right now. Her vitals are stable. Her brain function appears normal, but she's not out of the woods yet. We'll keep her in ICU for at least another day, but if I'm right, she'll be moved to a step-down unit tomorrow. We'll need to do more tests first."

"Can we see her?" Judy asked. She gripped Andy's hand hard enough her knuckles were white.

"You can. Try not to overwhelm her. You can answer any questions she has, but if she keeps repeating a question, let me know. There's a chance she'll have some short-term memory issues. A neurologist will look at her, and she'll be able to tell you more."

"Thank you, Doctor." Judy released Andy's hand and was off like a flash to Bren's room.

Andy turned to Sara and smiled for the first time. "She's awake."

"She is."

"She's lucky to have you, Sara." His hug was warm and kind, and Sara wanted to cry some more, even though she was pretty sure no more tears were left in her system. "We're lucky to have you."

"Thanks. I think I have to make a few calls. A whole team of people need to know she's going to be okay."

Two hours later, the waiting room was again full of people. This time there wasn't such a pall hanging over them. Bren was awake and asking questions, talking to anyone who came in, and even joking about the color of her bruises matching the color of her hair. It warmed Sara's heart to know she'd be okay.

In the midst of all the quiet celebration, she noticed Izzy wander off alone. It wasn't like Izzy. She followed her into the hallway and around a corner. When she reached her, Izzy was sobbing on the floor, leaning against the wall, her knees bent and her arms around her legs.

Sara dropped to her knees and pulled Izzy into an embrace. "Hey, it's okay. She'll be fine. A couple more tests, and they'll probably move her to another room. I bet she's home in no time."

"I hope so." Izzy swiped her hand across her tear-streaked face.

"Why the tears?"

Izzy turned her big brown eyes on Sara then looked away, as if she were afraid Sara might see something there. And Sara did. Izzy had a big heart. Everyone knew it. She was playful and boisterous and loved to gossip, but she was kind and sweet as well. Sara couldn't be sure, but she suspected there was more between Izzy and Bren than mere friendship.

"Talk to me."

"I can't. You're Bren's girlfriend. It wouldn't be right."

"Hey, look at me." She lifted Izzy's chin until they were face to face. "I'm not her girlfriend. We go out sometimes, and we have a lot of fun, but we're not seriously dating each other. I said I was her girlfriend because I figured they'd let me see her, and I was right."

"Does she know you're not her girlfriend?"

"She does. It might not be what she wants, but that's how it is. Bren's wonderful, but she's not wonderful for me."

"You're not her girlfriend?"

Sara allowed herself to laugh softly. "No. I'm not. Why? Do you want to be her girlfriend?"

"She's too blind to see me that way, but I've been in love with her forever. We're best friends, and I didn't want to screw it up. Then she got hurt, and I was scared she'd die without ever knowing how I feel about her."

"And now?"

"Now I'm afraid to tell her."

"You can tell her you love her. Friends love each other, Izzy."

"Not like I love her."

Sara stood and helped Izzy up. "Tell her you love her and you're there for her. Make sure she knows, and when the time is right, you'll tell her there's more to it."

"Even when I see her going out with women who aren't right for her? No offense."

"None taken. And yes. Even when you see her making mistakes. You'll know when the time is right." Sara put an arm around Izzy and led her back to the waiting room. "Trust me on this."

Izzy nodded, entered the room, and made it known she was next in line to see Bren.

Terry hugged Sara and pulled back to take a long look at her. Something was different about the way Terry stared at her, but it wasn't uncomfortable. In fact, it was quite the opposite.

Terry said, "I think it's time you went home, young lady. You need to sleep for a couple of days at least."

"I think you might actually be right this time."

"Oh, you're officially rescheduled for next Sunday at one. This is from Felicia, by the way."

"Is it?" Sara sported a silly grin and didn't care. She was light and happy for the first time in forever. "Does she often make her own appointments?"

"All the time. Even has a calendar she keeps on the fridge to make sure Mom and I know when and where she needs to be."

Sara laughed outright, until she saw the expression on Terry's face. "You're serious?"

"I am. You'll see."

"I can't wait." Sara realized she stood in Terry's embrace. Her hands still rested on Terry's hips, and if she leaned in a little... She forced herself to move away, breaking their warm contact. The time wasn't right, and she couldn't be sure Terry wanted to be kissed. Despite the look in her eyes.

"My car's here, but I'm tired. Would you drive me home?"

"Sure."

"Have I thanked you today?"

Terry smiled and led Sara to the parking lot. The drive home was spent in companionable silence. Once at her house, Sara dug the keys out of her purse, which Terry was smart enough to grab before their hasty retreat, and opened the door of the truck.

She stepped out and leaned in to say, "Thanks again."

"You're welcome. I'm glad Bren's doing better."

"Me, too." Sara hesitated before she asked, "Would you like to come in for a bit?"

"I thought you were going to bed?" Terry laughed nervously.

"I will, once I've had a chance to calm down. I could use the company."

Terry turned the engine off and was out of the truck faster than Sara thought possible. It made her feel slightly giddy. "I can't say no to you."

Sara captured Terry's hand, and they walked into the house together.

****

Terry stretched out her legs and crossed them at the ankle. She was quite comfy on Sara's couch, which held fond memories for her. She didn't bother to hide her smile as Sara handed her a cup of coffee.

"Do I want to know what you're grinning about?" Sara asked, settling on the opposite end of the couch.

Terry looked at the space between them and when she met Sara's eyes she found recognition there. The blush on Sara's cheeks was adorable. "It's still early. Want to order something in for dinner?"

"Sounds like a good idea. Anything in particular?"

"No. You know my tastes." The comment felt natural, but the awkwardness that followed nearly broke Terry's heart. She started to apologize for any missteps, but Sara gave a sad smile and tapped her phone awake to make the order.

Terry waited in the silence, wishing like hell she had some witty thing to say to help them bridge the gap between them. The literal one and the figurative one.

Terry's phone rang and she answered it immediately, concerned when she saw it was from Jackie. "Hey, what's up?"

"We won," Jackie said without preamble. "The judgment is in your favor. You have full custody, and William's lawyer says he is not going to contest it. Congratulations."

Terry nearly dropped the phone as she got to her feet. She couldn't stand still and at the same time felt like she could pass out with relief. "Seriously? It's over? For good?"

"For good. He signed paperwork to that affect. I'll get with his lawyer and set up a reasonable visitation schedule once you give me some dates. We can talk about it more tomorrow, but I didn't want to wait to tell you. Now give her a big hug from me and we'll talk later."

"Jackie, if you didn't have a girlfriend I might ask you to marry me."

Jackie gave her a hearty laugh. "I'll tell her. Good night."

"I can't thank you enough. Good night."

Terry disconnected the call and turned to Sara, who was staring at her. Suddenly, she was at a loss for words.

Sara got to her feet and stopped Terry's pacing. "Tell me you won. He's not taking Felicia away, right?"

"He's not. Ever. She's mine." Terry began to cry but found herself in the comfort of Sara's arms. It was the end of a nightmare and she simply wanted to hold on forever.

"I'm happy for you," Sara said, her voice shaking. "I know how much she means to you, baby. This is amazing."

Terry held tighter and let the endearment soak in. She was happy and sad at the same time. Elated to know her child wouldn't be taken from her; sad to realize how much she still loved the woman in her arms. She pulled away before to save herself any further heart ache. "Thanks. I'm sorry I broke down. It's such a shock. I didn't expect him to sign paperwork that he'd never try this stunt again. It's all surreal."

Sara handed her some tissues. "I'm sure it is."

"I need to go home," Terry said after blowing her nose. She grinned stupidly at Sara. "I need to tell Mom and I want to do that in person. She's going to freak out."

"But in a good way."

"Yes. In a good way." Terry felt the awkwardness return and rocked on her heels. Impulsively she pulled Sara into a fierce hug, released her and headed for the door. "Thanks Sara. I'll call you soon and set up a time to come over and meet Felicia."

"Sure." Sara had a strange look on her face and for a moment Terry considered kissing her. She resisted that sudden urge and left, putting her mind back on her good news and being thankful her daughter wouldn't to be taken from her.

Sara, however, would never be far from her thoughts.

****

Liv couldn't stop smiling. She stood in the kitchen of Sara's house and listened to her talk about Terry. And talk and talk and talk. After nearly a week, Bren's recovery was going well, and she was glad to see Sara return to what passed as normal. Currently, Sara was digging into a packet of Pop-Tarts. She offered one to Liv.

"Strawberry. Your fave."

Liv took the treat from her and enjoyed the sweet taste. "It is and that's the reason you keep them here. Will you tell me how things are going with you and Terry?"

"What do you mean?" Sara leaned against the countertop, clearly savoring her food.

"You know exactly what I mean, Sara Hyatt." Liv pointed at her with the Pop-Tart. "You and Terry. Not just friends."

Sara rolled her eyes and sighed dramatically. "We are absolutely just friends. I can't do more right now, much as I want to. Maybe rushing into the relationship the first time got us into this mess. If there's a relationship to be had, we need to take it slow."

"Why? You know you love her, and I'm willing to bet she returns the feeling. Go for it, Sara."

"Livvy, you do realize not every relationship works like your and Gracie's, right? You two were like a couple in ten minutes."

"So were you and Terry."

"Exactly my point. Besides, even though I'm not dating Bren anymore, I'm still her friend, and right now, she needs me to spend time with her."

"It doesn't mean you can't spend time with Terry, too."

"You are the most obstinate woman I know."

"I accept that. But you're avoiding the issue. What are you going to do about Terry?"

"I don't know. When she found out she'd won the custody stuff she cried on my shoulder for a long time and…it felt right. Holding her. I wanted badly to kiss her."

"Why didn't you?"

"Seriously? We're barely talking and everything feels fragile between us. Kissing would have been a bad idea."

Liv shook her head. "I don't think so. It's exactly what you should have done. You two belong together."

"You're crazy." She watched Liv finish the last of her Pop-Tart and brush her hands on her jeans.

"You need to trust me on this. I know what I see and I know you're still very much in love with her."

"Trust you? The world's worst matchmaker? Seriously?"

"I'm not that bad. I put you and Denise together, didn't I?"

Sara blushed at a flash of memory about Denise. They were good together for at least one thing. Though if she were honest with herself, sex had never been an issue for her. "Denise was great, but where is she now? Not here. She's married and living in Montreal."

"Not the point. You guys made a nice couple."

"Matchmakers are supposed to find you a match for the rest of your life. Not a few months, goofball. You so suck at this."

"Hmm. You and Terry. Work on it." Liv hopped off the counter and embraced Sara. "Seriously. The woman never left your side at the hospital unless Gracie or I took her place. When she wasn't there, she was sending me text messages to check up on you. Trust me, there's something there." Liv glanced at her watch. "I need to meet Gracie at the community center. We have to go over some stuff about the reception. You okay?"

"Sure. I've got your wonderful advice to consider."

Liv stuck her tongue out at Sara. "Don't be an ass. You know it's sound advice, and you're mad because for once you're doing what I tell you to."

"Get out of my house," Sara groused while gently pushing Liv toward the door. "I don't like you anymore."

"Bullshit." Liv gave her a kiss and left before she got into any more trouble.

****

Exhaustion slammed into Terry like a hurricane. Long days and nights with Sara at the hospital wore her out. She desperately needed sleep and regretted having gone to the office this morning. She never worked on Saturday, but she needed to get caught up and barely managed to stay awake on the short drive home.

Sara planned to visit tomorrow and finally meet Felicia, now that they knew Bren would be okay. Despite her lack of energy, Terry was excited about the visit. But her excitement waned when she noticed the elegant black sedan in her driveway. She parked her truck next to it and practically ran to the door. She had her fingers on the handle when she heard William's voice.

"You will not take my grandchild from me!" He stood in their living room, towered over her mother, and waved his finger in her face.

Shirley's eyes glared with anger. "You get the hell out of my house! You're not welcome here."

"I've got a right to see her!"

Terry bolted into the house and got between them. "William, get out. You don't have a right to come in here and yell at my mother like this. You lost your case. I never wanted to keep Felicia from you. I don't know how many times I have to tell you before you believe it. But right now, you're getting very close to having the police called to force you to leave. Felicia will be home any time now from her play date with our neighbor's daughter. I don't want her coming home to this."

"You took her from me," William said. His face was flushed from yelling, but he retreated a couple of steps from Terry. "You took them both, and I'll not have it. I want to see Felicia."

"I never took anyone from you." Terry tried hard to reason with him, but her patience ran thin. "I told Jackie to set up a visitation schedule with your lawyer. I want Felicia to know your family, but won't let her get upset or be caught in the middle."

"You expect me to fly out here every other weekend?"

"If you want to see her, yes. Jennifer seemed okay with it. Why aren't you? Don't try to tell me you don't want to spend the money. I know damn well you can easily afford it."

"That's not the point. I shouldn't have to do all this. She belongs with her real family."

"I am her real family. I'm her mother."

"No. My daughter was her mother. Not you."

Terry felt Shirley's hand on her shoulder and took a deep breath to calm her rising temper. She let it out slowly before she spoke. "I was there when she was born. I held her in my arms, changed her diapers, took her to the doctor, enrolled her in school, bandaged dozens of cuts and scrapes, and held her when she realized Ann wasn't ever coming home. I've spent hours fighting for her when a kid at her school called her a retard—a word, I might add, you're fond of using. Don't you dare tell me I'm not her mother."

William opened his mouth to speak but nothing came out.

Terry continued. "I'm going to ask Mom to call the police. I want you out of here. I'll make sure my lawyer knows about this stunt. Jennifer can come see Felicia whenever she wants to. I'll decide later whether or not you can." Terry marched to the door and held it open. "Leave."

She heard Shirley talking quietly on her phone. For a moment, she wasn't sure William would go. He stood, rooted to the spot. But something in his demeanor changed. His shoulders drooped slightly, and his eyes met Terry's. For the first time, she saw defeat on his features.

Clearly he didn't want to deal with the police as he slowly made his way to the door. He stopped on the threshold and said, his back to Terry, "I loved my daughter. I might have made some mistakes with her, but I loved her. I wanted to try and do right by Felicia. She's all I have left, and I want to be part of her life."

"I understand. Ann was the love of my life." Terry gentled her voice. "But you can't burst in here and take control of Felicia's life. You can't. Go home. We'll talk in a few days."

He nodded and walked away. Terry watched him get into his car and drive off before she softly closed the door.

"I didn't actually call the police," Shirley said. "I had a feeling it was all bluster. He's hurt and angry and taking it out on us because it's the one thing he has left to do. I might feel the same way if I couldn't see Felicia." Shirley put her hand on Terry's arm. "I love you, and if the situation were reversed...I can't help having some compassion for him."

"I know. I want him to stop being such an asshole."

"I think you made your point. I'm proud of you, honey." Shirley kissed her on the cheek. "Now come in here so I can feed you. Then you can tell me how Bren's doing."

"Deal."

****

Sara took off for the hospital after Liv went home. Izzy sent her a text message saying Bren was finally up to seeing visitors other than her parents. Sara went there once or twice to check on her, but each time Bren was either with her parents or Izzy or asleep. This time, Izzy promised Bren would be awake. Apparently she'd been sitting up and talking longer each day. By the end of the week, she'd be strong enough for the surgery on her leg.

According to the messages Izzy sent her, Sara understood not only was Bren improving, she showed signs of no lasting brain damage. Which enabled Sara to sleep better at night.

Around two in the afternoon on Saturday, she arrived at Bren's room. She peeked in, and Izzy motioned her to come forward. Sara was greeted with an enthusiastic hug from Izzy and a gentler one from Bren.

"How are you feeling?" she asked Bren as she settled in a chair beside her. Izzy leaned on the windowsill on the opposite side of the bed. Sara noted her eyes rarely left Bren.

"I'm better. Still have a headache, and my arm itches like crazy." Bren held up her left arm to show off the cast. Someone drew emojis all over it, everything from a smiley face to a slap-on-the-forehead face. The cast on her leg had matching art. Bren said, "It makes for a great conversation piece, thanks to Izzy."

Sara laughed. "I'm sure it does. Look, Bren, I've been wanting to talk to you about all this." Sara waved her hand in the air to indicate the hospital room. "I feel responsible for it."

"That's nuts, Sara. You didn't run over me. Angel Harrison did."

"I know, but I egged her on with the police reports and hanging up on her when she called. I should never have engaged in any contact with her to begin with. Which includes the first time she asked me to dinner back in the summer. I had a feeling she was bad news. I mean, I remember when she and Liv went out and how toxic she was for Liv. I should have known..."

Bren touched the side of Sara's face with her good hand and smiled sweetly at her. "You had no idea she was unstable. No one did. It's over now, and I'm going to be fine. Stop blaming yourself, okay? This wasn't your fault. I happened to be at the right place at the wrong time."

Sara took hold of Bren's hand and kissed her fingers. "You're a dear person, Bren. I wanted to kill her for hurting you. No one will let me talk to her, but I have a feeling she was either going for me or Terry next. I'm still sorry you got involved in this."

Bren shrugged and squeezed Sara's hand. "Don't worry about it. I wouldn't trade a minute of our time together. Regardless of the consequences. Okay?"

"Okay," Sara said. She glanced over at Izzy, who looked woefully uncomfortable. "When do you get out of here?"

"I'll probably have surgery on my leg at the end of the week, then maybe two more days in here. If I'm good."

"That's great."

"Izzy told me you wouldn't leave the hospital while I was in the coma. Not even when your mom tried to drag you away. Then my parents told me you kept sending them text messages about my condition, so they could know what was going on." Bren gave her that beautiful smile, and Sara blushed.

"I couldn't leave you, Bren. You're my friend. I had to make sure you were okay." She looked over at Izzy. "And that one's making herself crazy with worry. Her moms did manage to drag her out of here a couple of times, but many times she and I shared a lumpy, vinyl couch in the waiting room. Trust me, it was worth the wait. Neither of us was going anywhere."

"Thanks. I can't tell you how it makes me feel to know I have such good friends." Bren gazed at Izzy who now sported a very cute blush going up her neck to her cheeks. She kept her gaze on the floor, but Sara suspected they'd already discussed this topic.

"You do. We had to keep your hordes of friends away. Izzy set up one of those group apps to let them all know your status. Liv, Gracie, and Terry came in shifts to make sure we ate and slept. A team of people kept an eye on you, honey. Trust me."

"I do," Bren said. Her eyes drooped a bit.

"Listen, you need to rest. When you're feeling up to it, why don't you and Izzy come to my house for dinner? We'll get junk food and watch a sappy romance. Whatcha think?"

Izzy blushed more, and Bren gave her a tired smile. "Sounds like a plan."

"Good." Sara stood, kissed Bren on the forehead, and gave Izzy another hug. "Let me know if you two need anything." Izzy promised she would text her, and Sara left Bren in Izzy's very capable hands.

Chapter Seventeen

Sara couldn't remember giggling so much her sides hurt. When she was little, her dad would tickle her until she peed her pants. The sight of Terry dressed in her jammies, sitting on the floor with Felicia, had her in stitches. A blanket was laid out and adorned with Hello Kitty plates, cups, and matching sporks. The jammies Terry wore displayed Hello Kitty all over them in all her pinkness in many different poses.

She tried desperately to ignore Terry's braless chest. When Terry leaned forward to pour her tea, Sara was teased with the site of smooth, pale skin, which she knew would taste sweeter than... She gave her head a little shake to pull her thoughts back to the present.

Focus on other things, she told herself.

Cookies of various shapes, sizes, and flavors were assembled on different plates, and , Hello Kitty napkins were stacked nearby.

Sara enjoyed the serious expression on Terry's face. She played along with Felicia as if they were about to have high tea with the queen. She even pulled what Sara could described as a sour face at Sara's giggling. Which caused her to giggle harder, and before long, she was gone.

Felicia giggled along with her, though she probably didn't get the humor. Giggling was, after all, contagious.

"Mom," Felicia said after her laughter subsided. "Can Sara come over every Sunday? She's funny."

"Uh, it would be up to Sara, but I don't mind."

Sara realized she had about two seconds to say the right thing or she'd be screwed. What was the right thing? Commit to seeing Terry every Sunday? She'd already warned Sara Felicia never forgot anything. If she said yes, Felicia would expect her there every weekend. Could she do that?

"How about," Sara said, "we make a date for next Sunday and see how it goes? Sometimes I need to see my mom on the weekends. I might have to skip a few Sundays. Would it be okay?"

"To be with your mom?" Felicia asked.

"Yes. We like to go shopping. It's not as busy on Sunday, and let me tell you, she's crazy about shopping. And I like to go with her. It's fun."

"I like being with my mom, too. It's cool." Felicia moved on to other topics of importance, such as which cookies to start with.

Terry gave Sara an appreciative smile, and Sara's heart did a little flip. Damn. She swanted to kiss the woman so badly it hurt. Their eyes locked and she knew Terry's thoughts mirrored hers. Heat started unexpectedly as Terry woke feelings Sara was sure she'd shoved aside months ago. She squirmed a little under Terry's intense gaze and finally looked away, giving her attention to the adorable child seated between them.

Terry took the hint and joined in on the cookie discussion. The scene before her was like a live greeting card you might get at Christmas. The kind with the family doing something funny for their picture—like sitting on the living room floor in matching Hello Kitty jammies having high tea. It was a picture Sara could enjoy seeing for the rest of her life.

"Oh good. I didn't miss anything," Shirley announced as she came into the living room, her hair mussed from wearing a wool cap, and her cheeks rosy from the cold.

Sara looked up at her. "Hey, Shirley. Good to see you again."

"You, too. Are you enjoying your picnic? Or is it high tea? I'm never sure which is which."

"It's high tea," Felicia said, trying very hard for an English accent. "You may join us, Grams."

"It sounds lovely, but is it okay if I sit on the couch today? My knees can't take getting on the floor."

"Sure," Felicia said, already pouring a cup for her. "Which cookie do you want?"

Shirley settled onto the couch with a contented sigh, but Sara got the sense something wasn't quite right. Terry's face revealed a definite expression of concern as she watched her mother carefully.

Shirley said, "I'll take the peanut butter one, please."

"Here you are." Felicia served it up on a small plate and handed her a cup and went about serving cookies to Terry and Sara.

"Mom, are you okay?" Terry asked.

"Fine." Shirley ate her cookie faster than Sara thought possible. "A bit hungry is all."

"You skipped lunch."

"Not now." Shirley gazed pointedly at Felicia.

"Fine." Terry dropped the subject, but Sara knew her heart was no longer in the grand adventure with Felicia.

They stayed in the living room for another hour before Felicia decided it was time to pack it in. Apparently, her heart was set on watching a movie which came on at exactly three oh five. The kid was interesting to say the least. Sara hadn't spent much time around kids, but she was pretty sure she could get used to this one. She was smart, funny, and didn't hold back on her opinion. Especially when it came to comparing chocolate chip cookies with peanut butter ones. Chocolate chip won hands down.

Terry and Sara helped Felicia clean up, then Terry set her up with her movie. Once finished, she and Sara and Shirley moved to the kitchen for some adult time.

Shirley held up her hand when Terry started to speak. "No. I don't need a lecture. Yes, I'm exhausted. Yes, I know I wasn't on call but I was still needed. I'm the senior counselor, and this wasn't a cut-and-dried case. Not that they ever are, but this one was especially difficult."

"Can I ask what you do for a living? I know you're a psychologist, but Terry never gave me details."

Shirley smiled kindly at her while Terry placed a sandwich in front of her. "I work for an agency that mostly deals with juvenile offenders. Sometimes I'm called in to handle runaways or homeless kids, like today. We have to get them placed where they'll get the help they need. It might be a halfway house or a psychiatric unit at a hospital, but I'm usually the one who determines where they should go.

"Today we had a homeless boy. He didn't need psychiatric treatment—not urgently anyway—but we still needed to find a place for him to stay. Social services is limited in what they can provide. My agency has a wider range of options."

Terry said, "And it can mean spending an entire day working to get the kid somewhere safe. What my mom isn't telling you is she practically runs the place, and without her, they can barely operate. I talked her into removing herself from the on-call list, but it hasn't worked out well. They still call her."

"You do incredible work, Shirley."

"Thank you." Shirley nodded appreciatively. "But Terry's right. I have to slow down. Unfortunately, many of our staff are new and haven't got a handle on the nuances of what needs done."

"And they don't know everyone in the territory well enough to finesse them into getting what they want." Terry shook her head at Shirley. "I'm proud of you, Mom. But I'm also worried. Did you check your blood sugar?"

"I did and it was low, but not dangerously so. It's why I opted for the peanut butter cookie. I knew it'd last a bit longer in my system."

"Not good." Terry got up, poured a glass of orange juice, and handed it to Shirley. "Drink up."

"Yes, dear."

Sara watched the exchange with interest. Terry never mentioned her mother was diabetic. Nor had she mentioned how bad it could get. How much more was there she didn't know about Terry and her family?

Their physical attraction was most certainly still in place, but Sara worried about how well they knew each other. Was it a good idea for them to go down that road again?

"Okay, done," Shirley said and put the empty glass down. "I'm taking a nap now. Wake me about an hour before dinner." She kissed Terry on the cheek and turned to Sara. "I'm sorry to have to cut our visit short, unless you're staying for dinner."

"I'd love to," Sara said.

"Excellent. Terry's a good cook, and we'll have a nice chat while she does the work. I promise."

Shirley strode down the hall to her room.

"She likes you," Terry said.

"She just met me."

"And she likes you anyway." She sported a big grin. "I can tell. She invited you to dinner. That's huge from her. Ann was the first of my girlfriends my mother gave the time of day to. She's of the 'they aren't good enough for my little girl' opinion." She paused, her eyes showing sadness in them. "You're the second she's ever talked to."

"I'll accept the compliment."

"Good."

An awkward silence fell between them.

They both tried to break it at the same time.

"I didn't know—"

"How are things—"

They released nervous laughs. Terry held her hand out to Sara. "You first."

"I didn't know your mom was sick."

"She's a type one diabetic. Has been since the age of nine. She's supposed to keep a close eye on her sugar levels, but she's been bad about it lately. She's working too many hours, and it's taking a toll on her physically. I can't get her to eat properly, and sometimes her insulin pump shoots her up with insulin, but she's already processed whatever she ate—like a cookie or candy bar—and it brings her blood sugar down because the sugar is already gone. It can make her sick, throw up, pass out...all those things. She was in the hospital a year ago, and it was rough. She has an insulin pump now. I wish she didn't suck at taking care of herself."

"Wow. It couldn't have been easy for you when you lived in Quebec with her all the way out here."

"It wasn't. I called all the time and flew up as often as I could, especially after Dad died. I'm always worried about her. It's like having an adult child." Terry laughed softly. "She keeps saying I'm acting like her mom, and I guess I am. Someone has to."

"Has it gotten worse since your dad died?"

"Yes. Much worse. Moving here was the best thing I could have done. Having Felicia around has brought some of the spark back into her life, I think. Now if I can work on the eating and overworking stuff, I'd be very happy."

"Terry, I need to ask you something."

Terry stared at her for a moment, like a deer caught in headlights. "Okay."

"You never told me your mom was sick. I know we weren't together very long, I mean, five months is hardly a lifetime. But we talked—I can't think of anything I didn't tell you about. But you never talked about your family in any detail. I didn't realize until now, having met and spent time with them.

"I mean, Felicia is amazing. She's adorable and smart and witty and creative."

"Thanks. I think she's pretty damn amazing, too." Terry got up and poured them both a cup of coffee. She leaned against the counter and cradled her cup in her hands. "The thing is, I was scared of everything. If I told you too much, you might call things off. If I told you too little, you'd never get to know the real me. I thought I could find a balance of things to tell you, but it clearly didn't work."

"Why did you need a balance? What were you afraid of?"

"You."

"Me?"

"Yeah. I was afraid of my feelings for you, Sara. Ann was the only woman I ever truly loved. We knew we were meant to be together after the first few dates. I can't explain it, but for me, it was honestly love at first sight. Maybe for Ann, too, though she'd never admit it." Terry sighed and put her coffee cup down. "I've given this a lot of thought lately, and I realize I was afraid I might be falling in love with you. I didn't know where to go with that. I miss Ann, and I think about her every time I see Felicia. How was I supposed to find a place in my heart for someone new? Could I replace Ann? Did I have to shove her memory aside?"

"You never told me any of this." Sara got to her feet and stood inches from Terry. She wanted to take her in her arms. "I would have tried to understand."

"I know," Terry whispered. "I wanted to. I wasn't ready. Then William showed up, and I panicked. Somehow it seemed easier to break up with you than to work through all my issues and stay together. But it never meant I didn't/don't care about you. I'm sorry. I never wanted to hurt you. I can't tell you how hard it's been to live with myself knowing what I did to you."

"Shh." Sara gently held Terry's face in her hands. "Don't. You can't change what happened. But you can promise me something."

"Anything."

"Promise me you'll keep nothing from me. Not even your work calendar. Let me in, Terry. Please. I still need you."

"I need you, too." Tears streamed down her face, and Sara drew her closer.

Their lips met in a tender kiss that left Sara warm inside. She pulled away enough to speak, Terry's breath soft against her lips. "I can do friends. I can. But it's not what I want. I want to be with you, Terry. I want us to work this out. Please? Can we work on us?"

"Yes." Terry wrapped her arms around Sara's waist and tightened her grip as they met for another, soul-searing kiss. "I'll do anything for you, Sara."

"Mom, can I have a soda?"

Sara laughed into their kiss. "Right now I think you have someone else to do things for."

"I do." Terry didn't release her right away, instead holding her gaze intently. "She's always going to need something, Sara. She's the most important thing in my life."

"Do you think there's still room for me?"

"There is."

"Mom. Are you listening?"

Terry rolled her eyes. "She never lets up."

"I'm okay with it. I'm sure we'll work it out. Now answer her before she comes in here."

"No," Terry said to Felicia. "You had one before lunch, and it's too close to dinnertime. We'll save it for tomorrow, okay?"

Silence followed by a dramatic sigh. "Okay."

Sara tried to hold in a giggle. "Is it always this easy?"

"No way. She's on her best behavior because you're here. Wait until she's used to you. You'll see the real diva in all her glory."

"I can't wait." Sara placed a kiss on Terry's nose. "How about this coming Friday for another sort of date?"

"What would you like to do?"

"Dinner, movie, the usual," Sara said. She thought she saw a hint of pleasure in Terry's eyes when she mentioned "the usual." Her stomach fluttered.

"I think I can make room in my busy social calendar." Terry kissed her softly, and it sent a pleasant tingle through Sara. "What kind of movie?"

"Whatever's showing. You pick this time."

"Oh wow. I get to pick? You're very serious about this sort of date."

"I'm very serious about you." Sara cradled Terry's face in her hands and kept eye contact with her. "About us. It means sharing, and I choose to let you pick the movie. It's my way of sharing. Otherwise, I'd be picking the movie and you know it'd be a sappy romance."

"Are you sure that's not what I'll pick? I mean, maybe we could get some pointers from a sappy romance."

"Hmm. Maybe. I guess we're agreed on a sappy romance after dinner. Cool. Now, where were we?"

Terry grinned and leaned in for more kissing. "Right there. But you should know we could get interrupted at any moment. Once the movie is over, Felicia will be in here to see what we're doing."

"I don't mind." Sara found a lot of truth in her statement. "I want kids, Terry, and I think being around Felicia will be a great start." She pressed her lips to Terry's and sighed. "Since I'm here, maybe there is one thing you could do for me."

"What?"

"Show me pictures of Ann. I want to get to know her, too."

Terry's eyes welled with new tears. "I'll get the photo albums."

****

Sara stood at the door and kept watch on her driveway. The old adage, "A watched pot never boils," sprung into her head. But she continued to stare anyway. Terry was punctual, but a part of her hoped she'd be a bit early. She wanted the most out of her time with Terry.

They were still calling it a sort of date, but Sara knew otherwise. After the kiss last Sunday, she knew damn well where her heart belonged. There was no "sort of" about it. This was the real deal. She meant to show Terry how much she loved her. How much she'd missed her and how much she needed her in her life. When they kissed, Sara realized one thing: she never wanted to be apart from Terry again.

They spent most evenings this past week on the phone with a dozen text messages between them during work hours. Plus, Terry sent her tons of pictures of Felicia doing all manner of adorable things. Sara loved the kid the moment she met her.

She'd been thinking about this date all week, and the closer it got, the tighter her stomach got. Sara barely ate anything last night. Food was enemy number one—a rare occurrence.

Sara checked the text messages on her phone. She got one from Bren earlier in the day with her typical emojis. A broken arm, a smiley face with a bandage on its head, and a hand waving emphatically. It gave Sara a good chuckle.

The crunch of tires on gravel drew her attention to the driveway. She moved away from the window, grabbed her coat and purse, and hurried outside. She was locking the door when Terry joined her.

Sara took a moment to enjoy the view of her in shiny black boots, tight jeans, yellow Oxford button-down shirt tucked into her pants, and a belt buckle that held a tiny gold nugget in the center of it. She wore her leather jacket, and the dashing image left Sara weak in the knees. She accepted the welcoming hug and inhaled the familiar leather scent.

"Hello there," Sara said.

"Hey." Terry kissed her on the cheek. "I guess you're ready?"

"You guessed right." Sara put her keys in her purse and let Terry lead her to the truck. Terry helped her get in, closed the door behind her, and jogged around to the driver's side.

Once on the way, Terry said, "Would it be weird if I told you I'm nervous right now? This is the hundredth outfit I put on."

Sara laughed softly. "I somehow can't imagine you owning that many articles of clothing."

"I don't. But if you mix and match you can come pretty close."

"There's that." Sara fiddled with the strap on her purse. She con-sidered her own outfit, a pale, strapless, yellow cotton dress with a "V" neck she noted Terry kept staring at. Her matching yellow pumps weren't particularly comfortable but looked great with the dress. It was the third outfit she'd put on. "For the record, I'm nervous, too. I mean, it's not like we never went out together before. Right?"

"Right, but it's sort of like starting all over."

Sara let her hand rest on Terry's thigh and felt her muscles move under her touch. "Except it's not. We know each other, Terry. You got scared and couldn't tell me about William's custody claims—that's firmly in the past. You more than proved yourself by staying by my side while Bren was in hospital. You dropped everything to be there for me, and I can't tell you how much it meant to me."

"I would have been there even if we hadn't made up." Terry glanced briefly at her. "I've had such a hard time staying away. Being separated from you tore me apart. Every instinct I had told me to talk to you. To salvage something of our relationship. Even if I thought you hated me, I would have been at the hospital."

"I could never hate you." She gave Terry's thigh a little squeeze. "I never did, by the way. Hate you. Mad, sure, but never hate."

"You had every right to it, you know."

Sara shrugged. "Hate is pretty damn strong, and I don't know anyone I could say I truly hate."

"Not even Angel?"

"Not even Angel."

"Wow." Terry covered Sara's hand with her own and let go to park the truck at Chez Olivier. "You're one of a kind, Sara Hyatt."

"As long as you think so, I'm good with it." Sara leaned across the bench seat and kissed Terry firmly on the lips. "Shall we eat? I think I might actually be hungry now."

"Me, too, but not for food."

Sara smiled coyly at the comment and waited for Terry to open her door. Terry seemed in the mood to be gallant, and who was Sara to say no? She accepted Terry's hand, and they strode into the building.

They were right on time for their reservation, and the maître d' led them to an intimate table for two in a far corner. The lighting was low but not so much Sara couldn't clearly see her date. Terry removed her coat and hung it on the stand beside the table. Terry's hand brushed her bare shoulder, sending tiny shivers down Sara's spine. The look in Terry's eyes was enough for Sara's stomach to flip-flop, and she wondered about her decision to eat.

Once seated, Sara ordered the wine. She hoped the alcohol would calm her down. Her hands were shaking, and she smiled a little when Terry took hold of one of them.

"Hey, you're cold. Want your coat back?"

"No. I'm still nervous, I guess. I thought I was ready to eat, but my stomach has other ideas. It's weird."

Terry brushed her lips over Sara's knuckles. "How can I make it unweird?"

"I don't know." Sara took a sip of her wine.

Terry lifted her gaze and captured Sara's eyes in a way that made Sara all giddy inside. It didn't help Sara's nerves one bit. Terry said, "There's something I've been wanting to say to you, and I guess now is as good a time as any."

Sara opened her mouth to comment, but the server showed up and asked for their food order. They both rattled off what they wanted to eat, Sara uncharacteristically asking for a salad. Their gazes never left each other, and when the server was gone, Terry gave her a wry smile.

"Where was I?"

"You have something to say," Sara reminded her, though she was sure Terry was stalling.

"Oh, yeah. I want you to listen carefully because this is incredibly important. Got it?"

"Got it."

"I love you."

Sara's face broke into a grin. "That's it?" she asked with a laugh.

"Um, yes." Terry's smile lit up her face. "Should there be more?"

"I don't know. Your lead-up sounded like some kind of story was about to come out of your mouth. Like it might be something I wouldn't like or something I couldn't handle."

"Those are three powerful words. They can be hard to handle for some people."

"Good thing I'm not some people." Sara moved so their chairs were nearly touching and brought her hand up to caress Terry's face. "I'm pretty good with this stuff, actually. Even if my nerves get the best of me once in a while."

"Define pretty good."

"I love you, too," she said, pleased the words came out easily.

"I didn't know that was even possible."

"It's more than possible," Sara said against Terry's lips. She took her lower lip between her teeth and gently nibbled. "I can hardly list all the possibilities."

"Don't. Let's leave it as a surprise." Terry returned her kisses, her hand resting on Sara's waist. "I think it's going to be fun uncovering them. Don't you?"

"I do. But let's go a little slower this time. Take our time with it." Sara watched the desire play across Terry's face. "We already know we're good in bed. Let's find out if we're good in all the other, more important places."

"Like being a family?"

"For instance."

Terry nodded but didn't move away from Sara. Instead she leaned in again for another kiss. "I think you should maybe spend more time with Felicia and my mom. I'd like you to get to know them. Though I think Felicia already has you on her list of friends."

"She's got a list?"

"Oh yes. She keeps it in her diary. She moves people around on the list to show who's more important to her. For example, she struck Bryce Preston off the list completely." Terry shook her head with a laugh. "I did have to ask her to put his name back up there. I want her to try to be friendly with him. It's the how he'll learn she's not different from the other kids."

"I see why you're such a good mom. You think this stuff through."

"I try. Felicia can be a challenge sometimes, but it's okay. I don't mind." Terry took her phone out of her pocket and set it on the table between them. "What do you think about coming over more often and getting to know my kid?"

"I could start by spending some time on the weekend at your house, if it's okay."

"You do have a standing invitation for Sunday," Terry said.

"Sunday it is. Maybe one of these times I'll bring my mom for tea. I don't think Dad would be into it. We can make arrangements for him to meet your mom and Felicia some other time."

"We're doing this then? Bringing our families together while we work on our relationship?"

"Totally. There's nothing more important to me right now. I want to be with you, Terry. Always. I love you. And if we're going to be together, we have to do it right. Get to know each other through our families. By hanging out, talking to each other—those sorts of things."

"Done." She kissed Sara. "I love you, too. And I have one last thing to ask you."

"Yes."

"Yes? You don't know my question." Terry laughed.

"Doesn't matter. That's my answer."

"Cool. You'll make an awesome date to Liv and Grace's wedding."

"Well, hell. I was going to ask you to be *my* date."

"Then I'll take the yes, and we'll make plans for it."

The server showed up with their food, and Sara eyed the salad for a few seconds, before getting his attention. "Um, can I have the steak, too?" She grinned at Terry. "I think my appetite is back."

Chapter Eighteen

"Stand still," Sara admonished Liv for the tenth time. She was trying to fix her bowtie, but Liv wouldn't stop fidgeting. "I'll tie this around your neck like a noose if you don't quit."

"Why did I agree to a tie? I hate these things."

"Because it goes with your tux." Sara finally got it done and took a step back to admire her best friend. She was dressed in white tuxedo slacks, vest, and cummerbund. The vest had silky designs on it that reflected bits of light. Liv's hair was as unruly as ever, but it was Liv, and she looked handsome. Sara felt a well of emotion again, as she had when she helped Liv try the outfit on the first time.

"Gracie is one lucky woman," she said.

"You have it backwards." Liv caught her gaze in the mirror. "But for once, I'll take the compliment. You sure this looks good?"

"You look good in work overalls, Livvy. Gracie is going to grow all weak in the knees when she sees you. You're such a beautiful pair, and I'm damn proud of you right now. I never thought you'd get to this place—where you found a woman who could hold onto you. It's amazing."

"It is." Liv stepped away from the mirror and let her gaze rest on Sara. "You'll get here, too. I'm sure of it."

"Maybe, in a few years. Right now I'm happy with the way things are going with Terry." Her outfit matched Liv's, and as she stood beside her and gazed into the mirror, Sara thought they made a nice pair. She adjusted her cummerbund. The stupid thing didn't want to stay around her slim waist. "I also want you to know how honored I am to stand up for you today." She put a hand in her pocket and let it rest on the plain, gold bands lying there. "You know I love you, right?"

"You're the best friend I have in this world." Liv gave her a quick hug. "And I love you right back. Now stop being sappy or you'll make me cry."

"We wouldn't want that."

"Hell, no. There's no butch crying at weddings."

Sara rolled her eyes. "Bullshit."

Liv's mom came in. She was lovely in her pink dress and white wrist corsage. Her curly hair, much like Liv's, was pulled back into a simple twist with a few curls draping the sides of her face. Her eyes were darker than Liv's, and when she took in the sight of her, she started to cry.

"Mom..."

Jeanette Templeton held a hand over her mouth to stifle a sob.

"I'm sorry. I never expected—I—you're beautiful."

The blush was adorable as it spread across Liv's face. Sara put a hand on Liv's shoulder. "See. I'm not the only one."

"You two are biased," Liv groused, though her smile said otherwise.

"I'm your mother. I'm allowed," Jeanette said. "I came to let you know we're about to go. Your dad's waiting to walk you to the altar. Are you ready?"

Liv was shaking, and Sara gave her a one-armed hug. "I'm going on ahead. See you in a few minutes. Remember to breathe."

****

Breathe, Liv repeated to herself. She had one hand tucked into her dad's arm as they made their way to the altar of the church. She smiled and nodded to people as they went but couldn't remember a single face or name. The walk to the altar was all a big blur, and it took everything she had not to pass out.

She'd never been such a bundle of nerves in her life. When they got to the altar, her dad paused. "I got you a little something, you know, for the something old you're supposed to have."

"I thought it was my underwear," she said, smiling up at him.

Jonas Templeton took her hand in his much larger one and placed a piece of gold jewelry in it. "This was my mother's favorite locket. It has a picture in it of her and my dad. I decided a long time ago I'd give it to you on your wedding day. Your *real* wedding day. I'm proud of you, honey." He kissed her on the cheek and moved to his seat in the front row, beside her mother.

Liv's throat constricted. Her grandparents died before she was born, but she knew everything about them from her dad. To have something so precious to him—the thought threatened more tears to come. She felt Sara's comforting hand on her back.

"Um, I think you might want to look toward the entrance of the church," Sara whispered.

Liv tucked the cherished keepsake into her pants pocket as the music began to play. She hadn't noticed Grace's sister-in-law, Sherry, already standing at the altar.

All peripheral sounds and sights disappeared the moment she saw Grace coming toward her.

She wore a simple, strapless, white-satin dress with a low neckline. It hugged her figure perfectly, showing off her girly curves. Grace's sculptured arms were bare, and one of them was hooked into her father's. Harry wore his US Air Force dress uniform; he was a dashingly handsome man with his beautiful daughter on his arm. The sight of them caused Liv's heart to swell.

Grace chose not to wear a veil, and Liv was glad because she could see her face and her smile as she drew closer. Grace was obviously nervous, and it had a weird calming effect on Liv. Grace cradled a bouquet of flowers, and the rainbow colors stood out in contrast to her white dress.

Grace's dad, Hariku Kato, Jr., stopped in front of Liv, and for a moment, she watched him assess her. She was used to it because she understood no one would ever truly be good enough for Grace. Not in his eyes. But he silently gave her hand to Liv and then did the most incredible thing. He smiled and it reached his eyes.

Liv had to consciously close her mouth when he walked away.

Grace chuckled. "He likes you," she whispered.

"I had no idea," Liv muttered before they turned as one to face the vicar. She didn't think it was possible, but her day got a little bit better. She kept a tight grip on Grace's hand as the vicar began the ceremony.

****

An hour later, Sara and Terry entered the community center, a few minutes ahead of the happy couple. The place was decorated with all the appropriately white streamers and balloons. Tantalizing aromas issued from a sumptuous buffet ready to be enjoyed. Izzy, their hired DJ, waved from her corner of the room where Bren sat beside her.

Most of the wedding guests were already there and seated, anxiously awaiting Liv and Grace's arrival. Sara led Terry to the wedding table, waving at a few friends on her way there. "I can't believe it went so fast. I've been to weddings before, but wow. Was the vicar in a hurry? Do you think he had a hot date?"

Terry giggled. "Doubt it. And I don't believe it went as fast as you think. Seemed pretty normal to me as far as weddings go. At least nothing went wrong, and you didn't drop the rings, like you kept worrying you would."

"Oh my God. My hands were shaking. I'm super glad I won't have to do that again. Ever."

"You don't want to get married?" Terry asked.

Sara scrutinized Terry, enjoying her in a dark suit with the pale-yellow shirt. Her hair was freshly cut, and Sara ached to run her fingers through it. "I didn't say that. I don't think I can do the best person thing again. I do kind of like the idea of getting married someday."

"Seriously?"

"Seriously." She kissed away Terry's next question. "I love you. Now let's celebrate my best friend's wedding."

"Let's." Terry grabbed a confetti popper as Liv and Grace arrived. Izzy did a fine job of announcing Mrs. and Mrs. Templeton, and the crowd erupted in cheers.

Once the noise died down and Liv and Grace were seated beside Sara, it was time for Sara's best-person speech. She'd worked on it for weeks, and realized whatever she wanted to say would have to come to her in the moment. She went with her gut and raised a champagne flute.

"There's a ton of stuff I could say about these two, most of it not to be repeated in polite company. I'll keep it short. Livvy, you've been my best friend forever. I've seen you go through women like a ski cuts through snow. I never expected you'd stop and find yourself settled. But here we are, and I'm happy. Gracie, you are the best person I know, and I don't think anyone could've found a better match for Liv. That being said, let us raise our glasses to the brides and toast to their future."

The crowd lifted their drinks and joined in the toast.

Sara caught Liv's eyes and winked at her. When she was seated, she said, "Weddings make me sappy."

"No worries. I loved it." Liv kissed her on the cheek. "Thanks, best person."

"You're welcome. Now can we eat? I'm starved."

Liv laughed out loud. She took Grace's hand, and they led the line for the buffet.

Izzy queued the music, and Sara took a good look at Bren. The two had their heads together in conversation, laughing as they talked. Sara hoped Izzy was taking her advice about Bren. They'd make a cute couple.

Terry wrapped an arm around Sara's waist as they got in line for food. "I'm glad to be at this part of the wedding."

"Oh? You hungry, too?"

"No. But I'm looking forward to dancing with you. It's been awhile since we've gone out on the town, so to speak."

"It has. I'll make sure I eat enough and have the energy to dance all night. Or until they kick us out of here."

"I think it's a great idea."

Sara grabbed a plate and unashamedly dug into the buffet.

The reception lasted well into the night. Several times Sara caught herself watching Liv and Grace slow dancing—regardless of the musical tempo—holding each other and gazing into each other's eyes as if no one else existed in the world. In that moment, she imagined no one did.

She saw Terry chatting with Bren. It was nice to see them getting along because Sara felt, deep down, Bren would remain her friend. More importantly, she realized Terry wasn't going anywhere. She wondered if they'd have a wedding such as this one in the not-so-distant future.

Terry caught her staring and waved at her. She waved back and leaned against the wall as Terry joined her. The song was a slow, romantic number, and Terry pulled her onto the makeshift dance floor. They wrapped their arms around each other and began to sway to the music. Terry nibbled on her earlobe, sending pleasant tingles through Sara's body.

"Bren told me this is the last song. They have to pack it up for the night. Hardly anyone is left. I thought we could say goodbye and get out of here. What do you think?"

Sara noticed Liv and Grace were on the way to the door, saying goodbye to the few folks left over. Most of them were family and sort of formed a line to get hugs from the newlyweds.

"I think you've got a great idea. Let's go see them off and head to my house. Unless you have to get home?"

"Mom's fine and as is Felicia. I said goodnight to her hours ago. She won't miss me until morning. I need to be there to make her peanut butter pancakes for breakfast."

"I think I need to be there, too." Sara lightly kissed her lips. She and Terry gathered their coats and waited patiently for their turn at Liv and Grace. After several hugs, Sara said, "We're heading out. We'll see you tomorrow night at the extra party."

"You better," Liv said, hugging Sara again. She whispered, "Go home and don't worry if you're too tired to come to the party. I'll understand if you can't get out of bed."

Sara knew the blush on her face was deep red, and she hit Liv in the arm. "Asshat."

"But you love me."

Grace pushed Liv out of the way and hugged Sara one last time. "Ignore her. Go enjoy yourself."

"I plan on it." She waved at them as she took Terry's hand and practically dragged her out of the center. "I'm glad to be out of there. It was fun, but weddings are exhausting."

"You need to go to bed?" Terry asked with a hint of innuendo and Sara giggled.

"Why yes, I do. How about you?"

"I could sleep." Terry gave her a sideways glance. "Tomorrow some time."

"Good to know." Sara put her hand on Terry's arm. "Don't break any laws getting us home, but don't take your time either. Okay?"

"Yes, ma'am."

****

The days and nights since October were a torrent of emotions for Terry. Breaking up with Sara, William trying to take her child from her, Felicia being bullied at school, work getting busier. At times, it was hard for her to keep up. But standing on Sara's porch, waiting patiently as she opened the door to her house, Terry realized she'd been missing one emotion for far too long.

The love of another woman.

She followed Sara into the house, and once the door closed, she helped her out of her coat. She badly wanted Sara to know how much she loved her, but she couldn't come up with any words to convey what was in her heart.

That they managed to reconnect at all was a miracle. To know Sara loved her as well was almost too good to be true. Yet here she stood, in Sara's home, staring at the woman she wanted more than anything. Her guts were tied in knots as she gently brought her hand to Sara's cheek.

Their eyes met. Terry's voice was barely a whisper. "I love you."

Sara tilted her head, and the kiss that followed sent shivers down Terry's spine. "I love you, too. Want to come all the way into the house? Or would you rather stand here by the door?"

"I'd rather go to your bedroom," Terry said as she stepped into the house. "I know it not the most romantic way to put it, but it's what I want." She caressed Sara's face with her fingers and trailed them over her lips. "I get the feeling you want it, too."

"I've wanted it since that day in your kitchen when we decided to date again."

"Same here, but you were right. We needed to take the time to get to know each other."

Sara took her hand and gently tugged her toward the bedroom. "It worked. Right?"

"Felicia called your mother 'Granny.' I'd say she's given us her seal of approval."

Sara opened the bedroom door, flipped on the light, and led Terry inside. "I think there's a distinct possibility we'll be married eventually. Plus, she loves being called Granny. Even my dad has accepted his new role in all this."

"We're talking marriage?" Terry teased. Though the thought of marriage was exciting and scary all at once, Terry easily imagined them together for the rest of their lives.

"Not right now." Sara untucked Terry's shirt and lifted it over her head without bothering to unbutton it. "Right now, I want to make love to you. Right now, I think you need to know how I feel about you, and there's one way I can do that."

"Only one?" She closed her eyes when Sara removed her bra to touch Terry's bare breasts.

"Well, one at a time." Sara placed kisses on each breast, her lips stroking Terry's skin and setting a fire deep in Terry's belly. She ran her fingers through Sara's hair and removed the band that held it away from her face. It fell in soft waves around her shoulders.

Terry released Sara's cummerbund and tossed it to the side. She wanted to feel Sara's skin, and she wanted it now. The shirt was easy enough to remove, and she was delighted Sara didn't wear a bra. Not that she needed one. The sight of her pert breasts made Terry's breath hitch.

"You're beautiful," she said.

Sara laughed and tossed her head to shake her hair from her shoulders. "I'm very sure it's not true."

Terry pressed her lips to Sara's. Their bare chests pressed together and the connection sent tingles along Terry's spine. "Never doubt me, Sara," she said between kissed. "I think you're the most beautiful woman in the world."

Sara's eyes searched hers, and she smiled bashfully. "Okay."

"I plan to make you accept it, even if it takes the rest of our lives." Terry continued her kissing, not letting Sara respond. Her hands moved to Sara's trousers. She unsnapped them and slid the zipper down, pleased to find her wearing silky bikini undies. Terry gently pushed her hands against Sara's flesh, moved under the bikinis to her ass, and returned to the front. Her fingers tangled in Sara's damp curls.

Terry backed Sara up until they were at her bed and eased her onto it. Sara kicked off her shoes, and Terry pulled the slacks off in a slow, deliberate pace, her eyes caressing Sara's body as she went.

She settled astride Sara and her hand moved along the edges of the bikini underwear. The center was damp with Sara's desire. She hooked a finger under the band of the bikini and slid it over one hip, then the other, carefully removing it to reveal Sara's flesh.

Terry breathed in Sara's scent and felt heady with desire. She chanced a look at Sara who gazed back at her with darkened eyes filled with adoration and love. They connected and Terry realized it was far more powerful than before.

Her heart beat picked up as she slid the bikini underwear down Sara's long legs, raining kisses along Sara's heated center. She tossed the garment away, wanting to feel all of Sara—skin against skin— warm flesh in her hands while she loved the woman beneath her.

Her hand slid farther down, sliding into Sara with gentle pressure. Sara's hips rose with each movement of Terry's fingers.

Terry suckled on Sara's breast while her stroking continued. She could sense Sara was close and fulfilled her need faster than she'd intended. But Terry knew her well and this would was the first of many pleasant experiences for the both of them.

Sara's body shivered and Terry draped herself over her and kissed her softly on the lips. Sara smiled wickedly at her.

"You haven't lost your touch."

"Thanks," Terry laughed. "Always good to know."

"I didn't realize how ready I was for you."

"We've got all night," Terry said and grazed one taut nipple with her teeth.

"Awesome." Sara tugged at Terry's belt buckle. "Clothes off. Now. It's my turn."

"Bossy." Terry stood up to remove her boots, slacks, and undies in record time. She settled beside Sara and let her hand roam along Sara's soft belly, giving her a little tickle.

Terry leaned over Sara again and tucked a strand of hair behind Sara's ear, gazed down at her, and shared her breath as she allowed herself a moment of amazement. "I never thought we'd get here," she whispered.

Sara caught her hand and kissed her fingers lightly. "And yet we did. There was never anyone else for me. I always chose you, Terry. Even when you left me at the park that day, I still chose you."

"I'm not dreaming?" Terry half-joked.

"You're not. Let me prove it to you." Her hand snaked behind Terry's head and pulled her closer for a kiss that left Terry breathless.

Sara gently urged Terry onto her back and began a gentle exploration of her body with her mouth. She started at the hollow of her neck and moved to the apex of her legs. A small groan escaped Terry's throat when Sara's hand began to knead her breast. Her legs opened when Sara's other hand rested on her thigh.

Terry covered the hand kneading on her breast, increasing the pressure a little. Sara smiled through her kisses and released the breast to support herself between Terry's legs.

Eyes closed, Terry leaned her head back and sighed at the soft touches from Sara's lips. Exquisite. She wanted to watch her, but her body felt like a block of Jell-O. All she could do was wiggle to let Sara know she was very, very close to where she needed her to be.

Sara's hands lifted Terry's hips off the bed and supported her as her mouth found its mark.

Her tongue licked and sucked and sent shivers through Terry's body. She was close—so very close. It drove her crazy each time Sara would stop, teasing her with flicks across her clit. Maddening and hot all at once, and Terry loved it. Loved her.

Terry's hand tangled in Sara's hair as she tried to guide her closer to her flesh. She was pulsing with need and wasn't afraid to let Sara know it, either. "Baby," she whispered, "please...right there."

"I know," Sara answered softly, her breath warm against Terry's flesh.

The next moment robbed Terry of any speech. Her hips rose to meet Sara's mouth as she slowly, steadily brought Terry up and over the edge with such an amazing jolt and Terry cried out as she reached orgasm.

She arched her body, and Sara wrapped her arms around her as they rode the waves of pleasure together.

Terry settled down, and Sara nuzzled her inner thigh while her right hand traced a familiar pattern along Terry's belly. Her fingers slowly made their way to her curls and tangled in them as Sara moved on top of Terry and looked down into her eyes.

Terry felt more than sated. She held Sara's face in her hands. "I love you. More than I ever felt possible."

"I love you, too," Sara said. Her hand roamed over sensitized flesh, and Terry gasped. "It's why I'm here, doing this, connecting with you." When their lips met, Terry tasted herself and it fueled her passion.

They stopped chatting when Sara's fingers found their mark. Terry didn't think she had it in her to go again, but Sara proved her wrong.

Her fingers teased and stroked in a slow, building rhythm as Terry writhed beneath her. She nipped and licked along Terry's chest until finally she latched on to one breast with her mouth and suckled. It didn't take long for Terry's hips to buck against Sara's hand. They worked together in a frenzied rhythm that soon had Terry crying out Sara's name.

As the orgasm ended and Terry's breathing returned to normal, Terry kept her gaze on Sara's face. Their eyes locked, and a lump formed in Terry's throat. Sara's blue-green eyes were dark with pleasure, focused solely on Terry in this one, special moment.

Sara's hand reached up to touch Terry's cheek and her thumb gently stroked her skin. Terry leaned into the touch. Words weren't necessary, but somehow Terry felt she needed to say them aloud. She needed Sara to hear them again.

"I love you." Terry's heart filled with such emotion it felt ready to burst out of her chest. "Promise me forever, Sara. Please?"

Sara pulled her in for a kiss that spoke louder than any words could, but she said them anyway. "I promise you forever."

About the Author

Patty is the Goldie Award-winning co-editor of *Blue Collar Lesbian Erotica* with Verda Foster. She and Verda also coedited *Women in Uniform: Medics and Soldiers and Cops, Oh My!* and *Women In Sports*. Her first novel, *Souls' Rescue* was a finalist for the Ann Bannon Popular Choice Award. Patty is a retired paramedic and currently resides in The Netherlands with her wife, Sandra, and their kitties. Visit her website at www.pattyschramm.com

Books by Patty Schramm

From Flashpoint Publications

Finding Gracie's Glory
Book One In the Romance In the Yukon Series

Gracie Kato survived years of abuse at the hands of her wife. While her body has healed, her heart and soul remain damaged. Gracie seeks solace at her grandfather's home in the Yukon Territory of Canada. There she'll be able to work at his gold mine, named for her grandmother, Gracie's Glory. It's the perfect place for her to start over again.

Liv Templeton's heart was crushed years ago and she doesn't see any chance of recovery. She's never alone unless she wants to be, but never seeks any commitments. Instead she puts all her energy and time into running the family mining business.

From the moment they meet, Gracie and Liv's connection, physical and emotional, is obvious to them both. Is Liv ready for a serious relationship? Even if she is, will she be able to convince Gracie to trust again? To let her soul heal? Will Gracie open herself up to Liv? Or will she close her heart forever?

ISBN: 978-1-949096-15-6
eISBN: 978-1-949096-16-3

Reflections of Fate

Leoni Wolf lived and worked on the Qualla Boundry in Cherokee, North Carolina her entire life. It was her home and the place she belonged. Leoni once believed in fate and that everything happened for a reason. Until her wife, Tayanita, was killed in a tragic accident. What possible reason could there be for her death? The event shattered Leoni's world.

Each day Leoni awoke, gazed at her reflection in the old free-standing mirror and convinced herself she could get through one more day.

Nicola Daelis was tired of fate intervening in her life and wanted to throttle her. Before Nicola could act on the event that could change it all, fate landed a beautiful, dark-eyed woman in her lap and turned Nicola's world upside down.

Fighting for their lives, and often against each other, Nicola and Leoni must embark upon an adventure that could be the beginning of something new. Or the end of them both.

ISBN: 978-1-949096-12-5
eISBN: 978-1-949096-13-2

Better Together

Mac Bradenton has never been south of the Mason Dixon Line or across a body of water wider than the Ohio River. But her best friend is sick and on a quest to complete her bucket list. First stop is Paris, France. Mac goes along expecting to enjoy the time with Kristy, never anticipating just how much her life will change.

They meet up with Kristy's friend, Lenie, who has promised to give them a guided tour of Paris and while there, romance blossoms between Mac and Lenie.

Once home, life takes some major turns for Mac. As she struggles to deal with the challenges thrown at her, will everything fall apart? Or will she be able to lean on Lenie knowing that, no matter what happens, they are better together?

ISBN: 978-1-949096-09-5
eISBN: 978-1-949096-10-1

Souls' Rescue

Kelly McCoy is a firefighter and paramedic who's lived most of her adult life in New York. After 9-11, she relocates to Cincinnati, nursing a broken heart and looking for a new start. She takes one day at a time, trying not to let her losses overwhelm her.

Talia Stoddard is an insurance wiz who's always been smart on the job, but unlucky in love. After years of being told that she's too big, too tall, too black, too lesbian, and not a very snappy dresser, Talia has resigned herself to a life alone with only her dear gay friend Jacob for a diversion.

When Kelly and Talia's lives crash into one another, it's under the most stressful and threatening circumstances. Talia is in terrible danger, and it's up to Kelly to rescue her. In the horrendous situation they end up in, neither expects to find a friend, much less a soul mate.

Will they rescue one another and heal the wounds of their pasts? Or will they both continue to believe that they're not worthy of the kind of love the other might offer?

Souls' Rescue is the story of opening up to love, taking chances, and building a life that everyone dreams about, but few people ever find.

ISBN: 978-1-949096-06-4
eISBN: 978-1-949096-07-1

From Regal Crest Enterprises

Because of Katie

Siobhan Landry's granddad had one wish before he died. That she would travel from their small town in Indiana to the place of his birth in southern Ireland and become the artist he knew her to be. She never expected how much her life would change when she got there.

Katie O'Briain nearly lost her life, but that couldn't stop her from doing what she's always loved—being a marathon runner. However, no matter how much she pushes herself, or convinces herself life is good, there's something very obviously missing.

But Katie has a lot of scars and even though her attraction to Siobhan is immediate, can she bare those scars to the lovely American?

Siobhan also feels that attraction. Will she be able to move beyond her broken past and let Katie heal her heart?

Or will the scars they both hide keep them apart forever?

ISBN: 978-1-61929-380-9
eISBN: 978-1-61929-381-6

Love Is In the Air — w/Nann Dunne

Love Is in the Air is a collection of romantic short stories about   love that comes to us in different ways, different forms, and in ways we   might never suspect. Whether we feel worthy or not, love is there. And   it will find us all.

ISBN: 978-1-61929-278-9
eISBN: 978-1-61929-362-5

Women In Sports: Sweaty, Sexy and Hot, Oh My!
— w/Verda Foster

Women in Sports: A collection of romantic and erotic tales.

Hot. Sweaty. Tight shorts. Sports bras. Six-pack abs. What sparks your imagination? Muscular legs? Hands that are strong and sure? Baseball, soccer, hockey, track and field...does it really matter? She's sexy, she's incredible and she's all yours. Sit back, relax and enjoy some wonderful tales from this group of talented authors. Women in sports—does it get any better than that?

This amazing collection of romance and erotica includes stories from: Lee Lynch, Jessie Chandler, Mary Griggs, MB Panichi, Tonie Chacon, Kate McLachlan, A.L. Duncan, Jeanine Hoffman, Erica Lawson, Sharon G. Clark, Nann Dunne, Pat Cronin and Verda Foster.

ISBN: 978-1-61929-278-9
eISBN: 978-1-61929-279-6

Women In Uniform: Medics and Soldiers and Cops, Oh My! — w/ Verda Foster

Cops, medics, soldiers, chefs, forest rangers...let's face it...who doesn't appreciate women in uniforms? Whether it's a nurse in Vietnam, a lesbian about to deploy to Iraq, a horny football player, a cop who likes bondage, a medic who needs pampering, or a security guard who finds out she's not past her shelf date, these stories of erotica and romance will rev you up, touch your heart, and make you feel.

You'll be delighted by great stories from some of today's top writers: Catherine Lundoff, J.M. Redmann, Lee Lynch, AnaIza Otis, Lori L. Lake, Chris Paynter, Sammo, M.J. Williamz, Ms. M, Diane S. Bauden, Karen D. Badger, V.W. Massie, Victoria Oldham, Bliss, R.G. Emanuelle, Andi Marquette, Jessie Chandler, Pat Cronin, and Lee Coats.

ISBN: 978-1-935053-31-6
eISBN: 978-1-61929-046-4

www.ingramcontent.com/pod-product-compliance
Lightning Source LLC
Chambersburg PA
CBHW071152180726
48291CB00007B/2431